ESCAPE TO VAN DIEMEN'S LAND

Bob Mainwaring

Published in Australia by Temple House Pty Ltd,
T/A Sid Harta Publishers ACN 092 197 192
Hartwell, Victoria

Telephone: 61 9560 9920, Facsimile: 61 9545 1742
E-mail: author@sidharta.com.au

First published in Australia 2006
This edition published 2006
Copyright © Bob Mainwaring 2006
Cover design, typesetting: Chameleon Print Design

The right of Bob Mainwaring to be identified as the Author
of the Work has been asserted in accordance with the
Copyright, Designs and Patents Act 1988.

Mainwaring, Bob
Escape to Van Diemen's Land
ISBN: 1-921206-26-8
EAN13:978-1-921206-26-9
pp400
Printed in China by Everbest

Author's Notes

Bob Mainwaring is a Tasmanian born and bred. He has a lifelong fascination with the colonial history of Australia and has read widely on this topic, both the early writers who tell the story of the convict era and the modern, contemporary works that give us a more realistic understanding of the daily life in Britain in the eighteenth century that produced the most elaborate penal system the world had ever seen up until that time.

This is a work of fiction, but all the incidents in the story are based on true happenings and are well-recorded, both in respect to the convict system in Van Diemen's Land in the 1840s and the gold rushes of the 1850s.

About the Author

Bob Mainwaring can trace his ancestry back to his
farmer forebears who arrived in Van Diemen's Land in
1835 to help pioneer the fledgling colony. Their numer-
ous descendants include farmers and professionals of all
kinds as well as a wide selection of tradespeople.
He was educated in the public school system and
secured his first job at age fifteen as a messenger in the post office, later
returning to his first vocation of farming. He lived for twenty-five years
on Flinders Island where he developed a successful grazing property
running both sheep and cattle and subsequently became a member of
the Tasmanian parliament where he served for eleven years.

He and his wife now live in retirement in Launceston where he
continues to take an abiding interest in the early history of Australia
with a special interest in the settlement of the first colonies.

ESCAPE TO VAN DIEMEN'S LAND

CHAPTER 1

*T*he bewigged judge, in full regalia, was grim faced as he leant forward over the bench while wiping his nose and lower face with a white linen kerchief. Fixing his cold eyes on the young prisoner in the dock, he pronounced sentence on him.

'Martin Francis Maynard, you have been found guilty of stealing and also of consorting with Swing rioters. Therefore, it is adjudged by this court, with the authority of His Majesty the King, that you be transported upon the seas, beyond the seas, to Van Diemen's Land for the term of seven years.'

The twenty year old, fresh faced prisoner showed remarkably little emotion at this cruel sentence. His manacled hands rested quietly in his lap. He stoically kept his gaze upon the floor and his facial expression indifferent. His evenly sun browned features showed that he was a man who had spent all his life in the open, and his face showed a vigour that reflected the alertness of a country man.

The judge gave the order in a firm voice: 'Take him down,' whereupon the guard unlatched the door to the dock and grasped the prisoner's arm to lead him the few steps to the stairs that led to the cells below.

He was quickly bundled into a large cell already half full of newly convicted prisoners, most of whom were morosely staring into space while the rest were either weeping or pretending to laugh and make a joke of the proceedings.

He regained his balance and shuffled in his leg chains to the rear of the cell where he found a spot to sit on the bench extending around the four walls. He sat next to a dark-complexioned man whom he judged to be a little older than himself who pushed his way along the bench to make room for him.

'What did you get?' the man asked.

'Seven years in Van Diemen's Land,' Martin replied. 'It looks as if I'm going for a long cruise. What did you get?'

'The same,' he said. 'I hope they've got more food there than here, that's all I can hope.'

Three hours later, the last of the prisoners were returned to the cell and after it was securely locked, two warders came in and started removing their leg chains and handcuffs.

'You can have the irons off so you can eat and sleep, if you behave yourselves,' the head warder told them through the iron bars, 'but if you gives the slightest trouble you'll have them back on quick smart, and keep them on till you get down to the hulks, then you can please yourselves.'

Later in the evening, a bundle of dark grey blankets were thrown in and the prisoners were told to share them out, one to each man. The warders stood at the bars looking in to see that nobody got more than his fair share.

'Where do we sleep?' a young prisoner asked in a broad Lancastrian accent.

'You'll be all right in there,' one of the guards said. 'We'll see that none of your scum mates comes to disturb you.'

A little later, two buckets of food were shoved in, one containing boiled potatoes and the other fried mutton chops, exactly enough for each man to have one of each. There was a scramble around the buckets as the men rushed to get at the food until the warder again roared out instructions to line up in a single file so that everybody got their share.

The warder called two prisoners out to carry buckets of water into the cell for the men to drink as well as several heavier, iron slop buckets for their convenience. It wasn't long before the cell carried the stink of a cesspit.

It was now night-time and the few dim lights in the prison gave barely enough illumination for the prisoners to find a spot on the bench, or on the floor, where they could lay down to sleep.

Martin found a space under the bench and wrapped himself in the blanket before wriggling into position. He knew he had a long, uncomfortable night ahead and got settled as soon as he could. A lot of the men stood around in groups talking, but he was not the talkative type and preferred his own company and thoughts.

As he lay on the cold, hard floor his thoughts went to his mother back in the village of Ashfield. He knew she would be worrying about him and fretting about the disgrace to him and the family of his becoming a convict awaiting transportation to Van Diemen's Land. There was also the strong probability that she would never see him again, but even while his heart was breaking for her, he knew deep in his inner being that the course he had chosen to take was the correct one for him, and in the long run she would be the happier for it.

The hardest part was the knowledge that she was still deeply grieving the death of his father only eighteen months earlier. That had been the cruellest blow the family had ever experienced and had been the cause of cataclysmic changes to their lives.

For the whole of Martin's life and that of his two sisters, Anne and Ellen who were two and three years older than him, the family had lived an idyllic life on the great Ashburton Estate where his father, Frank Maynard, had been the bailiff in charge of all farm operations.

They lived in a comfortable cottage with a secure life within the tight little clan of the estate community where his father was a person of authority and was held in high regard for his skills as a farmer and manager.

The owner of the estate was Sir Reginald Palliser whose family had owned Ashburton for several generations. He was a Member of Parliament and was often away in London for months on end, but he took a close interest in his estate and was judged to be a good squire. He and Lady Palliser had five children for whom he had engaged a competent teacher and set up a small school on the estate. All the children of the estate workers were allowed to attend. This was a very enlightened practice and the Maynard children, along with the children of the other employees, were unusually privileged to have access to education from the age of seven or eight until they were twelve or thirteen.

The children's mother, Emily, used to take a close interest in what they were learning at school and after tea would hear them practise their reading. It was Frank Maynard's practice to read a short piece from the Bible every night before the children went to bed, and as soon as each child became proficient enough they would take their turn at reading.

The result was that Martin and his two sisters were good readers by the time they had to go to work on the estate, and they had the added advantage that their parents encouraged them to continue reading after they had finished their schooling.

Martin inherited his father's love of the land and from an early age he absorbed the farmlore of the English countryside. By the time he was fifteen, he was a competent ploughman and shepherd and fully earned his keep on the estate although he was too young to be paid for his work. The custom of the times amongst the landed gentry was that children under twenty-one were an adjunct to their parents' value as employees and any reward for their work went to the parent, mainly in the form of modestly improved conditions of employment and only seldom as increased pay.

But for all the lack of monetary reward and the long hours that were required of the workers, life on Ashburton was good. Martin was lucky he received an education and training in farming that would not have been available to him under conditions applying to the vast bulk of English boys and girls.

Sir Reginald was a keen horseman and bred both light horses for riding and coach work as well as draughthorses for farm work. He had for many years employed a steward whose job was the day-to-day management of the breeding horses and the breaking in and training of the young horses in preparation for sale. This man, whose name was Petala Smith, was a gypsy, a race of people with a long tradition of horse breeding and training. He lived with his wife Gwen and two sons and two daughters on the estate. He was highly skilled at his job and the Ashburton horses were known throughout the county as the best that money could buy. Sir Reginald made great profits from that part of his business.

Martin and all the Smith children, both boys and girls, were taught to ride and were given the job of exercising and training the young horses as they were broken in, with the result that Martin spent many hours in the saddle as he grew up.

Petala liked young people and was always willing to teach them many of his skills, both for work and recreation. Like many gypsies, he was an expert wrestler, and in the long summer evenings after work he taught the boys the fundamentals of the art and coached them to a high standard.

Martin was a well-built boy of average height, and by the time he was seventeen he was known in the village and the surrounding countryside as a noted competitor who was hard to beat. It was at that time that Petala started to teach Martin and his own boys, Eustice and Glenal, the practice of unarmed combat. He showed them how to divert the power of an attacker to cause their own defeat.

'If a man is coming at you, don't try to block him,' he told them. 'Seize him by the arm, or wherever you can get a grip, and pull him in the same direction, just stepping aside yourself so that he falls past you. That is the simple principle of the method. The same applies if a man is aiming a blow at you; just grab his hand or forearm and pull him towards you, diverting the power of his blow to throw him off balance. Once you get the knack, it becomes a simple thing to do,' he said. 'Practise makes perfect.'

But he cautioned them against using any skills they might develop in this regard irresponsibly or in a hostile assault. 'That is against all the ethics of wrestling,' he impressed on them. 'Worse still, you could easily hurt somebody and get into serious trouble with the law.'

Those lessons from Petala and the contests with the other boys on the estate made that time the happiest of Martin's life; and as he lay on the cold, hard floor of the cell, he thought of them with a mixture of sadness and appreciation for the times that had passed.

He remembered how he and his sisters as well as Eustice and Glenal and their sisters, Tilly and Matilda, were often called up to the manor house to work for an evening as waiters when the Squire was entertaining important people at dinner. They were given pageboy uniforms to wear which made them look bigger and more handsome, and they were required to help the butler and the kitchen staff with the preparations for the great occasions.

When the time came for the serving of dinner, they would be lined up around the walls of the big dining room with instructions to look ahead and not stare at the guests. The food was brought in on large buffet trolleys from where the plates were handed by the head footman to Martin and his fellow waiters to be served to the guests.

The butler, Mr Dudley Castairs, was a fierce old man who brooked no frivolous behaviour. He was known irreverently by the boys and girls as 'Old Dud', but they feared him. The stern old cook was a serious minded woman who kept a strict eye on the maids, but neither she nor the old butler were a match for the frolicsome young people who were full of high spirits. Not only were they adept at lifting the occasional glass of wine from the passing trays, but the boys were serious pinchers and jostlers of the girls, some of whom allowed themselves to be kissed while the old ogres were looking the other way.

Martin fell in love with Matilda and looked for every opportunity to be alone with her. Her mother, wise to the ways of boys and girls, was aware of the infatuation and kept a sharp eye on them, but she wasn't able to do that while they were working up at the big house. By a stroke of bad luck, Old Dud caught them canoodling in one of the pantries with Martin's hand in her bodice. He immediately kicked Martin viciously in the backside.

'What are you doing, you young yobbo,' he snarled as he aimed another kick at him.

Martin yelped in pain as he jumped out of danger, and in a temper he returned the snarl with interest.

'You cruel old bastard,' he said. 'A fellow ought to hang one on you for that.'

The immediate upshot was that Martin was sent home in disgrace, but the longer term result was more serious.

The saddest part of their lives came a few months later when Frank Maynard suddenly took ill and died at the age of forty-eight. Within a month, Emily had been moved out of the cottage on the estate and into a modest cottage in the village and Martin was desperately trying to find work for himself.

Once his father was gone, there was no place on the estate for Martin. Old Castair's report to Sir Reginald about Martin's transgressions worked against him, but in any case he was considered to be too young to be employed permanently on a wage, so he had to find whatever seasonal work was available. He was given a few days work on Ashburton from time to time, but only on a casual basis and at very low wages. In the chaotic times of the introduction of mechanisation on the farms, unemployment rose rapidly. The new mechanical reapers and binders had displaced thousands of scythe men and sickle men and the new thrashing machines, driven by steam engines, displaced thousands more workers who had been employed as hand threshers.

Martin scoured the countryside looking for permanent work but soon realised that the hordes of desperate and hungry men would keep the market glutted with cheap labour. Many of them were married with children and would work for little more than food. The ones lucky enough to get anything like a proper job were paid one shilling a day. In desperation, many of them turned to stealing food to feed their families and some to stealing anything else they could sell to the 'fences' for a few shillings. This often ended in the poor unfortunates being hauled into court from where hundreds every month, from all over the country, both rural and city parishes, were condemned to transportation.

It was during this time that Martin first heard any factual details about transportation and, more particularly, about Van Diemen's Land.

He had walked twenty miles out into the country to visit his uncle to inquire about the opportunities for work in that district and it was while they were discussing the prospects for Martin's future that his uncle told him about a local boy who had been transported for stealing an axe. The boy had written home to his mother, telling her how much better off he was as a convict in Van Diemen's Land than he would ever be as a farm worker in England.

'You ought to go down and see her,' his uncle said. 'She'll show you the letter. You can make your own judgement of whether it is true or not.'

The next day Martin walked the mile along the lane to the woman's cottage. When he told her who he was and about his situation in life, she gladly showed him the letter. It had the date, 1 February 1844, in the top corner and said:

Dear Mother,

I have been assigned to Mr Davey near Hobart. He is a good master and the mistress is good. The bondage is easy. I have to go to church every Sunday and answer my name. As to my living, I find it better than I ever expected, thank God. I want for nothing in that respect. As for tea and sugar, I could almost swim in it. I am allowed 2 pounds of sugar and a quarter pound of tea per week and plenty of tobacco and good white bread and sometimes beef, sometimes mutton, sometimes pork. This I have every day. Plenty of fruit puddings of all sorts in the season. I have two suits of clothes a year and three pairs of shoes a year.

Your loving son,
David.

Martin was convinced the letter was genuine and it gave him plenty to think about. He discussed it with his uncle and pressed him to tell all he knew about transportation. He thought of nothing else for the few days he spent with his uncle and aunt, and when he returned to the village he asked several others of the better educated people what they knew about it and, in particular, about Australia and Van Diemen's Land.

The countryside was rife with discontent and talk of revolution. A movement called the Swing Labourers Revolt was led by agitators who were literate enough to write pamphlets attacking the government for its disregard for the plight of the unemployed people. These found their way into the villages, and one Sunday afternoon Martin, one of the few young men of his village who could read, was asked to read out one of these pamphlets to a small gathering of farm workers. He thought nothing of it at the time, but later he learnt that the authorities had been informed of the incident and that it represented a black mark on his record.

The village blacksmith, George Latimer, had been Martin's friend for many years and this friendship had been strengthened when he and Martin's sister Anne were married a year earlier. George was an educated man and Martin had faith in his judgement. Martin confided in him that he was considering ways and means of getting transported to Van Diemen's Land and sought his advice.

'You could do worse,' he said, 'a lot worse. It is a new country and it is bound to prosper as more people go there to live.'

'It couldn't be any worse than here. If I stay here, I'll surely finish up in the poorhouse, or dead. I would go as a free settler if I had the money to pay my passage,' he said, 'but there's no hope of that ever happening. I can't even get a job, let alone save at least twenty pounds to pay my way.'

George was sympathetic. 'I would lend you a bit if I had it, but that kind of money is way beyond my modest means. If you're game to give it a go, however, I will do what I can to help you. You never know,' he went on, 'if you handle yourself cleverly out there, you might get on. By the time your beard has turned grey you could well be a rich colonial squire. That would be better than being a downtrodden English farm labourer.'

That was when the discussion turned deadly serious, and when Martin went home that evening, their plans had been laid. He knew his biggest problem would be to persuade his mother to agree to his plan, but he had decided to stress on her the importance of the opportunity for him to 'get on', something that she and his father had always impressed upon him.

As the floor of the prison grew colder and harder on that first night of his sentence, his thoughts were in a turmoil, but somehow he managed to convince himself again that he was doing the right thing. At last he drifted off into a restless and uncomfortable sleep.

In the morning, the prisoners were given a large slice of bread and more fresh water.

'Is this all you're giving us?' one prisoner asked the warder.

'You'll be going down to the hulks later. You might get more down there,' was all he would say.

An hour later, the warder came to the door of the cell and called Martin Maynard out.

'You're wanted,' he said. 'Go with the turnkey.'

The turnkey led him around the main corridor until they came to a door with 'Waiting Room' on it. The turnkey pushed Martin inside, saying, 'I'll wait ten minutes for you, don't tarry longer.'

Martin was surprised to see the village vicar waiting for him.

'Good morning, Martin,' he said. 'How have you been through the ordeal of the last few days?'

'I'm all right, Sir. It hasn't been any worse than I expected. I'm surprised to see you here like this, is everything all right at home?'

'Yes, I saw your mother last evening. She is very upset, and worried about you, but she is being brave. I told her I had to be in Lancaster today to see the Bishop and that I would make a point of seeing you while I was here.'

'Thank you, Vicar, I appreciate it. I know you will do what you can to comfort Mother, and I thank you for that. I'm very thankful that my sisters are living in the village so she won't be left on her own.'

The Vicar sounded disapproving as he said, 'I must say, Martin, that I've been disappointed with your behaviour over the past few months, and I don't think you have been completely open and honest with me. I only hope you know what you're doing.'

Martin turned his head and looked directly into the Vicar's face.

'There are some things that I haven't been able to tell anybody, Sir, not even you. But this might be the start of a new life for me. I'll be in a new country with all my life before me. Once I get through the first few years, I'll have a good chance of getting on; not like here where nobody like me has a chance to get on – ever. Please don't think too badly of me.'

The Vicar put his hand on Martin's shoulder and gently shook it. 'I don't think badly of you, boy. I know that deep down you are a good man. Even though you haven't told me in so many words, I suspect you have deliberately got into trouble so you can get a free passage to Australia. You know that if the authorities found out what you are doing, you would be in more trouble, real trouble. I don't approve of what you are doing, but you have my blessing. All I can say is: Be careful, think of what is right and think of your father. If you model yourself on him, you won't go astray. But be careful who you make friends of. Most of the prisoners you are with now are country men and basically not bad, but as you go through the system you'll come up against the trash of London and the other big cities and you'll encounter wickedness that so far in your life you've never seen. You'll have to be strong to survive.'

'I'll manage, but I know it won't be easy. My biggest worry is about Mother. Please help her when you can.'

With that they parted and Martin was marched back to the cell.

To the prisoners' surprise, they were treated to another meal about eleven o'clock that morning. It was boiled potatoes and mutton chops served up in the same way as the evening before. They were urged to eat it quickly and were then manacled and leg irons were attached before they were marched out into the yard. There they saw two, long, covered wagons hitched up to six horses each. Four soldiers with muskets were stationed around the yard.

The warders roared orders for the prisoners to line up in single file and then they were loaded into the wagons by way of a short ladder at the rear. They were pressed in close together, but there were enough benches along each side of the wagons to accommodate them all.

'Where are we going?' the prisoners were asking the warders, and each other.

'Blackpool, if you're lucky,' the head warder said, 'but if we strike trouble, you'll be back here and in double irons before the day is out. Make your choice!'

A soldier mounted the driver's platform along with the driver of each wagon and the other two got in with the prisoners, taking seats at the back so they could keep them under close scrutiny the whole time.

When all were loaded to the warder's satisfaction, the wagons rattled out of the yard and headed down the road towards the coast at a slow trot.

After four hours, they reached a staging depot where the horses were changed and the prisoners were allowed to step down, four at a time, to relieve themselves.

'Don't try any tricks,' the corporal warned them. 'We shoot first and ask questions later, and we shoot to kill.'

The dark man who had been friendly towards Martin the day before, whose name was Thomas Carter, guffawed at this and said, 'We'd be easy targets with these iron manacles on us. We couldn't run, that's for sure.'

The fresh horses had a faster turn of speed for the first hour, but as time dragged by they slowed down and night fell while they were still a long way from Blackpool. The prisoners became restless as the tedious journey continued.

'Can't you stop for a while and feed us?' the men at the back demanded.

'The Corporal's in charge,' the guard told them, 'and he's under strict instructions not to let you out of here until we reach the barracks at Blackpool.'

They finally reached that destination late in the evening and were immediately locked up in another large cell where they were eventually fed and watered and allowed to settle down for the night on the cold floor.

The next morning, after another bread and water breakfast, they were marched down to the wharf to embark on a coastal freighter for a voyage around the south-western coast of England to Portsmouth. By the time they had shuffled in the leg irons a mile and a half from the barracks to the ship's side, they were tired and hungry. It was a great relief to make their way aboard and descend into the hold where they could throw themselves down on the deck.

Another long and tedious wait followed for the ship to get under way, and once again the more insolent started calling out to the guards for food and water.

There were four soldiers stationed above the open hold, all with loaded muskets pointing down into the ship and it was plain that they had little sympathy for the convicts.

'Stop your squealing, you useless scum!' the corporal in charge called out. 'You'll get fed in good time, but only after we've had our dinner. Rats before mice you know!'

Another couple of hours passed before a bucket of food was lowered into the hold. Again, it was measured out so that each man got his portion. This time it was a hunk of bread with a generous piece of cold pork, washed down with water.

The ship finally got under way about two o'clock in the afternoon, and as she worked her way out of the harbour, the prisoners' leg irons were removed. The sails filled and the ship was soon rolling and tossing her way south with a stiff westerly on her starboard side. It wasn't long before the more experienced travellers amongst them were giving out bits and pieces of wisdom.

'This will be good experience for you lads,' one said. 'It will give you a taste of what to expect on your cruise to Van Diemen's Land.'

'I've been told it takes six months to get there, and it's howling gales all the way,' another said.

Most of the convicts had never been to sea before and were understandably nervous, not knowing what to expect. They had heard frightening tales of seasickness and terrible storms with people being injured by the violent movement of the ship. The ones who pretended to be experienced sailors delighted in feeding these fears by telling tall tales about some of their own voyages in times gone past.

Night fell and they were given another small meal and then ordered to settle down for the night.

'You can shut your noise!' the Corporal yelled down to them. 'We don't want to be pestered all night by your yabbering and squealing. Don't think we won't fire down onto you if you give us trouble. The bullets don't care whether it's dark or daylight.'

The voyage became ever more tedious and the prisoners suffered from tiredness and hunger. The hold by this time was a stinking pen full of cesspit smells and vomit from the weaker stomachs. The men became restive, but apart from yelling snide insults at the soldiers, they were powerless to do anything about their situation.

It was with a profound sense of relief that they reached Portsmouth late the next night. There they were fed and allowed to spend the night in the hold pending their transfer to a hulk. They were thankful the latrine buckets had been hoisted out and that the ship was lying still, making it possible for them to get a better night's sleep.

Early the next morning, they were again manacled and loaded into longboats manned by sailors. The experienced rowers propelled the boats across the harbour at a fast clip and the prisoners got their first look at the infamous hulks which would be their prison for the next few weeks while they waited for a convict ship to take them to Van Diemen's Land.

As they drew near to the old warships, the men fell silent. The high, steep walls rising from the sea were a joyless and forbidding sight. They were covered in a rusty coloured grime that forewarned of an even grimmer interior. They had the look of slum tenements with bedding and clothes hung out to air on lines rigged between any convenient points above the many-layered decks.

The longboat carrying Martin and his friend Thomas pulled into a landing stage built out from the side of the hulk where they were ordered to disembark and go aboard. They splashed through the water that sloshed up through the gaps in the decking of the landing and were marched up to the quarterdeck where they were lined up like soldiers on parade. There were more soldiers with muskets stationed around the large, open deck and also a number of other men dressed in the peculiar uniform of the convict and who were anxious to speak to the new arrivals.

The tall, red-faced sergeant in command of the soldiers shouted orders to the prisoners to be silent and hear the lieutenant. That officer demanded their attention to hear the standing orders that applied to daily life for the convicts in the hulk: They would be allocated to groups that would make up the various messes and working parties; they would obey the orders of the warders without question; they would be punctual for parade every morning in readiness to be taken to work and any disobedience in this respect would be severely punished; they were not allowed to have any tobacco in their possession; any prisoner caught smoking in the hulk would be flogged.

'Before you are issued with your convict uniforms, you must surrender any money you have with you for safekeeping by the Captain. It will be returned to you at the completion of your sentences.'

'Not bloody likely,' somebody behind Martin said in a low voice.

'Your clothes will be purchased by the dealers, if they are worth anything, and the money kept for you.'

'Stolen, he means,' the same low voice said.

'You will be inspected by the medical officer and deloused if necessary.'

Then the process of being integrated into convictry commenced in earnest. It was akin to being recruited into the army. Several convict barbers were kept busy clipping the prisoners' locks to a very short cut. The medical officer and his convict assistants quickly inspected them for head lice and any other disability that could pose a health problem in the ships. Those who were found to be infected were ordered away to be soaked for an hour in a cold bath of disinfected water. Finally, they were issued with their uniforms: two shirts of coarse material, two pairs of canvas trousers, a grey jacket of similar coarse material and a pair of shoes.

An old Jewish clothes dealer had set up in a corner of the quarterdeck and was offering to buy the prisoners' clothes, albeit at very low prices. He was offering only half a crown for a new suit, but the convicts had little choice of whether to accept it. The only other choice was to throw it onto the heap of worthless old clothes that the more poorly clad convicts had discarded.

While this activity was proceeding; a number of old, experienced hulk convicts were circulating around the group of 'Johnny Raws' – the name given by the convicts from the big cities to the country bumpkin men from the rural areas – to work their confidence tricks to swindle them out of any money or items of value they had on them. No lie or trick was too base for them to use.

A shifty looking character of about forty years of age approached Martin and asked him if he had a comb. Martin did in fact have a small comb in his pocket and in his innocence showed it to the scoundrel who made a show of inspecting it.

'I'll give you a penny for it,' he said.

'No, I don't want to sell it,' Martin replied, but somebody at his other elbow distracted his attention momentarily and when he turned back, the fellow was walking away towards a group of his mates. In two quick strides, Martin caught up with him and grabbed his forearm.

'Give it back,' he demanded.

Something in his grip and the look on his face made the scoundrel realise that he had picked a nark, and he passed it back without a word.

Thomas Carter was nearby and saw the incident.

'How did you do that?' he asked Martin. 'You must have had some pressure on his arm to convince him to give it back so easily.'

Martin grinned as he said, 'No, it was nothing special, just a wrestling grip I learnt as a boy.'

Thomas had a look of wonderment on his face, but he smiled knowingly and said no more.

By this time, the convicts were dressed in their uniforms and were ready to start their new careers as prisoners of the Crown. Martin and Thomas were put into the same group and duly taken down into the dark and mysterious bowels of the hulk to their mess where they would eat and sleep. This would be their home for the next few weeks or months while waiting to be put onto a convict ship for the long voyage to Van Diemen's Land.

During this time, they were taken in a longboat every morning, except Sundays, to the naval dockyards where they laboured on a variety of jobs all day before being taken back to the hulk as darkness descended in the evening. The worst thing was that they were manacled in light leg chains before being taken out in the morning and worked all day in them. The authorities took every care not to give the convicts any chance to escape; everybody knew that it was impossible to swim in leg chains and the convicts knew that if they attempted to leave the dockyards, they would be shot down like dogs.

Martin quickly adjusted to life in the hulk. He was a healthy and fit young man who had had the benefit of a good education and being raised in a well-ordered home by loving and wise parents. He was strongly committed to his plan to start a new life for himself in Van Diemen's Land and had prepared himself to handle the hardships he knew he would meet. He had been shocked and disgusted by a lot of the treatment that was meted out to them, but he never deviated from his plan.

He quickly learnt that every kind of corruption flourished in the hulks. Almost anything a convict desired could be bought with money if he knew the right channels to go through. Even the daily meals varied between adequate and very poor depending on how much of the rations that were issued to the different messes were dissipated in various forms of corruption.

Thomas Carter was similar to Martin in many ways. He was the son of a village wheelwright and had been trained in that trade. He could read and write and was an intelligent man who had been led astray by too much grog and the wrong woman. He had been sentenced to seven years transportation for stealing money from his employer.

As things turned out, they were both listed for transportation on the *Emma Eugenia* fourteen weeks after being sent to the hulk – an unusually short time. The Governor of Van Diemen's Land asked the authorities in England to send certain tradesmen that were in demand ahead of others who had no particular qualifications. Martin was entered in the lists as a ploughman and shepherd and Thomas was a wheelwright, both trades that were in strong demand in the colony, a circumstance that worked to their advantage to get them away from the hated hulk.

They were put aboard the *Emma Eugenia* on 7 February 1845 and sailed from Portsmouth a week later.

CHAPTER 2

*T*he *Emma Eugenia* caught the full force of the stiff westerly wind as she left Portsmouth Harbour on a cold and cloudy February day in 1845. Within two hours, she was out of sight of the English coast.

The few convicts who were allowed to go on deck, where the soldiers and their wives were watching England disappear over the horizon, gazed back with mixed emotions. The convicts were confined to a section of the foredeck, while the soldiers and their women were congregated towards the stern to get the best view. Many of the men, both convicts and soldiers, were weeping and most of the women, both soldiers' wives and women convicts, were wailing.

Along with most of his fellow convicts, Martin was manacled in his cramped mess below decks and was not given the opportunity of a last look at his homeland before it faded from his view, more than likely forever. He was one of the few on board who had no mixed feelings about the departure. His feelings were simply that of relief that he was finally on his way to Van Diemen's Land and the start of what he hoped would be a new and better life.

He had been able to send a letter to his mother after boarding the *Emma Eugenia*, something he had been unable to do from the hulk. As on the hulk, he soon found that corruption of many variations reigned on the ship, and a convict could get almost anything he desired if he had money to pay for favours. He had managed to retain a few shillings, which he had carefully kept hidden in his clothes. A guard had agreed to take his letter and post it for the modest reward of three pence.

'How will I know that you have posted it and not just thrown it away and gypped me out of my money?' Martin asked him.

'You won't know, will you?' the man had replied with a sly grin. 'You'll have to trust me.'

By this time, Martin knew enough about the convict system to realise how lucky he had been to serve only a short time in the hulk. In addition to that piece of good fortune, he had the great good luck to be sent to the *Emma Eugenia* for the voyage, the fastest ship on the run; in 1838 she had set the record by completing the passage in ninety-five days.

The convict world was full of folklore and legend about the old days of convictry, much of it fables and simple exaggeration, but a surprising amount was factual information about the ships and their masters. This was passed down by the 'old lags', the long-serving convicts who had, by good conduct and cooperation with the authorities, been given jobs as guards and minor officials. Some of them had completed several trips in the same ship.

The *Emma Eugenia* was known to have a good master, Captain Wilfred Birch, and a good surgeon superintendent, John Wilson. These two posts were the key to what little comfort the convicts would get on the voyage. Of the two, the surgeon was the more influential. It was his job to ensure that the convicts were properly fed and exercised and that they received their tonic to ward off scurvy as well as their ration of port wine every day to further boost their health.

Conditions below deck were very cramped and already this was causing friction amongst the convicts. A fight had started on the first morning out in Martin's mess because one of the convicts; a big, raw boned Irishman, had encroached over onto his neighbour's bunk and refused to move. Two guards had rushed in and arrested the interloper and marched him off to spend the rest of the day, and that night, in the 'Black Hole'; a small, dark isolation cell where the only food he would get was bread and water until his punishment was completed. The worst feature of the voyage for most convicts was the tedium and social friction caused by too many bodies being crammed into too small a space.

Martin and his friend Thomas had remained in the same group and had managed to stay together on the *Emma Eugenia*. They were sent down to a long, narrow deck that was the width of the ship, lined on both sides by bunks measuring exactly six feet square. There were two levels of bunks, and whether the convict got a lower or upper bunk was determined by the toss of a coin. Each bunk accommodated four men sleeping side by side on straw-filled palliasses. The passageway between the lines of bunks was less than three feet wide.

The bunks were merely squares delineated by wide boards placed on edge, and there was no passage or other space between them. The occupants gained access to them by climbing in the bottom from the central passageway. When all the convicts were in their bunks, the long line of bodies crammed together reminded Martin of how the pigs on the farm habitually slept in the same fashion. Many a time he had stood watching the domestic scene with mother sow sleeping surrounded by her little porkers all arranged in neat rows; when one moved to another position, they all moved in sympathy.

The second night in the bunk, Martin was woken by the man next to him fumbling around his groin. He shoved the hand away, but within a few minutes it was back, trying to get inside his trousers. He grabbed the wrist, giving it a sharp twist as he put his face close to the man's ear and, snarling, said: 'Stop that, or I'll break your arm. Keep your hands off me.' The man took the hint and never troubled him again. It was clear from the moaning noises that came from a few of the bunks that homosexual activities were indulged in by some. Martin was disgusted but not surprised; he had seen enough on the hulk to know that such behaviour was common only with a minority of them.

Once the ship was under way and well out to sea, the leg irons were removed from the convicts, making it easier for them to cope with the cluttered conditions of shipboard life and to climb and descend the stairs while going on deck for exercise.

'There you are,' the corporal who unshackled Martin said. 'Don't say that we fail to give our passengers good service. You can run up and down stairs like a young'un now.'

Despite this freedom, the bunks were fitted with leg chains and manacles so that if the necessity arose, the convicts could be fettered down for periods.

As on the hulks, every aspect of shipboard life was controlled by rules and regulations and any infringements were punished by deprivation of exercise, or in more extreme cases, by incarceration in the 'Black Hole'. Overshadowing these benign punishments was always the possibility of attracting a flogging although by the time of Martin Maynard's voyage, this was a rarity compared to the 'bad old days'.

The first morning of the voyage, Martin's group were ordered on deck for exercise. They were put to work washing down the decks and polishing all the woodwork around the bridge. The sight of the endless ocean, uncluttered by any land, was a new experience for them. Most had been born and raised in rural parishes, seldom travelling more than ten miles from their birthplace and few of them had any comprehension of the magnitude of the world, let alone the enormous distance they would travel to reach Van Diemen's Land.

'Gor blimey,' one fellow said as he gazed out across the endless ocean, 'it's a long way across, ain't it?'

Martin noticed the long red-and-white pennant flying from the rear mast and asked his letter posting guard, whom he now knew to be Basil Eldon, what it meant.

Basil chuckled as he said, 'You're still learning, aren't you, mate? That's the 'whip'. It tells all the other ships that we're a convict ship.'

Within two days the convicts in each group, most of whom had known each other in the hulks, had learned the names of their fellows and something about them, including their crime. By the end of the voyage, they would know every convict on the ship and would recognise them years later as former companions and associates, in the manner of old school chums.

During periods of good weather, the various groups were allowed to spend extended periods on deck. The surgeon-superintendent liked to have as many groups as practicable on deck at all times, but the individual convicts were not allowed to come and go as they pleased; they had to stay with their group.

The big difference Martin noticed in the first few days was that the food on the *Emma Eugenia* was much better than on the hulk. The difference was that corrupt officers could not sell rations that were meant for the convicts while out in the middle of the ocean; the result being that all the food reached them. The staple part of the diet was salt meat, supposedly beef but always referred to by the convicts as salt horse. Some of it undoubtedly was, but the rations were varied with pork a couple of times a week. Plum pudding was a special treat, often served on Sundays.

The surgeon-superintendent and the Captain were both careful to keep the convicts in good health. They had their professional reputations to preserve and the company got a bonus for every convict they landed in good health. The basic contract rate was eighteen pounds per convict with a bonus of twenty-five per cent at the end of the voyage if the Governor gave a good report and a favourable health certificate regarding the condition of the convicts.

Once a day, each mess was organised to receive their dose of tonic – a mixture of lime juice, sugar and vinegar – to guard against the scourge of scurvy. This was resisted by some convicts, but they were coerced into taking it by the threat of the 'Black Hole'.

'Please yourselves,' the Corporal said. 'It's either drink this stuff willingly, or go into starvation in the Black Hole until you're ready to cooperate.'

In addition, they were given half a pint of port wine with their evening meal to keep their spirits up. This was considered a great luxury and was not refused by anyone.

A week into the voyage, the weather changed with the wind veering around to the north-east bringing cold squalls of rain, lightning and heavy, rolling seas. The speed of the ship was not much affected, but the rolling and pitching increased alarmingly. Soon most of the passengers were seasick. All exercise on deck was halted and the unventilated lower decks became stuffy and oppressive, stinking of sweaty bodies and vomit. For several days most stayed in the bunks. Even though it was hot and uncomfortable, it was better than standing in the passageway clinging to the bottom end of the bunks. Attendance for meals was low and the consumption of food plummeted.

It was a melancholy ship by the time the storm finally blew past, but Martin noted how quickly the mood changed as the sun emerged and the wind abated. The Corporal went through the mess calling out: 'Select your volunteers for water duty! I want ten men to carry buckets of water down here so the rest of you can clean this place up! We've got plenty of water topside, all I want is a few men to carry it downstairs!'

It took two or three days of hard work to clean the ship and get everything back into order, but the shared experience generated a spirit of camaraderie amongst all aboard. They had now all become seasoned sailors.

Two days after the storm, Martin's group was working on deck when he noticed a smudge of land a long way off to the east. Basil Eldon happened to be on guard duty and Martin asked him what it was.

'That's the Cape Verde Islands,' he said. 'We're about halfway to Rio.'

'Why don't we call in and have a bit of a rest?' Martin asked.

'They used to, in the old days, but not so much these days,' he replied. 'We'll keep going till we reach Rio De Janeiro. We'll stop there for a few days and then we'll be off to Hobart. Our skipper likes to do a fast voyage and this time of year the westerlies never fail to help him. The word is that he wants to sail direct to Hobart without calling at The Cape if conditions are right.'

The strong westerly wind continued and the ship made good speed.

The convicts had become conditioned to shipboard life and found ways of filling in their time by fishing from the lower decks and playing games of their own making. Occasionally they would strike a good patch of fish and haul in great quantities in a short time; a welcome change to their diet. The surgeon and the captain encouraged these activities; they were well aware of the dangers of unrelieved boredom with regard to both health and behaviour.

Rio de Janeiro was reached about six weeks after sailing from Portsmouth and the ship was serviced with water and provisions. None of the convicts were allowed ashore, but some were employed in getting the new provisions stowed in the ship. Martin was given a job of carrying firewood from the deck down to the woodhouse near the kitchens, a job that took several men three days.

It was a blessing to have a still ship to sleep in for a few nights, but most of the convicts were pleased to get out to sea again. They missed the open air and exercise on deck and by this time, most of them were anxious to have the voyage over.

Mr John Wilson, the surgeon-superintendent, had been interviewing the convicts individually since leaving Portsmouth, and Martin was ordered to report to him one morning a week after leaving Rio. When they had reported to the ship for the voyage, they had been told this would happen. The word was that this interview would be a preliminary to being individually assessed on arrival at Hobart as to their suitability for employment.

John Wilson was about forty five, an age that made him seem old to Martin. He had a round, open face and a quiet way of speaking. Martin liked the look of him from the first. There was something about him that reminded Martin of the Reverend Willings, the Vicar of Ashfield. He had been trained by the Royal Navy as a surgeon and had been the surgeon-superintendent on the *Emma Eugenia* for five voyages.

'We'll start with a review of your record and bring it up to date, if that is necessary,' he said.

He checked off the facts of Martin's life as recorded in his papers; date and place of birth, where educated if at all, where employed and in what capacity. He had a fine knack of eliciting personal information, and after fifteen minutes he felt he had a good idea of what kind of man Martin was and what he was qualified to do.

'You have been a fortunate young man so far in your life,' he said. 'What happened to slew you off the straight and narrow?'

'I never had any trouble, Sir, until my father died and we had to leave Ashburton. I could not get work of any kind. I tried desperately, but I couldn't get on anywhere. I had to eat so I started stealing.'

'What would you like to do?' the surgeon asked him.

'Get a job on a farm, and one day have a farm of my own, Sir,' Martin said. 'In a new country I might be able to get on.'

Martin had made a good impression on John Wilson. He saw a healthy, well set up young man before him who would make an ideal servant for some farmer in Van Diemen's Land. He noted his obvious strength and confidence of character.

He then wrote a note on Martin's papers, and looking up at him, said, 'It is the government policy in Van Diemen's Land at present that all new convicts have to serve for a year on public works, mostly clearing and making roads, before they are eligible for assignment to a master'. 'I can't encourage you to think that anything else will happen for the first year, but my advice to you would be to do any work you're given as best you can, and be patient. In your new life, patience will be the main thing. Above all,' he continued, 'keep out of trouble and keep your record clear. You've got one big advantage that will stand strongly in your favour,' he concluded. 'You've had a good education and you can read and do calculations. That's more than most working men in Van Diemen's Land can do.'

Martin returned to his group well pleased with the interview. A spark of confidence had been lit within him and his hopes for a better life in Van Diemen's Land had been boosted.

A week after leaving Rio, they were far enough south to pick up the full force of the westerly trade winds and the ship was bowled along at a fast rate. The huge swells were evenly spaced out and did not affect the speed of the ship although the rough conditions often made conditions on board unpleasant.

A couple of weeks later, word went around the ship that the captain had decided to sail directly to Hobart without calling at Cape Town. According to the crew, conditions for a fast passage were ideal and if all went well, they should reach their destination about the first week in June.

The tedious daily routine went on with little to break the monotony. Any opportunity to make time pass more pleasantly was seized upon. The weather was often too rough for fishing and at those times, gambling of one sort or another was the only pastime available. The convicts manufactured playing cards out of anything suitable they could get, including prayer books and Bibles. Not being allowed to carry knives or scissors of any kind, they had to prevail upon sympathetic guards to lend them either one to cut the pages into the right size and shape.

Church services were well attended on Sundays, not because the congregation of convicts and soldiers were particularly religious, but because during the hymns they could ease their frustration's by loud and enthusiastic singing to the tunes blown out by a crewman with his accordion. The chaplain was urged by the surgeon to pick the catchy hymns that all could sing. The quarterdeck was crammed with men and women, and the chaplain, standing on an upper deck with the wind blowing his hair about, was inspired by the large congregation to preach moving sermons. Many would be the chaplain who would, in later life, look back on their experiences on the convict ships with fond memories of the big and enthusiastic congregations.

As the *Emma Eugenia* progressed into the Indian Ocean, she ran into the dreaded doldrums and was becalmed for five days. Although it was late autumn in the Southern Hemisphere, the weather was still quite warm and the ventilation in the lower decks – never good – quickly became nonexistent. By the third day, all aboard were tense and uptight. As many as possible were allowed to stay on the open decks to get what little air there was, but a large number had to be below decks at all times because the decks were too small to accommodate everybody at the same time. The crew rigged wind sails to divert air down into the ship but without much success.

Tempers were frayed and scuffles constantly broke out amongst the convicts, both male and female. On the fourth day, Martin's group were up on deck with several other groups when a big, raw boned redhead from another group took exception to something Martin had said, or not said. Martin was a quiet person who, unlike most of the men, was a man of few words.

'What's wrong, you stuck up bastard? Why can't you talk to a man, civil like?' he demanded.

Thomas Carter, who was nearby, tried to calm the redhead down, but he was determined to pick a fight.

'No!' he roared. 'Bloody Maynard! He's always the same, sulky bastard. Never says a civil word. to anyone.'

Martin grinned at Thomas but said nothing. This enraged him further and he stepped towards Martin with his fist poised to land a blow.

'Don't do it, Mate,' Martin said. 'I don't want to hurt you, but I will if you push me.'

This was the final slur that triggered him off. He stepped up closer and aimed a blow at Martin's face. All Martin's training and practise came into play as he calmly caught the man's wrist in his hand and jerked him forward as he turned his back and quickly crouched down. The fellow tumbled across his back and landed heavily on the deck where he lay winded and dazed. Thomas and several other men rushed in to settle the fray.

'Gawd's truth!' one said. 'If the guards see this going on, they'll have us all in irons.'

The assailant's mates got him to his feet and dragged him off to the other side of the deck. Martin's mates crowded around him, laughing and patting him on the back.

'You sure dealt with him good and proper,' one said. 'How did you do it?'

'It's just a wrestling hold I know,' Martin replied, not anxious to say any more.

Needless to say, the story of the affray soon got around amongst all the convicts, and Martin's reputation as a silent mugger was enhanced at every telling, and he became known as a man not to be messed with.

At last the doldrums lifted and the westerlies returned. As soon as the ship started to move at a good pace, the mood on board returned to normal; that is to say, relatively happy.

These better spirits were rudely dampened one morning a few days later when all the convicts were ordered on deck to witness the punishment of one of their number by ten lashes of the 'cat o' nine tails' for stealing. The man had broken one of the strictest rules on the ship. He had been caught in the act of stealing a pair of trousers from the bunk of a convict in another group with the idea of selling them. The captain knew that stealing by convicts from their fellow prisoners, if unchecked, would end in disaster for good order and discipline and the only way to stamp it out was to apply the punishment firmly and quickly. To reinforce the rule in their minds as many convicts as possible were crammed onto the quarterdeck to see the punishment applied first-hand. Others were lined up close enough to hear the punishment even if they couldn't actually see it.

The offender was spread-eagled and tied to a grating that was attached to the mast. The lashes were applied by a big corporal who looked as if he had experienced the task on previous occasions. The surgeon stood close by and kept a watch on the condition of the victim during the flogging. A fierce sergeant counted out the lashes. The assembled convicts looked on impassively, but as the first lash raised an angry weal on the naked back, there was an audible gasp from more than a few.

The count went on remorselessly as the offender screamed in pain and terror. When it was over, the man was released from his bonds and led away between two soldiers to the sick bay where he was allowed to recuperate for a few hours.

The mood amongst the convicts as they were returned to the routine of daily life on the ship was sombre, but within a few hours their behaviour had returned to normal. Martin noticed that most of them had no sympathy for the thief who had been flogged.

'He got off light,' he heard one tough character say. 'He could've got thirty or forty for what he did.'

The faithful westerlies held for the next few weeks and the captain continued to steer south-east to be sure of staying well to the south of Van Diemen's Land.

At last he was able to steer north in the direction of Eastern Australia, and a day later they caught their first glimpse of land. It was a mountain peak; a lone, blue peak it seemed at first, but soon other peaks came into view until all on board could see that Van Diemen's Land was covered in mountains; massive, towering things that stood out as far as the eye could see.

Word quickly went around the ship that it was indeed Van Diemen's Land and that the voyage would be over within a few days. This was received with relief and thankfulness by all on board, but many a convict breast was filled with foreboding of what lay ahead of them.

After a frustrating two days in getting across Storm Bay and a slow trip up the Derwent River where the clean smell of eucalyptus and myrtle forests drifted out to welcome the weary travellers, the *Emma Eugenia* was finally tied up at Hobart on 15 June 1845 after a voyage of 115 days.

Within a few hours of berthing, the first of the convicts were disembarked and escorted to the holding depots; the women were taken in covered wagons to the Female Factory at the Cascades and the men were marched, in light chains, the half mile to the convict barracks.

The convicts were carefully checked individually by an officer sitting at an upturned barrel near the gangway, a slow and tedious job, but according to the local authorities essential for future reference.

Martin and Thomas were not taken off until the next day although they got a good look at the town and the surrounding countryside from the ship when they were allowed to go on deck later in the afternoon.

It was a sunny day and the main feature of Hobart, the massive Mount Wellington stood out as the dominant feature of the landscape. The towering bulk of it dwarfed the surrounding mountains that marched off to the west and the south. The valleys between them that looked as if they had been slashed out by giant axes were filled with dense and mysterious forests of a muted green colour. The town was bigger and more substantial than they expected, and the dense forest that covered the foothills of Mount Wellington came right down to the outskirts of the town. The Derwent River made an excellent and beautiful harbour, and the two friends were surprised at the number of ships that were either tied up to the jetties or moored in the river. Many of them could be picked as whalers.

Martin wondered what the rest of the island would reveal. He felt a wave of excitement pass over him as he stared around the four corners of the scene. Would it cast a spell over him that would involve him in an adventurous life for the rest of his days, a spell that would help him to get started and to 'get on'?

As they shuffled their way in light irons along the muddy road to the barracks the next day, they got a good look at the wharfside shops and houses. There were plenty of people about the streets, all of whom stared at them.

The barracks were a vast improvement on conditions on the ship. At least here each man had his own bunk, and the latrines and bathing arrangements were adequate if primitive. The food was no better, except that it was healthier by virtue of including more fresh vegetables.

Apart from jobs around the barracks and a little gardening, the men were not put to work for the first few days. They had to be held close to the office where each convict was being examined again to determine where he would be sent to work. A committee of three army officers were charged with the task which had to be done in accordance with the government policy that all convicts, except in special cases, had to serve a year on public works before they could be assigned to a private employer.

Because there was a shortage of skilled wheelwrights in the colony, Thomas Carter was assigned immediately to a coach builder in Launceston, an order that he was pleased to receive.

Martin's qualifications as a ploughman and shepherd were not in such short supply that would demand that he be excused from the public works gang. He was ordered to join the government gang at Deloraine and was told that he would be taken from the barracks within the week to march there.

CHAPTER 3

*T*he long walk from Hobart to Deloraine in those June days of 1845 gave Martin his first introduction to his new home of Van Diemen's Land and his first lesson in the differences between the Northern and Southern Hemispheres. The morning the company of convicts left the barracks in Hobart was sunny and bright, but the men were stamping their feet and flinging their arms around themselves to ward off the bite of the frost.

There was a shining cleanness and magnificence about the country that was a new experience for the convicts after the dreary months at sea in the cramped convict ship. Even the dullest of the outcasts from the city slums felt excitement and a lift of their spirits. Martin, as a true country man, was burning with curiosity to see what the land was like.

Fifty-four convicts were in the charge of a sergeant, two corporals and three privates all armed with muskets or pistols; two of the privates were leading large, savage dogs.

As the squad reached the outskirts of the town, one of the corporals marched in front to lead the way, a private with a dog was stationed about halfway along each side of the marching convicts and the second corporal drove two horses drawing a light wagon in the rear. The sergeant was mounted on a horse and continually drifted from the front to the rear while the remaining private marched along with the wagon but was available for any messages or tasks that the sergeant might require.

The convicts' worldly possessions; consisting of a blanket, a second pair of issue trousers and shirt plus a small amount of personal gear, had been rolled into a swag by each man and tied with a length of thin rope. These swags were carried in the wagon and would be issued back to them at the end of the day's march.

The early morning parade had been told by the captain in charge of the barracks that they were starting on the long walk to the probation stations where they would serve a year on government work before becoming eligible for assignment to an employer or a master, depending on their behaviour and performance.

'Some of you will have a long walk, but it has been organised in short marches you can do comfortably in a day. The first two days will be easy stages so that you'll get toughened up to handle the longer ones. Don't think about escaping. All the guards are under orders to shoot any man who runs. These dogs are trained at Port Arthur and are fast and savage. Even if you got away alive, you wouldn't last long; every man's hand would be against you and the blacks are savage. They hate white men and spear them whenever they get a chance. Sometimes they eat them depending on how much tucker they've got at the time. Any misbehaviour will be punished severely, firstly by flogging and then by your dispatch to prison at Port Arthur.'

The first hour passed quickly. The new experience had the men chattering amongst themselves, pointing out things of interest to each other and making ribald remarks about the other travellers they saw on the road.

The sergeant rode along the ranks and shouted at them. 'Quieten down! Keep the noise down! If you want to get your hourly rest, keep quiet, or we'll keep marching – that'll soon quieten you!'

His shouts had the desired effect, and after a period of silence, the conversations were renewed in muted voices.

The sergeant cantered to the front and held up his arm. 'Halt, and rest easy for ten minutes!' he ordered.

The men threw themselves to the ground and stretched out their legs. Under the supervision of the corporals, they went back to the wagon and were given a measure of water. As they returned to the ranks, they stepped aside and turned their backs to urinate on the ground. A few more minutes of lying on the ground and they were called back to the ranks in readiness to resume their march.

Occasionally they would meet a bullock team pulling a heavy wagon loaded with bales of wool or other farm produce. The sergeant would canter to the front and order the convicts to halt, line up along the roadside and remain silent while the bullocks strained their way past.

Martin was surprised to see how much traffic used the road. It was plain to see that Van Diemen's Land was a land of plenty and that business was thriving.

Another hour brought them to Austin's Ferry where they would cross the Derwent River before heading north on their journey to the convict stations in the Midland and the Northern Districts. Getting across the wide and deep river was a tedious and slow job. The ferry was a strongly built craft propelled by a mixture of oarsmen and sail, depending on weather conditions. Half the men and the wagon were taken across and rested on the other side while the ferry returned for the second half. The whole operation took over three hours.

They were back on the road by 2 o'clock and after another two hours of marching, by which time the winter sun was well down, they reached their destination for the first day, a delightful little village called Pontville about fifteen miles from Hobart. The barracks at Pontville had been built twenty years ago from sandstone quarried from the extensive deposits on the outskirts of the village. It was a light, golden brown stone that had been used extensively in Hobart and on farms throughout the Southern Districts. The early settlers liked it for its natural beauty as well as for the sense of solidity and permanence it gave to their homes, a sentiment eagerly sought by them to compensate for the homesickness for their old homes in England.

By the end of the day, the convicts were footsore and very weary. They were given a good feed and slept that night on straw palliasses in the barracks. After the hardest day's work they had done for many months – indeed for some it was the hardest day they had ever had in their lives – peace and contentment prevailed and most slept soundly.

Martin was well-pleased with all he had seen during the day and went to sleep convinced that he was well started on the great adventure.

After much foot stamping and slapping of arms to get the blood circulating, plus a substantial meal of oatmeal and mutton chops with bread and tea – the only food they would get until reaching Green Ponds that evening – the squad was on the road by half past nine the next morning.

By the time of the first spell, the men were so hot that most of them asked permission to put their jackets in the wagon and march on in shirts only.

'And they call this winter!' a big, raw boned convict from Northern England said with a scornful laugh. 'Seems more like summer to me.'

The marchers quickly got used to the routine of marching and spelling. They learned to lie on their backs and put their feet in the air to get the most benefit from the spells.

The winter sun shone on them all day and the atmosphere was quite calm. By the time they reached their destination at Green Ponds, the sun was going down and they were again exhausted. Climbing the last big hill to the south of Green Ponds during the afternoon had been the last effort that drained them; but once over the top, the track had been downhill for the rest of the way and they were still in good spirits when they reached the barracks.

Their successful completion of the first two days of the long march had given them confidence and pride in themselves. They were noisy and high-spirited as their dinner was served out to them that evening.

The convict station at Green Ponds was a substantial stone building large enough to accommodate the whole company. They were locked in overnight and slept on the usual straw filled palliasses.

The Sergeant roared them out of bed early the next morning. 'All out! We've got a long march ahead of us today and I want an early start. You milksops are soft and have to go slowly, so we'll start early.'

They were given a good meal for breakfast, including the usual mutton chops. It would be the last food they would get until reaching Oatlands that evening. Four of the convicts were left at Green Ponds to be sent to work on local properties.

The guard dogs were left behind to be returned to the barracks at Hobart. 'We won't need them any more now,' the Sergeant said. 'Nobody would be silly enough to make a run for it while we're going through blackfellow country for the next few days.'

It was another bright, sunny morning. The men were stamping their feet and slapping their shoulders as they started out, but by the time the first rest came after an hour, most were so warm they again shed their jackets and marched on wearing only shirts.

The flat country they were passing through was easy walking. The large, open plains were rich farming country and the individual farms looked prosperous and well-managed. The paddocks stretched back from both sides of the road; on the eastern side to run up into undulating, low hills that were a series of rich valleys while on the western side the mountains in the far distance marked the boundary of the flat Midlands plains where the country rose steeply to ascend to the central plateaux marking the centre of the island.

During the second hour, the road started to rise into higher country and the grass paddocks gave way to bush. As they climbed Spring Hill which would be the longest climb of the whole journey, the bush became dense right down to the roadsides. About halfway up the long, winding climb, they took their second spell.

When they sauntered back to the wagon for a drink of water, they found the Corporal examining one of the horse's front hooves.

'What's up?' one of the convicts asked. 'Don't tell me the poor bugger's getting blisters like us.'

'No,' he replied, 'he's cast a shoe.'

Thomas Carter pushed his way to the front and after taking a quick look, he said, 'Martin Maynard can fix that for you. He's good with horses.'

The Sergeant arrived on the scene at that moment and heard what was said. He looked around and caught Martin's eye.

'Is that right?' he asked. 'Can you put the shoe back on?'

'If you've got some tools, I can,' he said.

The driver quickly produced a small, wooden box from under the wagon and opened it to reveal some rudimentary farrier's tools sufficient for the simple job of replacing a shoe. The horse was unhitched from the wagon and taken to one side where Martin quickly cleaned the mud and clay from the animal's hoof before trimming the frog and removing the old horseshoe nails. A few quick strokes of the rasp shaped the hoof to allow the shoe to be replaced. Fifteen minutes later, the horse was back with its mate, hitched to the wagon.

The Sergeant had watched the episode with interest.

'That's not the first time you've done that, I'll bet. Where did you learn to shoe a horse?'

'On the farm where I worked,' Martin replied, 'and my brother-in-law is a blacksmith and he showed me a lot.'

An hour later, the company reached the top of Spring Hill and were halted for a rest. From the vantage point, they could see Oatlands in the distance away to the north.

The sun was sinking below the mountains to the west as they reached the large prison and barracks where they would spend the night.

After the usual evening meal, they were locked into a large dormitory in the barracks where they found the straw filled palliasses waiting for them. As the Sergeant supervised the lockdown, he said, 'For a bunch of milksops, you've done well for the first three days. You deserve a day off. We'll be staying here tomorrow for a rest day, so you can lay in a bit tomorrow morning.'

This was greeted with a variety of responses, some of which were churlish, but most were strongly appreciative.

After breakfast the next morning, seven more convicts were taken out of the company to start the final journey to their places of employment under their new masters in the Oatlands district.

Later in the morning, the corporal horse driver said to Martin, 'The Sergeant thinks it would be a good idea for you to check the shoes on all three horses before we leave here. It could save any more trouble on the road.'

'Yes, all right, I can do that,' Martin replied. 'Can I have Thomas Carter to help me?'

'Yes, I think so. I'll check it out with the Sergeant.'

Martin was pleased to be given the task. It would be a good way of filling his day. He was a man of few words, but he hated inactivity. He could sit with a book for long periods, but without something to absorb him he soon became restless.

They did the job in the blacksmith's forge that was in the yard adjacent to the barracks. There was no blacksmith on the staff at the time, so Martin and Thomas had the run of the place. A private with a musket was placed to guard them to see that they did not abscond or steal anything.

The job took up most of the afternoon and when it was finished, the three men fell into a good yarn. The soldier was more than willing to talk to them about what it was like to be a soldier in Van Diemen's Land compared to back home in England.

'The climate's a lot better, for a start,' he said. 'This is supposed to be winter, but apart from a bit of frost, you'd never know. Not like back home where I come from. We'd have freezing snow on the ground for weeks every winter. And the grub's a lot better too,' he went on, 'and the meat. Back home, we seldom ever got a feed of meat, but here we get it every day. Good stuff, too.'

'What's it like working for a master?' Thomas asked him.

'That's a bit chancy from what I've heard,' he said. 'There's good ones and there's bad ones. It's a matter of luck.'

The soldier was a mine of information about life in the colony, and by the time the two young men returned to the barracks, they were a lot better informed about many things including the soldier's view of service in Van Diemen's Land.

The next morning, the company got away to a good, early start. The first two hours passed pleasantly, but towards midday a south-westerly breeze blew up and within an hour, light showers were passing over. As the afternoon progressed, the wind grew stronger and the rain colder. The only aspect of the situation that favoured the marchers was that the wind was coming from behind them.

The Sergeant timed the spelling stops to make the best use of whatever patches of bush along the road were available for shelter, but within an hour the men were drenched and cold. The showers became more frequent and laced with hail. For the convicts, it was the first experience of how the usually temperate winter weather could become cold and wet. The only thing to do was to quicken the pace in order to reach the barracks at Ross as soon as possible.

The last hour was full of drenching rain. It was an exhausted and dispirited company that finally got under cover in the barracks, by which time it was almost dark.

The cooks had prepared a good hot meal in the knowledge that the company would be in poor shape after a long day in bad weather, and they served up an extra ration that night. It wasn't long before the big dormitory was hung with wet clothes from every conceivable point. Fortunately, the swags in the wagon had been well-covered with a tarpaulin and had stayed dry, so the men had comfortable clothes to put on and a warm blanket to sleep in.

The next morning dawned better. A pallid sun and a light breeze promised an improvement in the weather for the next section of the journey which would take them to Powranna, a spot in a patch of empty country halfway to their next major destination at Longford.

The day passed uneventfully and they spent that night in a

ramshackle and draughty barracks built many years before with split slabs, a kind of construction that left many a gap for the cold winds to blow through.

After another long day, they finally arrived at Longford where they found a large, stone barracks to shelter them and some competent cooks to feed them, the best food they had been given since leaving Ross.

They were given another rest day to build their strength in preparation for the last stage that would take them to Deloraine. They needed the rest; the hard day after leaving Oatlands and the final two long days after Ross had knocked the stuffing out of them. In spite of that, they were a much fitter and stronger body of men than when they left Hobart eight days previously. The good food and the regular hours had benefited them all, and although few would have admitted it, they were in better shape to do a day's work than they had been for a very long time.

They were all enjoying the day off at Longford. The guards had been lenient with them that morning and allowed them an extra hour in their bunks.

Thomas knew he would be leaving the gang to be taken into Launceston to join his new master where he would be employed at his trade of wheelwright. Neither of the young men were happy about the prospect of being parted, but they well understood that as convicts they were obliged to go where they were sent and do whatever job was given them. Their only hope of an eventual release from bondage was to build a reputation as good, reliable workers. The most important thing for the next few years would be to stay out of trouble at all costs.

Martin was tidying and organising his swag as a big, tough Irishman he knew well said to him: 'I suppose you'll be doing a few extra jobs for the Sergeant again today.'

Martin was surprised by the question and was slow to comprehend the inference in it. 'No, not that I know of,' he replied. 'What makes you ask?'

'It's just that you like to be in good with the bosses. I thought you might be crawling to him again today by shoeing more horses.'

Martin felt a shaft of anger well up in him and his first reaction was to respond in kind, but his natural caution made him hesitate. To get into a fight with another convict at this stage could blacken his record before he was even properly started.

'Think again, Murphy, before you start that tack. You could start something that would get us both into big trouble.'

The Irishman had a sneering grin and raised eyebrows and was on the verge of saying something more when Thomas came through the dormitory. Martin got up and followed him out into the yard where he told his friend what Murphy had said. Thomas quickly said, 'Don't get into a fight with him; that would be the worst thing to happen. The authorities don't like convicts fighting amongst themselves and you don't want to get a name as a troublemaker.'

'Yes, I know that,' Martin replied, 'but he could turn into a real nuisance. He's a bully by nature, but I can't let him bully me.'

'Just be careful how you handle it,' Thomas said. 'It could land you in trouble.'

'I will be, don't worry,' Martin said. 'In the meantime, I'd like to keep in touch with you after we leave here, but I can't see how we'll be able to do it. I know you'll be somewhere in Launceston, but you won't have any idea where I am.'

Thomas had a grin on his face as he said, 'It's all in the lap of the gods now, Martin, whatever happens to us. We'll just have to see how it all turns out, but I reckon we'll meet again. After all, Van Diemen's Land is not a big place.'

It was a refreshed and cheerful company that started early the next morning on the last stage of their long walk to Deloraine. The Sergeant told them it would be a long stage and that it would take all day.

'It is twenty-three miles and it will be a test for you, but we'll take it in easy stages. You're in a lot better condition now than when we started and I know you'll be able to do it.'

The Sergeant called Martin out and said, 'Corporal Madson the horse driver is sick and can't work. Can you drive the wagon today?'

Martin was taken by surprise and stuttered, 'Yes, yes, I suppose I can,' and then, feeling foolish by this reply, said, 'Oh yes, I can do it.'

The two light draughthorses were quiet and well-trained, and as he helped to hitch them to the wagon, he knew he would have no trouble with them. Many months had passed since he had had reins in his hands and the feel of them gave him a sense of elation. Old memories of the plough teams and the carthorses he had driven on Ashburton came flooding back to him and he felt his spirits lift. No matter how hard his life would be at Deloraine, if he could be involved with horses and other farm work, he would be happy.

The Sergeant called a halt for the first spell of the day and most of the convicts sauntered back to the wagon for a drink. The other corporal was on hand to supervise the issue of the water.

As the red-bearded Murphy took his mug, he glanced at Martin and said, 'I see you're at it again today, you'll get on.'

The corporal, a Welshman by the name of Morris, heard the remark, and when the men had returned to the main company, he asked Martin what it was about.

'I'm blowed if I know,' Martin said. 'He seems to have developed a hatred for me since I did the bit of shoeing. Reckons I'm crawling to the Sergeant.'

'Oh, it's like that, is it? We get a few like him going through the system. They're a nuisance and can cause trouble. You need to watch him; he looks like a nasty character to me.'

Martin grinned as he said, 'I'm not frightened of him. I could handle him all right, but I don't want to get into trouble fighting over his stupid bullying.'

'Don't worry, if he pushes you into a situation where you have to defend yourself, we'll look after you. I'll tip the Sergeant off to what's going on.'

The weather was good and the company made good progress through the morning. The Sergeant gave them an hour off at midday and some of the convicts threw themselves down in the sun and went to sleep.

Martin was fascinated by the range of mountains that lay in the distance to the west and the south of the road they were following. One of the guards at Longford had told him that the mighty rim of mountains that ran from the centre of the island far away to the west were called 'The Western Tiers' and that on top of them lay a vast plateau containing many lakes. He could see that between the foothills and the road they were travelling on lay thousands of acres of dense forests so tall and thick that a company of men like the one he was following that day could easily be swallowed up and lost within them. But now the bright sunlight that bathed the scene for as far as he could see gave a wonderful atmosphere of peace and tranquillity that made Martin think that paradise would be like the vista that lay before them.

The men were given more water before starting again, but there was no food. The difficulties of catering in the field made it impossible to feed them during the day, so the practice was to give them a good breakfast and nothing more until dinner in the evening, but by the middle of the afternoon, hunger was gnawing at empty stomachs and fatigue was taking its toll. The Sergeant increased the number of spells but gave them no sympathy in regards to hunger.

'You'll get a good feed tonight,' he told them. 'Convicts can't expect to be mollycoddled. Anyway, if you were back in England, most of you wouldn't be getting even one decent feed a day, let alone two.'

Most of them knew he spoke the truth and fell silent for the next hour or two.

The barracks was a large, brick building situated on the banks of the Meander River in the village of Deloraine. They reached their destination as the sun was rapidly disappearing behind the mountains. After leaving a few convicts behind at every station along the journey, the company was now down to twenty-nine. They knew they would be allocated to various gangs that would be employed on government projects of one kind or another in the Deloraine district for the next twelve months.

The kitchen of the barracks turned out a good meal that evening and the bunks and palliasses in the big, slab-built dormitory were on a par with what they had found at all the other convict stations on the way from Hobart. For those who wanted to wash themselves or bathe their feet, there was plenty of water, and buckets to use as wash dishes.

By the time the convicts were fed, darkness had fallen and everybody was looking to get into their bunks. As they were preparing for bed, there was plenty of talk about how tired they were and how well they would sleep.

'There's one lazy bugger who's not too tired,' Murphy said in a loud voice. 'Sitting on his arse all day in the wagon while the rest of us had to slog it all the way.'

Silence fell over the dormitory as all eyes looked at Martin. He was flabbergasted at the childish charge and didn't know whether to respond rationally, or treat it as a joke.

'Don't be a silly fool, Murphy,' he said. 'Somebody had to drive the bloody horse. Try and be a bit grown-up for a change.'

Murphy was quick-tempered and couldn't control his jealousy. 'I might be a fool, but I'm not a crawler,' he snarled. 'You're always at it. First it's shoeing the boss's horses, now it's driving his bloody wagon. You'd like his job, wouldn't you? Then you could boss us all around.'

'Don't be wet behind the ears, Murphy. You're acting like a jealous kid.' Martin laughed as he taunted him.

At that, Murphy completely lost his temper and, jumping up, he ran at Martin, yelling, 'I'll give you something to laugh about, you stuck-up bastard!'

As he got close, Martin's right hand flashed out and grabbed Murphy's wrist and, jerking it savagely, he sent him crashing up against the brick wall at the end of the dormitory. Murphy collapsed on the floor, completely winded and more than half senseless.

Martin stood and watched him as he struggled to gather his wits and stand up.

'Don't try anything more, Murphy. I don't want to hurt you, but I will if you come at me again.'

Murphy didn't say anything. A couple of his mates went to help him to his bunk.

A crowd quickly gathered around Martin, laughing and slapping him on the back.

'That's the same way you handled that bloke on the ship that day,' one of them said. 'Where did you learn to fight like that?'

'I was lucky I had the chance to learn wrestling from an expert when I was a boy on the farm,' Martin said. 'It's just learning the right holds that does it. But I don't want to fight anybody. All I want is to get along well with everybody, even with Murphy, the silly bugger.'

The excitement kept them all chattering and laughing for a time, all the fatigue temporarily forgotten, but after a while they crept into their bunks and the only noise to be heard was snoring.

As they gathered for breakfast the next morning, Martin went up to Murphy, holding out his hand. 'I'd be just as pleased to bury the hatchet and forget anything ever happened,' he said.

Murphy looked sulky and unfriendly.

'Go on, shake hands and be mates!' somebody called out, a cry that was taken up enthusiastically by the majority. Murphy didn't say anything, but he did take Martin's hand and gave it a half-hearted shake.

Later that morning, the Sergeant spoke to Martin while he was waiting to be paraded before Captain Bellinger to be told where he would be working for the next few months.

'I hear there was a ruckus in the dormitory last night,' he said. 'I also hear that you handled yourself well at the time, and again this morning. I've put in a good report on you, and I hope it helps.'

'Thanks, Sergeant,' Martin said in some confusion. 'I appreciate it. I don't want to get into trouble, but the silly fool gave me no choice.'

'You've done well,' the Sergeant said, 'but be careful in future. If you get a reputation as a brawler, there'll always be some pug around wanting to take you on.'

Captain Bellinger, the officer in charge of the Deloraine convict station – a fresh faced, forty year old Scotsman – was reading Martin's file when he was escorted into his office.

'I see from your file that you are an experienced farm worker and that you have had experience with horses.'

'Yes, Sir,' Martin replied. 'I can drive horses in the plough and in the wagon. I was taught how to handle horses by the horse steward on the farm where I worked.'

'Right, you've got a mark on your papers for good conduct, so you will be allocated to Mr Kentish's gang. You'll be taken out to Kimberley's Ford to join him tomorrow. Dismiss for now.'

When they returned to the yard, the Sergeant told Martin that Mr Kentish was a government surveyor who was engaged in surveying a road through the unexplored wilderness to the south-west of Deloraine and that his gang of twenty men were supplied with food and other requirements by packhorse.

'The next supplies will be going out tomorrow, so you can help with the packhorses and stay out with Mr Kentish's gang. You'll be camping out, so it'll be a bit tough for a few weeks until the weather improves. You'll be issued with more clothes and an extra blanket to take with you.'

Martin returned to the barracks wondering what lay ahead; there was something ominous in the need for more clothes to go to his new job.

CHAPTER 4

*T*he morning after their arrival at Deloraine, the convicts were told they would have a rest day while being assessed and allocated to the various gangs where they would serve their obligatory twelve months in the probation system before being either released on a ticket of leave or assigned to an employer.

Captain Bellinger had their files before him and interviewed them individually. The files contained all their personal information including behaviour reports from the time of their trials through to that day.

By being asked questions based on the information in their files, the prisoners soon realised the Captain knew a great deal more about them than they liked, so they felt impelled to be truthful in their answers to him about their work experience and capabilities. Most were sent to road building gangs. Those who had building skills were used appropriately, some on bridge construction and some on building barracks and other facilities needed by the convict system.

Mr Kentish's survey gang, to which Martin had been allocated, was made up of the better qualified and hand-picked men who could fit into the lightly supervised life in the wilderness. Only well-behaved and reliable men were placed in this job that was well away from the strict discipline of the probation station.

'Your record shows that you have been well-behaved and that you are capable of driving and looking after horses. You have been put into Mr Kentish's survey gang and it will be up to you how you fit in out there. Conditions in the bush are bad during the winter, but it's only a few weeks before the good weather returns. If you can't handle the work, you'll be brought back here to go on to a pick and shovel job on the road gang. Have you any questions?'

'No, Sir. I think I'll be able to handle it,' Martin said.

The convict population consisted of men and women from every layer of society and of individual character. Many were worthless characters content to be swept along in the general tide of convict life with little thought for their future prospects. There were many others, however, like Martin Maynard, whose only thought was to avoid trouble and serve out their sentences quickly, and to their own benefit if possible.

Martin was placed under the supervision of Private John Spinks, the soldier in charge of the packhorse team. He was an easygoing, blue-eyed man of medium height and slim build. He greeted Martin with a friendly handshake and immediately asked him if he could handle horses.

'Yes, I can drive a plough team, and in the wagon. I like working with horses.'

'Good. That will make a nice change. Most of the blokes I get don't know anything. These are packhorses, so they carry the freight on their backs, not by pulling it in a cart or a wagon. There are no roads good enough for wagons where we go, but you handle them the same way as carthorses.'

The team of eight packhorses were kept in slab-built stables at Deloraine, and as soon as Martin saw them, he recognised them as well-bred horses ideal for the job. They were half-bred Shires, too light for a plough team and too heavy as saddlehorses, but just right for a pack team; big and strong enough to carry a heavy load, yet light and nimble enough to travel along rough tracks.

The supply party left early the next morning, the eight packhorses in the charge of Private Spinks assisted by Martin, and four convicts who were also to join Mr Kentish's gang under the charge of a corporal.

John Spinks told Martin they would be travelling that day to Kimberley's Ford where Mr Kentish's camp was set up. 'Mr Kentish's job is to survey and clear a track through the wilderness twenty miles in from the coast, right through to Emu Bay, far away to the west. They've got as far as Kimberley's Ford, but they'll move the camp with them as they get further west. It's a bugger of a job at this time of year because the bush is so wet,' explained the private.

The first few miles out from Deloraine ran through settled farmland where the road was adequate although very muddy and soft. Martin was interested to see how red the soil was, although judging by the colour of the grass and the few crops that could be seen from the road, it was obviously fertile. A few paddocks adjacent to the road had been cleared and made into farms, but most of the country was covered in bush.

After a little over two hours travelling, John announced that they were halfway to their destination and ordered a halt to rest both the horses and the walkers.

The further west they travelled, the fewer cleared paddocks were to be seen and the road petered out into a rough track where the horses had to walk along in single file to get through the narrow path between fallen trees and rocky outcrops. Progress became much slower. Every now and then, they had to negotiate patches where the mud was deep and sticky, hard going that tested the horses to their limits.

They reached Kinberley's Ford in the late afternoon and had the horses unloaded and the provisions securely stored away within an hour. The horses were kept in a sheltered yard where they were fed on hay and a measure of oats.

The camp was a cluster of tents laid out in the lee of a bank of gum trees on the western banks of the Mersey River, only a hundred yards from the stony ford that gave the place its name.

Martin and the other newly arrived convicts were taken into Mr Kentish's work tent to be presented to him and to be briefed on what their work would be.

Nathaniel Kentish was a little above average height and of slim build. He stood behind a work table littered with charts. He had a shock of brown hair and wore a short beard. He had an open, friendly looking face and greeted the men with a smile. Martin noticed that he introduced himself to them as if he were talking to a group of free men. He also introduced his chief assistant, Lakin Boyes, who was standing beside him.

'The job we're doing here is to explore the country and survey a new road to Emu Bay,' he told them. 'As we complete the survey in sections, we open up a track one chain wide by felling the trees and scrubbing out the undergrowth. We'll clear the narrow road of timber so that it can be used as a track by people and horses. It's important work and will be a boon for this part of Van Diemen's Land. In these wet, winter conditions the work is unpleasant and hard; however, in a few more weeks, the spring will be here and everything will be better. In the meantime, we'll try to make the camp as comfortable as possible. We've got plenty of good food and we've got good tents. Finally, if any of you want to speak to me or Mr Boyes at any time, you can feel free to do so.'

By the time they left Mr Kentish's tent, the work gang had returned from the job to the camp for the night. The head man of the gang, a convict by the name of Bill Thomas, showed Martin to the tent he would share with three other men and showed him which bunk to use. Bill Thomas was about forty years of age; a small, wiry man whose beard was showing a tinge of grey.

'You'll be all right here,' he said. 'We've got a good boss and he runs a good camp. The worst part is that the bush is so wet, and it'll be weeks before it gets better.'

The new men were pleased to see that Mr Kentish's remarks about the food were correct. The cook and his two assistants, working in a makeshift kitchen knocked up from bush poles and a tent, produced a good spread of hot meat and potatoes that warmed them up and put them all in a good mood as they ate outside around a big fire. The meal was finished with big mugs of hot tea, and the men lounged around talking in the glow of the fire for a couple of hours before going off to their tents.

Martin was surprised the next morning when Bill Thomas told him that he was to return to Deloraine with John Spinks to get more experience at packing the provisions out to the camp.

As they set off up the track, John said, 'I think they want to train you up to take over the packing on your own a bit later when they've worked their way further west. It's a good thing you can handle horses, and it'll help you get a good report as well.'

After they had been on the track for half an hour, they stopped for a spell. 'A couple of these horses are quiet enough to be ridden; the rest will lead along behind,' said John.

They rigged the leads to hitch the horses one behind another and mounted the leaders to resume the journey, this time in ease and comfort.

They reached the Deloraine station in the afternoon after a leisurely journey from Kimberley's Ford and then spent an hour organising the pack loads for the next morning.

Martin was interested to meet his old friends again at the barracks that evening. Most of them were working on roads not far from Deloraine and were able to walk to work in the mornings and walk back to the barracks in the evenings. They said the best part so far was that they got cold meat and bread – with cold tea – for a midday meal which was a big improvement on what they got on the long walk from Hobart.

John Spinks knew his job well and Martin took particular note of how he did it, showing a close interest in the method of filling the packs and loading them onto the horses. By the time they arrived back at Kimberley's Ford the next evening, Martin felt confident that he could handle the job if he was called upon to do it. John Spinks usually did three trips a week to keep the camp supplied, but Martin would not be required on every trip.

The next day, he was taken with the other men out along the new track as far as it had progressed and got his first taste of working in the wet bush. The men were organised into small groups that took turns to work at the head of the trail where the dense bush was most saturated by the frequent rains. The first blow of the scrub hook or the axe brought down a torrent of water from the higher limbs and leaves. Within half an hour, they were soaked to the skin and bitterly cold. They would then be replaced by another group and sent back to widen out the trail they had blazed.

The dense bush covered most of the ground, but every now and then they would strike a patch of lightly covered ground that would allow the work to bound ahead for a short distance.

Either Mr Kentish or Mr Boyes would be on hand frequently to check the direction of the slowly lengthening track and to mark out where to head by crawling over or under the impenetrable bauera undergrowth and blazing bark off the lead trees.

The men complained continually about the conditions and mumbled threats about going on strike, but they never refused duty because, in spite of the discomfort, they had too much respect for Mr Kentish. They believed him when he told them that it was important work and well worth doing. They also knew that he did all he could to make their lives bearable. On bad days, he always got them back to camp early where they could shelter in the tents. He always had two men employed on gathering dry firewood to keep the kitchens going and to provide big, roaring fires at night to dry out their wet clothes.

There was often an interchange of convicts from the road gang at Deloraine which kept the men well-informed about conditions on that job. The result was that the men at Kimberley's Ford knew that in spite of the wet and cold bush, they were on a better wicket than the road gangs, so while they continued to complain, they didn't press their case too hard.

The men were allowed to find the wallaby's tracks and set snares to catch them, both for their meat, which made a welcome addition to their meals, and for the skins they were allowed to keep for sale. The men were fascinated by the small wallabies and the larger kangaroos. There were no animals like them in Britain or Ireland, so they had nothing to compare them with.

The country around Kimberley's Ford had a wide selection of native animals, some of which the men saw while working in the forest, but many others; being small, timid and nocturnal, would seldom be seen. The small wallaby was about as big as a medium sized dog and, like all the members of the kangaroo family, it ran about by hopping along on its back legs. The larger animal, called a kangaroo, varied in size from that of a medium sized dog up to that of an Alsatian dog.

The animals made 'runs' through the bush that led out to their feeding grounds on the open plains, and they could be caught in wire or cord snares set in a way that would catch them around the neck and hold them until they choked to death, or when the trapper came he would club them to a quick death.

The soft, furry skins were carefully 'tacked' out to dry on the trunks of trees or some other flat surface and were readily saleable to an insatiable furskin market.

Nathan Kentish was a humane and kind-hearted man with a genuine concern for his fellow men, and his good treatment of his gang was repaid by their loyalty and hard work. In this atmosphere, Martin settled easily into life in the camp and soon made friends with the men he lived with. He continued to help with packing provisions out from Deloraine and, after only a few weeks, was often ordered to handle the job himself, mostly alone but sometimes with the assistance of another convict.

As the winter drew to an end, the camp was moved a few miles further west. They found a small patch of lightly covered high ground on which to build the new camp. The tents were quickly and easily moved, but the kitchen and the heavy gear was more difficult. Martin was put in charge of a packhorse that was kept at the camp for several weeks to assist with the move.

Bill Thomas identified a tall gum tree near the site of the new camp that he claimed would be a good 'splitter' and suggested to Mr Kentish that the men could get enough slabs and palings from it in a day's work to build a kitchen. He was given approval to proceed and the men took up the project with enthusiasm. Much to the cook's delight, within a few days the camp had a far better kitchen which made his job a lot easier.

The slow job of hacking their way through the dense bush continued with impatient speculation as to when some open country would be found, but there were no encouraging signs; however, success was nearer than the weary scrub cutters knew.

One early morning, Martin went with Bill Thomas to check his wallaby snares that were set in the bush a little way ahead of the track. They found the snares and took out three small wallabies. Bill pushed his way a little further into the bush and called out, 'Look at this! There's some fresh tracks here, and they're too big for wallabies! They must be kangaroos! I reckon there's clear country nearby if there's 'roos about!

The two men excitedly followed the track and came to a place littered with cattle dung still steaming with warmth that indicated the animals weren't far away. They continued on and suddenly emerged onto a vast expanse of beautiful, open country that stretched away to the west as far as they could see. Bill was excited and let out a wild 'hurrah'.

'We'll hurry back to camp and tell Mr Kentish what we've found,' he said. But as they turned to go, he paused and said, 'We'll leave a mark to show that we've been here.' He handed Martin his pocketknife. 'Cut our initials and the date on this tree,' he said, putting his hand on a big, smooth-barked tree.

Martin quickly carved:

B T M M

OCT 1845

They were back in camp within half an hour and told a delighted Mr Kentish what they had stumbled onto.

As soon as breakfast was over, Mr Kentish announced that he would immediately go and see the open country for himself. He instructed

Martin to get some bread and meat sandwiches in a carry bag from the cook and accompany him on his trip.

Martin led the way past the place where they had snared the wallabies, then past the spot where the cattle had camped and again they suddenly emerged into the sun-drenched, open country. Mr Kentish was astonished.

'It's amazing,' he said. 'How could we be so close and yet not see more signs?'

After looking around the immediate area and taking a bearing on a hill that could be seen about a mile away, he set off to climb it and get a good look at the surrounding country.

It was easy walking through the open country that was covered in a tall, silvery grass with the occasional eucalypt or wattle tree dotted about. Within half an hour, they were at the summit of the low hill and could see that the open country continued on into the distance.

'This is magnificent!' Mr Kentish exclaimed. 'We've found something important. This could be a new farming district in times to come. We'll keep going to the west and see what we can discover.'

He carefully took bearings on landmarks as they proceeded and kept the time so that he could estimate how far they had walked. Martin saw with interest how he could make a map of the area as they travelled across it. About midday, they found a spot on some rising ground and sat down to eat their bread and meat.

'This is a great day, Martin,' Mr Kentish said. 'You'll be able to say that you helped discover a new, unexplored part of Van Diemen's Land.'

'This place ought to be called Kentish Plains, seeing that you are the discoverer of it,' Martin said.

Mr Kentish chuckled as he replied, 'No, I'm not one to expect my name to be tacked onto new discoveries. I'd rather see it called something more poetic and beautiful, but we don't know yet what we've found. We'll have a spell and then go on to see more of it.'

They lounged on the grass covered hill and rested. As usual, Martin was quiet, and after a few minutes Mr Kentish asked him about his home in England. He was by nature a generous and kind-hearted man who had the knack of communicating easily with other people and he drew Martin out to talk about his early life and his growing up on Ashburton. A half hour had quickly passed before Mr Kentish got to his feet and led off to resume his exploration.

They came on to a herd of about thirty cattle, all in good condition and healthy looking. They were not frightened of the men but were very curious. They bunched up together and stared at the men as they slowly approached them. Suddenly, when the two men had got within a chain of the cattle, they snorted loudly and stampeded away with their tails held out horizontally behind them and disappeared behind another hill.

The men covered a further four miles of similar country during the afternoon and then turned to walk back towards camp.

Finding the open country was a turning point in the progress of the exploration and survey project. Mr Kentish spent many days exploring and measuring it before spending two days in his tent writing up a report to send off to his chief in Hobart. After that, the survey progressed so well that it was necessary to move the camp further west again in the early summer.

Mr Kentish's road ran ahead into increasingly rugged country and it was impossible to find a workable gradient along the route he had been given. He finally had no option but to find a different way further to the north, but while searching for a way through the original route, he made several new discoveries, including a large river that he named the Wilmot.

From the new camp, it was quicker and easier to bring supplies from a place called Forth, a small village near the coast to the north, than to travel all the way back to Deloraine. Mr Kentish blazed a trail through the wilderness to Forth and the men scrubbed it out to make a bridal path sufficient for packhorses.

He had taken Martin with him to act as his chainman when he first surveyed the route to Forth, a job that took several days to complete because the country was rugged and finding a suitable track through the mountains was difficult. They carried enough food in knapsacks to keep them going for the few days it took to reach their destination: a farm on the banks of the Forth River owned by a Mr Fenton, an old friend of Mr Kentish's. They carried blankets in a swag on their backs and camped out in the forest overnight.

The farm had been settled by Mr James Fenton several years previously, long enough to clear and plough several large paddocks with the assistance of six convicts who had been assigned to him several years before.

Mr Kentish stayed with Mr and Mrs Fenton for two days. Martin was given a bunk in the convict's hut and enjoyed meeting and talking with the other convicts. They were eager to exchange experiences of Van Diemen's Land and any scraps of news that they had heard about their old homes in Britain.

'What's it like, working for a master?' Martin asked them.

'Depends on who you get,' one man said. 'There's good masters and there's bastards. This one we've got is good.'

'Do you get paid?' was the next question.

They laughed. 'If you call two shillings a week pay, yes we get paid, but you'd be a long time getting rich on it.'

'It's a good thing we get plenty of good tucker, and some clothes, even if they are only convict garb,' said another.

'Some masters let their servants earn a bit on the side,' another man said. 'A lot depends on how well off they are.'

'Yes, you could say that,' the first man said. 'The better off they are, the stingier they are. The old lags usually make the best masters; they know what it's like to be a convict in servitude.

With the atmosphere of the farm with its modest house, the barn-yard where the stables and huts were enclosed with a post and rail fence and the talk with the convicts in the huts, Martin was reminded of his old home and his mother when he settled down to sleep that night. I wonder how she's getting on, he thought.

His thoughts ran on for a while and he felt a wave of homesickness come over him. He resolved to ask Mr Kentish to help him get a letter to his mother and to find out if it would be possible to get a letter from his family in return.

The next morning Martin, for the first time, saw the man who would become his master within a few months although at that time neither of them knew it. He was lounging outside the hut with the other con-victs before they were to go off to work when a chaise cart, pulled by a high-stepping horse, came into the yard. The driver was a big man of middle-age, wearing a large beaver hat. One of the convicts stepped forward to hold the horse's head.

'Good day, Mr Drewitt,' he said as the man got down from the cart. 'Mr Fenton's up at the house.'

'Right, I'll go over. Keep an eye on this rig, would you?'

'Who is that?' Martin asked the man standing near him.

'That's Charles Drewitt,' he replied. 'Got a big farm over at the Don, a few miles from here.'

'He's an old lag, made good,' another said. 'Very tight with money, he's a hard nut.'

A few minutes later, Mr Fenton and Charles Drewitt came out to where the men were waiting to be given their orders for the day. Martin noticed Drewitt was taller than anybody else in the yard and very thick around the chest and shoulders.

After a few minutes discussion, the men left the yard to go to their various tasks. Mr Kentish then said to Martin, 'Just wait here for a while. We'll start back soon.'

An hour, later they had started the long walk back to the camp. Most of their walk was uphill and through bush. They stopped at midday to rest and eat the lunch Mrs Fenton had packed for them. They sat down on a fallen tree on the side of a hill that gave them a good view over Bass's Strait, shining blue in the distance. Martin took the opportunity to raise the question of writing to his mother.

'Yes, of course you can write to her. I'll post it to go on the first ship to England and she can write back to you. She can send it care of my address and I'll see that you get it.'

After a long day struggling uphill and through the bush, they got back to the camp as darkness fell.

Mr Kentish was as good as his word and produced paper and envelope for Martin the next day. 'You can write it on the table in my tent,' he said. 'I'll start it on its journey when I'm in Deloraine next week.'

Within two weeks, the men had opened up a bridle track to Forth and from then on, all their provisions came by small ship into Forth where they were collected and stored by Mr Fenton before being packed up country by Martin with four packhorses.

Mr Kentish periodically walked down to Forth to spend a couple of days at Mr Fenton's farm where he worked on his reports. Depending on the weather, Martin often stayed overnight in the convict huts, becoming friendly with all the people who worked at the farm, including the cook and the housemaid, the only women he had spoken to since being arrested in the village over a year earlier.

The cook was a thirty year old Irishwoman, mostly of a cheerful disposition but capable of a flash of temper if the mood took her, but she was always inquisitive. She wanted to know all about Martin, but he was a man of few words and information always had to be prised out of him. Soon after she met him, she said, 'You don't say much, do you? Cat's got your tongue? Or perhaps you've got something to hide, eh?'

The housemaid was a good-looking young Londoner, convicted at the age of fifteen for stealing a few pieces of cloth. Now eighteen and as a result of being fed properly and living a decent life, she was starting to bloom into womanhood. She gave Martin a bit of cheek, as much to see how he would take it as anything else, he thought. Nevertheless, she caught his interest and made him think of Matilda Smith and the old days.

Mr Fenton always greeted him with a relaxed and amiable manner he used with all his men. He was considered by them to be a good master, authoritative but good-hearted and fair.

Progress on the survey had improved greatly after the breakthrough into open country, and the arrival of summer had made life in the bush much better. The long, mild days and the balmy evenings put everybody into a good mood and it was a happy and contented camp.

Most of the convicts in the gang were now nearing the end of their time in the probation system and would soon be eligible to apply for a ticket of leave which would release them from full-time bondage and make them free to take paid work, if they could find it.

Even though they seldom emerged from the bush to talk to other people, they knew enough about conditions in the colony to know that since the end of the assignment system, the labour market was very tight and there were thousands of unemployed people, all competing for the few jobs available. Ironically, it was a repeat of the same conditions in Britain that had got most of them into trouble in the first place.

As the summer gave way to autumn, it was apparent to all that the job was rapidly coming to an end. Mr Kentish made it known that he expected to finish the job within a few weeks and then all the convicts would return to the probation station at Deloraine.

In the meantime, unknown to Martin, his reputation as a steady and reliable worker had been growing. Mr Kentish had praised him to Mr Fenton, telling him about his training on Ashburton and his capabilities as a horseman and bushman, and he in turn had recommended him to Mr Drewitt. Charles Drewitt's business at the Don had thrived to the extent that he needed one or two men who could be trained up as overseers to take responsibility for helping to run his farming and timber businesses.

Mr Drewitt was a man with a mixed reputation; on the one hand he was mean, even stingy, where money was concerned, but on the other hand he was a very successful businessman because he knew how to manage both money and people. He had arrived in Van Diemen's Land at the age of twenty-nine as a convict. He had served his time and, after being released on a ticket of leave, had started a little business in Launceston as a carrier with one horse and a cart. From that modest start, he had built up a fortune by hard work and thrift, plus a large measure of cunning – animal cunning, some said. However, when the occasion demanded it, he knew how to be generous. He provided land and money to erect a church and finance to pay a pastor for the little community where he lived at the Don.

He treated his employees with strict fairness, albeit with a tight purse. His own experience had taught him that being a convict was not necessarily an indication that a man was worthless and of low intelligence; for him it was better business to take a good convict on a low wage and train him for the job he wanted done than to take another man on a higher wage and run the risk of getting a dud. In the end, the convict would invariably develop a stronger loyalty to him and be the more valuable employee.

He had a friend in the convict system in Launceston who had directed good men to him in the past and when he heard about Martin Maynard, he applied to have him released to his service on a ticket of leave. Although Martin had not completed his twelve months probation, his good conduct and work reports, plus the influence of Mr Drewitt's friend, got him his ticket of leave as Mr Kentish's survey was completed.

Mr Kentish called Martin into his tent a few days before they struck camp for the last time and told him that Mr Drewitt had been told that Martin was to be released to work for him on a ticket of leave. Martin was flabbergasted; he didn't know whether it was a great stroke of fortune for him, or whether it was a sentence of further punishment.

'Well, I'm pleased to get the job, Sir,' he said, 'but I'm surprised, and I don't really know what to think.'

Mr Kentish chuckled as he looked at Martin, by now a well-built, strong young man with a dark brown beard and a good-looking, open face.

'You'll be all right with Charles Drewitt,' he said. 'Don't believe all the silly things you hear about him. I know him well and I think it is a lucky break for you. If you do as well for him as you have on this job, you'll get on.

'We will all be leaving this camp for the last time in a few days,' he continued. 'The rest of the camp will be going back to Deloraine, but I want to visit Mr Fenton, so you can come with me to the farm and Mr Drewitt will pick you up from there.'

CHAPTER 5

*I*t was a warm and shining morning in April 1846. Martin, full of apprehension and suspense, waited at the convict's hut on Mr Fenton's farm for his new master to come to take him to his property, Norwood, on the Don River a few miles to the east.

Martin had arrived at the farm the day before in company with his previous master, the surveyor Mr Kentish, and now faced a new experience in his life as an assigned convict servant in Van Diemen's Land. Somewhat to his surprise, he had been told only three days ago that he was being released from the probation gang at Deloraine to work for Mr Charles Drewitt.

He would be under the control of his master by virtue of the fact that he could be returned to the probation gang at any time for misbehaviour in respect to the many regulations controlling the convict system. In essence, he would be free to move around the police district and take paid work from his master – and with his approval, from other people as well – subject to the obligation to report regularly to the police .

Martin's mixed feelings had been aroused by Mr Drewitt's reputation as related by the convicts on Mr Fenton's farm. According to them he was a well-known miser, more interested in making money than anything else in life. He had been branded as a demanding master and a hard man in business and had come to the colony as a convict who, by extreme thriftiness and hard work, had made good and was now a successful farmer and businessman.

This reputation intrigued Martin whose secret ambition was to do the same. He had conspired with his brother-in-law to be convicted for stealing blacksmith's tools and transported to Van Diemen's Land because his future prospects in England were hopeless and he had no way of getting the money to pay for the voyage.

The irony of his situation that morning, the details of which were not known to another living soul, gave him cause for inner hope, and he smiled as he thought about it.

Mr Drewitt himself drove into the yard in a chaise cart about mid-morning and greeted Martin with a friendly smile and, somewhat to his surprise, a handshake. Martin didn't know how their personal relationship would be conducted and was hesitant in how he greeted his new master until the ground rules were established.

The situation was complicated by factors that were unique to Martin, and for that matter, to the colonial society. While Mr Drewitt was undoubtedly entitled to the full respect of society and his employees, the unspoken fact that he was himself an ex-convict added a special flavour to the situation.

Having been reared on a large English farm and accustomed to dealing with a squire and his family, Martin was confident of fitting in with whatever his employer wanted. If he wanted to be called 'Master', that was what he would get, or if he wanted to be called 'Squire', that would be just as easy.

Mr Drewitt climbed down from the cart and said, 'I'll go up to the house for half an hour before we go. We can have a good talk on the way home. Just take care of the horse, would you.'

An hour later, they were climbing the steep road from the Forth Valley over the hills to the Don Valley, only about three miles away.

'Well, we can talk about a few things as we go along,' Mr Drewitt said. 'I want you to work on the farm mainly. I hope you can do a lot of the horse driving. Mr Kentish said you were good with horses.'

'Yes, I have had experience on the farm. I can handle the plough team and the wagons.'

Mr Drewitt said, 'That's good. I'll pay you four shillings a week and your keep for the first six months and then six shillings until the end of the first year, and throw in two sets of work clothes as well. After a year we'll look at it again. This job I'm giving you; it will be up to you as to how well you get on. If you treat me right and please me, I'll treat you right. If we can't get along, or if you get into trouble, I'll take you straight back to the gangs.'

'That's all right by me,' Martin replied. 'What am I to call you?'

'You can call me Mr Drewitt,' he said.

After a while, he asked Martin where he had grown up and about his father. Martin was not a talkative man, but knowing that making a favourable impression on his boss was important, he tried hard to give him a sensible answer. He told him about his father and his early life on Ashburton, about his mother and his two sisters and about his brother-in-law; the village blacksmith, George Latimer.

As they drove along, Mr Drewitt pointed out to Martin where his land started and the lay of the land out to the Don River heads. A lot of the land had been cleared and cropped, but there were hundreds of tall, dead trees dotted all over the countryside as far as the eye could see. He asked about this and Mr Drewitt said, 'Yes, they're the result of the system we use to clear the forests. All the good, valuable trees are used for palings and the like and the others are ringbarked to make them die. When the land is cleared, they are left there to eventually fall over in the storms. They're a great nuisance, but we can't do much about them. It's too expensive to grub them out until they fall over.'

'Yes,' Martin said, 'I can see that. They're big, aren't they?'

'Yes, they are. Most of them would be hundreds of years old. What you see now is the first stage in developing a new country. In times to come, all this will be a rich farming district as good, if not better, than any in the world,' Mr Drewitt said with pride.

As they drove up the road to the house, a substantial building on the rising ground back from the river banks, Martin noticed an avenue of young oak trees that had been carefully protected by a post and rail fence. The whole place had a well-kept and cared for appearance, and as they drove into the spacious barnyard, he caught sight of a large orchard at the back of the house.

They stopped at a stable where the horse was unhitched and taken into a stall. Mr Drewitt said, 'Bring your swag and I'll show you where you'll be living.

'Is that all you've got?' he asked as Martin took his swag of blankets from the cart.

'Yes,' Martin replied with a grin. 'I've been travelling light.'

'We'll have to see what you can accumulate here over the next few months,' Mr Drewitt said with a laugh.

He led the way across the yard to a row of three huts. Going to the smallest one, he said, 'In here, you'll have this one to yourself. You'll be king of your own castle. Now you can come up to the house and see where you'll get your meals.'

The path went through a vegetable garden and up to the back door of the kitchen which was separated from the house by a covered walkway. There was a large room with a skillion veranda all around it. Mr Drewitt walked straight inside and Martin followed.

'This is Mrs Smith, our cook,' he said. 'You'll have your meals here in the kitchen.'

Her strong Welsh accent betrayed her land of origin as she greeted him. 'It's just about dinnertime now,' she said, 'so don't go too far away.'

'I'll leave you here now and we'll have a look around the stables and the horses after dinner,' Mr Drewitt said as he went through into the house.

'You can sit down on that bench until it's time,' Mrs Smith said. 'This here is Ellen Brown, she's the kitchen maid and chief washer-upper.'

Ellen Brown was a dark-haired girl about eighteen years old. She gave him a quick, toothy smile as he sat down on a bench running down one side of a large table.

Martin sat down and looked about the room. It had a vaguely familiar look about it and he realised it wasn't very different to the big kitchen at Ashburton. He noticed that almost the full width of one end of the room was taken up by a deep, bricked fireplace. A large, iron, colonial oven made in the shape of a box with a door in the front occupied one end of the fireplace. It had a fire burning on top and a smaller fire burning under it. The remainder of the large fireplace was fitted with two swinging cranes that would allow kettles and large pots to be suspended over the fire. From where he was sitting, he could see a large, bricked baker's oven under one of the kitchen verandas. The furniture in the kitchen consisted of the large table where he was sitting and a massive sideboard, together with other sundry cupboards and chairs. Martin noted all these things and surmised that this was a substantial home, the property of a wealthy man.

Ellen Brown went outside and rang a large bell that could be heard clearly around the house and the nearby paddocks.

Another young woman came into the kitchen and Mrs Smith introduced her to Martin as Joyce Salmon, the housemaid. She was a little older than the kitchen maid and she had fair hair and blue eyes. She looked Martin in the face with an inquisitive smile as she said, 'Hello, pleased to meet you.' Mrs Smith and Ellen then proceeded to get the food ready for serving.

Shortly, two men came in who were introduced to Martin as Allan Freeman and Jock Masters, both of whom he knew were, like him, ticket of leave farm workers.

The first plates to be filled were taken by Joyce into the house to be served to the Drewitt family in the dining room. She soon returned to the kitchen and immediately started gobbling down her own meal before going back to attend to the wants of the family.

It was a substantial meal of stewed meat and vegetables, followed by a boiled pudding. It was easily the best meal Martin had enjoyed since being arrested in England almost a year earlier. Always a quiet man, he ate his dinner in silence. The others around the table eyed him in bafflement. It was so unusual in convict circles to encounter a person of silence that they didn't know how to respond to the situation.

After a few minutes, Allan Freeman said, 'Where have you been?'

Martin's response was restrained, and in a quiet voice he said, 'Up on the survey with Mr Kentish.'

As this was quite mysterious and unintelligible to the others around the table, they too remained silent.

As a last resort to find out something about their new workmate, Mrs Smith asked, 'How long have you been out?'

Again Martin responded in a quiet voice. 'Only about ten months. I came out on the *Emma Eugenia*.'

The others passed a few words amongst themselves about current affairs on the property by way of conversation and the meal came to an end. Martin felt slightly discomposed at this sudden initiation into the farm community. It was the first meal he had shared in a civilised family situation with both men and women since his trial.

The two farmhands got up and departed the scene. Fifteen minutes later, Mr Drewitt came into the kitchen and said, 'Right, Martin, we'll go and look around.'

Martin followed him out and they went to the stables where most of the horses were kept.

Martin was immediately impressed by the quality of them. The draughthorses showed a definite cast of the Shire breed; big, strong horses with a placid temperament.

'We've got two teams,' Mr Drewitt said. 'One four-horse team and the other a three-horse team, and of course we often use just two of them as a team to handle light jobs.'

There were two matched, grey light horses that were obviously the team used to draw the carriage or whatever vehicle the family used as the ordinary mode of transport. 'They look like a good lot,' Martin said.

Mr Drewitt, who was also finding Martin's habit of silence somewhat disconcerting, responded enthusiastically to this sign of normality by talking more about the horses, including the fact that he liked to breed as many mares as possible every year.

He announced that he wanted to show Martin the paddocks that needed ploughing over the coming winter months in preparation for early spring sowing with crops of grain and potatoes, so together they hitched up the carthorse to the chaise cart.

The farm extended back over undulating paddocks to the west of the Don River and was a beautiful tract of country. Martin could see at once that it was a fertile farm and he felt a sense of enthusiasm to get to work welling up inside him.

As they returned to the homestead, Mr Drewitt said, 'I want you to tackle the ploughing as best you can. The other two are good workers, but they are not ploughmen and they need a bit of leadership to carry them along. Let's see how you go over the next month.'

That was the start of a happy and constructive term of employment on Norwood.

Martin, although a silent man and thought by some to be morose, was nevertheless a perceptive and sensitive man who instinctively knew how to get along with other people and was careful not to antagonise the other two farm workers.

Mr Drewitt had told him that work started on the farm at half past seven in the morning and finished at six o'clock in the evening with an hour off for dinner in the middle of the day .As was common in those times, very few people carried a watch, or even owned any type of timepiece. To keep time on the property, a bell was rung to summon everybody to breakfast, dinner and tea which served the dual purpose of splitting the day into work periods.

On his first night at Norwood, Martin felt quite strange having a hut to himself. Once again, it was the first time he had not shared a sleeping arrangement with others since his arrest.

The hut was constructed of split timbers, both walls and roof, and was of ample size for one or two bunks. A small, stone-lined fireplace was built in one end and an opening draped with sacking at the other end served as a window. A bunk against one wall had the usual straw-filled palliasse to sleep on. He had brought his two convict issue blankets with him.

The other two farm workers shared one of the larger huts. They told him that the third hut was kept in reserve for use by itinerant workers who came to the farm from time to time.

On his first morning, Martin was out and about before the breakfast bell rang and was the first to greet Mrs Smith in the kitchen.

'You're an early bird,' she said. 'Are you always an early riser?'

He smiled, saying, 'Yes, I've been brought up that way. My father was strict about being early for work, I'm used to it.'

The other two men came in a few minutes later to join in a hearty breakfast of porridge followed by fried chops, and they all walked back to the barnyard together.

Martin asked them to help him locate the gear he would need to get the horses harnessed and hitched up to the plough, a request they readily accepted. The shared task helped the men to get to know each other and was the start of a closer personal contact that developed quickly over the next few days. They were soon talking freely and Martin rapidly gained a good working knowledge of the farm operations and of the nearby village.

'The boss will be out in a few minutes,' Allan Freeman said. 'He nearly always comes every morning to tell us what to do.'

The plough team was harnessed and ready to go when Mr Drewitt came on the scene a few minutes later. In the meantime, Jock Masters had saddled a strong cob the boss used to ride around the farm while supervising operations.

'I'll come up to the paddock to get you started with the plough,' he said to Martin. 'You go ahead with the team and I'll follow.'

So started a routine of farm life that suited Martin. His love of the land and all that was connected to it gave him a close interest in the seasonal activities of cultivating, sowing and harvesting. He had quickly settled into life on the farm and soon felt himself developing an affinity with it.

As the weeks went by, Mr Drewitt left more of the day-to-day farm management to Martin while he spent his time organising his timber business. He employed up to twenty men at various places in the forests splitting palings and other products from the tall eucalypt trees that grew across vast areas of Van Diemen's Land, especially in the northern districts. The rapidly growing cities of Melbourne and Adelaide provided a ready market for all the timber he could deliver to them. He had a small ship of his own, and he also used other ship owners whenever he had more orders than he could deliver himself.

Martin's fellow workers, Allan and Jock, urged him to accompany them on a Saturday evening to the village of Don only a mile or two further up the river from Norwood. Martin was hesitant because he wasn't sure whether that would be allowed under the conditions of his ticket of leave and he wanted his master's approval for whatever he did at this early stage of his employment; too much depended on getting a good report at the end of his first year.

'It's all right,' they said. 'He doesn't mind us going up there on a Saturday if we're home by ten o'clock.'

But Martin decided to have it straight with Mr Drewitt before he started leaving the farm to go anywhere. He broached the subject with him one morning a week or two later.

'No, I've got no problem with you going to the village, providing you don't get drunk or get into any other trouble. I've told you what my attitude is to that, but I know you've got to live a life and in your situation, a new man in Van Diemen's Land just finding your feet, mixing with a few of the locals will do you good. The others know the rule. I won't have you staying out all night, that's the quickest way to get into trouble. Be home by ten o'clock.

'While we're talking about the village,' he added, 'we need to talk about church. It's part of your ticket of leave conditions that you attend church on Sundays if it's possible, and while I don't believe in forcing anybody to go to church, and in the ordinary course of events it's unlikely that the police will be checking up on you, I do think it's a good idea for anybody in your position to do it. It'll help you learn something about the colony and it'll look good on your record, if you get what I mean.'

'Yes, I understand you,' Martin replied, 'and I'll start going next Sunday. Thanks for the advice.'

'My family and I go regularly,' Mr Drewitt said. 'I'm not too strong on religion myself, but I've seldom seen anybody hurt by it and it's good for families. The other men go sometimes and the girls from the house always go. It's a good outing for them. You could all go together.'

'Can I ask you about money?' Martin said. 'I haven't got any at all.'

Mr Drewitt laughed as he said, 'Yes, that's fair enough, I'll pay you like the others, once a month. The last day of the month is pay day, and my months have just four weeks.'

Martin grinned at this but made no comment; it seemed to be in line with his boss's reputation for stinginess

Martin started going to the village with the other two, an experience that brought back many memories of his old village in England. They went to the tavern, a place by the name of The Red Bull where they could buy beer for three pence a large glass and where they met a lot of other men from the district, some of whom were farm workers, some timber workers and some shop hands.

When Martin got back to his hut that night and sat on his bunk in the faint glow of a candle that Mrs Smith had given him, he was in a philosophical mood and reflected on his experience so far in Van Diemen's

Land. He had consumed two glasses of beer so he had spent sixpence of his first pay. It was the first money he had been paid for well over a year, but the knowledge that he would get more every month from now on gave him a feeling of confidence, even though it would be in small amounts. He knew he had been given a lucky break by the way things had turned out, especially with getting a good job on Norwood. After a while, he threw off his clothes and settled down for a good night's sleep, the happiest he had been for many a long day.

Martin's knowledge of life in Van Diemen's Land grew apace. Mrs Smith, who had been in the colony for five years, including three years on Norwood, was full of knowledge about the various police districts and the small towns scattered about the island. She had a good understanding of the way the convict system worked and how it was constantly changing. Most importantly, she knew that nothing was impossible under the system and that although strict policies and rules were laid down, if circumstances demanded it, certain people in positions of power could always circumvent them.

'Take your own case,' she said with a mischievous grin. 'You were supposed to serve twelve months in the probation gang, but you were released after nine months. How do you suppose that happened?'

'I don't know,' he said, genuinely puzzled. 'What do you think?'

'I think some of Mr Drewitt's friends in the right place knew he wanted a good ploughman, that's what I think,' she said with a grin and a wink.

He told her what Mr Drewitt had said about church and asked her whether she went.

'Yes, I and the two girls usually go, unless the weather is bad,' she said. 'You can come with us if you like.'

'The only thing I'm worried about is that I've only got old convict clothes. I'd look a right berk turning up like that.'

'You'll have to ask Mr Drewitt to tell the shop to give you credit to buy a decent pair of trousers and a shirt,' she said. 'Now that you're working here permanently, you will qualify for credit at the shop.'

Martin tackled Mr Drewitt about it the next morning.

'Yes,' he said, 'I understand what you're saying, and I did say that I'd throw in a couple of sets of work clothes in the first year. I'm going up to the village on my way out to the forest first thing this morning. You can come with me and I'll fix it up with the shop. You can buy something and walk home.'

When they pulled up outside the general store, Mr Drewitt said, 'Just wait here a minute while I go in. I'll give you a call soon.'

The man who served Martin said, 'Mr Drewitt's fixed it all up with the boss. You're to get a pair of work trousers, a shirt and a pair of boots on his account and a pair of good trousers, a shirt and a pair of shoes on credit.'

Martin had a large parcel to carry back to Norwood, but he was thrilled to be doing it. He had a bill for twenty-two shillings to pay off within three months, but the experience of being fitted out and set up for entry into village society had given his confidence a boost. While at the store he had bought some writing paper and pen and ink and would write to his mother to tell her of his good fortune that night. Now that he was settled at a permanent address, he hoped it would only be a matter of time before he had a letter from her with news of the whole family.

The next Sunday saw him go off with Mrs Smith and the two girls after he had harnessed the two greys and hitched them to the phaeton for Mr Drewitt to drive his family to church. The other two farm men decided to join in when they heard that a party was being made up to walk to church, so Norwood was well-represented that morning. The Drewitt family passed them on the outskirts of the village with a wave of hands while sitting up in the carriage in style.

Martin was interested to see that the church was well filled with worshippers, and it reminded him of the old days when his family went to church every Sunday without fail. An interesting sidelight to proceedings was that the names of all in attendance were carefully noted in a little book. He noted that, as was the practice back in his old village, the Drewitts and some others who were obviously quality people sat in the front pews while the ticket of leavers and other workers sat at the rear of the church.

The party of Norwood workers walked home in a happy group, laughing and joking amongst themselves like old friends. Ellen walked alongside Martin, asking him about going to church at his old home in England, and telling him about her old life in London.

'Most of the people in our street used to go to church. Mother used to make us go, but she seldom went herself. I think about my mother and my sisters a lot,' she said with a sigh. 'I'm often homesick, but now that I'm here, I'd rather stay. At least there's plenty to eat and we're warm at night.'

The other girl, Joyce Salmon, fell in on the other side and joined in the conversation. She too made it plain that being a convict was not what she wanted, but under the circumstances, she felt satisfied that life at Norwood was as good as it got in Van Diemen's Land. 'One of these days, when my ship comes in, I'll go back for a holiday just to see what it's like now,' she said.

The first two months had passed very quickly for Martin and the days had shortened. It was now dark black at teatime and they often sat at the table in the warmth of the kitchen for an hour or more after finishing eating, idly chatting and exchanging items of news or scandal they had picked up in the village.

The men and the girls would start drifting off after an hour, often leaving Martin alone with Mrs Smith. She loved a good talk and would offer him another cup of tea to prolong the evening.

A month after Martin's first attendance at church, Mr Drewitt asked him to take Mrs Drewitt and the girls to church in the phaéton on the next Sunday.

'I've got to go to Launceston on business for a few days,' he said, 'and I'd like them to get their usual outing on Sunday, so I'll get you to drive them.

'And another thing,' he added. 'I want to have a good talk about the farm when I get back. The spring is only a few weeks away now and we'll have to start thinking about what crops we'll be sowing.'

He didn't mention anything to Martin, but it was obvious he was depending on him increasingly as each month passed to manage the farm while he spent more time on his timber business. He had secured more land, some of it on the verges of the settled farms in the Don district and some in large areas further inland secured on long leases that entitled him to harvest timber there.

He left for Launceston on board his ship, the *Water Witch*, the next morning.

At breakfast on the Sunday morning, Martin asked Joyce to inquire from Mrs Drewitt as to what time she wanted the phaeton ready. He was surprised when she came back within a minute or two, saying that Mrs Drewitt wanted to see him in the dining room.

He had seen her often enough but had never spoken to her. She was a middle-aged woman who looked short alongside her husband simply because he was tall and big in stature. She had a good head of hair, and while she could not be described as beautiful, she was always immaculately groomed and was a reasonably attractive woman.

Her two daughters, Rebecca and Sarah, who were fifteen and twelve, were in the same cast as their mother although an inch or two taller. They were pleasant enough with the staff and although Martin had very little to do with them, he liked them and felt at ease in their company.

'Good morning, Martin,' Mrs Drewitt greeted him as he entered the dining room. 'Thank you for taking us to church today. It's afternoon service this week, so we'll be ready to leave at two o'clock.'

'Very well, Ma'am,' he replied. 'I'll have the phaeton ready for you.'

⚓ — — ⚓

Martin had a wry smile to himself as he drove the smart pair of greys up the road at a stately pace, passing the two younger housemaids on the way. He gave them a wave and a big grin. He had an inner, humorous reflection on the irony of life in Van Diemen's Land. Here he was, acting as coachman for the leading family in the district and the final irony was that they were the respected family of an ex-convict.

After church, Martin was waiting at the phaeton when Mrs Drewitt approached him and said, 'There are only three of us, so there is room for Mrs Smith and the two girls to have a ride home if they so wish. Mrs Smith can come inside with us and the two girls can sit up with you.'

'I'll ask them,' Martin said.

He caught them as they were heading off to the churchyard gate. They showed a great surprise and confusion by the sudden and unexpected offer.

'You'll have to come,' Martin said in a low voice as he saw that they were hesitating. 'You'll hurt her feelings if you don't.'

Joyce quickly climbed up to sit beside Martin on the driver's seat while Ellen squeezed into the seat beside her. Mrs Smith climbed into the phaeton and sat beside Rebecca.

There was some good-humoured badinage at the tea table that evening; Martin noted that the two girls were thrilled, and impressed, by the little experience.

After tea, Martin and Joyce were left sitting at the table on their own for a few minutes while Mrs Smith and Ellen tidied up in preparation for washing up. It was a rare occasion that Martin had any time alone with either of the girls. He spent quite a few hours alone with Mrs Smith of an evening, but seldom ever with the girls.

'You've been in your new castle now for months and you've never invited me to visit you to see what it's like,' she said in a low voice.

'You'd be welcome any time,' he murmured with a grin, 'but what would Henrietta say? More to the point, what would her ladyship inside say?'

'Yes, it's a bit tricky,' she whispered, 'but don't be surprised if I find a way to see how you live up there in your hut.'

The little tete-a-tete came to a sudden end when Joyce felt Mrs Smith's eyes on her. She quickly got up and grabbed a tea towel to help with drying the dishes.

Charles Drewitt was developing increasing confidence in Martin's ability to organise and manage the farm work as each month went by and he spent more time away from home on his other business interests. He developed the habit of having a weekly farm inspection with Martin during which they planned a schedule of works for the coming weeks. He engaged another man from the village to increase the farm workforce and in October, true to his word, he increased Martin's wage to six shillings a week.

One evening, Mr Drewitt came up to the huts after he had returned from the village and called out, 'Are you here, Martin?'

When Martin appeared from inside the stables where he had been giving the horses their end of day feed, Mr Drewitt held out a letter.

'This came today from Nathan Kentish. He sent it care of me. It's obviously from England, so it will be from your family.'

Martin had been in Van Diemen's Land for over a year and this was the first letter he had received. The ships that carried the mail took at least four months to make the voyage either way and to complicate matters still further, for the first few months he had no address he could ask his mother to write to. He felt a wave of emotion threaten to overwhelm him as he took it and mumbled his thanks.

As soon as he got to his hut, he lit a candle and sat on the bunk to examine the letter. It was addressed to him care of Mr N Kentish at a Launceston address which told him that it was in reply to the letter he had written to his mother during his days on the survey gang.

Tears blinded him as he read the first few words:

My dear son,

Your last letter arrived here yesterday and I hasten to reply to tell you how pleased we all are to know that you are in Van Diemen's Land and that you are well. I had two other letters from you, one from the Emma Eugenia and one from Hobart. Thank you for writing to me. I hope you continue to do that often, we all want to know what fortune is upon you.

Your camp in the bush seems like a terrible place, but we are pleased that you have a good master and that you have a lot of food. I am well but often lonely for you. I know it is for the best, but I can't help worrying about you.

Anne has had her baby, a little boy now nearly one year old. He was christened Robert George. She and George are very happy and still getting enough money to live. Sarah is well, but she can't get permanent work. Sir Reginald has promised to give her a place at Ashburton, the first vacancy that occurs. There are still

thousands of people out of work all over the country and little
hope for the future. Maybe you have been fortunate in getting to
Van Diemen's Land.
Your sisters and brother-in-law all send you their love and best
wishes, as I do. Please write again when you can.
Your loving mother

Only a month later, during his usual weekly inspection, Mr Drewitt
again raised the matter of their working arrangement.

'My timber business is growing at a pace where I've got to spend
more time on it,' he said. 'That means I'm depending more on you to
keep things going here. I'm pleased with the way you've fitted in and
with your work generally. I believe in treating good people fairly and I
have decided to promote you to be my overseer. I'll pay you ten shillings
a week and your keep from now on. Does that suit you?'

Martin was astonished. Suddenly, his world seemed to be opening
up. It was like a miracle. He covered his feelings as best he could and
tried to keep his voice under control as he said, 'Yes, I'd be pleased to
take the job, and thanks for having the faith in me. I'll try my best to
live up to it.'

'Right, I'll tell the other men what I've done and put it around the
village.'

Chapter 6

Christmas 1847 drew near and life at Norwood flowed on happily and successfully for all concerned. Martin Maynard had grown into his elevated position of overseer and, after an early hesitancy in exerting his authority, had developed an easy confidence that drew the respect of his fellow workers, both on the farm and in the house. At first, the two older men who had been on the property when he came on the scene showed a degree of resentment towards the Johnny-come-lately who had been promoted over them. He was not only younger than them, but had been in the colony for less than two years; however, they soon came to realise that he knew his job and that he was a good boss.

Mrs Smith, as always the wise one amongst the staff, settled any further discussion by saying to them one day after Martin had left the dinner table to go to his hut: 'You can be pleased to have a nice young man like him over you. Better him than some jumped-up, self-important slavedriver.'

They understood the language she used and could see the truth of it. From then, rather than resent young Martin, they chose to praise him and boast to their friends in the tavern about his abilities as a farmer.

Mr Drewitt continued to expand his business interests and build his fortune. He now had two ships trading between the Don and other rivers on the north coast and Launceston, with frequent trips to Melbourne and Adelaide with cargoes of palings and other split timbers from the rich forests he controlled.

During the busy spring sowing period, he put on another two men from the village to help out on the farm. To run a large property like Norwood, at least one man was engaged full-time on homestead duties which entailed milking two or three cows to keep the establishment supplied with milk, cream and butter and working in the vegetable garden, a vital part of the food supply. As well as these jobs, sheep and other animals had to be slaughtered and the meat butchered and, as far as the kitchen staff was concerned, the adequate supply of good firewood was essential. All the cooking and water heating as well as all the fireplaces that warmed the house were fuelled with wood. Having good and bad wood made the difference between having a happy cook and household, or the opposite. A big house like Norwood used an enormous amount of wood every day – winter and summer.

During Mr Drewitt's last inspection of the farm before Christmas, he expressed his satisfaction in terms – for him – quite lavish. 'Yes,' he said, 'you've got the place looking well. I'm pleased with the crops; everything seems to be coming on as planned.'

The Christmas season passed very happily for everybody. The family inside had many friends call on them over the week and the staff had a happy time in the kitchen. They still had to work as hard as usual, but as a concession to Mrs Smith, the additional kitchen maid from the village was retained to help out.

On Boxing Day while the staff were all lounging about, either in their rooms or huts or in the grassy orchard, Joyce and Ellen cleverly concocted a good excuse to visit Martin in his hut. They had both been very curious to see what his living arrangements were, but Mrs Smith ruled with a rod of iron and she had no intention of getting the boss offside by too much fraternising between the men and women staff. She had warned Martin in his early days on the property not to get frisky with the girls.

'You've got to be careful, especially a man like you. You've got too much to lose by getting a girl into trouble,' she said. 'You couldn't get married, even if you wanted to. It'll be years before you'll have enough to marry on.'

But that was before he was promoted to overseer and given a good pay rise. She could see now that he was on the way up and her respect for him rose accordingly. She still encouraged him to linger in the kitchen of a night to talk and drink cups of tea, but she restrained her advice on personal matters to a lower level of frankness.

The two girls came into the hut full of giggles and laughter.

'This is where you hide,' Ellen said. 'My word, you've got it fixed up good.'

Joyce looked around the small room with approval. 'You're a bit of a homemaker, I can see that,' she said.

Martin was flattered. He was proud of the way he had improved his living conditions. Like a lot of farm boys, he had been reared to be handy with tools, and by the clever use of wooden packing cases he had been given from the village store, he had knocked up a wardrobe and a storage cupboard as well as a small table and a couple of chairs. His mother had drilled cleanliness and order into him as he grew up and the habit had stayed with him over the years.

'I'd offer you a cup of tea,' he said with a laugh, 'but I haven't got any decent cups and saucers for visitors yet.'

'You'll make some woman a good husband one of these days,' Ellen said cheekily.

'Yes,' he responded, 'that's when I find a girl with a fortune, one who can keep me in the style to which I am accustomed.'

It was all good fun and he didn't think any more about the visit, but he got a shock on New Year's night when Joyce arrived in his hut at midnight. She had sneaked out of the house, leaving Ellen asleep in their bed, and quietly pulled the latch cord on his door to get in. The first he knew of what was happening was when her hand was gently caressing his cheek.

'What are you doing here?' he asked in surprise and alarm.

'Just paying you another visit to see that you're behaving yourself,' she said coyly.

'Well, thanks for the kind thought,' he said, 'but if you're caught, we'll both be in big trouble. You know that, don't you?'

'We won't be caught,' she whispered. 'We'll be very quiet, just talk in whispers.'

She sat on the side of his bunk and put her arm around his neck. Without conscious thought, his arm went around her waist. He was a healthy young man and had the usual mating urges, steamed up by a strong flow of testosterone that constantly stoked his libido. He felt a wild urge to crush her to him and let nature take its course, and within a minute they were kissing and stroking each other. She was naked under the nightdress she wore and all he had on was a pair of underpants. His hands found her breasts and her soft, round tummy and her hands were exploring private parts of him. After a few moments, he groaned and pulled away from her.

'This is crazy,' he moaned. 'You don't want a baby, do you?'

'Depends,' she murmured.' If I was married to the right man, I'd want one, straight away.'

'Well, I can't marry you, or anyone, so we can't carry on like this,' he said. 'You'll have to go straight back to your own bed.'

'I'll just stay for a little while. It won't hurt to have a little time together,' she said.

'Don't get me wrong,' he said with a little chuckle, 'I'd love to have you stay all night with me. I feel randy like any man would, but it's just too risky for both of us, especially you. You'd be in a fine pickle if I made you pregnant. The first thing would be back to the convict's house. You wouldn't want that, would you?'

'No, but that won't stop me giving you a little relief from the terrible stiffness you've got in your leg. That *is* your leg, isn't it?' she said as her hand wandered under the blanket.

He was a mass of confusion as her hand started its cunning work, and it was only a couple of minutes before he was groaning in ecstasy. As sensibility returned to his mind, he found her cradled in his arms.

'You're a naughty girl, a very naughty girl, but a lovely one,' he murmured as he kissed her, 'but you'll still have to go back to your own bed.'

'I'll go in a minute,' she said. 'Just let me stay for a while. I get so lonely here at times. I know it's good, and we're lucky to be here, but I do think about my mother and my old home a lot,' she murmured.

He knew he was playing with fire, but he felt sorry for her. He caressed and comforted her and they enjoyed the closeness of each other for another half hour before he sent her to sneak back into bed beside Ellen.

The summer months continued to be busy on the farm. The main harvest of all the crops took place during the summer and in addition to that, they were bringing more of the rich, chocolate coloured soil into production. Any slack periods were used to clear more land.

The relationship between Martin and his master had developed into a genuine friendship. As Martin got to know Charles Drewitt better, he recognised that he was a decent and good man. Tough in business he might be, but always fair and honest. He never welched on a deal, his word was his bond and he was a good community man.

They sometimes fell to yarning while they were doing the farm inspections and Charles confided something of his early years to Martin. He talked about his days as a convict and the struggle he had to get a start as a free man when he finally won his freedom.

'I know a lot of people condemn me as a miser and a skinflint,' he said, 'but I've never robbed anybody deliberately, and the only way I had of getting on was to be careful with money, both with the making of it and the management of it.'

He surprised Martin again one day a few months later when he said, 'You've been here for well over a year now, what about a bit of a holiday? The *Water Witch* is going up to Launceston later this week. You can go up on her and have four days in town while she unloads and loads. What say you?'

Martin grinned widely. 'I say yes, thanks a lot. I'll see my old mate Carter while I'm there. It'll be a nice change being a proper passenger, not like my last voyage by ship,' he said with a grin.

In spite of Martin's stern warnings and discouragement Joyce persisted in sneaking up to his hut two or three times a month. They never engaged in real sex, but they did manage to comfort each other's passion without running the risk of pregnancy. He told her he would never be in a position to marry for many years and, without being cruel, he made her understand that he would not be asking her to marry him.

'When the time comes and a good man courts you and wants to marry you, you'll be a sensible girl and accept him,' he told her, 'and the time will come, probably sooner than you think. There are far more men than women in Van Diemen's Land and they all want to get married eventually.'

He never knew what arrangement Joyce had with Ellen, but he often wondered how she managed to remain asleep every time Joyce sneaked out.

Martin was excited by the prospect of a visit to Launceston and the chance of meeting up with his old mate. He had often thought about Thomas Carter whom he had met for the first time on the day of his trial in 1844. They had remained together all through the ordeal of the hulks and the long voyage to Van Diemen's Land in the *Emma Eugenia*. The walk from Hobart had been the last experience they had shared before parting at the probation station at Longford, Thomas to go to Launceston to serve a master wheelwright and Martin to walk on to the probation station at Deloraine.

The last part of the voyage to Launceston in the *Water Witch* was the tedious passage south along the Tamar River to the town. With the help of a gentle westerly wind, the voyage from the Don to the Tamar Heads was a pleasant cruise; but the long, sheltered Tamar Valley cut off most of the wind and it took two days to traverse the last forty miles. The final few miles had been accomplished by putting the longboat out front, manned by eight strong rowers, to slowly pull the ship into the wharf. All the able-bodied men on board, including Martin, took turns at rowing.

Martin told Captain Dickson, the Master of the *Water Witch*, that he intended to track down Thomas and asked him the best way to go about it.

'There's a fellow in our agent's office who knows his way around town better than anybody else. I'll take you in to see him when we get tied up.'

Following the directions he had been given, the walk up Charles Street was Martin's first good look at the town of Launceston. It had a surprisingly settled look about it in spite of the fact that it was only a little over forty years since thick tea-tree bush and eucalyptus jungle had covered the whole expanse of where the town now stood.

He followed the directions he had been given to the bottom end of Canning Street where he saw the sign on the side of a big, wooden building that told him he had found Joseph Linnell's Coachbuilders premises. The first person he saw as he walked into the workshop was his old friend, Thomas Carter. He was bigger and more mature, but there was no mistaking him. He was dressed in blue overalls with a hammer hanging on his belt and a carpenter's ruler sticking out of his back pocket.

He caught sight of Martin and after a moment's hesitancy burst out, 'Well, I'll be buggered! If it's not the great Martin Maynard. Where did you pop up from?' he asked with a big grin on his face.

'I thought it was time I checked up on you,' Martin replied with a grin of his own. 'I see you're walking around free, so you must be going all right.'

They quickly exchanged inquiries about their state of health and the like and chatted for a few minutes before Thomas said, 'I can't talk for too long just now; the old man will have his eye on me. Meet me at noon and we can have a sandwich together down at the shop on the corner.'

'Where are you staying?' he asked.

'At the moment, nowhere,' Martin said. 'I've only just got off the ship.'

'Well don't book in anywhere. You can stay with me tonight,' he said.

They met at the small shop that sold sandwiches and cups of tea at noon as arranged and had a good but hurried chat as they gobbled down their snack.

'We can have a good feed tonight,' Thomas said. 'In view of the occasion, I think we can treat ourselves to a good counter meal up at the Brown Dog tavern. I've got a spare bunk in my hut, so you can sleep there.'

Martin had no trouble filling in the afternoon. After he had returned to the ship and told Captain Dixon what he was doing, collected his portmanteau and then explored the main part of the town, he was ready to find a quiet corner at the Brown Dog to wait for his friend.

He didn't have long to wait. Thomas was anxious to get together and he found Martin soon after six o'clock. He bought two glasses of beer and settled back on the bench with a smile.

'Right,' he said, 'now give me a full report on what you've been doing since I said goodbye to you that day at Longford. What was the probation gang like?'

They spent a wonderful evening together. They had the best meal the tavern could serve as a special treat to celebrate their meeting along with several glasses of beer. They exchanged accounts of their experiences and the kinds of men they were working for and, inevitably amongst convicts, discussed what they now thought of Van Diemen's Land.

'The way things have turned out, I haven't got too many complaints,' Thomas said. 'I haven't been really hungry since I've been here and I like the climate; it's certainly better than the old country, especially the winters. My master is not bad; a bit of a slavedriver, but not too bad. He's tight with a shilling and doesn't believe in paying good wages if he can get out of it, but I've been here nearly two years now. Only another year or two and I'll be able to apply for my ticket of leave, then I'll be able to look for a better job if I want to.'

'Do you miss your old home?' Martin asked him.

'Yes, I do, but I got into such a mess with my matrimonial affairs and everything, I wouldn't want to go back. I reckon I'll be a Van Demonian for the rest of my life. I might even get married. I've got my eye on a nice sort that I met at church. The old man is very strong on church which was a bit of a drag at first, but it may have helped me.'

They returned to Thomas's hut in the backyard of the coachworks where they spent another couple of hours yarning before finally settling down for the night. Fortunately, Thomas had a spare blanket and a couple of heavy coats that helped keep Martin warm in the spare bunk.

The next three days passed quickly and pleasantly for Martin. He and Thomas spent their evenings together, one of which was at a tavern where Thomas was in the habit of meeting a few of his friends from other workshops around the town. A large number of them were ticket of leave men who, like Thomas and Martin, were in their present jobs because of being placed there by the convict system. Most of them were content with their lot, but a few were under harsh masters who demanded the most out of them with the least expense possible.

One man said to Martin, 'There's only one word to describe my master. He's a mean old bastard, and the sooner I can get away from him the better.'

Another said, 'I've only got another twelve months to put up with him and I'll get my ticket of leave, and then it's off to Port Phillip for me. I've had enough of Van Diemen's Land.'

Several of them talked about the high wages being paid to tradesmen in Melbourne and their desire to go there as soon as they could.

The next morning, Martin had a few errands to attend to for his boss, all of which took him into various business places around the town, an experience he found interesting because it gave him a good look at Launceston and a first-hand feel for the business community. He had been told to buy two ladies' side-saddles.

'The girls want to learn to ride,' Mr Drewitt had said, 'and I've got my eye on two nice ponies that should be right for them. I'll get the ponies home soon. In the meantime, you can get the side-saddles.'

'Will the ponies be broken in?' Martin asked.

'Yes, they're supposed to be, but we won't know what they're like until we get them home.'

'If you don't mind me making a suggestion,' Martin said, 'it might be a good idea to get the girls started on a quiet old horse that is easy to manage before they go on a younger, and maybe friskier pony. What about your own old cob you use on the farm?'

'I hadn't thought of that. Yes, it's a good idea. I'll get you to help them. You know a fair bit about horses, and riding too, I wouldn't be surprised.'

Martin chuckled. 'I don't know about being an expert, but I've certainly done enough of it. Old Petala Smith used to have us riding saddlehorses he was breaking in for the Squire all the time, and some of them were frisky.'

Martin carefully selected the side-saddles to suit the young girls and the appropriate bridles and other gear that would be needed. He also had a list of other harness that was needed for the farm horses. By the time he had finished, there was quite a large package to be taken to the *Water Witch* for the trip home.

The Captain picked a time of departure to catch the outgoing tide so the trip north to the heads was much quicker and easier. They were lucky to get a favourable wind in Bass Strait which gave them a good trip home. They caught the tide at the Don Heads that carried them into the village wharf barely twenty-four hours after leaving Launceston.

Martin arrived back at Norwood during the afternoon and went to the kitchen to inquire whether Mr Drewitt was about the place or not.

Mrs Smith gave him a cheerful greeting and a warm smile. 'I suppose you're hungry,' she said. 'I'll get you a cup of tea and some biscuits. No, Mr Drewitt is up the river seeing to his paling splitters today. He'll be back late this evening.'

Martin sat at the table drinking his tea while she quizzed him about the trip. Joyce and Ellen appeared on the scene and got themselves cups of tea, so it quickly developed into a cosy little homecoming.

Joyce sneaked into his hut late that night and stayed for two hours.

Mr Drewitt hadn't forgotten their talk about the girls learning to ride. The day after Martin's return from Launceston, he inquired whether he had bought the side-saddles and when told that they were hanging in the stable, he immediately asked for them to be brought to the house.

Rebecca and Sarah were waiting with their father in the back-yard and were full of interest in the saddles and the idea of learning to ride.

Mrs Drewitt came out to join the discussion and raised the question of whether Sarah would be too young to learn as she was only twelve, three years younger than her sister.

Mr Drewitt looked at Martin and asked, 'What do you think? Did girls as young as that learn at your old place?'

'Yes, they did. In many ways it's easier for the young ones to learn as long as they're tall enough to reach the stirrups.'

Then Mr Drewitt said to his wife and girls, 'Martin has suggested you ought to start learning on old Maggie to get your balance properly before going on the young ponies. He knows a lot about horses and I've asked him to teach you. We'll have the first lesson after dinner today.'

So it was that Martin put in many hours teaching the girls to ride. He had been reared amongst horses and had seen Petala Smith break in all sorts from heavy drafts through to ponies and had been trained by him in all the basic principles of the craft.

He started off by leading the old mare Maggie around the yard with a girl in the side-saddle until she had developed the confidence to take the reins and walk the horse herself. The first thing that became apparent was that the girl who was waiting her turn found it frustrating and boring and asked her father for another horse so they could both ride at the same time.

'Haven't we got another horse on the farm that I could use, Father?' Rebecca asked.

A few days later he asked Martin to collect a horse from a farm a few miles away. 'If you go and get it yourself and ride it home, you'll know whether it's safe for the girls,' he said.

The girls came with their father and Martin when they drove the few miles in the chaise cart to get the new horse. They immediately fell in love with the quiet old pony. From that time, they made fast progress with their riding and were soon trotting around in great style, and then came the big day when they graduated to cantering. By the time the new ponies arrived a month later, both girls were well-started on the road to being accomplished riders.

The ponies, a beautiful pair of chestnuts showing a touch of Arab, were young and newly broken in, and Martin was very careful to thoroughly test them for tractability and temperament before allowing the girls to mount up. The last thing he wanted to happen was for one of the girls to have an accident of some sort. Of course, it was inevitable that they would take the occasional fall as all learner riders do, but he wasn't going to risk upsetting their parents for the sake of a little extra training.

'I hope you don't think I'm wasting too much time with the girls and their ponies,' he said to Mr Drewitt, 'but considering their age and the fact that the ponies are only just broken in, I think it's best to be careful.'

'You are right,' he said emphatically. 'Don't worry about the time. You've got plenty of others to handle some of your work. Just carry on as you are.'

Martin taught the girls to pat and fondle the horses to quieten them and to win their confidence. 'Don't forget,' he taught them, 'these horses are not used to being handled by people and they are nervous, even frightened of you. But at the same time, you've got to master them and let them know that you're the boss, but the trick is to do it without being cruel or silly.'

Within three months, they were accomplished riders and able to ride into the village and beyond on their own. By then, Martin and the girls had become good friends and they often consulted him about their horses and the various finer points of riding. Rebecca especially appreciated the relationship that had developed between them and showed in a dozen different ways that she liked being with him and talking to him, not only about horses and riding, but about the farm and the village.

Mr and Mrs Drewitt showed their pride in the girls' achievements and thanked him for what he had done. Mrs Drewitt, normally a quiet and thoughtful woman, surprised him with her obviously sincere appreciation.

A few weeks later, during one of their periodic farm inspections, Mr Drewitt said, 'I've been thinking lately that I'd like you to give me a hand with my timber business. What I should do is find somebody like you to be my overseer in that part of my business, but they are hard to find, and if I put the wrong man in there to deal with my crazy forest workers, it could ruin the business. We've got the farm running well now and I don't think you need to be here all the time. What say you?'

'I understand what you want,' Martin replied. 'I could give it a go and see how it pans out. But if I'm to be away for a few days, we really need somebody here who is next in charge. Maybe you could make Allan Freeman a sort of leading hand to be in charge of the others when I'm not here. You'd probably have to give him a little more money. In fact, the more I think of it,' Martin said, 'that would have a good effect on the others too.'

'Right,' Mr Drewitt said. 'What you say makes sense to me. You can have Freeman in the yard tomorrow morning and I'll speak to him. You be there too; I don't want any misunderstanding about this. I don't want your authority weakened in any way.'

Martin had learned the ropes well over the past two years and realised that the present opportunity to advance his own cause was too good to miss.

'Are you thinking about looking at my pay as well?' he asked.

'Well, yes, I suppose it is time to review our arrangements. What did you have in mind?' Mr Drewitt asked, taking Martin somewhat by surprise. Fortunately, Martin had been thinking about things, especially since his trip to Launceston, so he was prepared to say what he wanted. He had also come to know and understand Drewitt and instinctively knew that he would respect him for being forthright.

'There are two aspects to it, both of which are very important to me. Firstly there's money. I hope you could see your way clear to raise me to two pounds a week and keep. Secondly, there's the matter of my eventual release from bondage. Would you help me to obtain my pardon?'

'Well, that's a mouthful! That would double your pay for a start. And about the pardon ... you're not thinking of leaving me, are you?'

'No, I'm not. I like working for you and I've learnt a lot from you already, but I've got to think of my future. I'm twenty-three now and it looks as if I'll spend the rest of my life in Van Diemen's Land, so I need to start building a kitty. About the pardon, I know it takes a long time, so the sooner the procedure is started the better. And I know you've got a lot of influence with the authorities.'

As Martin had suspected, his boss responded with good humour and seriousness to this frank statement. He laughed as he said, 'You've got it all worked out, haven't you? Yes, I do have some small influence in certain quarters, and yes, I will help you when the time comes, but I'd say that is at least a year away yet. But I told you in the first place, if you serve me well and faithfully, which you've done up to now, I'll treat you right. You can have your two pounds a week as from now, but I don't know how you've got it out of me. I'm usually a lot tougher than that.' He burst out laughing, then continued: 'You've obviously got me at a weak moment. Don't tell anybody, I might lose my reputation.'

Martin grinned as he said, 'Thanks for everything. I do want you to know that I appreciate having the job here with you. I know I'm lucky. I could still be out there on the road gangs. But you know me now, and I'll not let you down.'

'One last thing,' Mr Drewitt said. 'While we're in this confidential mood, there's something else. We have come to be friends and maybe it's time to drop the formality a bit. While we're on our own away from the other men, which we will be more now, you ought to call me Charles.'

'Why don't I just call you 'Squire'. That's friendly and not too formal,' said Martin.

He laughed again. 'Have it your own way.'

CHAPTER 7

*O*n the morning that Mr Drewitt and Martin interviewed Allan
Freeman in the farmyard and promoted him to the position
of Leading Hand, with an increase of two shillings a week in
his wages, they boarded a twelve foot rowboat at the village
wharf and headed upstream to reach a gang of splitters who
were working in one of the forests that Mr Drewitt leased from
the Crown.

The boat was loaded with provisions for the gangs, a service that
was part of the deal they worked under. Mr Drewitt explained to Martin
that he had an arrangement with the store at the Don to supply him
with provisions at a large discount so that he could on-sell them to his
splitters.

'It suits all parties,' he said. 'That way the store gets the business
and is guaranteed to get their money and the splitters are assured of

getting their supplies every week. This makes it easier for me to get the splitters and keep them on the job. I take my profit when I buy the split timber at an agreed contract price. When I finally sell the timber, wherever I can find a market, I take my chances on making a profit. If the market is good, which it has been for the last year or two, I do well, but sometimes it turns against me and I lose money.

'I've got to be sharp and on the ball all the time. Most of the splitters are shiftless types and, given half a chance, will rob you blind. You'll get used to dealing with them, but don't be surprised by what you see. My strong advice is: don't trust them to honour a deal to the letter of the law and never put yourself under an obligation to them. My policy is that I fulfil my side of the deal fairly and fully, but I insist that they do the same for me.'

They were both rowing, sitting side by side in the wide middle of the boat. Martin had seldom seen him do physical work on the farm and he was surprised to see how fit he was and how deftly he handled the boat. He surmised that it must be the boat work and the riding that kept him in such good shape.

They rowed at a steady but constant rate which covered the distance more quickly than Martin would have expected. An hour after leaving the wharf, they were tying up at a camp on the banks of the river. Martin saw a large pile of palings neatly stacked in the open space and a rough hut off to one side.

The sound of splitters working could be heard from a little way into the forest and the two men walked towards the activity along a narrow track. As they drew near, Mr Drewitt stopped and, putting his fingers to his mouth, blew a loud whistle. The noise of the axes and the thumping of the mauls stopped and a loud voice called out, 'Over here!'

The three splitters waited for them to arrive on the scene of operations.

A large tree had been felled and was in the process of being split into thin palings five feet long and about nine inches broad. Martin was fascinated to see how it was done.

The tree, about five feet thick at the butt end, was first cut into five feet logs by a crosscut saw and after the bark had been removed, the log was split into halves. The splitters could tell at a glance the best place to start the split by hammering in a small iron wedge. When the split was opened up enough, larger wooden wedges were hammered in with a heavy, wooden maul. The timber was very 'free' and split easily. Within minutes, the first log was in halves and then those halves were split into quarters, and they in turn were halved again. This process was continued until the logs were reduced to billets of the desired width. That was when the art of paling splitting was displayed with pride by the expert splitters. The palings were split away from the side of the billet individually by using a special tool called a paling 'knife'. The knife was a sharp, iron blade a little over a foot long and three inches wide with a large 'eye' at one end to take a wooden handle. It was tapped into the billet at the appropriate thickness by a small, wooden hammer and then pushed – or tapped – through the side of the billet to produce the paling. A skilled splitter could produce several hundred palings a day, depending on the quality of the tree.

After the usual greetings had been exchanged, Mr Drewitt introduced Martin to the men and explained that they would be doing most of their dealings with him in future because he had put him on as overseer of his forest operations.

They were silent for a minute while they eyed him off; and then the big, craggy-faced man who had been introduced as Badger said, 'Will this make any difference to our deal?'

'No,' Mr Drewitt replied firmly, 'everything will stay the same. The only difference is that Martin will be dealing with you on my behalf, but I have to approve of any arrangements he agrees to.'

They discussed the number of palings they had ready for delivery and their plans for the next few weeks. They had identified twenty good trees within a short distance of the river and there were more further back.

'We'll be a long time cutting this area out,' they said.

'As soon as you've got ten thousand ready, I'll arrange for the punt to come up to take delivery,' Mr Drewitt told them

Badger said, 'If you come back to the camp, I'll take whatever you've brought up for us and give you an order for next week. You can have a cup of tea then, if you like.'

All three walked back to the camp where they quickly had the camp fire blazing under a tea billy. Mr Drewitt produced a notebook and made a list of what they wanted brought up next week while he sipped the scalding hot tea. He then walked over to the heap of palings and pulled a few out to get a good look at them. He made a show of calling Martin over and showed him how to assess the quality of a paling. They were joined by Badger who said, 'Not a bad lot, eh? There's plenty of good palings like that here.'

Martin noticed that Badger gave Mr Drewitt his full title – or 'boss' – as he talked to him.

Mr Drewitt completed his explanation about the quality of the palings by saying, 'My buyers in Melbourne and Adelaide are very fussy and will refuse to pay for any they don't like, so we've all got to be careful.'

When they returned to the boat, they went upstream for a short distance and landed on the opposite bank where another gang was based. The same procedure was gone through with them.

By the time they started downriver late in the afternoon on the long row home, they had visited two more gangs. As they glided along, Mr Drewitt said, 'Well, you've had your first look at the splitters. They're a tough lot, eh?

Martin chuckled as he said, 'Yes, Squire. I could see what you mean, but I think I'll be able to get along with them. Do you own the punt you mentioned, or is that another contractor?'

'No, I don't own it. It belongs to a fellow called Sam Ling. He lives at a small place upriver of the Don and he brings a lot of timber down for me, all on contract. You'll be dealing with him. He's a good bloke – and reliable.'

At first, Martin found himself engaged on his new duties for a day a week, but as the months slipped past, Mr Drewitt expanded his timber operations, both on the Don River and the surrounding districts and on the Forth, a few miles to the west. Martin was soon spending several days every week on the timber business. The demand for high quality split timber was increasing every month as a result of the huge number of timber houses being built in Melbourne and Adelaide.

Charles Drewitt was not the man to let opportunities for money making slip past him. He bought another sixty ton ship and put more men on to work both in the forests and on the farm. It was obvious to Martin that he was making huge profits, especially from the timber operations. Fortunately, Allan Freeman was handling his duties as leading hand well. With the extra men, the farm was running profitably.

It was a busy life but enjoyable, and Martin liked the challenge of his increasing responsibilities. He got great satisfaction from the fact that he was being educated by example by a very clever and able man and he looked forward to the day when he would be able to spread his wings and launch out into business for himself.

He emulated his employer and became a dedicated saver of money.

Since getting his big pay rise, he had been saving at least one pound a week, and often more.

Rebecca and Sarah Drewitt continued to be keen horsewomen and thought nothing of riding to the Mersey or the Forth to see friends or attend functions. Rebecca often had occasion to consult Martin on matters relating to their horses and sometimes just for a talk. He had developed a great liking for her and sensed that she reciprocated similar feelings for him.

Joyce still sneaked up to his hut late at night. Martin had to be honest and admit to himself that he enjoyed her visits, but he feared more and more that she would eventually be caught. But she wouldn't be dissuaded. It worried him that they both had too much to lose; he his job that he could never hope to equal anywhere else and she her good conduct record that would be equally as important to her future.

Of course it was inevitable, and it happened late one night when Henrietta Smith was taken short and had to make a hurried dash for the dunny on the far side of the kitchen garden. She almost collided with Joyce on the verandah. Another few seconds and they would have passed in the night without seeing each other, but fate decreed otherwise.

Henrietta had to curb her first impulse to start yelling at the girl and instead obey the call of nature, but on return to the house, she went into the girls' room and called Joyce out to the kitchen. Poor Joyce was petrified and shivering like a leaf as she shuffled into the dimly lit kitchen.

'Where have you been, you little hussy?' Henrietta demanded. 'Up there with the men, I don't doubt. Who was it?'

At first Joyce could only stutter inanities, trying to avoid saying a name, but her brain started to function again after a few moments and she quickly decided that a straight and honest answer would be her best chance of avoiding too much trouble.

'I've been with Martin,' she said, 'but we've done nothing wrong.'
Henrietta was staggered to hear that her favourite young man had
been misbehaving. She would have staked her life that he was far above
seducing housemaids, and she knew she would have trouble believing
anything bad about him.

'What do you mean, nothing wrong? Is that what you're going to tell
the parson when you take your little bastard to be christened?'

Joyce had her hands over her mouth to keep from bawling outright
which she knew would wake the whole house. The tears were streaming down her face as she mumbled, 'There'll be no baby. Martin didn't
do anything.'

'What did you do? Tell me that! I'll bet you haven't just been holding hands.'

'No, we've just been talking. He's like me; missing home, and
lonely.'

Joyce was a bright girl and her brain was quickly working out the lay
of the land. She knew Henrietta was besotted with Martin and wouldn't
do anything that would get him into trouble.

'Do you always go to talk to young men in the middle of the night
almost naked in a skimpy nightdress like that?' Henrietta demanded
as Joyce cringed before her.

'Oh no, please don't. We've done nothing wrong. You can ask Martin, he'll tell you,' she said, and then a stroke of inspiration dawned.
She said again, 'He'll tell you. He likes you.'

She struck a golden chord in Henrietta. In spite of her anger, she
hesitated at this. Her mind started considering the full implications
of what could happen if the whole story became known to Mr and
Mrs Drewitt. Joyce would be sent back to the female convict factory in
Launceston with her future prospects in tatters and worse still, Martin
could be sacked and sent back to the road gangs.

But who would be held responsible for allowing the domestic discipline to erode to the stage where the convicts were able to misbehave to this extent? This thought sent cold shivers through her soul and disgrace was staring her in the face.

But she had to exert her authority. Without that, she was a nobody, no more than the housemaids she worked with. It was a matter of image. Being the cook and a person of authority at Norwood was a badge of honour she truly treasured. After a life of disappointment and failure back in the old country, she was desperate to establish herself as a person of note in her new life in Van Diemen's Land.

'We'll see about that,' she said. 'Go up and bring him down. I'll talk to him myself.'

Martin got a shock when he was wakened again by Joyce. He was in the midst of a dream about swirling waters and a tea billy boiling madly when he felt a soft hand on his shoulder. He was confused and she was crying as he said, 'What? What? What's happened?'

'Mrs Smith caught me going back to the house. She's carrying on like crazy,' she sobbed.

'Where is she? What's going on?' he demanded.

'She's in the kitchen, she wants to talk to you.'

He came back to full consciousness with a sick feeling in his stomach. After a moment, he asked, 'What did you tell her?'

'I told her we'd done nothing wrong, that we were only talking together and were both lonely.'

He got up and quickly pulled on his trousers and a shirt and took her arm. 'Come on,' he said. 'We'll go and talk to her.'

As they walked down the path to the kitchen, he asked her in a low voice: 'What else did you say to her?'

'I told her that you would tell her we'd done nothing wrong. I told her that you like her.'

He recognised instantly that that was the key to the looming interview. 'Good girl,' he said.

As he walked in through the kitchen door, he looked Henrietta full in the face and said, 'Well, old friend. What's up?'

She met glance with glance and said, 'I caught this girl sneaking back from your bed, naked, at this hour of night, and you ask me what's up? There's plenty up, I'd say.'

'Let's talk sensibly about this, Henrietta,' he said. 'I don't think there is all that much to get excited about. Whatever we've done, we didn't want to cause you any worry, and we've done nothing that will cause you any worry either now or in the future.'

She was red in the face and obviously upset. 'What the hell is going on?' she asked. 'What are you thinking of, being in bed with a naked housemaid at midnight? I'd say there's something going on.'

Looking her in the face again, he replied, 'Henrietta, please hear me out. I know it looks bad, but I can explain what happened. It's just a case of two young, healthy people who are desperately homesick and lonely looking for comfort of some kind and trying to help each other. I can tell you honestly that we have not been having sex. There is no way that Joyce can be pregnant so there's no chance that you will be embarrassed later on. If we've made you angry, we are both very sorry and apologise. I hope you can see your way clear to let us off this time.'

When Martin saw the tears come to Henrietta's eyes, his heart leapt. He knew that she would do the right thing by them.

She was silent, and Joyce slipped around the table to put her arms around her.

'You're a very naughty girl,' Henrietta said to her. 'You'll get us all into trouble. What do you think Mrs Drewitt would say, if she knew? We'd all be down the road with the sack, if not worse.'

After a minute she sent Joyce off to bed.

'Don't tell anybody about this,' she said as Joyce got up to leave. 'I don't know how you're going to handle Ellen, but nobody is to say anything to anybody. This is all to be kept a secret between us. Now, off you go.'

As Joyce quietly closed the door on her way out, Henrietta looked at Martin and said, 'How the hell did you let this happen? What's the full story?'

'Well, for a start, I'm only flesh and blood. I'm twenty-three years old and I've got my full measure of sex drive. Sometimes I think I must have more than my full measure, I'm so driven.'

'I understand that. I'm thirty-five and I've been through the mill, married and all, so I know about sex. You don't have to tell me about that,' she said with a bold look on her face.

'This wasn't all Joyce's fault,' he said. 'She's a very lonely girl. She's like the rest of us; we think a lot about our old home and our family. You've no idea how I miss my old mother. Joyce came to me and I should have sent her packing, but I couldn't. But I'm telling you the truth when I say we haven't been having sex, so I can assure you she is not pregnant and not likely to get so.

'Anyway,' he went on,' I know I can speak honestly and plainly to you and you'll understand. Yes, I've fondled her, and given her some sexual satisfaction as a person can, you'll understand that. I hope you're not disgusted, but I let her masturbate me, and I'm honest enough to say that it gave me tremendous relief. So, there you are. I hope we can continue to be friends.'

She was silent for a minute and then said with a wry smile, 'Silly boy, of course we will be friends. I know what it's like to be flesh and blood. All I can say is: For God's sake, be careful. You've got a big future ahead of you in this country, so don't put it all at risk.'

With that he kissed her on the cheek as he would his mother and slipped back to his hut.

Henrietta decided not to report anything about the affair to her mistress. From her point of view, there was nothing to be gained by trouble and turmoil in the house, but a lot to be lost by all the house staff, including herself. It was true that she was more than half in love with Martin herself and had sometimes indulged in daydreams that she knew would never eventuate into reality. She could understand when Martin talked about his loneliness and the forces of nature that drive a man of twenty-three, and in her heart – if not in her head – she felt sorry for him. She was immensely impressed by his self-control in abstaining from making the most of the opportunity presented to him by Joyce. She knew enough about men and their powerful sex drives to appreciate the strong temptation he would have been under to take full advantage of the girl and to hell with the consequences. From her experience, there wouldn't be more than one in a hundred men who would behave like he had. She admired Martin more than ever, and by the time the morning dawned, it had slowly occurred to her that this way of handling the situation would put Martin and Joyce, and even Ellen, under more obligation to her than ever and this, in effect, would increase her power at Norwood.

*   —   —

Joyce had been thoroughly frightened by the experience and made no move to resume her visits to Martin for three weeks, but in the mild summer nights of the new year, she screwed up her courage and sneaked up to his hut every week. If Henrietta ever suspected what was going on, she never gave any indication of it.

Martin had written to his mother and family several times since coming to Norwood. He wrote his letters on the table he had built from packing cases. There was no organised postal service to Van Diemen's Land that was available to the wider community, especially in the outlying country districts, but letters were taken by ships to England where a service did exist. Martin could take his letter to the manager of the store at Don who had an established contact with a Launceston businessman who regularly sent mail to England. He was concerned that his mother would have to pay to take delivery of the letter, probably several shillings, an amount that would be significant in her poor circumstances, but there was nothing he could do to save her this problem in 1849. Only three years later, a better postal service between England and Van Diemen's Land was established and then he could pay at the time of posting.

Martin was working harder than ever. Mr Drewitt's time was taken up with managing the sales of timber and organising shipping to take it to the markets, leaving Martin to engage the splitters and make all the necessary arrangements. In addition to the gangs they had working in the Don district, they had others working on the Forth and Leven rivers, all of which had to be visited regularly. Mr Drewitt had engaged two more men to assist Martin, but he continued to rely on him to keep the production side of the business going full swing.

One day when Martin was returning to the Don after a trip upriver to service Badger's gang and half a dozen other gangs in the same area, he had his first experience with bushrangers. The occasional newspapers that turned up at Norwood had been carrying stories about robberies throughout the colony and Martin was aware that Mr Drewitt and his friends were worried that the villains would eventually inflict themselves on the coastal settlements.

Martin had Jock Masters with him to help with the rowing, and as they neared the wharf at the village, he said, 'Marty, who's that calling out?'

Martin turned his head and caught sight of a group of men on the wharf. Something about their stance and the way they were staring at another four men who were facing them suddenly made him apprehensive. He sensed that trouble was afoot.

One man, who Martin recognised from the village, was gesticulating at him and calling out, 'Keep away! Don't land!'

One of the four stepped up behind him and hit him in the back of the head with a pistol. He dropped to the wharf and laid still.

Before Martin or his mate could do anything, the boat had glided into the landing steps on the side of the wharf. The man with the pistol was holding it out at arms length, aiming it straight at Martin. He was coming down the three steps to the small landing platform.

'Don't do anything silly,' he said. 'We just want to borrow your boat for a while.'

Jock looked at Martin and was amazed to see him smiling at the man with the pistol. Martin stood up in the boat and said, 'What's that you say? Where do you want to go?' and he held out his hand as if to shake hands.

The man with the pistol was momentarily nonplussed and made a slight movement as if to change hands with the pistol. That was what Martin had hoped to achieve. As quick as a flash, his right hand reached out and grabbed the man's arm and he savagely jerked him forward. The man stumbled into the boat and as he fell, Martin gave him a heavy blow to the back of the neck, sending him over the far side of the boat and into the water. The man appeared to be lifeless.

'Get him out if you can,' Martin said to Jock as he sprinted up the steps and onto the wharf.

There were five men standing in two groups, all agape and staring at Martin. One of the three bushrangers was holding a pistol and another an old shotgun.

'Help!' Martin roared out. 'Help us get him out before he drowns!'

They were all staring at him. He didn't pause but bounded as quickly as he could straight up to the man with the pistol and knocked his hand up as he shoved him over the other side of the little wharf.

Martin swung around in time to see the third man coming at him with a large butchers knife and he dropped to one knee as the naked steel whistled past within an inch or two of his right ear. He grabbed the hand that was holding the knife and jerked forward as hard as he could as he turned his back on the attacker and leant over. The manoeuvre that Martin had practised a thousand times as a youth resulted in the villain falling over his back and crashing on to the wharf where he lay winded and senseless. As he looked around, Martin saw that the fourth bushranger had thrown down the gun and was turning to run.

'Grab him!' Martin roared at the two village men who were staring as if mesmerised. 'Grab him! Quick! Grab him!'

The village men suddenly regained their senses and darted after the man who by this time was almost off the wharf. They managed to grab him and hold him.

Another man from the village ran onto the wharf at that moment, calling out, 'What's happened? Is somebody hurt?!'

Martin grabbed him by the arm and said, 'Get some rope, quickly! We've got to tie these bushrangers.'

The man was shocked. 'There'll be some in the hut on the wharf,' he stammered.

'Well, get it!' Martin ordered him, 'but be quick!'

Martin picked up the old shotgun and gave it a cursory glance. It was loaded, but how lethal it would be was anybody's guess.

He looked over at his own boat and saw Jock holding the first bushranger to keep him afloat, so he ran to the other side where he found the second man clinging to one of the piles. He waved the shotgun in his face and threatened to shoot him. 'Don't go away,' he said with a grin, knowing that it was extremely unlikely that the man would be able to swim at all, let alone be able to escape.

The village man suddenly appeared with an armful of rope.

'Now, you fellows,' Martin ordered, 'tie all these blokes up tight. Put their hands behind their backs, and do it properly. Don't let them go,' he cautioned. 'They'll be trying to escape.'

He told one of them to help Jock get the senseless man out of the water and then to secure the swimmer on the other side. Martin then ran up the track to the village and into the store. There he found pandemonium reigned. The manager was in the middle of the shop as white and shaken as if he had just returned from an earthquake, surrounded by an equally frightened male assistant and three women, all crying and moaning.

'What's up?' Martin demanded.

'We've been held up and robbed by bushrangers,' the manager said, his voice verging on hysteria.

'Were they four shifty looking fellows who looked like escaped convicts?' he asked.

'Yes, that's them, and they had guns too,' the manager croaked.

'Oh, right! That's it!' Martin said. 'We've got them caught and tied up down at the wharf.'

The manager's eyes suddenly enlarged to the size of goose eggs. 'Are you serious?' he asked. 'How did you catch them?'

'You'd better come down and have a look at them yourself,' Martin said. 'Somebody will have to decide what to do with them.'

The manager, who already had a good opinion of Martin because of his success as Mr Drewitt's overseer, was effusive in his praise of the capture of the bushrangers.

'Did they get away with money from the store, or was it goods?' Martin asked him.

'Yes,' he replied. 'They seemed more interested in money than goods; they took over two hundred pounds from the safe and the tills.'

'We can search them when we get down to the wharf,' Martin said. 'You might get it back. I'll question them about the money if you like. They might respond a bit quicker to me.'

'Yes, whatever you think best,' he replied.

Martin was pleased to see that Jock and the other village men had carried out his orders to tie the miscreants securely. They were trussed up and shut inside the hut. Martin made a show of threatening to kick the man he thought to be the ringleader. 'We know exactly how much money you took from the store. Give it back now and you might save yourself a good belting,' he said to them. Turning to the weakest looking of the four, he leant over him and snarled, 'Where is it? Tell us where it is, or we'll start on you first.'

'Dudley's got it,' he squeaked. 'That big bloke there.'

Within a minute or two, the manager had the money in his hand and was looking a lot more confident. Again he thanked Martin and the village men who had helped catch the robbers. 'I'll make a point of recommending you all to the police for what you've done; you especially, Martin,' he said.

'Thanks,' Martin said, 'but the first thing is to deliver them to the police. You'll know how to handle that better than me. The important thing is not to let them escape. They will have to be restrained and guarded all the time until you get the police involved. Now, if you can manage here, Jock and I will get back to Norwood. We've got duties there to attend to before dark.'

Jock was full of excitement and talk on the way home, and when they pulled up in the barnyard, he ran down to the kitchen and told Mrs Smith about the whole drama.

'Martin did it all, practically single-handed,' he said. 'I've never seen anybody fight like him. He's a bloody marvel!'

Henrietta went into the house and told Mr Drewitt who, by good fortune, was home early that evening. He immediately asked to have Martin sent to him in the dining room. When Martin walked in with a grin on his face, he said, 'What's this about you catching a whole gang of bushrangers? Tell me all about it.'

'Well, Squire, it wasn't all that much really. They were pretty weak desperadoes and went to water under a bit of good bluffing.' Suddenly, what he had said struck him as comical and he burst out laughing.

'Sorry, Squire,' he spluttered. 'Two of them finished up in the river and had to be fished out. It just struck me as funny.'

Mr Drewitt thought it was funny too, but he insisted on having a detailed account of all that had happened.

'It's a good day's work you've done,' he said, and then as if to reveal the way his brain worked in response to any situation, he continued, 'It'll look good on your record with the authorities, and I hope the company is pleased enough about getting their money back to give you a decent reward.'

It was a response typical of the man. Since arriving in Van Diemen's Land as a penniless convict fifteen years earlier, determined to lift himself to wealth and respectability, he had developed the habit of spontaneously assessing every daily experience and incident as to the likely effect it might have on his future fortunes.

Martin told him he had no thought of a reward when he attacked the bushrangers.

'Yes, I know that would be the case, but it would be a just and reasonable thing for them to do,' Mr Drewitt said. 'I'll speak to Earnest Valentine about it. But don't go just yet,' he said with a broad smile. 'I'm sure Mrs Drewitt and the girls would like to hear about the capture.'

He went out into the hall and within a minute was back with all three. Martin had to relate the story again and answer a lot of questions from the excited girls. He related the story in humorous terms as he had with Mr Drewitt, saying again that the desperadoes were not very bright and that they had a fatal weakness of succumbing to bluff.

'Yes,' Rebecca said, 'that was very clever, but what if he had pulled the trigger? You couldn't ward off a bullet speeding towards your head with bluff.'

Sarah chimed into the conversation by saying, 'I think you were very brave.'

Martin didn't know how to handle that kind of adulation and settled for a hearty laugh. 'Thank you, I'm sure.'

Mrs Drewitt said, 'Well, we can all have a good laugh at the happy outcome, but no matter which way you look at it, it was a very bold response to a frightening situation. We are all proud of you, and I hope you get a reward.'

Charles Drewitt was as good as his word, and by virtue of the fact that he was a shareholder in the trading company as well as a man of standing in the community, the directors quickly agreed to award Martin ten per cent of the money recovered from the bushrangers, an amount that was calculated to be twenty-four pounds. At Mr Valentine's suggestion, a deposit account with the company was opened for Martin with a credit balance of that amount.

'This will be the best way for you to handle the money,' he said to Martin. 'You won't want to keep it under your bed, and as there are no banks within a hundred miles the next best thing is a deposit account with the company. If you want to deposit any more money for safekeeping, you can do it easily, and it will all be earning five per cent interest per annum.'

News of the episode spread quickly throughout the length and breadth of the north coast and within a week, the Devon correspondent for the *Launceston Examiner* arrived at Norwood by horseback looking for Martin to get the story first-hand. The result was a headline story in the newspaper the following week and Martin's name became a household word across the northern districts of Van Diemen's Land.

Wherever he went for the next few weeks, people of all sorts wanted to shake his hand and congratulate him on his bold capture of the bushrangers. Bushranging had been a problem in Van Diemen's Land from the earliest days, but the Devon district suffered only occasional attacks, unlike the older and more thickly populated southern districts. But people on the north-west coast were fearful of the danger and lauded anybody who had the wit and courage to stand up to the villains, especially those who managed to capture them.

On 15 February 1850, Martin turned twenty-five. He had never told the Drewitts his birth date, but Mrs Smith had extracted that information from him, along with other family details, in his early days on Norwood. She told the others in the kitchen what an important day it was for Martin. Joyce told Rebecca and she, in turn, told her mother who mentioned it to her husband. The upshot was that Mr Drewitt mentioned it to Martin the next morning.

'It's been a good year for you,' he said, 'and we congratulate you

– that's all of us, wife and girls. You've done well, and I wish you well. I'm very pleased about the way you've taken over the timber management and how well it's going. I always seem to be raising your wages since you came here three years ago,' he laughed, 'and I'm doing it again. From today, you'll be getting four pounds a week.'

Martin was surprised, not so much that he was given a rise, but because the doubling of his wage was more than he expected.

'Thanks, Squire, I do appreciate it,' he said. 'At this rate, I'll be able to put a bit more into my account at the store.'

'Yes, well, you do deserve it. I told you in the first place that I'd do the right thing by you if you proved yourself, and you are certainly doing that.'

By this time, Martin always felt relaxed and at ease in his boss's company and there was a genuine friendship between them. As Martin had got to know him over the years, he had developed a strong admiration for his success in Van Diemen's Land and wanted to emulate it.

'That brings me to something else,' Mr Drewitt said. 'I've been thinking about your future, especially after the bushranger capture. I think we could soon apply for a conditional pardon for you, say before June this year. I've got in mind now that we might even get a full pardon. We could make a good case; you've got good behaviour right through. I'm sure Nathan Kentish will put in a strong word for you, and to top it off, capturing the bushrangers will be a powerful recommendation. The Governor is very concerned that the colony is still troubled by bushrangers and he'll be anxious to show everybody, including the convict community, that anybody who helps to capture them will be rewarded.'

'That would be good as far as I'm concerned, very good,' Martin said. 'I have always hoped that I'd somehow get a pardon, but I didn't think it could happen this quickly.'

'There are big things developing in the country now,' Mr Drewitt said. 'Not just in Van Diemen's Land, but on the mainland too. You can see how the growth of Melbourne and Adelaide has helped us with our timber business, and I think other opportunities will open up in the next few years. It's certain that transportation will end soon and that's bound to bring about more changes, some good and some bad, but for men who can change with the times and grab the opportunities as they come, the future looks good.

'Anyway, for us this year looks full of opportunities,' he said. 'You never know, by the end of it you may be a free man again. I will help you all I can, but I want you to concentrate on the timber. That's where the money is at the present time.'

CHAPTER 8

*I*t was the first of December 1850 when Martin was advised that the Governor had been graciously pleased to grant him a full pardon and that from that date, all his entitlements as a free citizen were restored to him. This momentous decision had been transmitted through his employer Charles Drewitt who had been advised through his good friend in the Launceston convict establishment.

A month later, Martin was notified through Mr Drewitt that he could attend the police station in Westbury to take delivery of the official document that constituted the pardon.

Martin was overjoyed by his good fortune and within an hour of learning about it, he was busy writing to his mother with the good news.

He reflected on the turbulent course his life had taken over the past five years: the death of his father and the hard times that followed, the bitter frustration of failing to find employment after being sent away from Ashburton, the final desperation that made him conspire, with the help of his brother-in-law George Latimer, to get himself transported to Van Diemen's Land, hopefully to find more opportunities to 'get on' than he could ever hope to find in England. The harsh life on the hulk and the months of agony during the voyage to Hobart were stamped on his memory, never to be forgotten, but already he had accepted that the experience was part of the price he had to pay for a new life in Van Diemen's Land, a price he now regarded as a bargain.

Martin believed that his life had started to improve as soon as he reached Van Diemen's Land. The long walk from Hobart to Deloraine had been a great experience and, in spite of the strangeness of the bush and the forests, there was a spell working on his mind that made it all seem familiar and comforting. The first experience of kindness and civilised working conditions that he found in the colony took place, ironically, in the depths of the rainforests where he met the kindly Nathan Kentish. Finally, there was the incredible stroke of good fortune that had installed him at Norwood in the employ of Charles Drewitt.

He was convinced that his future was mapped out by a kindly fate to spend the rest of his days in Van Diemen's Land. He missed his mother and would dearly love to see her again, but somehow he found their letters made up for the impossibility of that, and he had reconciled himself to the life of an exile.

Martin resolved to serve Charles Drewitt with even more loyalty and to patiently wait for the opportunities that he had spoken of to open up and launch him on his course. While Charles Drewitt and his family were congratulating him on this latest achievement, Charles said with a wide smile: 'Now that you can come and go anywhere you like, even return to England if you wish, I hope you don't leave me too soon.'

Martin smiled. 'No, I've got no immediate plans to go anywhere. I'm happy here. As for going back to England, no thank you! I had a fair bit of trouble leaving the poverty ridden place and I certainly don't fancy going back to it. The only thing I'd like to do is see my old mother again, and the others too. Maybe I'll go for a holiday some time in the future.'

'Van Diemen's Land is the place for you, my boy,' Mr Drewitt said. 'You've made a good start and you'll get your chances as time goes on.'

'There is something I'd like to say,' Martin said. 'I want to thank you and Mrs Drewitt, and the girls too,' he interjected on himself with a smile, 'for the way you've treated me since I came to Norwood. I know I was lucky to get a good chance like this and no matter what happens in the future, I'll never forget your kindness.'

'Thanks, Martin,' Mrs Drewitt said in her usual quiet way. 'We've all become very fond of you and we wish you well for the future. We hope you'll be around for a long time.'

The first important development to affect Martin and his fellow servants at Norwood in 1850 was the marriage of Joyce to Gordon Brownlow, a shipbuilder who lived at Forth. He was about ten years older than her and had been on a ticket of leave for several years after being transported for seven years for stealing. He had served his apprenticeship with a master shipbuilder at Woolwich in England and had been married to a woman about his own age, but poverty and the temptation to get more money by stealing from his employer had been powerful influences in his eventual downfall. He had arrived in Van Diemen's Land in 1843 and was assigned to a shipbuilder in Launceston. His wife back in England, like hundreds of other convicts' wives, took up with another man and that was the end of his marriage.

He first saw Joyce when he attended church at the Don and gradually developed a friendship with her that led him to ask Charles Drewitt for permission to court her. He was given permission to visit her at Norwood, always under the chaperonage of Henrietta Smith, and two months later she accepted him.

The close relationship Joyce had with Martin quickly came to an end when Gordon came on the scene, a development that was something of a happy release for him as the relationship had become more of a problem as time went on; he had no intention of marrying her and was feeling more guilt about the situation than he cared to live with.

Mrs Drewitt took over and insisted on helping Joyce get a nice dress to be married in, and also one for Ellen as bridesmaid. The wedding was held on a Saturday afternoon in the church at the Don and was followed by a reception at Norwood where Henrietta Smith was in her element as proxy mother of the bride. Twenty people were entertained to a lavish afternoon tea in the dining room at Norwood before the happy couple left to drive to Forth in the groom's stylish jinker, drawn by a smart cut of a horse.

Another housemaid, this time by the name of Estella Summers, came to take Joyce's place and was soon absorbed into the life of Norwood.

Mrs Drewitt was always on the lookout for ways to improve the little community of Don. She got the idea of starting up a lending library in the village for the use of the whole community and persuaded her husband to finance the venture. She and the girls travelled to Launceston that autumn before the roads became too boggy and made quite a splash by purchasing the first consignment of books. The selection available in Launceston was somewhat limited in both quantity and width of selection, so she left an order with the bookseller for a second consignment to be sent down on the *Water Witch* in due course. The little library, which was open for business after church on Sundays, was popular and well patronised. Martin, who had been reared to be a reader, had missed the opportunity to read all through his days in Van Diemen's Land and started borrowing from the first day the library was open.

Charles Drewitt's business ventures continued to flourish and Martin's life was a busy mixture of farm management and organising and servicing the gangs of timber getters in an ever widening area of forests.

The small settlements that had taken root on the rich soil of the Mersey, the Don, the Forth and in recent times at Ulverstone and Penguin – all situated on the north-west coast of Van Diemen's Land – were slowly growing as more people arrived to make new homes on the 'Coast' as it was being called. Many of these people were convicts on ticket of leave releases and pardons along with a strong stream of emigrants from the British Isles.

The area had suffered bad times through the 'hungry forties' when potatoes and other crops had to be sold at very low prices, but as the new decade dawned, better times brought more prosperity and confidence. The trade in timber had made Charles Drewitt a rich man and was helping more farmers as well as hundreds of splitters as it continued to grow.

The advent of the gold rushes in the early 1850s affected Van Diemen's Land in much the same way as it did the larger colonies on the mainland. The first reliable news of the gold rushes came to Norwood about the middle of 1851 by way of the *Launceston Examiner*. Whenever the small coastal ships returned to the Don from Launceston, they brought copies of the paper. The Don Trading Company store always had copies of the last few weeks issues in stock and Norwood had a standing order in place.

Martin was excited to read of the big discoveries of gold at Ballarat in August and September of that year, and as the reports gained in drama each week, he became more interested. He read of the storekeeper at Buninyong who had been prospecting for gold in the nearby ranges as a hobby for two years when he decided to go around to the other side of the hill to try his luck. There he struck it rich, and in a few days it was the site of the first gold rush in the Ballarat district. From there the diggers branched out in all directions, finding gold everywhere they went.

The sensational reports continued week after week. By the middle of October, Ballarat had a population of diggers calculated at between six and ten thousand and more were arriving on the scene daily. The glimmer of gold was an immediate attraction for thousands of low paid farm workers, as it was to thousands of city workers of all kinds.

The thought uppermost in Martin's mind was: is this my first opportunity? He was in a torment of indecision. His first thought was to go and try his luck. Now that he was a fully pardoned man, he could go anywhere he liked at any time that suited him. Two diggers from Ballarat had arrived in Geelong with sixty pounds of gold in a flour bag, an event that had fuelled the gold fever to a new madness. If he missed this opportunity, would another occur later, or would he miss out entirely?

But his second thought was of the obligation he felt to Charles Drewitt. It would be unthinkable to go off and leave him in the lurch at short notice. After agonising over the decision for two weeks, he talked it over with his boss and friend.

'Yes,' Charles said, 'I know how you're feeling, but I hope you don't do anything rash too quickly. I've never been in a gold rush, but I know a lot about them. I've got a good friend who had five years away in the Californian gold rushes and he told me enough about his experiences to give me a knowledge of what is going on in Victoria right now.

'The first thing to keep in mind is that this rush will not come to an end quickly; at the very least it will last for three or four years. The second thing is that it's not always the gold diggers who make the fortunes; it's the storekeepers and the others who provide the services for the thousands of people who will continue to flock to the fields. They too make fortunes, especially if they have a business head on their shoulders.'

Martin said, 'I can feel the gold fever stirring in my bones, Squire, and you're right. My rash feeling is to catch the next ship to Melbourne and go straight to Ballarat, but I'm not going to walk out and leave you in the lurch.'

'Good, I'm relieved and pleased to hear that,' Mr Drewitt said. 'I know that if this lasts for a few months, my timber business will boom, and because all those people in Melbourne and the goldfields will have to be fed, the farm will boom too.'

'But I can understand how you feel. This could be a good chance for you. You're young, with no ties like a family to think about; of course you'll be thinking about what's best for you. I don't want you to rush off too soon, but I'll help you when the time comes. In the meantime, I'd like you to go to Launceston and talk to my old friend, George Wilson. He could give you advice to help you decide what to do.'

After a moment or two, he grinned and said, 'As an old horse and cart man, I can see the prospects for making money carting freight up to the goldfields that would be more reliable and easier than digging for gold you may not find.'

Martin was interested immediately. 'I hadn't thought of that. I have enough money now to buy a wagon and a couple of horses.'

Mr Drewitt laughed and said, 'You can see an opportunity when it's staring you in the face, can't you? If you're serious about going to join the rush, you ought to go and talk to George soon.'

The result of this conversation was that Martin rode to Launceston and met George Wilson in his modest home in George Street. He told him who he was and that he was there on the recommendation of Charles Drewitt.

'Ah, old Charles Drewitt,' he chuckled. 'Now there's a man with a good head on his shoulders. A fine man too although a lot like to run him down because of jealousy. So he told you to come and see me, did he? I don't mind talking to you, especially if it'll please old Charles.'

Martin spent two hours with the wise old man and in that short time learnt more about gold rushes and goldfields than he had ever gotten from newspapers or books, or from other people.

'Once you get gold fever, it never completely leaves you,' he told Martin. 'Even now, if I were twenty years younger, I'd be off to Ballarat. Not to dig for gold, but to set up a business on the fields and be part of the game.'

As Martin left, George shook his hand warmly and said, 'Good luck to you. I hope you find a few good nuggets, one way or the other. Come and see me again in a few years and let me know how you get on.'

Martin went downtown and found his old mate, Thomas Carter.

'What are you doing in town? You haven't got the sack, I hope.'

Martin laughed. 'The main thing at the moment is, can you let me have a bunk for the night?'

'Yes, I can, but it won't be in the hut. I'm married now and I live in a cottage that belongs to this old skinflint, but the wife will be pleased to meet you. You can sleep on a bunk in the back room.'

'I've got a lot to tell you,' Martin said, 'including how to capture bushrangers,' he added with a big grin on his face.

They arranged to meet that evening at Thomas's cottage, only a short distance from the coachworks where he still worked. A few minutes after meeting, Martin was being introduced to his wife; a short, plump woman with a pleasant face and a ready smile.

'This is Aileen,' he told him, then to her he said, 'and this fellow is that bloke I told you about on the ship who was my good friend. But first of all,' Thomas said, 'I've got a couple of bottles of ale on hand. Let's have a drink.'

As on their previous meeting, now many months in the past, they had a lot to talk about. Somehow Aileen managed to find enough for the three of them to eat and they spent a pleasant evening.

Martin told them he was considering going to the goldfields and setting up as a carrier. 'How much would your boss charge to build a decent sort of a light wagon?' he asked Thomas.

'Depends on what you want,' he replied. 'You'd get something really decent for twenty-five pounds.'

'I've got a few ideas about what I'd need to handle the tough conditions over there,' Martin said. 'From what I hear, the roads in Victoria are either dust bowls or bogs, depending on the season.'

They talked on into the night. Eventually Aileen pleaded tiredness and retired to bed. The two men chatted on until midnight.

The next morning, Martin rode out of Launceston along the Westbury Road, well-pleased with his visit and anxious to get back to Norwood to help Charles Drewitt organise his business so that he could fill the vacancy when Martin departed.

During the next few days, he and Mr Drewitt had several discussions about finding somebody to take Martin's place and also planned the best way for Martin to get to Melbourne and what to do when he got there. Martin was lucky that Mr Drewitt, who had many years experience over a wide range of activities in the colony, including operating his own carrying business, was available and willing to advise him.

'From what I read in the newspapers and from what people who have been in Melbourne tell me, it's just chaos over there now,' Charles said. 'There is a desperate shortage of labour; everybody has run off to the gold rushes. I think your idea of having a wagon built in Launceston is good because you may find it impossible to get one over there at present, and the same thing would apply to horses. I think you ought to keep your eye out here for suitable horses and take them over with you. It will be vital to have good ones.'

A few days later, he told Martin that he would be talking to a man who was living at the Mersey whom he hoped to persuade to take Martin's job. 'I heard yesterday that he has just sold his land and is looking for another opportunity. I know him well, and I know he would be better off with me than taking on another small farm.'

A week later, he told Martin that the man, Ben Campbell, had taken the job and would be available to start in two weeks.

'I'm sorry I am causing you this trouble,' Martin told him. 'It's a pity we didn't have more time to get organised for it.'

'Now, listen to me. Don't think that I will hold this against you; I can see things from your point of view. You're in the same position as I was when I first got my freedom. I had to grab every opportunity as it came along, and that's how you need to go if you're to have great success, which I think you can. As a matter of fact, I'd think less of you if you weren't set to have a go.

'The only thing I want you to do is to spend a month getting Ben Campbell trained up to handle the job the same way you've been doing it. A month won't make much difference to you,' he said, 'but it will help me a lot. Another thing, it will take that long to get yourself organised. You've got to get your wagon built and horses found. Have you worked out how you're going to finance the deal? It's going to cost a lot.'

'I've got a hundred pounds in my account at the company. I hope that will do it.'

Martin rode to Launceston again soon after this conversation and made arrangements with Mr Joseph Linnell, coachbuilder and Thomas

Carter's employer, to build a light wagon to his specifications. Martin was pleasantly surprised by the man's interest in him and his plans and his willingness to do the job quickly.

'Yes, we can do it within a month, once we get to know exactly what you want. It will cost at least twenty pounds and we'll need a deposit before we start.'

Martin told him he would have the cash in his hands within a few days, an arrangement that satisfied him immediately.

'Before we start talking about the specifications, could I bring my old mate, Thomas, to listen in? He knows pretty well what I want and he might be able to suggest something as well.'

The old man, whom Thomas had described as a skinflint, agreed readily and went out into the workshop to call Thomas into the office where they were talking.

'The first thing to decide is what size you want this wagon to be,' Mr Linnell said.

'I will only have two horses,' Martin replied, 'so I don't expect to be hauling any more than two tons.'

'What size wheels do you want?' was the next question.

'I'll be looking to you fellows for advice on that,' Martin said. 'I am told that the roads over there are very bad, either dust bowls in summer or bog holes in winter. Do you recommend a wider wheel for conditions like that?'

So the discussions went on. Thomas suggested that a good toolbox would be essential to carry some spare horseshoes and shoeing gear as well as the usual axe and digging tools, heavy ropes and other items that would be handy in emergencies.

'There's one more thing I think would be more than handy,' Martin said. 'Could you put a false floor on it so that I can hide small items, such as money or the like?'

Joseph Linnell sparked up at this suggestion. 'What a good idea,' he said with a grin. 'You might want to put gold in it. After all, you're going to be on a goldfield.'

They were words spoken in gest, but time proved them to be prophetic.

In the end the deal was made. The wagon, built to all these specifications, would be ready in a month and the cost would be twenty-four pounds. Martin returned to Norwood full of confidence and in high spirits.

Ben Campbell moved into the third hut two weeks later and Martin started to get to know him. He was in his mid thirties and a large lump of a man with dark hair already showing faint signs of grey. Martin saw that he was full of confidence and sure of his own capabilities and sensed that he was not a man who liked to be argued with. Martin had seen many like him in his convict days and resolved to handle him carefully.

For the next month, Martin moved nowhere without him. They visited all the gangs at least once and spent many hours on the farm. The madness of the gold rush was by this time affecting every farm and business in the colony. The workers, including the splitters, were departing the scene as quickly as they could raise the fare to the goldfields. Martin could see that within a few weeks, Ben wouldn't have much to do because unless he could find a new source of labour, he wouldn't have any splitters left to supervise.

After the years of hardship and poverty during the 'hungry forties', the small farmers and the labourers of the Devon district saw the gold rushes as their opportunity to lift themselves to prosperity and a better life. The stories of the diggers digging up fabulous fortunes in a day with nothing more than a shovel and a tin dish were too much to resist.

They continued to leave Van Diemen's Land by the hundreds every week to join the rush.

Even Norwood itself was being affected. Jock Masters had left as had three of the four village hands Mr Drewitt had put on during the past year, and Allan Freeman was showing an unhealthy interest in the goldfields. Henrietta Smith had told Mr Drewitt that she wouldn't be surprised if the fever took him. He reacted in his usual pragmatic way and made a deal with Freeman to increase his pay by two pounds a week on condition he stayed on the job for another year.

The exodus proved to be something of a blessing for Martin. A small land-holder at Forth was desperate to raise money to finance himself to the goldfields and wanted to sell his matched team of light plough horses. Charles Drewitt heard about it, as he heard about almost everything that was happening in the district, and went with Martin to look at them.

'I'm not coming with you to interfere because I know that you know as much about horses as me, but maybe my being there will help you get a good buy.'

He was right. The man accepted thirty pounds for the two horses, less than half of what they would have cost in Melbourne.

'There's your first stroke of luck,' Mr Drewitt said. 'They're not only cheap, but good horses into the bargain.'

'Thanks, Squire,' Martin said. 'I appreciate your interest, and if you don't mind me saying so, your friendship as well. Maybe you ought to be coming with me. You'd be right at home on the goldfields from what I've heard.'

Charles burst out laughing. 'At your age, I would be going, but that part of my life is behind me now. I'm sure you'll be able to manage without me.'

One last inspection with Ben Campbell around the few forest gangs still on the job and Martin was ready for the big adventure.

When it came time to say farewell to all at Norwood, Martin was surprised at his own – and everybody else's – emotional goodbyes. Charles Drewitt gave him the biggest surprise of all by giving him a big hug and pressing fifty gold sovereigns into his hand. Martin had never seen him show emotion before.

'You deserve it,' he said. 'You've earned it, and I want to see you succeed. Keep in touch with us.'

Mrs Drewitt kissed him and gave his shoulder a warm squeeze. 'Good luck, dear boy,' she said. 'I hope things go well for you.'

The girls both kissed him goodbye. 'You will write to us, won't you?' asked Rebecca.

'Yes, of course I will,' he said as he squeezed her hand.

Henrietta Smith clung to him with tears streaming down her cheeks. 'Now you be careful, won't you,' she said.

'Yes, I will,' he replied, 'and thanks for your friendship and all you've done for me while I've been here.'

At last he got away, riding one horse and leading the other one loaded with his swag.

After two days of travel, Martin reached Launceston where he found stables near the wharf to leave his horses while waiting for the *Water Witch* to sail for Melbourne.

The day before, he had taken delivery of his wagon from Liddell's coachworks. He was delighted with the finished job and had told Mr Liddell as much.

'You've made a great job,' he said, 'and I'm more than satisfied. I'm looking forward to trying her out on the Ballarat road.'

'Don't overload her with gold. It's heavy stuff, I believe,' the old man had said with a grin.

'I wish I was coming with you,' Thomas Carter had said as he helped Martin hitch up the horses. 'You'll probably have lots of adventures.'

Now, on the way back to the stables, Martin stopped at a hardware store and bought the few tools and the odds and ends he would require on the road. When it came time to board the ship, the wagon was loaded into the hold first and the horses were lowered down in turn by a canvas sling and tethered it. There were several others horses to go as well. Martin spoke to the skipper again about their arrangements.

'You will be unloading me on to the wharf at Williamstown, won't you? Mr Drewitt was very firm in his advice to me not to unload by lighter at Melbourne. It's too risky for the horses.'

Martin knew that the use of Mr Drewitt's name would be the most influential factor in how they treated him. In those days, the ships had a bad name for pushing people off by lighter onto the boggy banks of the Yarra before they got anywhere near the Port Melbourne wharf.

'Yes, that's where we're going first. We'll unload you first and anybody else who wants to get off at Williamstown. That will lighten us enough to get up the river.'

As the ship prepared to leave, four policemen came aboard and went around amongst the passengers, demanding of many to see their passes. The only convicts allowed to leave the colony were those with a ticket of leave or a pardon. As the policeman approached Martin, he withdrew his pardon and flashed it in his face. One glance and the policeman mumbled, 'You're right, mate.'

The ship was crowded with a motley lot of rough cut people. Some of them were diggers who had done well on the goldfields and had been home to Van Diemen's Land to show off their newfound wealth. Some had bought horses while they were in the colony and were now taking them back to Victoria. Martin heard enough of their talk to realise that he had been very lucky to get his horses at a low price. According to them, horses in Melbourne were up to a hundred pounds each and there was not much to choose from in the way of quality.

Every spare space in the hold was filled with goods of some sort from bags of bran and oats to large bundles of hay, all crammed in to within five feet of the deck. This low space was where most of the passengers slept that night. Martin noticed a long, wooden box tucked in under the rear end of his wagon and idly wondered what was inside it.

The December weather was warm and stuffy and he could already feel the perspiration breaking out on his own back. Martin was concerned that his horses would not get enough air, so he went up on deck where the air was sweet and fresh to speak to the mate about the stifling conditions in the hold. He pointed out that the few horses and the people down there would need more ventilation. The man seemed interested and said he would speak to the skipper about it.

The afternoon grew hotter as the ship sailed down the Tamar with a gentle south-east breeze behind her. The diggers and their friends were gathered in small groups, drinking rum and talking, and as the rum took effect they talked more and louder. They talked incessantly about the respective merits of Mount Alexander and about Ballarat versus Bendigo. Martin kept his ear cocked to pick up any bits of folklore that could be useful on the road.

As the sun set, Martin climbed down into the hold to check on his horses. The hold was open and an attempt had been made to rig a windsail to drive more air down into it, but the atmosphere was hot and humid. He asked a man on deck to pass down two buckets of water which the horses sucked up greedily. As he was idly checking his wagon, Martin fancied he heard a noise coming from the long box under it. He got down on his knees, and crawling up close to it, he knocked gently on the side. His knock was immediately answered by a knock from within. He took a closer look all over the box and found a slit at one end that was obviously a breathing hole for somebody inside. Putting his face close to the slit, he said in a low voice, 'Who are you?'

A woman's voice answered him. 'I'm a stowaway and I'm suffocating. Get me out.'

'Is there anybody on board who knows you?' he asked.

'Yes, find Sam Jessup and tell him I'm suffocating and will never make it to Melbourne.'

Martin realised at once what was happening. The woman was a runaway convict and was escaping to Port Phillip.

'I'll go and find him,' he said to the slit. 'It might take a while because I don't know him. Is he a digger?'

'Yes,' she replied, 'but you won't give me away, will you?'

Martin's mind worked quickly. It was an unusual situation, and with an element of danger involved. It was a serious crime to help a convict escape, but he was loath to turn her in. As he was confident that nobody had seen him 'talking' to the box, he made a quick decision to take the risk.

He climbed back onto the deck and went to the first group of diggers he saw. It wasn't difficult to pick the diggers from the other passengers. They were mostly rough cut and noisy and by this time, under the influence of rum.

'Is Sam Jessup anywhere about, mate?' he asked one of them.

'He was here, but he's gone now. He might be down with that mob at the stern.'

Martin went to the stern of the ship and inquired there for Sam. He was soon facing him.

'Good day, mate,' he said. 'Can I have a word? Come over here.'

Sam Jessup was a typical digger, dressed in his moleskin trousers and flannel shirt with a big cabbage tree hat on his head. He had three or four days growth of beard on his round, chubby face and looked as if he could do with a good wash.

'What's up, mate?' Sam asked in an offhand way.

'Nothing with me, mate,' Martin replied, 'but I'd say you've got a big problem. Your woman in the box is suffocating and I'd say she's on the verge of making a big noise.'

Sam suddenly looked astounded and very worried. 'How do you know about that? Who are you, anyway?' he demanded.

'I know because she is in the long, wooden box under my wagon in the hold. Let's not waste time here, come down and see for yourself.'

In a few minutes, they were back beside the box and Sam started talking through the slit. All he got in reply was a series of moans and the few words that were spoken were a repetition of: 'I'm suffocating, get me out.'

'Bloody oath!' Sam swore. 'What the hell do I do now?' he asked.

'I'd say you'll have to get more air to her, or she'll be dead within an hour,' Martin told him.

'I haven't got any tools to get her out,' Sam said. 'Bloody oath, what a right bloody mess.'

'I've got a few tools here in my wagon. I'll lend you something, but you'll have to cover for me. If I'm caught helping a convict to escape, I'll be back inside myself, and I don't want that,' said Martin.

'No, well, I'll do the best I can and if we're caught, I'll say I stole your tools. What's your name, anyway?'

'I'm Martin Maynard, and I'm on my way to the diggings.'

Martin was terrified somebody would see them releasing the woman and then alert the crew, so he quickly arranged a few bags of bran and other goods on the wagon to provide some small measure of protection from prying eyes.

Martin crawled around to the back of the wagon and opened the small toolbox. He brought a hammer and a pair of blacksmith's pincers back to Sam who quickly crawled in close to the box and started fiddling with the boards that formed the lid.

To Martin's great relief, he managed to get one board loose without making too much noise. By this time, no more sound was coming from the box and Martin despaired of seeing the woman alive, but Sam persevered and soon had the other two boards off. Within a few minutes, he was able to lift the woman up to a sitting position. She looked ghastly, but after a minute or two, with Sam gently rubbing her face and shaking her as best he could, she started taking a few deep breaths.

The other passengers in the hold were grouped up at the bow end where they were lying on bags of bran and other soft cargo. Many of them were asleep and the others were talking amongst themselves, unaware of the drama taking place behind Martin's wagon.

Within an hour, the woman, whose name Martin learnt was Nellie Houseman, was sitting up and almost fully recovered from her ordeal. They gave her water and she ate some of the food she had in the box with her.

'Thanks a lot, mate,' she said to Martin. 'You've been a brick. I would have been dead only for you.'

'What do we do now?' Sam asked. 'I don't suppose you want to go back in the box?'

'Not on your bloody life!' she exclaimed. 'I'll take my chances with the crowd. With a bit of luck, I'll just walk off in Melbourne and nobody will take any notice of me.'

'We're calling at Williamstown first. That will be your best chance of slipping off unnoticed. My advice is to get off this ship as soon as you can,' said Martin.

'I'll put the lid back on the box in the morning,' Sam said. 'They'll just unload it amongst all the other junk in Melbourne, but by that time we'll be gone to Ballarat.'

By this time it was almost dark, and with the help of the good south-easterly breeze they were approaching the Tamar Heads. Once out in the open sea of Bass's Strait, the wind picked up and by midnight the *Water Witch* was sailing along at twelve knots.

CHAPTER 9

*B*efore midnight, a good draught of air was coming down into the hold where the horses and the passengers, including Nellie Houseman, were refreshed and able to sleep well even if somewhat uncomfortably. By midafternoon they were in Hobson's Bay, opposite Williamstown with its little huddle of houses and small jetty.

As the *Water Witch* entered Hobson's Bay on 12 December 1851, she had to wend her way through a large number of big sailing ships that were anchored there. The tall, bare masts, stripped of their rigging, stood out like dead trees. Martin was reminded of the forests of dead trees that covered thousands of acres of the fertile soil of the Devon district back in Van Diemen's Land.

'Why are all these ships waiting here?' he asked one of the mates.

'They've been left stranded with no crews. The crews have all deserted and run off to the diggings,' he replied. 'This country has gone so mad with gold fever, Melbourne is almost a deserted city. All these people on this ship are the same; they're all chasing the pot of gold. Poor buggers, most of them won't find enough gold to buy a feed.'

'What will happen to the ships?' he asked.

'Eventually, when the silly fools find out what it's really like on the diggings and that only one in ten ever finds anything worthwhile, they'll come back and sign on again. Some of the masters and mates have gone with the crews. They're going to look, silly buggers. Serve them right, I say.'

An hour later, they were tied up at the jetty. A good number of the passengers had decided to disembark and find their own way to Melbourne rather than take their chances of being stuck on the mud in the Yarra River where the Port Melbourne wharves were situated. Nellie Houseman blended in with the disembarking passengers and walked off unchallenged, followed closely by Sam Jessup.

'We'll see you ashore,' she said to Martin. 'We'll wait for you to get your stuff off. We might be able to help you. If we can, we will; we owe you a lot.'

Martin's horses, along with the four others in the hold, were hoisted out in a canvas sling and landed on the jetty. Martin led his pair off the jetty and tethered them to a post and rail fence a short distance up the street. They immediately put their heads down and started cropping the grass like mowing machines.

Martin had to wait while more of the smaller freight was unloaded before his wagon was hoisted up and swung out onto the jetty. He had planned to hitch the horses to it on the jetty, but when he saw a group of men, most of whom he judged to be diggers, standing idly watching the unloading operations, he said to them: 'What about a hand here, mates. I just want to get this wagon off the wharf, out of the road.'

A couple of them grabbed the shafts and the others pushed from behind. The wagon rattled its way to a cleared spot on the street and a moment later, Sam Jessup and Nellie Houseman were by his side, all smiles and cheerfulness.

'Hi, mate,' Nellie said. 'That went well. At least we're all ashore safe and sound.'

'I'll just have to wait a bit to get the rest of my stuff,' Martin said, 'then I can work out what to do next. I suppose to find a place here where I can camp for the night would be the best. At least that would give the horses time to rest up after the voyage.'

'Yes, that sounds good to me. I could do with a good night's sleep. That bloody box wasn't any bed of feathers, I can tell you,' said Nellie.

'We could go to the pub. I believe there's one here not too far away. I've got plenty of money,' Sam Jessup said.

They hitched the horses up to the wagon and set off up the road. Soon they found a colonial hotel that agreed to accommodate Sam and Nellie inside as paying guests, and Martin was told he could camp, with his horses, in a little paddock at the back of the establishment. Sam wanted Martin to stay at the hotel at his expense, but Martin wouldn't hear of it.

'No thanks, all the same. I'll be all right out here in my tent. It'll be a good chance for me to practise pitching it and getting organised to live in it. That's what I'll be doing all the time I'm on the road.'

'Well, just come in with us and have a good feed. That will do you the world of good and it'll be a way for us to thank you for your help on the ship.'

He agreed to that, and he enjoyed the meal. He said as much to Nellie. 'Thanks for that,' he said with a grin. 'I was hungrier than I thought. That's the best feed I've had since I left Norwood a week ago. I don't expect to get too many like that where I'm going.'

They fell to talking between themselves about their plans. Sam and Nellie were heading for the diggings at Ballarat. Sam and three partners had done well on that field in the previous two months and he was intent on going back to round out his fortune.

'I did all right the first time,' he said. 'I walked away with six hundred pounds for two months work. I know a lot more about digging now and I can do better next time.'

'Are your old partners still there?' Martin asked him.

'Some of them may be,' he replied. 'They were good fellows, but if I have to find new partners, I wouldn't expect to have too much trouble.'

'What is your plan?' Nellie asked Martin.

'It's simple,' Martin said. 'After taking advice, I decided not to go digging but to get into some sort of business on the goldfields where I could build up a good stake and eventually to go back to Van Diemen's Land to buy a farm.'

'So you decided to go into business as a carrier?' Sam asked.

'Yes. I know a bit about horses and I don't mind steady work, so it might suit me better than the more chancy work of digging for gold. Only time will tell.'

'From what I've seen on the fields, I'd say you were on the right track. If you're reliable and get a reputation for honesty, you're bound to get plenty of business. The only thing is it's very hard work. You'll be getting bogged in the winter and famished out in the summer. What are your plans for the next few days?' Sam asked him.

'Go to Melbourne and get myself organised to start my business. My old boss told me about a firm of wholesalers in Elizabeth Street that could be helpful. One of his friends works there and he urged me to call on him first.'

'That sounds like a good idea. We'll come with you if you like. I know my way around Melbourne and I might be able to help you a bit.'

'Right, thanks, I would like to have you with me. It might save me getting lost and wasting time. We'll get going early in the morning.'

Martin went back to his wagon and put up the tent for the first time. It took longer than he expected and he wondered whether it was worth the trouble. As he unrolled his swag and prepared to settle down for the night, his mind was working on ways to improve the design to make it quicker and easier.

He spread a canvas ground sheet and, using a bundle of clothes as a pillow, he stretched out under a blanket. There was no problem keeping warm, but the hard ground was soon making every joint ache. He spent a restless night and was pleased when the sun brought daylight and warmth. There was plenty of firewood laying about and he had the billy boiling within a few minutes. Some good, strong tea and bread and jam made a breakfast for him. Sam and Nellie appeared on the scene as the sun was well up and Martin was getting impatient to be on his way.

Half an hour later, they were trundling along the track to Melbourne. The country was flat and the only features were occasional patches of tea-tree scrub and a few scattered eucalyptus trees that Martin saw as very second rate, not in the same class as the majestic giants on the banks of the rivers in Devon.

The closer they got to the city, the better the road became and the more houses were seen. An hour after leaving Williamstown, they were entering the outskirts of Melbourne, and within the next hour they had located the firm of Moles & Keane in Elizabeth Street. Martin left Sam and Nellie to look after the wagon and horses while he went into the large, double-fronted store to find Mr Cameron Ralph whom Martin knew from Charles Drewitt to be the assistant manager.

Martin was directed to where Cam Ralph was working in a small office at the entrance to a large warehouse that stood a few yards away from the front retail store.

Martin introduced himself and quickly outlined his connection with Charles Drewitt and his present situation, plus the fact that he wanted to go into business as a carrier servicing the goldfields.

'Well I'll be blowed!' Cam exclaimed. 'Here's a bloke who actually wants to start a business rather than rush up to Ballarat and dig up his fortune. I don't see many like you these days; most of them have the gold fever so bad all they can think of is digging holes in the ground, not working at some sensible job that will make more money for them anyway. Of course I'll talk to you, and be pleased to do it.'

'Before we start talking seriously,' Martin said, 'I've left my wagon and horses on the street in the care of a couple of friends. Can you tell me where I can safely park my rig while I talk business with you?'

'Yes, I can,' he replied. 'There's a good stable less than a block away from here. I suggest you go there and then come back to talk to me. We'll probably have quite a bit to say to each other.'

Martin returned to the wagon and told his friends what was happening. They found the stables and arranged to leave the horses there until the next morning.

'That'll be ten bob each,' the stableman said. He noticed the look of surprise that crossed Martin's face and chuckled as he said, 'Sorry, mate, that's the going rate at present. It's the gold rush, you know.'

Martin arranged to meet Sam and Nellie later in the afternoon.

'Do you plan to make a trip up to Ballarat in the next day or two?' Sam asked him.

'Yes, if I can get a load to take, I'll go as soon as I can,' Martin replied.

'In that case, we'll come with you if you'll take us. I'm prepared to pay something towards the trip,' Sam said.

Martin was pleased to get the request. He already had the idea in mind, but in keeping with his cautious nature, he didn't want to mention it to them until he had made his business arrangements. It would be a big advantage to him on his first trip up the Ballarat road to have an old hand like Sam to show him the way and the customs of the huge exodus that was taking place. He had already seen and heard enough to know that there would be hundreds of others travelling the road and there would be a lot to learn.

'How long have you known Charles Drewitt?' was the first question Cameron Ralph asked him upon his return.

Martin had been told enough about him by Mr Drewitt to have a good idea of what sort of man he was dealing with, and he had decided that a straight out account of his own background would be the best way to win his confidence. He was right. Within fifteen minutes, Cam Ralph had summed Martin up to be an honest and reliable man and one who could be trusted.

'What made you decide to go into the carrying business and not go gold digging yourself?' he asked.

'It was mainly because of what Charles Drewitt and his old friend George Wilson told me about gold rushes. I think a good, steady business would suit me better than the risky life of a digger.'

Cam burst into a short laugh again and his blue eyes twinkled as he said, 'You're a bit of a serious thinker, aren't you. Of course you're right; only about ten per cent of the diggers ever make more than wages.' He chuckled again. 'Well, you've come to the right place. We can't get enough carters to service our customers in both Ballarat and Bendigo, so I can give you a load today if you want it.'

'I wasn't thinking about today,' Martin said, 'but tomorrow would suit me well. But before we go too far, let's talk about money – freight rates and the like.'

Cam had a big grin on his face. 'You like to keep your eye on the main chance, don't you. I can see that Charles Drewitt has trained you well. But I like that, it shows that you know what you're doing. The rates vary with the seasons. Winter rates are the highest because of the wretched state of the roads. The rate right now is forty pounds a ton to Ballarat. You can pick up two tons of flour here in the morning for your first trip.'

'Right, that's a deal then. But there's a couple of more details you could advise me about. Firstly, is it true that bushrangers are on the roads often and secondly, is there anywhere here in Melbourne that I could make my headquarters? I need somewhere to keep my horses, and where I can get a feed and a bed, that sort of thing. And another thing,' he continued. 'Where's the best place to buy horse feed?'

'As far as a headquarters and lodging to live in is concerned, I know what you want, but finding it will not be easy. I'll get my ear to the ground. If I can't put you onto something before you leave tomorrow, I'll likely have a place for you when you get back in about a week.'

The upshot of their discussion was that Martin purchased a pistol and ammunition and found that he could buy oats and bran, and sometimes chaff, at Moles & Keane, the wholesale merchants who would be his main customer.

Cam Ralph showed him how to get his wagon around to the loading bay at the back of the premises and showed him over the store. From what Martin could see, they stocked just about everything that people, both country and city, would ever need.

He bought a palliasse and some light rope and wire clips that he planned to use to make his tent better suited to his needs. He planned to have more comfortable sleeping arrangements than on his first night at Williamstown.

He met Sam and Nellie as arranged for later that evening and told them that he planned to leave for Ballarat first thing in the morning.

'You don't muck around, do you?' Nellie said with a smile. 'I thought you might like to stay and sample life in Melbourne town for a few days before you head up country.'

'No, there'll be time for that later, after I get going. I've got to earn some money, I've spent all I had saved up on my outfit.'

'You'll be right, mate,' Sam said. 'You'll soon start making a few pounds, especially at this time of year while the roads are good.'

Sam and Nellie spent that night in a hotel three blocks away from the stables where Martin had his horses and wagon parked while Martin slept on the hay in the barn at the same stables.

They were loaded up and on the Mount Alexander Road, passing through Flemington by 10 o'clock the following morning. The payload was two tons of flour which was spread out over the floor of the wagon with Martin's swag and other gear stacked on top, together with Sam and Nellie's luggage, all covered by a canvas tarpaulin tied around the sides of the wagon. The all-up load was a little more than Martin felt comfortable with for the two horses, but the way things had worked out, he didn't have much choice.

Nellie was up on the load, but the two men walked beside the horses. The day was already hot and the horses had started to sweat. The road near Melbourne was good, but Martin knew that they would soon be on a much rougher road that would get worse as it reached out into the country, so he stopped about every hour to rest the horses for a quarter of an hour.

The road was cluttered with traffic of all kinds. There were dozens of one horse carts of every imaginable kind and almost an equal number of wagons similar to his own but of various sizes. He noticed one particularly big one being pulled by six horses harnessed in pairs. There was an equally big wagon being pulled by eight bullocks, lumbering along at a steady pace under the stern voice of a swearing driver. Mixed in with this conglomeration of vehicles were hundreds of pedestrians, many of them carrying swags and odds and ends of luggage. The strained looks on their faces showed clearly that they were already feeling the fatigue that would defeat a large number of them over the next few days.

The whole cavalcade moved along the road like a colony of ants travelling to a new source of food at a speed that Martin estimated to be a little faster than two miles an hour. It was slower than he would normally expect to travel with a wagon, but mindful of the softness of his horses, he was satisfied to maintain his place in the parade.

'This place up ahead is Five Mile Creek,' Sam said. 'There's a public house there where you can get meals. If you're agreeable, I'll buy any meals we can get along the way like this and we can save our chops for tonight.'

'That's all right by me,' Martin replied. 'You're the one who knows the ropes and I'm quite happy to follow your advice.'

A large, wooden building fronted the road with a fading sign on the front gable that proclaimed it to be the Lincolnshire Arms. They pulled into the yard and Martin quickly unhitched the horses and tethered them to the post and rail fence. He carried buckets of water to them and then slipped nosebags containing a measure of oats and bran over their heads.

'Now,' he said with a grin, 'I'm ready to get my own nosebag on.'

They went inside where a crowd of diners were making short work of the only items on the menu: cold meat with a slice of bread and a bottle of ale.

'Not much of a choice, but it's better than a kick in the arse. I've had to work on a lot less at times in the past,' said Sam.

Martin was surprised – and impressed – when he saw that the cost was ten shillings each. This publican would soon be a rich man.

They lingered around the Lincolnshire Arms for the full hour to give the horses a rest before starting off again.

About a mile along the road, they came across a cart that had overturned, spilling its load over onto the dusty verge. A woman with a tear-stained face was sitting on a stump while her man was trying to get the cart back onto its wheels.

'What happened?' Sam asked.

'The near side wheel dropped into a bloody great hole as I tried to get past that tree on the side just there,' the man said angrily. 'You'd think the useless bastards could do something to the road when there's thousands using it every week!'

'Never mind,' Sam said. 'It could've been a lot worse. Come on, we'll give you a hand to get it back on its wheels.'

With all three of them helping, plus three more who happened along at that moment, it was soon back on its wheels and the horse was being hitched up again. They spent ten minutes helping load the cart before Sam said quietly to Martin, 'We'll slip away. They'll be all right on their own now.'

'This flat country we're going into now is the Keilor Plains,' Sam told Martin. 'Diggers Rest is up ahead about five or six miles. If you take a good rest in a little while, we should be able to get there before dark.'

Martin steered the horses over to the verge of the road and stopped them as Sam had suggested.

They rested for another quarter of an hour before driving on. The road, except for patches in very bad condition, was not too rough, and the sun was still well up in the sky when they reached Diggers Rest. As they pulled into the cleared camping area, Martin was surprised to see old camp fires from previous visitors still smouldering. Some of the tall, dead trees were puffing out clouds of smoke, obviously alight inside their hollow centres.

Sam and Nellie made themselves busy setting up camp for the night amongst the hundreds of others who had arrived before them. Martin had insisted that they take the tent for the night and he would sleep under the wagon. While they were erecting the tent and getting a fire started to cook their chops, Martin unhitched the team and looked around for whatever feed and water was available. There was none. He took a quick walk out onto the open plains in the hope of finding grass on which to hobble the horses, but the long dry spell that had affected the country for the previous six months had finished all the grass. The waterhole that was the main reason for the camp's location was reduced to a slurry of poisonous looking mud, quite unfit for horses or any other animal. He had been warned in Melbourne by Cam Ralph what to expect and had brought a five gallon keg of water on the wagon. He broached that and gave each horse a ration of a gallon with a carefully measured feed of bran and oats. As there was no point in hobbling out the horses, he tethered them, one each end of the wagon.

As he finished these chores, Nellie was ready to start the chops, but Sam said, 'Hang on a minute. We can take the time for a little sip before tea. I've got a small flask here that I want you two to share with me.'

With that he produced the flask and poured a measure of rum into their mugs. Martin was not a great rum drinker, but after the long day's walk in the hot and dusty conditions, he was ready for a reviver.

The fiery liquor crept over his tongue and the fumes drifted into his nose. 'Ah, yes, good. I can feel that doing me good. Thanks a lot,' Martin said.

Sam laughed and said, 'You can't manage in this country without a sip now and then. The trick is not to let it take more out of you than you take out of it – that's the trick.'

Half an hour later they were eating their grilled chops and slices of bread, all washed down with hot tea. All around them, dozens of other travellers were doing the same chores in preparation for the night. They were a good-humoured, boisterous crowd; many of them drinking and talking in voices that were becoming louder by the minute.

It was the best part of the day and Martin felt relaxed, and happy with his first day on the road. He was weary but relieved that the great adventure was finally started. They had covered twenty miles, an achievement that pleased him and settled a few questions that had been in his mind from the first. How would the horses stand up to the hot conditions and the heavy work? How far would they be able to pull the wagon in a day? How would he himself stand up to the work, especially the walking? He knew that if he loaded up with payload to the full capacity of the wagon and the horses, then he would have to do a lot of walking to ease the strain on the horses.

They continued lounging around the camp fire and several fellow travellers from nearby groups wandered over to chat. The opening questions were always the same: 'Where are you heading? What's the news from there?' It was part of the easy camaraderie that pervaded the whole camp. Somebody on the other side of the camp struck up a tune on a guitar and it wasn't long before somebody else was serenading the crowd with an accordion.

The evening passed quickly. The talking, yelling and singing culminated in somebody taking pot shots at a possum up a tree and Martin was beginning to wonder what sort of a night they would have, trying to sleep in the midst of such noise; however, by midevening the fatigue of the day's march started to have its effect and the camp gradually quietened down.

Martin checked his horses for one last time and then made his bed on the ground under the wagon. He had brought a bag stuffed with hay from the stables in Melbourne and he used that to fill his palliasse; the result was a much better sleep than he got on his first night in the tent.

He was awake early the next morning to give his horses another gallon of water and a feed in preparation for the day's march.

Sam and Nellie were proving themselves to be good travelling companions. They were out early and soon had the fire crackling under the frying pan and the tea billy.

'You've got to have a decent feed for breakfast,' Sam said. 'We're just like the horses; we can't work for long on an empty belly, and it's best to have meat for breakfast if you've got it.'

Nellie was showing that she was a good camp cook. She was adept at toasting the bread and brewing the tea as well as keeping a close watch on the frying pan.

The sun was starting to give a warning that another hot day was coming as they pulled out onto the road amongst the first half dozen groups to get started.

'It pays to get started early,' Sam said. 'That way, if we do come across a waterhole, it won't be too stirred up for the horses to drink.'

By the time they reached the second hourly rest, the road started to rise up towards two low mountains. The road passed between them at a place called The Gap.

'Gisborne is down in the lower country and it's downhill all the way, so we should get there by dinnertime,' Sam said.

After giving the horses a good rest, they proceeded on the easy run into Gisborne. The last stage was down a steep section known as Breakneck Hill because of the many accidents that happened to bullock wagons and other heavy vehicles while descending into Gisborne.

Another country public house fronted on to the road, this time under the banner of The Bush Inn. There was no grass anywhere to be seen, so Martin unhitched the horses and fed them more bran and oats. Fortunately there was still a good supply of water in the several pools remaining in the Gisborne Creek, so the horses got a good drink and Martin took the opportunity to refill the water keg.

Again Sam insisted that Martin eat with them at the inn at his expense. When Martin resisted on the grounds that it was unfair for him to be buying all the food, both he and Nellie wouldn't hear of it.

'No,' Sam said. 'That's my share of the costs. It's only fair; we're getting our luggage carted and Nellie spends a lot of time up on the wagon. We're still getting a good deal. Anyway, I'm enjoying the trip.'

Nellie backed him up. 'We're only too pleased to help you. If it hadn't been for you, I wouldn't be here today. I was nearly done in that box when you came down and saved me.'

The menu at The Bush Inn was slightly better than at the Lincolnshire Arms, but the price was even higher. Martin was again surprised and shaken to see that it cost them one pound each.

'No worries, I'll soon make a lot more than that when I get back to Ballarat,' Sam said.

They travelled across rising country, some of it open paddocks, for two hours after dinner. At the second rest stop, they found a patch of good grass near the road and at Sam's suggestion they unhitched the horses and gave them an hour of good feeding.

'We'll be getting into the Black Forest within a few miles,' Sam told Martin. 'Too early to stop for the day, but most people these days do stop. They think it's a bad place for bushrangers, so if they can't get through it before dark, they camp on this side. I think the stories about bushrangers are just that – just silly stories. My advice would be to keep going and camp in the middle of it.'

That is what they did. Martin was surprised to see that the forest had been burnt out by bushfire the previous summer, so the name 'Black Forest' was appropriate. As usual with a eucalypt forest after a bushfire, the blackened skeletons of the trees had sent out a mass of young, fresh leaves which still looked fragile because of the continuing drought, but which gave a firm promise of restoration of the forest once the rains came again. The big trees and the obvious denseness of the forest was in stark contrast to the other bush seen on the road which was thin and open enough for a horse to canter through.

They travelled on through the weird forest of skeletons for another couple of hours before they reached a good place to camp. They unhitched the team and busied themselves setting up for the night and were soon joined by several other groups of travellers. That evening and night was a replay of the previous night, but with fewer travellers to keep them company. It was obvious that the reputation of the place, whether warranted or not, was enough to dissuade most people from camping there.

Sam Jessup told Martin that from time to time bushrangers did stick people up on the road, and even on the goldfields, but it was not as often as some of the gruesome stories would have it. 'Just the same,' he said, 'it's something you'll have to keep in mind. There are lots of villains on the goldfields that will pinch the eye out of a needle if it's left lying around, so as far as possible, travel in groups and be aware of the danger.'

The fact that they were over halfway through the nine miles of forest gave them a good start the next day. By midmorning they emerged from the forest and a short distance on, they came to a large tent set up as a tea and food stall and, they assumed, also as a sly grog tent for anybody looking for a reviver. They had a light lunch and travelled on to their destination for that day which was Kyneton.

Kyneton was situated on the banks of the Coliban River and in 1851 was already a settled town. The Coliban Inn fronted the main road through the small town and, like all the other public houses on the road, it was then enjoying a surge in business. They all charged very high prices for meals and any other services they provided, yet there was no shortage of customers who philosophically paid up the inflated gold rush rates. If Martin had been alone, he wouldn't have gone near them, but under the circumstances he was able to sample their wares and learn a lot about life in Victoria in those heady days at someone else's expense.

Once again, Sam and Nellie stayed overnight in the inn and Martin camped out in a paddock not far away. By this time, Martin had developed quite a good opinion of Sam in spite of the poor impression he got from his first experiences with him, but he noticed that, like most diggers, when he had money in his pocket he was overconfident and inclined to be a spendthrift. His attitude was: I succeeded in finding gold once and I will do it again, so if it's easy go, it'll be easy come again.

Sam had warned him about camping on the banks of the creek. 'All the creeks in the country are subject to flash flooding and many people have been drowned by floods that sweep down in the dead of night completely unexpected. The rain that causes it has often fallen twenty or thirty miles away and people on the spot are completely unaware that there is rain about. Always play it safe,' he said. 'Camp well back from the creeks and rivers.'

They continued on the next morning in what was now becoming a daily routine for Martin. Up early to feed and water the horses, cook breakfast over the camp fire, double-check the load and hitch up the horses, then out onto the road again for another day.

By dinnertime they had reached Sawpit Gully, notable as the site of the last licensed premises before reaching the Mount Alexander and Ballarat goldfields. As the sale of liquor was prohibited on the diggings, it was the last chance for anybody who needed his daily tipple to stock up.

The pub had the most outrageous prices of any place in the Port Phillip District, in preparation, it was said, for the diggers before they got their first shock at the cost of living on the goldfields.

Martin and his party had to continue for another five miles before approaching the diggings through Golden Point and Forest Creek. Rearing high into the sky on their right was Mount Alexander, the namesake for the field, but Martin found in the ensuing weeks that many diggers still called it Mount Byng, its old name.

As they passed by the boulder strewn foothills, Sam said, 'We're getting close to the diggings now. Only a mile or two further and we'll be on the goldfield.'

Martin remarked about all the people travelling out from and away from the diggings. 'How come there are so many going the other way?' he asked Sam.

'For a start, there are thousands of people here, and in the ordinary course of events there is bound to be a big two-way traffic,' he replied. 'Some are going on holidays, some are going home for Christmas, some are clearing out because they can't hack the life any longer, and a few are going home to retire,' he said with a laugh.

Just when Martin was beginning to wonder if they would ever see a sign of a goldfield, they finally saw evidence that they had arrived. There was an occasional pile of dirt, presumably beside a shaft, and Martin noticed that a large number of trees had been cut down in the bush they were passing. They plodded on a little further and then the road curved and the horizon opened out ahead of them to reveal the most amazing vista of a rural area that Martin had ever seen. He was shocked that the first impression he got was of utter desolation; the banks of the creek on both sides for as far as he could see were a mess of piled up soil through which there seemed to be no organised way, and through all this muddle were thousands of human beings moving about like ants.

His second surprise was hearing the constant, loud noise coming from the diggings. Nobody had told him that the hundreds of cradles being 'rocked' by the miners generated a great din that could be heard from one end of the scene to the other. Mixed in with this was the sound of picks being thudded into the gravelly ground and the shouts and curses of miners trying to communicate with each other above the din.

'How do you find you way through this?!' he yelled into Sam's ear.

Sam just grinned and said, 'There's the road, that takes you down along the creek and through this part of the fields!'

'I've got to find Zac Bellchambers to deliver his flour!' Martin said. 'How the hell will I do that?!'

'You said his address was The Junction, didn't you?!' Sam roared back. 'I know where that is, it's not far from here! Come on, I'll show you!'

They set off down the road. Once they got started, Martin could see that it was leading somewhere and he put his faith in Sam to find his way to The Junction. They turned off the road after about a mile and headed up a narrow valley. Within minutes they came to a rough, bushbuilt store with a big sign on the front that told the world it was Bellchambers Emporium. Sam went inside and came out again within five minutes with a stooped man of about fifty who was sporting a large apron and a skullcap.

'This is Zac Bellchambers,' he said as they approached the wagon. 'He wants that flour you've got for him.'

Martin held out his hand and Zac Bellchambers took it with a firm grip. 'You're new on the job, eh?' he said in a grunting kind of voice, but with a grin on his face.

'Yes,' Martin said, 'this is my first load. I'm just starting in business.'

'You can get your wagon round the back to unload,' Zac said as he led the way.

Martin quickly got the team round the back and the flour was unloaded within twenty minutes.

'Have you got a back load to take to Melbourne?' Zac asked him.

'I've got a heap of empty barrels to go back to Moles & Keane when I can get them taken by somebody.'

Martin was suddenly confused because he didn't know who would pay him for taking empty kegs and the like back to Melbourne. He thought quickly and decided to confront the question head on.

'I haven't got a back load and I am looking for business, but the question is, who is going to pay me if I take them?'

Zac and Sam both burst out with a hoot of laughter.

'You're a quick learner,' Sam said. 'The first rule of business: get your deals worked out straight before you start.'

'It's sometimes a matter for negotiation,' Zac said with a grin. 'They want me to pay and I want them to pay because the kegs and casks are their property. But I'll make a deal with you. If they don't do the right thing by you, I'll pay you myself when you make the next trip.'

Martin caught Sam's eye and saw the little nod he gave. He accepted the deal and accepted twenty-four casks and kegs of various shapes and sizes as a back load.

When they got away from the store and found a place to camp for the night, Sam said, 'You did the right thing agreeing to take the back load. He's held in good regard here on the diggings and I think he will stick to his word. The other thing is, he will be in a position to put a lot of business your way as time goes on. It'll pay to be in good with him.'

The drought had taken a tight grip on the country and there was no free water to be had on the diggings. Martin watered his horses from the water keg again that night, but he knew he would have to leave the diggings as quickly as possible in order to get back to where he could find a supply of good, cheap water.

Martin and his friends camped with the wagon again that night. It was taking Sam a little longer to find his old partners than he expected.

'They've moved on to another claim while I've been gone,' he said. 'I heard it was at a place called Anderson's Flats, about five miles from here. We'll walk out there this morning. I don't expect to have any trouble finding them; it's a new strike on the diggings.'

It was with a sense of regret that Martin said farewell to Sam Jessup and Nellie Houseman as they broke camp after another breakfast of mutton chops that morning. They too were loath to lose touch with him.

'Make sure you come to see us sometime,' Nellie said. 'It won't be too hard to find us.'

'That's right,' Sam said, 'keep in touch. You never know, we might have business to do to our mutual advantage.'

Martin double-checked that his load of empty barrels and kegs were securely tied onto the wagon, and after giving the horses the last of his water he headed out the road to Melbourne.

He was anxious to get back to Melbourne, but he had to consider his horses. The worst blunder he could make in this early stage of his business would be to have his horses break down through overwork. He remembered the one good patch of grass he had seen just before they entered the Black Forest on the way up and resolved to return there and rest himself and the horses for a day.

Once again the road was busy with traffic going both ways and he spent the first night amongst a large crowd at the roadside camp.

He reached the grassy plains about midday on the second day and found a good spot to get off the road where he could park the wagon and unhitch the horses. He hobbled the horses and turned them loose although he kept a sharp eye on them. They were ravenously cropping the grass, but he knew they would be content to rest once they had their bellies full.

He noted that what Sam had told him about gathering fellow travellers was true. Several other groups caught sight of the wagon parked behind the small, scrappy patch of scrub and came to join him. By nightfall, he had about twenty people as fellow campers.

He had bought a pistol on Cam Ralph's advice, but he hadn't actually fired it. He was anxious to get some experience with it in case he had to use it seriously, so when a good crowd had gathered at the camp that evening, he brought the pistol out and told them that he would walk out onto the plain and fire off several shots, explaining that he had to learn how to handle it.

One man, dressed as a gold-digger, said, 'I've had a bit of experience with pistols, I'll come with you if you like.'

As they walked along; the man, who said his name was Jake Simms, told Martin that he had been employed for a few months as a guard on the gold escort. 'It was a good job,' he said, 'but I wanted to have a go at digging myself, so I gave it up.'

'How has it worked out, moneywise?' Martin asked him.

Jake chuckled as he replied, 'About evens, I'd say. I never struck it rich, but I made about the same as wages, so it wasn't too bad. I'm going back to try it again, for a few months at least, after Christmas.'

Martin had some knowledge of firearms but had never used a pistol. Jake showed him the basics, together with a bit of advice about the safety angles.

'The worst part about pistols is that you can easily shoot yourself,' he said, 'so make sure the thing is always pointing away from you.'

The night passed uneventfully and Martin was on the road early the next morning. It was another bright, sunny morning with a promise of a hot day. Martin was riding on the wagon and the horses were showing the benefit of the day's rest he had given them.

As the wagon trundled along, he worked out in his head what profit he had made since picking up his first load in Melbourne seven days ago. Two tons at forty pounds would gross eighty pounds, a huge sum to Martin who had never had more than a hundred pounds at any one time in his life, even taking into account the twenty-four pounds reward he got for capturing the bushrangers. If he got paid well for carting the empty casks back to Melbourne, that would be in addition, so the trip could gross him upwards of a hundred pounds, as much as a highly paid professional would make in six months.

Three days later, he was reporting back to Cam Ralph at Messrs Moles & Keane in Elizabeth Street, Melbourne.

'So you got there and back safely,' Sam said. 'It hasn't taken you long, so things must have gone well.'

Martin gave him a quick report on the trip and told him that Zac Bellchambers had sent twenty-four casks back and that he had said that the firm would pay the freight.

Cam grumbled about Zac being too sharp by half, but agreed to pay one pound return freight on the casks and ten shillings on the kegs. This was good news to Martin because it more than met his expectations.

The next question to Cam was: 'Did you have any luck finding somewhere for me to live while I'm in Melbourne?'

'Yes, it's a place about five miles out on the road you'll be using to go to Ballarat. It's got an acre of ground and a small stable. I'll tell you all about it when you've finished unloading and we've had a settling.'

CHAPTER 10

*C*am Ralph had a settling with Martin and paid him one hundred and one pounds less twenty-four pounds contra account for horse feed and a pistol plus one or two smaller items. He had made a profit on the trip of seventy-seven pounds.

Martin's mind leapt ahead and he could see prosperity looking his way, but of course he couldn't be on the road all the time. Some trips would be quick and easy; others were bound to strike trouble at times, but now that he had a feel for the job, he felt very confident.

Cam gave him Mrs Alice Bunce's address in Alexander Road, Flemington, and said that he had agreed to pay her two pounds a week whether he was there or not. When he was there, she would give him full board, including washing his clothes, but when he was away on the road, he would still have to pay her.

'She drove a hard bargain, but I can see why,' Cam said. 'The way things are now, all sorts of accommodation are in desperately short supply and the landlords, or landladies, can demand – and get – what they want. But this will suit you down to the ground, so I advise you to go and try it.'

Christmas was only three days away, so it wasn't practicable for Martin to think of heading straight back to Ballarat. For one thing, he would have to rest his horses and for another, in spite of the chaos caused by the gold rushes, there would still be time off for most workers in Melbourne over the Christmas period, so the warehouse would be closed.

'But if you come here first thing the day after Boxing Day, we will have another load for Ballarat, so you won't have much time kicking your heels,' Cam said. 'Anyway, you'll need a rest and your horses certainly will.'

It was early afternoon when Martin left the town and headed out to Flemington. He found Mrs Bunce's house and drove his team into the spacious yard between the house and what he took to be the stable. His eyes quickly passed over the set-up and his first impression was favourable; it looked like a yard that would suit a local carrier.

He tethered the team and walked over to the house, meeting Mrs Bunce coming down a garden path towards him. He greeted her and introduced himself.

'Yes, I've been expecting you to turn up today,' she said.

She was a small, slim woman in her early thirties with light brown hair and a fair complexion. Two grey-green eyes were giving him a frank assessment.

'Have you been in Melbourne today?' she asked, more to carry the conversation forward than to get information.

'Yes,' he replied, 'I've just got back from Ballarat and I had to deliver goods to the warehouse in Elizabeth Street.'

'Well, you'd better come in,' she said, 'and I'll show you around.'

'You'll be sleeping here in the hut,' she said, turning towards a solid looking, timber hut not far from the back door. 'You can make yourself at home here,' she continued. 'You've got a good, comfortable bed and plenty of storage cupboards.'

Martin glanced around the room. It was about twelve feet square and he could see at once that it would be ideal for him.

'Come into the house and I'll show you the kitchen and where you'll be having your meals.'

He followed her through the back door into a hallway from which various rooms were accessed. The kitchen was the first room on the right and was typical of farm kitchens throughout the colonies; one end was taken up with a large open fireplace and a large table occupied the middle of the room. Several cupboards and a small sideboard completed the furnishings.

'I suppose you'd like a cup of tea,' she said.

'I'll just unhitch the horses before I do anything,' he replied.

She walked out to the yard with him and opened the stable door. It had two good sized stalls and a chaff house at one end.

'Yes, it looks good, just what I wanted,' he said.

'My husband used to be a carrier, like you,' she said. 'That's why it was built in the first place.'

'Has he given it up now?' Martin asked.

'Yes,' she said in a brusque tone. 'He's run off to the diggings to find his fortune.'

She watched him unhitch the horses and take them into the stable. He gave them a measure of bran and oats and then turned to her and said, 'I'll have that tea now if it's still on offer. I'm a bit parched myself.'

She led the way back to the house and quickly brewed a pot of tea and poured two cups.

'Let's sit down,' she said, pulling out a chair from the table. 'We can talk comfortably here. I suppose there'll be things you want to know.'

'Yes,' he said with a grin, 'there are one or two things. For a start, are you well off for water? The horses need a lot, especially when it's hot.'

'Yes, we've got a well that's never gone dry yet. It's at the back of the stable. You have to pull it up in a bucket but it's good water.'

'Cam Ralph told me you would be charging me two pounds a week for full board. How often do you want me to pay?'

She had a stubborn look on her face as she replied. 'I don't want to sound too hard, but I'm depending on this money to live. I want you to pay me every four weeks in advance.'

'That's eight pounds in advance?'

'Yes, I know it's pretty steep, but these are unusual times and every-thing has gone sky-high. The fact is, I could get more, but I've got to be careful who I take in. Cam Ralph recommended you as a decent man.'

Before he could answer, she went on. 'You may as well know now, my husband got gold fever and ran off to the goldfields and left me with very little to live on. He hasn't been home for four months and I don't know how he's getting on, or when I'll see him again, and in the meantime we have to live, me and my little girl.'

'I understand what you say,' he said. 'I'm willing to pay in advance and if you treat me right, I'll treat you right. One thing I would like to get straight though. If I'm to pay every week whether I'm here or not, you won't let my room to anybody else while I'm away, will you?'

'No, I won't. I'll make you a promise on that. It won't matter whenever you come back. You'll find your room waiting for you.'

'One other thing while we're talking like this,' he said, 'especially living in the same house. You'll be wondering who and what I am, especially as you'll soon know that I've come over from Van Diemen's Land. I have been a convict, but I have a full pardon now and am just like all free men; I can come and go as I like. But that is something I don't go telling everybody and I'd like you to keep it to yourself.'

'Yes, Cam Ralph told me you are a good man, but thanks for telling me just the same.'

He rummaged in his pocket and brought out eight pounds in banknotes and coins and paid her, saying, 'This is my first payment. We'll have to keep account of it, I suppose.'

'Yes,' she said. 'I'll write it down.'

At that moment the door opened and a young girl came into the room. She was well grown and pretty, and Martin judged her to be about twelve years old.

'This is Gwen,' Mrs Bunce said, and to her daughter, she said, 'This is Mr Maynard.'

After a few minutes of light pleasantries, Martin said, 'I'll go and look around and get settled into my room.'

Because of the drought, there was very little grass on the small paddock, but Martin was relieved to discover that the well had a good supply in it although about twenty feet down. He immediately set to and pulled up buckets of water until he had filled the trough that sat nearby and then brought the horses out to drink. They relished the water and sucked it into themselves with alacrity.

He unpacked his swag and kitbag in his room and stored his modest stock of clothes in the cupboard. He noticed the kerosene lamp on the table beside his bed and looked forward to a good read as opportunities arose.

The evening twilight was coming on when a knock came on his door and Gwen told him, 'Mother said it's time for tea now.'

Mrs Bunce served up a very tasty beef stew with potatoes and carrots followed by stewed fruit and custard as a dessert. Martin thanked her, saying, 'That's the nicest meal I've had since leaving Melbourne with my first load. We had some pretty scratchy ones on the road, I can say with honesty.'

'When do you go again?' she asked.

'The day after Boxing Day,' he replied. 'I'm to be at the warehouse to pick up my load first thing in the morning.'

'Oh well, that will give you a few days off over Christmas,' she said. 'I'll pack a hamper of sandwiches and cold meat that will get you through the first couple of days.'

The next few days passed pleasantly while he impatiently filled in the time until he could get back to work and earning more money. He had become aware of his hairy and wild appearance and asked Mrs Bunce where to find a barber.

'There's one up the street,' she said. 'It's only about half a mile and there are some good shops there.'

Once there, he instructed the barber to trim his beard and hair short and neat and got a shock when he asked him for five shillings in payment; another sign that the gold rushes were affecting all items in the cost of living.

He looked around the few shops in the village that was the centre of Flemington and purchased a few small items of clothing and a few utensils that would make camping a bit easier. He also bought a couple of newspapers and a *Bulletin* magazine.

The experience of having a pocket full of money gave him a relaxed and confident mood that was already making him feel rested and ready for the next instalment of his great adventure.

Once home again, Mrs Bunce got a surprise by his groomed and suave appearance when he came in for dinner at midday. He was a very good-looking young man, and she wondered again about his background and his story.

Mrs Bunce had a plum pudding for Christmas Day and a bottle of ale as a special treat. By this time, Gwen had become used to having him around and was happy to chat to him. He was surprised how quickly and pleasantly the time passed until he was ready to go into Melbourne to start the next delivery run to Ballarat.

Martin was waiting in the loading yard at Moles & Keane's warehouse early on the day he had arranged with Cam Ralph, and that worthy gentleman gave him a warm greeting and best wishes for a happy – and prosperous – New Year. He was loaded with another two tons of flour, but this time for delivery to two different storekeepers.

Before he left, he arranged with Cam to leave fifty pounds on safe deposit with the firm rather than keep all his money in his pocket and run the risk of being robbed on the road.

He reached his lodgings at Flemington in the late morning where Mrs Bunce gave him a meal and a hamper of food to keep him going for the next couple of days, and then he was on the road to Ballarat.

Amazingly, the roads were still crowded with travellers in the same variety of vehicles as he saw on the first trip, all heading for the diggings. All thoughts of Christmas and holidays were completely finished with and the one aim was to get to the Ballarat or Bendigo fields and start using their new picks and shovels.

As the wagon wasn't loaded quite so heavily this time, Martin was able to ride behind the horses where the road was good.

He was surprised at how quickly he reached the Lincolnshire Arms at Five Mile Creek. As he stopped to rest the horses, he thought of Sam Jessup and Nellie Houseman and wondered what they were doing at that precise time. He pictured them working away at a claim somewhere on the Ballarat field, him swinging a pick in a half sunk shaft and she busily engaged on tent keeping duties.

While the horses were resting, he had a sudden impulse to be extravagant and went into the bar and bought a bottle of rum at the outrageous price of three pounds. He had a fond recollection of the tipple that Sam had produced as they had waited for their chops to cook on the first night of their trip together.

The worst feature of the road was the dust caused by the continuing drought. It lay inches thick on the road and the horses' feet continually stirred it up to get into every crease in the travellers' clothes as well as into their noses and mouths. Windy weather made it a hundred times worse.

As the team plodded through the dust all afternoon, he looked forward to the relief of getting into camp at the end of the day and relaxing with a mug of sweetened, strong tea fortified with a slug of rum.

When he reached Diggers Rest late that evening, he found the camp already full of weary travellers busily setting up camp for the night. He had no sooner pulled up on the outskirts of the camp when a woman came up to him offering clothes and a camp oven for sale.

'We didn't realise how hard it would be to carry so much,' she said. 'We've brought too much stuff with us and now we have to get rid of some of it.'

She was holding out the items for his inspection and he felt a mixture of sympathy while being irritated by her attempt to impose on his good nature – or gullibility; he couldn't decide which.

'I don't need the clothes,' he told her. 'I've got all I can manage, but I'll give you a pound for the camp oven.'

She immediately accepted the offer which made him think that she had been unable to make a sale anywhere else in the camp; however, he knew that what he had given her was only a fifth of what the same camp oven would cost in Melbourne, and he looked forward to trying it out. He had heard a lot of wonderful tales about cooking in camp ovens and now he would find out for himself.

Thanks to Mrs Bunce's hamper, he didn't have to worry about cooking anything for himself that night, so he went over to a group camped near him and begged permission to swing his billy over their fire.

There would have been upwards of two hundred people in the camp that night. It was a wild and picturesque scene with people continually moving about between the blazing fires, with groups seated around talking amongst themselves and the animals munching away in their nosebags in the background. The hum of conversation was often overshadowed by the laughing and shouts of the travellers, and not infrequently by the loudly muttered oaths of somebody who had dropped their food in the dust or spilt their hot tea down their legs.

Two hours later, as he settled on his well-stuffed palliasse in the tent he had modified to be quickly attached to the side of the wagon, he smiled to himself with satisfaction. He had certainly improved his 'plant' and he felt that he was rapidly becoming a genuine wagoner.

He woke up later, well after midnight, and was struck by the silence in the camp. He thought of all those two hundred souls sleeping peacefully on the wide plains of the Port Phillip District, the only sound an occasional bark of a dog and the muttered oath of a camper as he stumbled out to find a vacant space to urinate.

As he pulled out the next morning, he noticed various items of clothing and pieces of equipment lying along the side of the road and realised that it had been thrown away by people who had found the load too heavy to carry further. He picked up a shirt, and a pair of boots which he could see were too small for him but which might come in handy later, and a little further on a 'bluey' coat in new condition.

He passed through Gisborne the next day, watering his horses and filling two five gallon water kegs from the pools of good water that remained in the creek. He continued on further that day to reach the spot he had discovered where there was a good cover of grass. The rest the horses had been given over Christmas was reflected in their strong condition and the fact that they were able to travel the extra distance without showing signs of distress.

He reached Ballarat about midday two days later. This time he found Zac Bellchambers's store without trouble and soon unloaded his ton of flour.

'Did they pay you for taking the empties back?' Zac asked him.

Martin laughed as he replied, 'Yes, no worries, they paid me.'

'I've got some more to go back if you can take them,' he said. 'Anyway, you'll have time for a cup of tea before you go on, won't you?'

Martin accepted his offer and followed him into the living quarters at the back of the store. A spacious room extended across the width of the store that accommodated a kitchen-living room at one end and a storeroom at the other. Like all colonial kitchens, it had a large table in the middle that was used not only for dining but also as a business desk and office as well as the drawing room for serving cups of tea and for other social intercourse.

Zac asked him how he was settling into his new business and a little about his previous experience. Martin realised at once that he was pushing him for information about himself and his capabilities and he himself had the good sense to respond with patience and civility. As a businessman himself, Martin understood the importance of building trust between people with whom you hoped to do business, so he told him about his family background in England and his experiences in Van Diemen's Land. He told him that he had got himself transported in order to get away from England and that his long-term plan was to make enough money to buy a nice farm back in Van Diemen's Land.

Zac responded with a similar account of his life. He too had been born and raised in England. 'But I wasn't as lucky as you,' he said. 'My father was a stonemason in Birmingham and while he made enough to keep us fed most of the time, we were always dirt poor.

'I became a shop boy when I was twelve and had to stay in that line all my life until I got lucky and managed to get enough together, one way and another, to buy a passage to Australia in 1832. I've done a variety of jobs in New South Wales over the years and got enough together to get a start in this business which has turned out to be the best thing I've ever done. I'm fifty-two now and this is my last chance to make something against the day when I'm too old to work.'

After an hour's yarning together, Martin left to deliver the rest of his load. He had decided to look for Sam and Nellie if he could find out where they were.

Zac told him how to find the other storekeeper he was looking for and gave him a few hints on how to find people on the diggings.

'Asking everybody you see is the quickest and easiest way, but not always the most effective. You can always go to the police. They know where everybody is because of the gold licences, but most of them expect to be paid for any favours they give.'

As Martin left, he said, 'You'll be back to pick up the empties, won't you? I want to see you about something else.'

Martin found the next storekeeper only half a mile further on. His name was Derek Miles and he was a fat man of about forty years of age. His big, round face gave him a look of openness and honesty, but Martin felt his gaze through half closed lids was calculating and suspicious.

'Thank goodness you've come,' he said when Martin told him who he was. 'I've been out of flour for the past week and my customers don't like it. When are you going to bring another load?'

Martin laughed. 'As soon as I can get back to Melbourne and get organised for another load. Have you ordered it from Moles & Keane?'

'Yes, I did send an order, but I'll give you another one to take back as you go. I could handle two tons if you can bring it.'

Martin thought of his new friend Zac and said, 'I've got to do as the firm says; they decide who to send me to.'

'Do you know Sam Jessup? He's around here somewhere. Is Anderson's Flats in this area?' Martin asked him.

'It's not far, another mile down the road and turn right up towards the gully you'll see.'

Martin decided to invest an hour or so in the search for his friends and set off down the road. Within half an hour, he found Anderson's Flats and soon after found Nellie at their camp. She was delighted to see him.

'You did come to find us, then!' she said. 'We've been wondering how you're getting on. Tell me what's happened to you.'

He told her about getting good accommodation and how his business was going well.

'From what I've heard on the diggings again today, there's plenty of work for carriers, and from what I saw on the way up here, I'd say there'll be thousands of new diggers on the fields for a long time to come,' he said.

'What about this woman you're living with?' she asked with a wicked smile on her face. 'You might find more than accommodation there!'

'Cut it out, Nellie. I'm not "living" with her, I'm boarding with her and her daughter, and that's as far as it will go.'

She laughed and said, 'Oh yes, that's what you say, but I know you blokes. No woman is safe anywhere near you as a rule.'

'Anyway, how are you blokes going? Have you found any more gold yet?' Martin asked.

'Yes,' she replied, 'we've been lucky so far. Not making a fortune yet, but getting a good living.'

She went on to tell him that Sam had found his old partners and was working with them again. She was full-time camp keeper and was enjoying life on the diggings. She told him where their claim was and urged him to take a walk down to see Sam.

'I'll look after your team while you're gone,' she said.

Martin went the way she had indicated and within twenty minutes had found Sam working as he had imagined him, swinging a pick in a shaft that was about fifteen feet deep and nearing a bottom. His three mates were all doing various jobs around the claim, from hauling up the dirt to wheeling barrow loads down to the creek to be cradled and tested for gold.

His mate, who said his name was Jim Kelly, called Sam up. He greeted Martin with a hearty handshake and a thump on the back.

'Good to see you, mate!' he said. 'I thought you'd turn up some time. How's things going?'

Martin gave him a quick run-down on what had been happening to him since they had parted about a fortnight earlier. They stood chatting for ten minutes when Martin became aware of some organised activity happening on the neighbouring claims.

'It's the bloody police again,' Sam said. 'They're always coming around demanding to see our licences. They just about drive us mad at times.'

A couple of minutes later, two policemen came up to them, saying, 'Licences! Licences!

Sam and his mates all produced their pieces of paper which were given a cursory glance by the police and handed back with a grunt. One of the police looked at Martin and said, 'Licence!'

'I'm not a digger,' Martin said. 'I'm only here to see these men on business. I'm a carrier.'

'That doesn't matter,' he said. 'If you come on this goldfield for business of any sort, you've got to have a licence.'

'Since when?' Jim demanded.

'Since this week,' he said. 'It's something new, but it's in and we've got to see that everybody has a licence. I'll have to book you,' he said, looking at Martin with a mean glance. 'It's a five pound fine.'

'Oh hell!' Sam exclaimed. 'Give the poor bugger a go! He's only just got here from Melbourne an hour ago. He doesn't even know about the licence, let alone had time to get one.'

'Go to the police station and get one within the hour and you'll be right, I suppose,' the policeman said reluctantly. 'What's your name? I'll check up to see that you get one.'

A number of police were working around the area, visiting every claim, demanding that every individual show their licence. There was a good volume of complaint and swearing coming from the diggers and the atmosphere was far from pleasant.

'See that sergeant over there?' Sam asked Martin; pointing to a tall, well-built policeman talking to a group of diggers a couple of claims along. 'That's the famous David Armstrong, The Flying Demon, the worst bastard in the police.'

At that moment, the man turned his face towards them and Martin caught a glimpse of a striking, handsome face with a pair of flashing, bold eyes.

'He's a real demon,' Sam said. 'He never misses a chance to book a digger for not having a licence, unless you can slip him three pounds;

that's his price for letting you off. It's a couple of pounds less than the fine. He can fight, too. There's nothing he likes more than bashing up a digger.'

'He gives the sly grog boys hell,' Jim said with a chuckle. 'If they don't come up with twenty pounds quick smart, he burns their tents and all their gear. He's known far and wide for being a thoroughbred mongrel.'

Martin didn't linger too long with Sam and his mates. 'I'll get going,' he said. 'If I've got to go and buy a licence, it will probably take time and I want to be back on the road by tonight.'

When he got back to the camp, Nellie wanted him to stay for a while and have some tea, but he told her what had happened and said, 'I've already promised Zac Bellchambers that I'd go back and see him, and now that I have to find the police station, time is going to be short, so I'll have to go.'

'Come and see us again on your next trip,' she urged, 'but next time stay for a meal. I'm a good cook, you know.'

He laughed heartily as he said, 'Yes, I know. I've sampled your cooking before, remember?'

Zac Bellchambers wanted to load him up with empties, 'but before we do that, I want to ask you something else. Just step inside a minute, will you?'

Once inside, he addressed Martin, 'How would you feel about carting a small consignment of gold back to Melbourne? In my business, I have to buy a lot of gold from the diggers. They pay for everything with gold dust. As you will understand, I accumulate fairly large amounts each month. I can sell it on to a gold buyer here at the diggings, but they rob us blind, giving us at least ten shillings an ounce less than the Melbourne price. What do you think?'

'Come out to the wagon,' Martin replied. 'I'll show you something.'

Back at the wagon, Martin looked around to make sure nobody was watching and then carefully lifted a couple of boards from the false flooring he had got the coachbuilder to install when building the wagon.

'I don't know what gave me the idea when I was ordering this wagon, but something made me think a hiding place for valuables would be a good idea. If you'd like to try a consignment or two, I'd be happy to oblige. The only thing we've got to get straight is whose loss is it in the unlikely event of me being robbed on the road.'

Zac was immediately very impressed and said, 'Yes, I would like to try it out. I'll carry all the risk for a start and pay you two shillings and sixpence an ounce. That will give me another seven shillings and sixpence an ounce and, selling into a rising market like we are at present, there's a good chance I'll get more than that.'

He told Martin to take the gold to the Bank of New South Wales in Melbourne and ask for Mr Arthur Lees, the manager. 'I'll give you a note for him. It will only take a few minutes to scribble it out. I want to try fifty ounces as a trial this time,' he said.

He went back inside and a few minutes later emerged with three small, flat tins in his hands. He slipped them into the hiding place and Martin quickly replaced the boards. Zac looked carefully at the floor and satisfied himself that nobody would guess that the floor was hollow.

They loaded the wagon with thirty empty barrels and kegs, completing the camouflage of the hiding place.

Zac directed Martin where to go to find the police station. 'Yes, I know it's a damned nuisance having to buy a licence, but it's a good thing you are, I think. You may be surprised how handy it will be later.'

Martin headed back out onto the road and found the police station on the outskirts of the goldfield.

A sergeant was in the office and was being harassed by a number of diggers – and would-be diggers – all waiting to purchase a gold licence. After a tedious wait, Martin finally got his turn to be attended to by a man who, by this time, was obviously in a bad mood.

'Name?' he barked.

'Martin Maynard.'

'Address?'

'Mount Alexander Road, Flemington.'

The sergeant scowled and said, 'No, I mean where is your claim, here on the goldfields. I don't mean where your home is.'

Martin sensed a problem of misunderstanding and a bad temper looming, so he put on his most agreeable smile before he said anything more.

'Sorry to be a nuisance, Sergeant,' he said, 'but I'm only buying this licence to fulfil my obligation to the law. I'm a carrier carting to and from the goldfields and I only learned today that I have to have a licence to do business here.'

'Yes, well, that's right; you do have to have a licence. Who is your principal contact here at Ballarat?'

'Zac Bellchambers, the storekeeper,' Martin replied.

'Right, I'll put both addresses on the licence so I'll know where to find you, if necessary.'

With that Martin handed over the thirty shillings and departed with the licence in his pocket.

He was six miles along the road towards Melbourne before the sun went down too far to allow him to travel any further. Fortunately, he came across a good camping area, already occupied by a large crowd, and was soon sitting beside a crackling fire sipping a pannikin of hot tea laced with rum. As he sat, reflecting on all that had happened since leaving Melbourne four days ago, he felt a great surge of satisfaction. His visit to the goldfield had been hectic, pushed for time all day because he wanted to be away from the field by night – mainly because of the shortage of water – but in spite of all that, it had turned out to be a great success with good omens for the future.

He continued to mull over the day's experiences as he prepared his meal, the same old chops and bread washed down by tea. This trip would gross him even more than the first one. The freight on the two tons of flour and the returning empties would add up to over a hundred pounds, and the fifty ounces of gold at two shillings and sixpence would add another six pounds five shillings.

He went to his palliasse a weary but happy man that night.

The return trip to Melbourne was uneventful. The roads continued to be cluttered with all kinds of traffic including hundreds of pedestrians. He was learning the route by this time and knew where to buy meat and bread, where to find water and the best camps.

He paced his progress to arrive at his lodgings at Flemington in the afternoon so that he could complete his round trip to Melbourne the next morning. Mrs Bunce gave him a warm welcome, as did Gwen.

'I have been wondering whether you'd get back today,' Mrs Bunce said. 'I've got something I can put on quickly for tea.'

After stabling the horses, he had a stand up bath in his room from a bucketful of hot water, and a good tidy up before tea. Both Gwen and her mother wanted an account of the trip. 'What's it really like, up there on the goldfields?' Mrs Bunce asked.

'It's very crowded, with people everywhere all working like ants, and dust everywhere too. It's blowing about all day long,' he said.

The questions continued for an hour until Gwen was sent off to bed, to which she went reluctantly.

'I'll tell you more about it tomorrow evening,' Martin said as she went out.

Mrs Bunce was also looking for a chat. 'I'll get another cup of tea,' she said. 'When will you go again?'

'The day after tomorrow. I'll be back from Melbourne by midday tomorrow and the horses can rest all afternoon.'

'How did the trip go, really?' she asked.

Martin was careful what he said to her. She had left no doubt in his mind that she was angry with her husband for joining the rush when he could be home making more money than taking his chances on the goldfields, and he didn't want to heap more coals on the fire of her anger.

'So far it's going fairly well,' he said. 'The horse feed and everything else is terribly expensive, but we are getting a good rate and that will give me a profit as good as wages.'

He told her a bit more about the goldfields and his friends, telling her what a wild and lawless life many of the diggers led. They chatted on for another hour when he started to yawn and excused himself to go to bed.

He slept soundly all night and was up early to water and feed the horses in preparation for the short trip to Melbourne.

He was face to face with Cameron Ralph by midmorning and making arrangements for his next load. He gave him the message from Derek Milcs and told him that he had told Derek that he was under orders from Moles & Keane as to where to deliver his loads.

'So, if the occasion comes up, you'll cover for me, won't you?'

Cam laughed and said, 'OK, I will. The trouble is, there are so many orders coming in from the goldfields now that we can't keep up with the demand. The bottleneck is with the carting. You wouldn't like to put another couple of wagons on, would you?'

Martin said, 'I wouldn't mind, but I couldn't do it now. I've got to get started properly first, then I might look at it. How long do you expect the gold to last?'

'The way it's going, I'd say for a long time, three or four years at least.'

They made the final arrangements for the next load to Ballarat.

Martin said, 'I want to go to the Bank of New South Wales to open an account before I leave today. Can you tell me where it is?'

Martin had decided not to tell Cam about his gold carrying activities. The fewer the people who knew about that, the safer it would be.

'It's not far from here, only a five minute walk,' he said, and told him where to go.

Martin arranged with Cam to park his wagon and team in the yard for an hour. He found a spot where he could securely tether the horses without unhitching them and then recovered the tins of gold from the hiding place. He put them in a small carry bag that he had bought that morning from Mole & Keane's store and walked down the street until he found the bank.

He had taken the little extra trouble that morning to wear his best work clothes and appear as smart as possible for his first visit to the bank manager.

He told the young man behind the counter he wanted to see Mr Lees.

'Can I inquire what it is in connection with?' he asked.

'No, it's a private matter. I'll discuss it with him, thanks. If he asks, you can say I'm here with a message from Mr Zac Bellchambers of Ballarat.'

The young man left the counter and disappeared into an office. In a few moments, a man dressed in a blue serge suit came hurrying out and looked around. The young man behind the counter indicated that Martin was his caller whereupon he rushed over with his hand held out, saying, 'I'm Arthur Lees. I believe you've got a message for me.'

'Yes,' Martin said with a wide smile as he handed over Zac's hastily scribbled note. 'I can complete the message when we're in a more private place.'

The manager hastily read the note and said, 'Yes, yes, I think that would be best. Come this way,' and led the way into his office.

Once inside, he invited Martin to sit down and then sat in his own chair to read the note again.

'According to this note, you have some gold to deposit to Mr Bellchambers's account,' he said.

'Yes,' Martin replied, 'fifty ounces in all,' as he produced the three tins from his bag.

'I'll just get that weight checked,' he said. 'Come through here,' and he exited through another door.

In the back room, the manager addressed an older man who was wearing spectacles with thick, glass lenses: 'Check this gold for weight, Perkins.'

Perkins walked over to a set of gold scales on a bench at the rear of the room and carefully poured the gold dust into the scales' weighing dish, one tin at a time, keeping account of the individual weights on a docket. At the end of the exercise, he turned to the manager and said, 'There's fifty ounces there, sir.'

'Come back to the office, Mr Maynard,' Lees said.

Once seated, he continued, 'Thank you for delivering the gold to me. I'll post a receipt to Mr Bellchambers today.' He'll have it within the week.'

'What is the market price of gold in Melbourne this week?' Martin asked him.

He looked a bit startled, but recovered himself quickly. 'Three pounds two shillings an ounce. That is the price Mr Bellchambers will be credited with.'

'Thanks,' Martin said. 'I would like to open an account for myself while I'm here. Could you do that?'

'Of course,' he said. 'We would be delighted to have you as a customer of the bank. I'll just get some particulars from you.'

He filled in a large form with Martin's particulars of business and address. He gave his address as 'care of Moles & Keane, Elizabeth Street, Melbourne'. Martin produced seventy pounds as his initial deposit, signed his name several times and was given a receipt and a handshake.

Half an hour later, Martin was driving along the road to Flemington with a full load for Ballarat on board. He arrived at his lodgings less than an hour later where he unhitched the horses. After getting a meal, he prepared everything for an early start to Ballarat the next morning.

CHAPTER 11

'Oh, you're back on time,' Mrs Bunce said as Martin walked into the kitchen on his return from Melbourne. 'Have you had a good morning?'

'Yes,' he replied with a smile, 'I've got no complaints.'

Although his new life in Port Phillip was having a good effect on Martin's shyness and, some would think, taciturnity, he was still a man who kept himself and his private affairs to himself. Although he had taken a liking to Mrs Bunce, it would be a long time before he confided anything more than ordinary day-to-day routine matters to her.

Half an hour later, she had a nice dinner of roast beef cooked in a big camp oven. Martin took an interest in the camp oven and she gave him a few tips on how to use them.

Gwen was in a frisky mood, demanding attention, until her mother sent her outside to play for a while before dinner.

'Are you going to rest this afternoon, Mr Maynard?' Mrs Bunce asked him.

Martin smiled and said, 'You don't have to call me Mr Maynard, you know. My name is Martin and I'd be just as pleased if that's what you called me.'

'Righto,' she said. 'That's if you call me Alice. What's good enough for the gander is good enough for the goose!'

'Righto,' he chuckled. 'That's settled then, Alice.' Then he said, 'Yes, I am looking forward to a quiet afternoon. I've got some letters to write.'

'You can work at the table in the front room if you like, Martin,' she said after lunch, an offer he accepted.

He had written to his mother over the Christmas break, so this time he wrote to his brother-in-law George Latimer and sister Anne and included his other sister Ellen and his mother as well. He told them about his life in Port Phillip, now universally known as Victoria, and about his business. He downplayed any mention of how much money he was making because he had a suspicion they wouldn't believe him if he told the truth. He did finish his letter by saying that he was very pleased he had been sent to Van Diemen's Land and that he was confident about having a good future.

The next letter he wrote that afternoon was rather different and needed a bit of special handling. He wrote a short, personal letter to Charles Drewitt, telling him of the progress he was making with his business, including the contact he had made with Moles & Keane through Cameron Ralph. He thanked him again for the help he had given by way of advice and the wages bonus. Then he wrote another, longer letter addressed to 'Dear Squire and all at Norwood', telling them about the trip to Port Phillip – appropriately edited – and about what had happened to him since landing at Williamstown. He knew they would be interested in where he was living and the two trips to the goldfields that he had made. He tried to explain what the goldfields were like and the amazing numbers of people who had been stricken with gold fever so badly that they were abandoning their jobs and families to join the gold rushes.

He imagined the talk in the house, and the kitchen, about his letter and what their individual reactions would be. The realisation came into his mind that of them all, it was the dark-haired Rebecca who always came to his mind whenever he thought about Norwood. He smiled wryly and dismissed the thought from his mind.

Martin worked steadily through the afternoon until Alice brought him a cup of tea. She settled on a sofa and sipped her tea as she chatted about the price of meat and other housekeeping matters, all of which were being affected by the gold rushes. She was obviously wanting to chat with him and he wondered if she was lonely. She hadn't mentioned any family connections in the Flemington area, and he could understand that the absence of her husband would leave a big gap in her life. He felt sorry for her and tried a bit harder to be sociable.

He left the house to go to the little paddock to check the horses, with Gwen tagging along. She was a great little talker and told him all about Mother and the garden, and related matters, but Martin noticed that she didn't mention her father at all. He assumed that he had been gone for so long she had almost forgotten him.

Tea was sliced cold meat and a potato salad with bread and jam to follow, all washed down with the usual tea. They sat in the kitchen and read newspapers and chatted through the evening.

Gwen was sent off to bed after an hour or so and Martin and Alice continued in the kitchen, reading and talking for another hour when Alice swung the kettle over the fire and brewed up a fresh pot of tea.

After a while, Martin pleaded tiredness and the need for a good start in the morning and retired to bed in his hut.

He had been in bed for another hour and was sleeping lightly when he became aware that Alice was in the room with him, sitting on the side of his bed with her hand on his shoulder. He woke with a start, but soon realised what was happening. The thought flashed into his mind that he wasn't really surprised by the turn of events.

'Is there something wrong?' he asked.

'No,' she said, 'not as far as I'm concerned.'

'Can I do something for you?'

'You can give a lonely woman a bit of company, that's all I want.'

She leant forward over him and put her arms around his neck. His arms automatically went around her and he could feel her nakedness under the thin nightdress. She kissed him on the lips and put her face against his. 'Can I come in with you for a while?' she murmured.

He chuckled and whispered, 'It looks as if you're already in. All I can do is move over and give you some room.'

Within a few seconds, she was under the blanket with him and stretched out against his body with her lips on his mouth and her hands around his neck. His lonely body responded to her with force, and he felt any vestige of control he may have had desert him in a flash.

Within a couple of minutes, she mounted him and accepted his manhood with enthusiasm. A few minutes later, they were sated and lay in each other's arms.

'You're a lovely woman,' he murmured. 'I think you're beautiful and wonderful, but what brought that about?'

'You did,' she murmured. 'I like you; you're the best looking man I've seen in years, and to a woman like me, deserted and desperately lonely, I couldn't resist the temptation. Don't worry, I'm not a worthless hussy. You're only the second man, apart from my husband, that I've ever been with.'

'Well, I'm flattered … I think you should kiss me again.'

She again led the way and indicated her approval as only a woman can.

Later, as they lay together, sated, Martin said, 'Aren't you afraid of becoming pregnant? What will your husband say if he comes home and finds a strange man in his house and his wife pregnant?'

'The way things look, he may never come home again,' she said. 'To tell the truth, I don't think I'd care if he didn't. Anyway,' she went on, 'you needn't worry. I won't be falling pregnant, I'm barren, worse luck. I had Gwen when I was nineteen and I've never fallen pregnant since.'

Martin had jumbled thoughts tumbling through his mind. He wondered where this would lead. He knew that now it had started, it wouldn't stop unless something happened, like a husband coming home from the diggings. He felt he should say something, but not knowing how to say it, he kept silent.

An hour later she crept back to her own bed, leaving him to wonder what twist life would serve him next, and then he fell into a deep sleep.

Martin was out early the next morning to water and feed the horses before breakfast. He entered the kitchen wondering if anything in her behaviour would be different, but she greeted him with her usual smile and a 'Good morning, Martin'. She had evidently schooled Gwen on the use of his name because she continued to call him Mr Maynard as she had from the first day, in spite of hearing her mother call him Martin.

He was on the road an hour later on his third trip to Ballarat. When he arrived, he encountered the same gold rush in action as on the previous trips, the same busy camps and the same choking dust. The gold rush continued. Under the scorching sun, across the dusty plains and climbing the few hills that were on the road, the rush went on.

Alice's hamper was even better than the first one and saved him a deal of cooking for both the evening dinner and the breakfasts. She had bread and butter sandwiches for him to eat with the cold leg of mutton, and a jar of pickles to add a bit of zest to the cold fare. He became adept at toasting the bread and butter sandwiches and the thick slices of mutton at the fire. Some biscuits and apples all added to the finest camping fare he had experienced so far on his journeys to the goldfields. She had thought of everything and he hadn't even finished eating all the goodies when he reached Ballarat.

He managed the stages so that he was able to rest the horses at his special camping place south of the Black Forest for the whole of one afternoon and the night before going on early the next morning. By doing it that way, he was able to reach the goldfields about midday on the fourth day.

As he arrived on the outskirts of the field, he met a light southerly breeze that carried the odour of the diggings to him in its full power. The thousands of tents extending through the gullies and the undulations in every direction for about ten miles and the dozens of stores marked by the various flags they all flew all contributed to the unique odour of the place. Worst of all were the dozens of so-called slaughterhouses, mostly very primitive and unhygienic, which could be smelt from miles away. Few of the butchers made any effort to dispose of the offal in any sanitary way; it was simply thrown onto a heap near the killing yard and left to rot. Martin wondered how long it would be before the whole community was wiped out by disease.

He proceeded down the road to Zac Bellchambers's store, arriving there in time to be invited to join him in a snack lunch and a cup of tea. Zac had already received the receipt for the fifty ounces of gold Martin had deposited for him at the Bank of New South Wales in Melbourne and expressed his full satisfaction for the result of the trial run.

'I not only saved the ten shillings an ounce that the greedy gold buyers rip off us here on the diggings, but I got two shillings an ounce more because the market had risen. How did the job suit you?' he asked Martin.

'All right,' he replied with a grin. 'Nobody on the road had the slightest idea that I was carrying a fortune in gold, but I must say it was in my mind. It would be a nasty comedown if I did get robbed on the road and a big loss for you. For me, I made an extra six pounds five shillings on my trip, almost enough to pay for my horse feed.'

They continued to talk about the risks and benefits involved in Martin carrying the gold in the wagon and agreed that the most crucial thing was to keep it a closely guarded secret.

'If the word got out amongst the bushrangers, you could bet your life they'd be laying in wait for me,' Martin said. 'At the moment, the only people who know about it are you and me.'

'I fully understand the risks involved,' Zac said, 'but the rewards are good too. If you're agreeable, I want to send a hundred ounces every trip you make for the next few weeks. There's more gold about now than ever, and many of the diggers prefer to sell it to me rather than consign it down to Melbourne by the official Gold Escort. You ought to think about buying gold yourself. It would be a nice little sideline for you.'

Martin laughed as he said, 'If I started buying gold here on the diggings, the word would go around on the breezes that blow and the villains I spoke of would know in quick time. I'd like to be in it, because I'm anxious to make money, but I've got to be careful. You don't want a silent partner, I suppose?'

It was Zac's turn to laugh. 'Yes,' he said, 'I know what you say is right. If they found out you were carting gold, they'd be out to rob you. But I like the idea of going partners as gold buyers. I can buy a lot here in the store without people actually knowing I'm a gold trader. If I keep sending a portion of what I get to Melbourne on the Gold Escort, nobody would ever become suspicious of you taking more of it on the wagon. That way, we could be getting the best of both systems. If you want to have a flutter, I'm agreeable to giving it a go.'

It was agreed between them that Zac would secretly buy some gold on Martin's behalf. The sellers of the gold wouldn't know that Martin was connected with it in any way. Martin was to start leaving a hundred pounds with Zac on every trip to build up a trading kitty.

Even though the two men had known each other for only a short time, a mutual trust had grown up between them, reinforced for Martin by Sam's statement that Zac was well thought of on the diggings. Another strong factor in their mutual trust was that they were both refugees from a poverty-stricken and starved England, trying to make their way and build a future for themselves in Australia .

After lunch and their business discussions, Zac's share of the load of flour was unloaded. Martin then headed down to deliver the other half to Derek Miles before returning to Zac's place to load up with empties for the return trip to Melbourne.

Derek was obviously in a good mood. 'I got the message from Moles & Keane. They said you'd be bringing more loads on a regular run. You'll see that I get a fair share, won't you?'

Derek had a lot of empty barrels to return, but Martin had to refuse to take them all on the excuse that Cam Ralph had told him to take some for Zac. Martin knew that Derek would be hostile to Zac, so he had to be careful not to be seen to be favouring him unduly.

'I can take twelve this time,' he said. 'That'll help you a bit.'

'I wouldn't worry about the bloody things,' he said, 'except that they try to make me pay ten pounds for every one that's lost or stolen.'

They parted on good terms and Martin returned to Zac's store with a half loaded wagon.

—

Martin was able to lift the false floorboards at the front of the wagon's tray where Zac quickly stowed another hundred ounces of gold in four flat tins. They then loaded another sixteen empties to fully load the wagon and to complete the camouflage of their secret payload.

They shook hands as Martin climbed up into the driver's seat. 'I'll have my hundred pounds stake money when I come again late next week,' said Martin.

Zac grinned as he returned the shake and said, 'Yes, partner,' and then as the wheels started turning, 'Good luck, mate!'

As he pulled out onto the main road through the diggings that would lead him back through Golden Point on the road to Melbourne, he was met by a posse of police who stopped him with the cry, 'Licence! Licence!' He produced his piece of paper and stood near his horses' heads while it was examined.

'That's right, mate,' the officer said as he stood aside. 'You know you have to renew this licence every month, don't you?'

Martin simply nodded and they let him go on his way.

Martin arrived back at Flemington late in the afternoon on the third day to be greeted by a happy Alice and Gwen. As on his previous trip, he had to give them an account of the trip and what was happening on the fields.

As he expected, Alice came to his bed again that night.

Martin was waiting to do business with Cam Ralph when the store opened the following morning, and again he was paid in banknotes and some sovereigns for his work, again an amount slightly over one hundred pounds. With the extra money from Zac's gold, he would gross nearly one hundred and fifteen pounds from the trip, an amount that was a glittering fortune to Martin as it would have been to nearly all Victorians at that time.

As on the previous trip, he left the team securely tethered in the yard at Moles & Keane and walked the couple of blocks to the Bank of New South Wales. He had an inward smile in response to the prompt and courteous way he was received on this occasion. Mr Lees was out from his office with outstretched hand in sharp time and he was ushered straight through to the weighing room to watch Zac Bellchambers's one hundred ounces of gold being weighed. Once again, it matched perfectly with his weights and the receipt was made out accordingly.

The price of gold remained at three pounds two shillings an ounce, a price that would please Zac.

Before loading the wagon for his next trip to Ballarat, he wrapped the hundred pounds he would be paying Zac to establish their gold buying partnership in a shirt and tied it up with string before secreting it under the false floor of the wagon. Within the hour, he was fully loaded and heading out to Flemington where he arrived before dinnertime. He unhitched the horses and rested them – and himself – all the remainder of that day in preparation for another early start the next morning.

Alice had prepared a big midday dinner of beef stew with vegetables followed by a pudding after which he spent the afternoon reading and loafing about.

'You ought to take more time for resting,' Alice said as she gave him a cup of tea during the afternoon. 'You won't be able to keep this pace up for long; both you and your horses will break down.'

'No fear of that,' he said. 'I'm too good a horseman to have my horses break down. That's why I give them a good spell on the country near the Black Forest, going and coming. But thanks for you concern for me,' he said with a laugh, 'and thanks for the tucker you pack for me to take. It's a big help – and nice eating, too!'

'That's all right. I'll find a way to get paid for it,' she said with a wicked smile and a poke of her finger.

As he expected, she came to him again that night and didn't leave until the early hours of the morning.

As usual, he was on the road bright and early the next morning. He reached Zac Bellchambers's store at midday on the fourth day. Once again, he ate with Zac while they discussed their business. He handed over his stake money to finance their mutual gold buying venture and to that Zac added the amount he owed Martin for carting the one hundred ounces on his previous trip, an amount of twelve pounds ten shillings.

That was the start of a profitable and exciting venture for Martin. By the time he reached Ballarat on his next trip, Zac had bought eighty ounces of gold on behalf of their partnership at a price of two pounds ten shillings an ounce. That was the going price for gold bought by the regular gold buyers on the field. Martin asked Zac to write a letter to Arthur Lees, the manager of the bank in Melbourne, explaining the business partnership they had formed and asking him how he would handle the gold deposits Martin would be making on a regular basis.

The partnership thrived because they eliminated the cost of transporting the gold by the official Gold Escort and took for themselves the margin of profit that was usually claimed by the established gold buyers. The only thing they had to accept was the complete lack of insurance against loss of the gold on the trip to Melbourne. Both men knew that in the event of being robbed, they would have to accept the loss themselves; however, in reality this was not much different to using the official Gold Escort because the Government had made it clear that there would be no compensation to the users of the service in the event of the gold being lost in transit – for any reason.

On his next visit to the bank, Mr Lees carefully read Zac Bellchambers's letter. He looked up at Martin with a crooked smile and said, 'We live in interesting times, Mr Maynard. Only a few weeks ago, you came here as a young and inexperienced carrier looking to get a start, and now here you are, a gold buyer. I wish you luck.'

Martin fell into a routine of constant toil on the road to and from Ballarat, driven by the desperate need to make money and the thought that the gold rushes couldn't last for long; he would have to make the best of the opportunity while it lasted. After that, he couldn't imagine another opportunity like this ever coming again.

He kept that routine up for the following weeks. Alice pleaded with him to take more time to rest, but his only thought was to rest his horses and to feed them well enough to keep them in good working condition. His own physical strength and his careful lifestyle was the key to his ability to work so constantly. His consumption of alcohol was limited to a tot of rum at the end of the day, and the many miles he walked beside the horses had toughened and hardened him into a peak of physical fitness.

He was offered carting jobs to Bendigo at a much higher rate than to Ballarat, but now that he had entered into the deal with Zac Bellchambers, he wanted to remain on the Ballarat run.

The matter of most concern to Martin, and all the other carters servicing the growing number of goldfields, was the continuing drought. It was now early in March, the time of year when the farmers were looking for good autumn rains, but the weeks of drought continued with no signs of a break.

The road was gradually getting worse under the constantly increasing traffic, and the government was not making much effort to repair it.

The cry from the Governor was, probably with some justification, that he couldn't get contractors to take the work because all their workers had run off to join the gold rushes.

Already some of the carriers were cutting down on the number of trips because both they and their horses were being worn down by the bad roads and the constant work in the heat of summer. The carting rate to all the goldfields had been increased; in respect of Ballarat, it was now forty-five pounds a ton.

All these issues were exercising Martin's mind as he plodded along. He saw that the magnificent profits he was making from his simple and straightforward business were dependent on regularity of service. The single biggest factor in generating the profit was that he was completing three round trips a month while keeping his costs to a minimum. If the roads became so bad that he was forced to cut that down to two, or even one, his profit would disappear, even with a higher cartage rate.

The answer came to him one day a couple of weeks later when he was settling up with Cam Ralph after another successful, if slow, round trip to Ballarat. Cam told Martin that one of his carters had cracked up under the strain and wanted to sell his cart and two horses.

'You're the sort of bloke who might be interested in expanding your operations and I thought I'd mention it to you.'

'Yes, I'm interested,' Martin said, 'but what sort of set-up is it? Are the horses good? What's the cart like?'

'I think it's all good gear; not as good as your wagon, but it carries over a ton. He operates out of a small farm at Keilor, on the road to the goldfields.'

'He won't find it easy to sell right now,' Martin said. 'The road is getting worse all the time and it's slowing everything down. Now, all the old carters are saying that when the rain does come, it will turn the whole road into a mud river and close the road altogether.'

'I'll tell him you might be interested and to get in touch with you,' Cam replied.

'Well, if you do, don't build him up to expect a good deal. To put it bluntly, I'm only interested at a low price. I don't want to be hard, but the present time is not a seller's market for a carter's business to the goldfields.'

Three weeks passed before Martin and Max Matson, the retiring carrier, finally met to discuss a possible deal. In that time, the drought had tightened its grip and the road had got worse. Pessimism was strong amongst the carting fraternity and feelings against the government for its apparent lack of action were running high. The mood of the carters was: 'I'll pull out until they do something. That's the only way to get anything done. If we pull out altogether, they'll soon come to their senses.'

Fortunately for Martin, Max Matson was of this mind; he had done well over the year or more that he'd been in the job; but, now tired and feeling the onset of age, he had the one obsessive thought: to get out. He agreed to sell his dray and two horses to Martin for fifty pounds, complete with harness and gear. Part of the deal was that he was to deliver the rig to Martin's lodgings at Flemington at which time he would be paid.

Martin had inspected the horses carefully. They were both big, strong geldings about five years old. His opinion was that they were basically sound but a bit tired and undernourished. An investment of a few pounds worth of good feed and a few days rest would restore them.

He had no intention of putting the cart back on the run immediately. His plan was to convert his own wagon into a four horse rig, thus taking a huge strain off his own two horses and making it possible to maintain a thrice monthly service to Ballarat. The extra two horses in the rig, although increasing his feed costs dramatically without increasing his payload, would allow him to maintain the vital aspect of his business on which rested his success, that being the regular three round trips to Ballarat every month.

He parked the new dray behind the barn as inconspicuously as possible and tethered the horses, along with his own two, in a way that would get them used to each other as quickly as possible.

He had to buy a few items of harness and equipment to make it possible to hitch all four to the wagon. His old horses stayed in the shafts and the new ones would he hitched as leaders.

He spelled the whole lot for an extra two days while getting them used to working as a team. His early training by Petala Smith and his experience over the years since stood him in good stead, and he soon had the four working as a team.

Alice was very interested in all that was happening. 'You'll only have two stalls to stable them in. What will you do with the other two?' she asked him.

'I'll make some temporary arrangements at the back of the barn for the two new ones until I can organise something better before winter comes on. If you are agreeable, I'll knock up a couple of neat, covered stalls – at my expense. I won't ask you for any contribution, but it will be a nice improvement to your property,' he said.

'Yes,' she replied, 'that's good by me. I'd like a bit more money one of these days, but I can see that you're stretched at present.'

He grinned. 'Patience is the name of the game, old friend. Let's get things running well and then we can look at it again.'

Martin set out on the next trip to Ballarat with some misgivings about the way his expanded team would perform on the road, but for the most part the trip went well. His judgement that the extra power from the two new horses would make it easier to negotiate the bad stretches of the road proved to be correct. The trick to handling the worst parts was to slow the horses down to a slow, steady pull that glided the wagon over the holes, the submerged rocks and the tree roots at a slow but continuous pace that covered the distance without knocking the horses about. By the time he reached Ballarat, he was congratulating himself on his decision.

His partner Zac was looking anxiously for his arrival and met him with a warm welcome.

'I'm pleased to see you,' he said. 'I've been hearing more bad reports about the road and thought you might have been delayed. I see you've increased the team.'

Martin explained the ideas that had prompted him to buy the extra horses.

'A great idea,' Zac said. 'We need a regular service now more than ever. There are more people on this field and they all have to be fed. I'm selling more flour every week. And there's more gold; that means there's more for us to think about,' he concluded with a wink.

Martin unloaded Zac's share of the flour and took the rest down to Derek Miles who, as usual, wanted more and also had a lot of empties to be returned to Moles & Keane.

When he returned to Zac's store, they quickly stowed the secret cargo of gold in the usual place under the floor of the wagon and then completed the load with as many empties as they could cram on.

As he rolled out past the outskirts of the diggings, Martin was accosted by a lone digger with a swag and a portmanteau at his feet.

'Any chance of a lift to Melbourne, mate?' the man asked.

'Sorry, mate. As you can see, I'm fully loaded and can't handle any more,' Martin said.

'I'm not asking for a ride; I can walk it empty-handed, but I know

I won't make it carrying a swag. I can help you with the horses and anything you want.'

Martin had cast a quick eye over him and on the strength of his appearance as a genuine digger, he decided to take a chance on him.

'Oh, righto. If you're prepared to walk, you can throw your swag on the wagon. You can give me a hand with the horses tonight.'

He said his name was Bluey Bayles.

'How long have you been on the diggings?' Martin asked him.

'Nearly a year, and now I want to go home to Melbourne for a few weeks for a rest and a change,' he said.

'Coming back?' Martin asked him with a grin.

'Yes, I reckon I will. I haven't made any more than wages, but I like it and now that I know a lot more about it, I will do better next time.'

They travelled on for all the afternoon, the two men walking beside the horses at a steady pace. As usual, Martin stopped and spelled the horses every hour.

They camped the night uneventfully at Martin's usual first night camp site on the way home and were on the road again early the next morning. Their intention was to travel through the Black Forest to spend the afternoon spelling on Martin's spot south of the forest.

They had entered the forest and travelled about a mile into it when suddenly two men appeared on the road only ten feet ahead of them, one holding a rifle pointed at them. This was the moment Martin had been dreading since his first trip. Out of the side of his mouth, he said to Bluey in a quiet voice, 'Take it easy, watch me. Go to the horses' heads and hold them.'

'Whoa!' Martin called out to the team and pulled on the reins to stop them. 'What do you want?' he asked the men. 'It's Camel Jack, isn't it? I thought I knew you.'

'We don't know you,' the man said. He was the bigger of the two, with a bushy beard. 'All we want is a pound or two to buy some food. Turn your pockets out. What have you got on that wagon?'

Martin laughed heartily. 'You won't get much from us, Jack,' he said. 'All I've got is a couple of pounds. You can have that if you want it. The wagon's full of empty casks. Come and look for yourself.'

A third man appeared from behind the wagon, his face also bearded but in thin, dirty brown hair. He held a pistol and was pointing it at Martin in an unsteady hand.

'Don't make it hard for yourself,' he said in a whining accent. 'Just turn your pockets out.'

The first man had stepped over closer to the wagon and said again, 'What have you got here?'

'Nothing, Jack,' Martin said. 'Have a look for yourself. If you're stuck for a feed, I'll give you a couple of quid. Go on, have a look.'

Jack made his first big mistake: he lowered the rifle and stepped closer to the wagon. Catlike, Martin stepped beside him but a little behind. As quick as a snake strikes, he smashed a rabbit killer down across the back of his neck. The rifle clattered to the ground and Jack collapsed in a heap.

Martin spun around and, as he expected, the third man was looking with his mouth agape, the pistol pointing to the ground. Martin darted forward like a savage dog, raving at the top of his voice, 'Look out! Look out!' and collided hard with him. He went spinning away, dropping the pistol as he stumbled and fell over. Martin seized the pistol and ran around behind the wagon to check on the second man.

Bluey was struggling with the horses. They were trying to rear up and were plunging from side to side. The second man was moving towards Bluey as if to grab hold of him. Martin ran forward, again yelling, 'Look out! Look out! Danger!' He got close to the man who by this time was slightly confused and, putting the pistol close to his head but pointing it in the air, he pulled the trigger. The explosion ripped through the scene like a mighty clap of thunder.

The horses started to go berserk and Martin rushed to grab the bridles and settle them down. Both Bluey and Martin were fully occupied for the next two minutes with holding the horses and getting them quietened.

A voice suddenly cut through their consciousness. 'What's going on, mate?' a rough diamond digger's voice asked.

Martin swung around and saw a group of five travellers standing not more than ten paces away, looking in amazement at the scene before them.

'We're being held up,' Martin said. 'Grab this bastard, will you?'

Martin ran back behind the wagon and saw Jack still lying in a heap on the ground. The third man was on his feet but very groggy and frightened. Martin grabbed him by the arm and said, 'Stay still or I'll kill you.'

The group of travellers were now crowding around, asking, 'What happened?'

Martin picked up the rifle and pushed it in amongst the empty barrels on the wagon. 'These rotten mongrels tried to hold us up,' he said.

'Is this man dead?' another asked as he looked down at Jack.

'I doubt it,' Martin replied, 'but he'll be out to it for a while yet. Just watch that other fellow in case he tries to run away. I've got to check my horses.'

He walked up to where Bluey was holding the leaders by their bridles.

'Well done, Bluey. You certainly handled that little situation well. Thanks a lot for your help.'

'Bloody hell,' Bluey stammered. 'I've never seen anything like that. How did you do it?'

Martin chuckled and said, 'We'll talk about it later. Let's get this mess cleaned up and get on our way. I don't want to hang around here too long.'

He rejoined the travellers where they stood looking down at the inert figure of Jack lying in an awkward sprawl on the road. 'What are you going to do with them?' one of the men asked.

'I'm buggered if I know,' Martin said. 'I haven't got time, or the inclination, to take them all the way back to the police station. I think I'll just leave them here to look after themselves.'

What's your name?' the man asked.

Martin smiled. 'That's not really important and I'm not anxious to have it spread around that I was held up at gunpoint, but for the record, I'm Martin Maynard.'

Martin took care to gather up the revolvers the second and third men had been carrying and demanded that they hand over the ammunition in their pockets. He turned to the travellers who had happened along at a most opportune time for him. 'I want to search that fellow's pockets for ammunition. He's too dangerous to be let loose carrying that.'

To cover himself against any later accusations of robbery himself, he got two of them to hold the robber he had been calling 'Jack' while he went through his pockets. He recovered about twenty rounds of ammunition for the rifle, which he put into his own pocket. By this time, the man was showing the first, faint signs of recovering full consciousness.

Martin thanked his helpers and said, 'We'll have to get going. We can't wait here any longer. These scum will have to look out for themselves. Good luck to you all on the diggings.' With that he took the reins from Bluey and called 'giddup' to the horses.

They passed through the Black Forest and reached the grasslands where he turned off the road and drove a mile or more through the light, open scrub to find a good place to stop and unhitch the horses out of sight of the road. He hobbled the horses and turned them loose to feed on the little grass that was available but was careful to keep them in sight. The last thing he wanted was to lose more time searching for strayed horses.

With Bluey's help, he set up camp and boiled the billy. Soon they were enjoying pannikins of hot tea with plenty of sugar.

Bluey was still bubbling with excitement to talk about their encounter with the bushrangers and Martin was now able, and ready, to talk to him about it.

'It's the most amazing thing I ever saw,' Bluey said. 'How did you ever learn to fight like that?'

Martin laughed. 'I was taught a lot about wrestling by an expert when I was a boy,' he said, 'and that kind of combat is a variation on wrestling. It's a combination of bluff and conning your attackers, and knowing how to use their own strength and power against them.

'But I was serious when I said that you had done well, battling the horses like you did. It was a lucky thing I had you with me; otherwise I would have had to surrender to them. I couldn't run the risk of the horses being spooked and bolting. Thanks a lot.'

Martin was privately elated at the outcome of the encounter and experienced a tremendous lift in spirits and confidence. He enjoyed a good laugh with Bluey at the utter disaster that had befallen the would-be bushrangers who had not only failed completely to get anything of value from the hold-up but had lost all their guns to boot.

Chapter 12

*M*artin and his new friend Bluey Bayles had an uneventful trip back to Melbourne after the hold-up in the Black Forest.

They parted when Martin reached his lodgings at Flemington about midafternoon on the last day.

'Could I travel back to Ballarat with you after I've had a break at home for a few weeks?' Bluey asked.

'Yes, you certainly can,' Martin replied. 'We'll try and avoid any bushrangers next time though. You know where I live now, so you can come and see me when the time comes near.'

When Martin pulled into the yard, Alice and Gwen were soon on hand to greet him. He lost no time in parking the wagon behind the stable and unhitching the horses. Alice soon had a cup of tea ready and the three of them sat at the kitchen table.

'Have you had a good trip?' Alice asked.

'Yes,' he said with a wide grin, 'everything went well, except that I got held-up by bushrangers.'

'What?!' both females shrieked. 'What do you mean – bushrangers?'

Martin knew that, sooner or later, he would have to give them a full account of the episode, so he decided to do it earlier rather than later. They took a breathless interest in every detail and questioned him at length.

'All I can say is, thank God you had that Bluey fellow with you. Without him you could have been murdered,' Alice said. 'It makes you think you should have somebody with you on every trip, especially now that you have four horses to look after.'

'I think you were very brave,' Gwen said.

'It's a pity you couldn't get the police onto them. They deserve to be locked up for that kind of crime,' said Alice.

'Maybe,' Martin replied, 'but taking everything into account, I think it all worked out for the best. They've been punished already by the loss of their guns, and will be a lot more by public ridicule, and I doubt that I'll ever see them on the road again.'

Late that night, Alice said to him in bed, 'You're making light of the bushrangers and I think I understand why, but I hope you don't believe that in your heart. You will be careful, won't you?'

'Yes, I will, and you are right. I am treating it seriously and there are some things I can do to make it safer. Travelling in numbers for one thing. So far, I've avoided taking people on as fellow travellers, but now that I've got the extra horsepower, I could carry three or four swags on the wagon while they walk. That way I'd have more people around all the time.'

As she put her arms around him and murmured, 'I hope so!', he had a private smile to himself. If only she knew about the gold in the wagon!

The next morning, Martin was at Moles & Keane's warehouse to do business with Cam Ralph early in the day. As usual, when he had finished there, he went to deposit the gold at the bank. He now enjoyed the prestige of being a valued customer there and had become a good friend of Arthur Lees, the manager. On this occasion, he asked him how he could send money to his mother.

'I would like to send her a few pounds,' he said, 'but apart from sending her a banknote in a letter, which might cause her problems because nobody in the village would want to accept Australian money, I don't know how it could be done.'

'No trouble at all, Martin. I can send it to a bank in Lancaster where she can pick it up at her convenience.'

Martin smiled as he said, 'Right, I understand how that could be done and I do want you to arrange to send ten pounds for me, but you might be surprised at what a stir that will cause amongst the family. Why, she'll have to be taken into Lancaster, twelve miles away. A big trip!'

He was back home at Alice's house by dinnertime, all loaded up and ready to start for Ballarat the next morning. This had become a well-established routine for him, and by taking full advantage of being an early customer at the warehouse in Melbourne, it worked smoothly.

The road was continuing to be the subject of howls of complaint to the Governor, but apart from a few small repairs to bridges, nothing was being done. But Martin was now getting the full benefit of having the extra horses and he completed the trip to the goldfields in the same time as usual.

Zac Bellchambers had heard a garbled report of the hold-up and had been a worried man until Sam Jessup came into his store and reassured him about Martin's ability to look after himself.

'Don't worry,' he said with a wide grin. 'He'll be here in a week's time with your flour as usual.'

It's not my bloody flour I'm worried about, Zac thought grimly to himself.

So when Martin did arrive on time, whole and hearty, Zac was very relieved and gave him a warm welcome, including a good dinner.

'What happened?' he demanded. 'We've heard some tall stories, I can tell you. One going the rounds a couple of days after you left was that you had killed one fellow, shot another one in the head, broken a third fellow's arm and then thrown them all into the bush and driven on.' He was laughing. 'But I must say I'm anxious to get the truth from you, straight from the horse's mouth, you might say.'

It was Martin's turn to laugh. 'I'm not surprised to hear about the stories. I thought the travellers who came along to see the tail end of the action would soon put it about. I'll tell you all about it,' he told Zac. 'I felt good after I got going down the road again. For one thing, I got three good firearms at no cost, and it made me have even more confidence in the false bottom hiding place.'

Martin told him everything that had happened, including his lucky break in having picked up Bluey Bayles who turned out to be a real help. They discussed the whole episode and also the latest action in their gold buying business.

'I've got another hundred ounces in the pool that cost an average of two pounds ten shillings, so you'll have another good profit to take back to Melbourne today,' Zac said.

Martin made his deliveries and pick-ups as usual and by midafternoon he was trundling down the Melbourne road through Ballarat to reach his camping place as the sun went down. The camping place was full of travellers, some going north and others coming south.

As he packed up his camp the next morning, he noticed a group of four men in a camp nearby who looked like returning diggers. He made a quick decision to offer to carry their swags on the wagon. 'I can't let you ride,' he said, 'but if you want to throw your swags on, you can.'

Needless to say, they quickly accepted the offer and spent the next three days walking not far from the wagon. The best part of the arrangement was that the travellers offered to cook Martin's chops along with their own for the evening meal, not a big deal of itself, but one less chore he had to think about at the end of the day.

Another trip brought the year around to the end of April and the drought still had the country in its grip, but not for long. During the night of Martin's return from that trip, it started to rain, so quietly at first that he wasn't sure it was rain he could hear. When Alice paid him one of her nocturnal visits near midnight, her coat was wet and she said, 'Yes, it's rain and it feels as if it will come on properly soon.'

And it did. Within the hour it was pouring down, and by morning the surrounding countryside had been soaked.

Martin wore his 'bluey' coat for the first time that morning on the final leg of his round trip back to Melbourne. He had a strong, country-man's premonition that the drought would turn into a long, wet winter which prompted him to buy an expensive, waterproof stockman's coat while he was in Moles & Keane's store.

More heavy showers were falling when he set off for another trip the next day. He was amazed at how quickly the deep dust had turned to sloppy mud. The horses were sparky and full of renewed energy as a result of the change in atmosphere and the mud was flying from their stamping hooves.

The trip north was not much affected by the wet conditions, but by the time he traversed the same road on the way home, the mud was deep and sticky, a forerunner of what was to come.

The rains continued and within three weeks, the road to Ballarat – and, for that matter, all the roads in southern Victoria – were impassable. All traffic on the Mount Alexander Road ceased for a week towards the end of May, and for the first time since starting his business, Martin had to give up any idea of travelling for a week.

A few sunny days allowed him to start on another trip in early June. The few days of dry weather had dried out the surface, but the deep mud remained wet and sticky. Much valuable time was lost on the road assisting other carriers whose vehicles, sometimes carts but often large wagons, had become bogged.

Martin was frustrated by the muddle-headed efforts of some of his fellow carriers to keep going when they should have stayed off the road. The additional horses in his team were now paying off handsomely and if he hadn't felt obligated to help others, he could have maintained his normal schedule. The extra horsepower kept the wagon moving, sometimes very slowly, but at least it was not bogging and losing hours of time as a result.

The cartage rates to all the goldfields kept rising all through that winter in order to entice the carriers to keep working when many of them just gave up and went home for a couple of months. The rate Martin was being paid for freight to the Ballarat field had risen to one hundred pounds a ton.

'It's a problem,' Zac Bellchambers said to him, 'but the diggers want the flour and groceries and they know they have to pay. You just get as much up here as you can.'

Most of the diggers continued to produce gold, but some were flooded out and had to move to other fields. Many went to Bendigo which was drier country than Ballarat.

Zac continued to buy gold and Martin was now taking up to two hundred ounces back to Melbourne on each trip.

He wanted to stay the night at the diggings to rest the horses and decided to accept Sam and Nellie's invitation to visit them, so after completing his business with Derek Mason, he went on to Anderson's Flats to find them. Sam and his mates were just coming home at the end of the day when he got to their tent.

'Yes,' Sam said, 'there's a space big enough to hold you and your team a bit further up the gully. I'll show you where it is. One thing, you'll have no trouble finding water for your horses; it's been raining here nearly every day. Half the shafts on the diggings are flooded.'

Nellie produced hot tea for them all as they settled down in the tent for a good yarn, and somebody found a bottle of rum to add to the tea.

'The first thing we want to hear from you is the truth of what happened when you were stuck up by bushrangers,' Sam said with a big guffaw. 'We've heard some funny stories, I can assure you.'

Martin laughed heartily and said, 'Well, there's one thing you can be sure of: most of those stories will be bullshit. I know how they got carried back here. A party happened to come onto the scene to see the last of the action and I could tell that they were all agog to see a fellow laid out cold. They thought he was dead, but of course he wasn't.'

'Well, what happened?' Sam demanded. 'Tell us your side of it.'

Martin gave them a quick run-down of the episode from start to finish and they all had a good laugh.

'It's all very well to laugh now,' Nellie said, 'but you could have been shot, and maybe killed. I'll bet you weren't laughing when they had you in the sights of their guns.'

'You're dead right about that, Nellie,' Martin said with a chuckle, a response that brought another wave of laughter.

Nellie had made a good meal of mutton chops with damper, and as a treat, some Johnny cakes to finish on. After tea, the men lay around smoking their pipes and yarning about conditions on the field. They were having moderate success with their claim and were making good money.

'If we can keep the water out of the shaft, we'll soon be into some really good ground,' Sam said. 'Then, with a bit of luck, we'll start to make a lot of money.'

The talk turned to the unrest amongst the diggers because of the way the police were doing their work in relation to the gold licences and other policing duties on the goldfields. The police were widely perceived as being corrupt, and too many of them habitually acted the part of school bullies.

'We were asked to show our licences four times in one day a few days ago,' Sam said.

It was nearing the end of the evening and Martin was thinking of departing the tent to go to his own wagon and tent when a shot rang out not far from where they were.

Martin jumped up. 'What's that?'

One of the men said, 'It's the silly bloody diggers starting to fire off their guns; they do it every night. It's just a silly custom that's got established here on the diggings. They do it every night about this time.'

'Strewth!' Martin spluttered, 'my horses will be scaring like crazy. I'll see you blokes in the morning.' He bolted out to run to his own camp.

The firing continued for about ten minutes and swept from one end of the diggings to the other. Martin managed to soothe the horses and settle them down by giving them another measure of feed.

Nobody knew exactly why the custom had started, or why it

persisted, but it must have been a boon for the manufacturers of ammunition.

Martin was at the digger's tent for breakfast the next morning, as arranged, and on this occasion Nellie produced a big dish of beef sausages.

'Ah, mystery bags,' one of the men said with a laugh.

'No fear, there's no mystery about these,' Nellie retorted. 'They're made by the butcher at Gisborne and he brings them up twice a week. They make a nice change.'

Breakfast was finished and the men were preparing to go to their claim when shouting was heard in the distance. Martin heard the cry: 'Joe! Joe!' which was spreading towards them.

'The bloody police again!' Sam said. 'They're starting early today!'

The cry had been taken up all over that section of the diggings until it was a continuous roar. It was primarily to warn all those who didn't have a current licence to hide or run from the police because the penalty for not having one was the steep fine of five pounds. Lately, it had come to be a strident expression of the diggers' hatred for the police.

As the police posse got closer, the demand, 'Licence! Licence!' could be heard.

Sam and his partners all got their licences out, ready to show when the police rushed up to the tent. Martin too had his licence in his hand. The last thing he wanted was to be held up by an argument with the police.

It was all over in a few minutes and Martin hurriedly said goodbye to his friends and got back to his horses. The diggings is no place to keep horses, he grimly reflected.

Half an hour later, he was drinking tea in Zac Bellchambers's kitchen, giving him an account of the night's activities.

'Yes,' Zac said, 'the diggings are a madhouse most of the time. You never know what is going to happen next. But the diggers love it, even with the shooting and the barking dogs, and the fighting. It gets in their blood.

'The maddest thing of all is the way the police deliberately harass people all the time. It is crazy, but they do seem to set themselves out to be as mean and officious as possible. And of course, they are all on the take. You can buy your way out of any fine if you produce enough money fast enough. That's the reason the diggers keep up the "Joe, Joe, Joe" taunt whenever they go out on a licence hunt which they do almost every day. It's the only way the diggers have of telling them what they think of them and their corrupt ways.

'The police have got so fed up with the humiliation they feel because of the continual "Joeing" that they've persuaded the government to make it an offence. It's been classified as an obscenity and a five pound fine has been put on people using it in a public place. But the fine is another madness that only makes the bad feelings between the police and the diggers worse. It hasn't stopped them; they still shout it out when they know they can get away with it, which is most of the time. I can hardly believe that the authorities are so incompetent, and just plain stupid. Mark my words,' he said. 'One of these days soon, there'll be big trouble on all the diggings.'

'Have you heard of Inspector David Armstrong, the one they call "The Flying Demon"?' Zac asked Martin. 'He's the one you need to keep clear of, he's a holy terror. His speciality is burning the sly grog tents and all their gear unless they buy him off, but he's on the take all the time. The diggers reckon he's making a fortune.'

'Yes,' Martin said, 'it does make you wonder where it will all end; not too soon, I hope. You and I are doing well out of it, that's the main thing.'

'I'll bet you're pleased you went into the carrying business and not digging,' Zac said with a grin.

'You are right about that!' Martin replied with a chuckle. 'I was listening to my mates last night when the same thought came into my mind.'

Martin and Zac reviewed their gold buying business and then loaded the wagon with empties. Martin set off on the return journey with plenty to mull over as he trundled southwards along the muddy road.

The numbers of travellers going north to the diggings had decreased somewhat, but the numbers going south had remained high. The rain had been a blessing for the whole country, but it had completely disrupted the lives of many diggers who were operating claims in low lying places. Many had moved to higher ground, or to other fields on dry country, but many had given up and were returning to their old jobs.

The one big blessing at that time was that there were plenty of jobs available for anybody who wanted to work right across the state, in both city and country. The government was looking for contractors and labourers who were competent to undertake roadworks of all kinds, including bridge building, but many of those travelling south were only going home for a break of a few weeks with the idea of returning to the goldfields when the country dried out. As Zac had said, the goldfields get into your blood!

The remainder of 1852 was very good for Martin. The additional horses were costing a lot in feed, but because of them, he was able to continue without interruption and the higher rates he was paid all through the winter and spring were more than sufficient to cover the extra costs. He was one of only a very few carriers who were able to maintain a regular schedule over the dreadful roads during the winter.

Martin maintained his carriage of gold on every trip home, and he and Zac prospered greatly from their gold buying business. After his experience with the bushrangers in the Black Forest and the fact that he was not bothered again, Martin developed even more faith in his ability to carry large amounts of gold hidden in the false bottom of the wagon. He was confident that even if he were robbed by more capable bushrangers, they wouldn't find the hiding place.

He had long since accumulated over one thousand pounds in his account with the Bank of New South Wales, and taking into account the value of the plant and horses he owned, he was now a wealthy man, a far dream from the day he got off the *Water Witch* at Williamstown only one year ago.

He had built an extension onto the stable to accommodate two extra stalls and a skillion roof at the back to shelter the second cart and the wagon. He had agreed with Alice that he would pay all the costs and that when he eventually left, she would own everything. In the meantime, he volunteered to increase his weekly board to two pounds ten shillings, a move that delighted her and increased his already high standing with her.

He had received a letter from Rebecca and Sarah Drewitt in reply to his first letter to them. It was full of little bits of news about Norwood and the Don village and messages from Mrs Smith and the others. 'Father and Mother' sent their regards and best wishes. On the bottom of the two page letter was: 'Write again soon'.

It seemed to him that time had flown when he sat down to eat Christmas dinner with Alice and Gwen for the second time.

'Yes,' Alice said, 'the time has passed quickly, but it's been a happy year. Let's hope the next one will be as good.'

Alice was a bit grumpy when he set out again for Ballarat three days later. 'You should be staying home for all this week,' she said. 'You can't go on working every day of your life like you do.'

Martin thought she was sounding more like a wife as each month went by. He was very fond of her, but he had no thoughts of marrying her. He fully appreciated her many good points and knew that she would make a good wife ... if she had been available, which she wasn't. Even if she had been available, the fact that she was barren must be a bar to him marrying her. He knew that he would never be really happy in his new land until he had a family of his own. He didn't know how it was all going to end, and he put it out of his mind. In the meantime, his only thought was to increase his fortune, and working hard every week was his method of achieving that.

His first trip up the road to Ballarat after Christmas showed that the gold rush was still going as strongly as ever. As 1853 dawned, Melbourne was crammed with thousands of British migrants who had arrived in the last months of 1852, many of them living under the most awful conditions in rented hovels and in 'tent city' on the south bank of the Yarra River.

It had taken nearly a year for the news of the fabulous gold discoveries in Australia to reach England and to be spread around the country. Gold fever had taken hold and thousands who could raise the twenty-two pounds it cost for a 'steerage' passage decided to try their luck in the faraway colony, a place up until then they had regarded as the end of the earth and not fit for free people to live in. Married and single, young and not so young, they came in their thousands. The ships were crammed; they had never had trade so good. The flood of immigrants would continue for at least another year before it started to peter out.

Most of the would-be gold seekers were quite unsuited for the harsh and primitive life of a gold digger; and worse still, they knew nothing of the basic skills that were essential for success. One piece of advice that was given by an early gold digger that was right on target, and should have been heeded by all would-bes, was to dig a hole in the garden four feet wide and twenty feet deep as practise for what would be needed on the goldfield, but like most good advice, it was not heard or thought about. Unhappily, the newspapers had too many stories – often misleading – of people picking up a fortune in nuggets from the ground on the early goldfields.

As on Martin's first trip up this road a year ago, it was crowded with all sorts of horse and bullock drawn vehicles and hundreds of pedestrians, spread out like a line of ants. Martin had to refuse dozens of people permission to throw their swags and luggage on the wagon. He always had his load carefully covered by a canvas tarpaulin securely tied down all round the wagon. That gave the message that the wagon was full with no room for anything else at all, not even a swag.

By sticking to his carefully developed plan and working to achieve three trips every month, he continued to prosper greatly. His profits from trading in gold were greater by far than what he made from his carrying business.

His partnership with Zac Bellchambers had been his biggest stroke of luck. Their arrangement had worked to enrich them both, but Martin had benefited most because it had opened up a big opportunity early in his career as a carrier. No doubt he would have done well in carrying alone, but the gold trading had been the bonanza.

Zac and Martin had become very close friends and a genuine regard for each other existed between them. Martin appreciated Zac's understanding of the broader issues applying to the gold rushes. He always told Martin that these feverish days of plundering the alluvial gold that was easily got on or near the surface would not last for more than a few years. He also had a fine appreciation of the value of money and the importance of sensible, long-term investment.

'I never had enough to invest when I was young,' he said. 'For most of my life, all I could do was keep body and soul together. It wasn't until I had enough to invest in a passage to Australia that I started to make anything more than starvation wages. Even when I first got here, the system was stacked against people like me and it was hard, very hard, to get your foot on the first step. The gold rushes have made me. That was my one big opportunity and I thank God that I had enough sense to stick to my trade and take on storekeeping. I am wealthy now, and I'll take fine care to see that I stay that way. I'll be very careful of where I invest my money. Bank interest will be enough for me, I reckon.'

Martin listened and mulled it all over; that line of talk reminded him of Charles Drewitt and his advice to him that carrying goods to the diggings would be more profitable than digging for gold.

Early in 1853, Martin's friend Arthur Lees reminded him that he now had three thousand pounds in his account and suggested that he ought to think about investing some of it where it could make more profit for him.

'I'm willing to invest, but I can't see any good opportunities right now,' Martin replied. 'I don't think it would be sensible for me to invest more in my goldfields business, and as for anything else, all I'm looking for is safety.'

'Well, for safety you won't get anything better than the bank,' Arthur said. 'Why not put two thousand on fixed deposit for a year? I can give you four per cent. That'll bring you eighty pounds. Not a large fortune, but better than having it lay idle in your account.'

By the end of 1853, Martin had doubled his fortune and was looking forward to continuing to prosper in 1854.

Zac Bellchambers said to him, 'I wonder if we've seen the best of it? I wouldn't be surprised if things start to fade a bit here. I'll make a judgement at the end of this year on what to do. I might retire and go back to civilisation for a change.'

As Martin sat down to Christmas dinner with Alice and Gwen in 1853, he noticed how Gwen had grown and was now at the tall, leggy stage of development. He reflected on the two years that had passed since he joined the household and how they had grown together; almost like a family, he thought.

He picked up the glass of ale that Alice had put out for them all and said, 'Merry Christmas. Seems like no time since the last one.'

'That's what you and Mother said last year,' Gwen said with a laugh.

'It was too,' he chuckled. 'I must be getting old, repeating myself like that. But I don't mind saying it again. I can hardly believe it's two years since I came here to live with you.'

'That's because you've been so busy, working all the time,' Alice said. 'Are you going to take a few days off this Christmas?'

To her surprise, he smiled and said, 'Yes, I'm taking all next week off. I don't know what I'll do, but a good rest will do me, and the horses, a lot of good.'

After a day or two, she hinted that it would be a good idea for them all to have a day out together. 'We could go into the city to see the sights, or we could go to the beach and maybe have a swim,' she said.

He surprised her again by agreeing. 'Yes, that would be a good idea, but I don't know how we could do it.'

She laughed and said, 'You know, I reckon that's true. You've been so busy working all the time that you don't know how to get from here to Melbourne except by wagon. You can hire a pony and trap at the stables here in Flemington,' she said with a laugh. 'I suppose you do know how to drive a pony?'

CHAPTER 13

*I*t was on the second of January 1854, the first day back on the road after the Christmas break, when Martin first noticed that the crowd of gold rush travellers he had become so used to over the past three years was diminishing in numbers. It was a refreshing change after the pressure and heaviness of the pressing crowds on the road ever since he started on his first nervous trip three years ago. It suddenly felt as if a great burden had been lifted.

He enjoyed the feeling of freedom it brought and at the first resting place, the Lincolnshire Arms at Five Mile Creek, he wandered into the bar and treated himself to a rum and water.

As he drove his team back onto the road, he had a smile to himself in recognition of the change in his circumstances and also in his own personality. He remembered his uncertainties on that first trip up the Ballarat Road. He remembered his new friends of that time, Sam

Jessup and Nellie Houseman. I wonder what they're doing right now, he thought.

At the first camping ground, the well-known Diggers Rest, more memories came flooding back into his mind.

As the sun slowly went down into the end of another day on the road – this time a summer sun – he automatically went about setting up his camp for the night. He was so practised at the job now that he did it almost without thinking. The tent attached to the side of the wagon with half a dozen wire clips. His palliasse pulled out from its place on the wagon with a flick of the wrist and the camp fire tripod was recovered from under the wagon. All that remained to be done was to light the fire and boil the billy. Alice's hamper made the first three days of the trip very easy with its roast of cold meat, mostly mutton but sometimes beef and, on odd occasions pork. Three or four slices of meat, a cup of hot tea and a slice or two of toasted bread made a quick and satisfying meal.

The camp was quiet on this night and a couple of hours later, he fed his horses for the final time that day and crawled into his bed.

The next afternoon, he still gave his team and himself a rest at the grasslands south of the Black Forest. This year, the country was thick with grass and the lushness of the season made everything glow with the power of spring and early summer. His horses were all in good condition and fit. Seldom though it was, whenever he called on them for an extra daily march or a strong pull to get through a bog, they could and did respond with great power.

He was always pleased to reach the diggings and arrive at his old mate's store. The flag that identified his store from all the others on the diggings always flew, day and night. It was a large, white flag with a red cross drawn diagonally from corner to corner.

Zac believed in the philosophy of mass display as his main tool of selling, thus he always had a jumble of goods covering the ground out-side the substantial tent and timber building that was his store. It was a 'topsy' building that just grew and grew from the day it was built, so that now it was substantial with a lockup storeroom and a kitchen right across the back of the front tent.

Pillars of washing pans, cramps of buckets, gold washing cradles, puddling tubs, heaps of picks, shovels, gads, stone hammers, crow-bars and sundry small tools occupied one section of the display while camp stretchers, tin teapots and pannikins and coffee cans took up another. A clothes hanger sported moleskin trousers and jackets, and shirts of various degrees of quality from light summer weight through to hard-wearing, winter weight. Another important section was filled with coils of rope, hatchets, handsaws; small, crosscut saws and a selec-tion of chisels both large and small. To round off the display, flitches of bacon and barrels of Irish pork were placed on low benches with tins of preserved fish.

To assist him in keeping order amongst this apparent jumble of merchandise, and to keep a sharp eye open for thieves of which there were always a few about, Zac employed a miner's wife as his senior assistant. She was a reliable, forthright and honest woman who had been with him from his earliest days on the field.

As usual, Zac met him in the yard, one arm waving from his stooped shoulders and a wide grin on his face.

'You're back! Where have you been?!' he called out.

'Having my Christmas holidays!' Martin called back in reply. 'You know, holidays that all those city people in Melbourne have!'

'You'd better come in and have a feed,' Zac said. 'I suppose you're in need of it after your long trip.'

They exchanged news of what had been happening to them over the Christmas break.

'Things have been quiet here,' Zac said. 'That is, in comparison to how they used to be last year and the year before.'

They talked about business for a while and the prospects for the coming year. After eating, and another cup of tea, they unloaded the freight and Martin went on to deliver Derek Miles's share of the load.

Derek, as usual, wanted to know when Martin would be making his next delivery. He wanted more flour, and more empties taken back to Melbourne. Then, out of nowhere, he said, 'What about this story that was going the rounds about you? Is it true that you got held up in the Black Forest and that you bashed three men and turned the tables on them and finished up robbing them?'

Martin laughed heartily. 'Is that story still going the rounds? I thought that was finished months ago.'

'Well, what about it?'

Martin had to conceal his impatience and give him a measured and carefully structured account of the episode.

'Serve the bastards right. You should have shot a couple of them while you had the chance,' was Derek's comment.

They loaded twelve empties onto the wagon and Martin returned to Zac's place where he completed the load before heading off down the road on the homeward journey.

That first trip in January was followed by many others through the summer and autumn, and all too soon Martin was battling with mud and slush again as winter took hold.

He often got messages from Sam and Nellie, asking him to obtain some items in Melbourne that they couldn't buy on the field, or to run the occasional business errand. The messages were always accompanied by invitations to spend a night at their new claim which was only a short distance from their old one.

One day in early spring, Martin had an impulse to accept the invitation. It would be a good chance to rest himself and his horses. They were all in need of a little extra time off after the heavy winter work. He told Zac what he had in mind and to his great satisfaction, he offered to look after the team for the night. 'I've got plenty of room in the yard,' he said. 'I can feed and water them and if necessary keep them quiet if the silly buggers start firing their guns in the night although they don't do that so much nowadays. It seems to have gone out of fashion. I reckon they finally got sick of buying the ammunition just to fire it into the air.'

Martin left the team in Zac's care and walked the three miles down the road to find his friends coming in after a hard day on their claim. They greeted him warmly and Nellie soon had pannikins of tea brewed which, as usual at the end of the day, were laced with rum. The talk immediately turned to digging, how the luck was running and to the latest news on the field.

'This field has taken a new lease on life the last few days,' Sam said. 'Some fellows about half a mile from us struck a rich patch of ground about twelve feet deep and are doing well with it.'

'Yes,' his mate Jim said, 'that sort of find always puts new life into a field. I'll bet there will be a whole new crowd of diggers in here soon. When the word gets out that the field is far from finished, it'll set another rush going.'

Nellie produced another of her famous stews, this time with some potatoes and carrots she had managed to buy, and to finish the meal she turned out a rich boiled pudding. The men's appetites were satisfied and they lay about smoking their pipes and talking. After an hour, Jim said, 'We ought to go up to Notchy Mellors's store and see what's doing around the diggings. There might be some new strikes.'

Nellie was left to keep an eye on the tent while the men went off, saying, 'We'll be back in a couple of hours.'

Notchy Mellors kept a store at Anderson's Flats and it was an open secret in the locality that he always had sly grog for sale.

When Sam and his mates arrived on the scene, a crowd of diggers was jammed into the store, a canvas tent stretched over a frame of saplings. They all had pannikins in their hands, and judging by the scent coming from them they were not drinking tea. The place was humming with talk about the new strike and what it meant for the future of the Ballarat fields.

'It goes to show that there's plenty of gold left here,' one burly fellow said. 'It shows that those so-called experts don't know what they're talking about either.'

This was greeted with a gale of laughter and the evening became even more jolly. A good time was being had by all when a voice out the back yelled, 'Joe! Joe!' at the same time that four policemen rushed into the store. Martin saw at once that they were led by the infamous David Armstrong who had his trademark riding whip in his hand. It was a beautiful whip with a small, golden ball dangling from the leather lash. He was a cruel man and loved to lay the whip across the shoulders of any man who got too close to him in a brawl. As he came into the tent, he handed the whip to one of his troopers and immediately vaulted over the trestle table that served as a counter and started rummaging around in the goods that were laying in a jumble on the floor. He stood up with a bottle in his hand.

'You're gone this time!' he shouted. 'Caught you fair and square. I'll have you for this!'

'What do you think you've found?' Notchy Mellors said. 'That's vinegar you've got in your hand.'

Armstrong glanced at the bottle while a gale of laughter swept the tent. He swore and smashed the bottle against the end of the table. The contents spilled out in a gush and he dabbled his fingers in it before putting them up to his nose.

'It might be,' he snarled, 'but that's not what you're all drinking. Look around,' he ordered the troopers. 'There's sly grog here.'

He turned and pushed the trestle over to make it easier to look amongst the goods laying on the floor.

The diggers, fed up with endless months of this kind of heavy-handed and illegal behaviour by Armstrong, started to taunt him. 'Give the poor bugger a fair go!' one man called out. 'There's no need to smash the place up!'

'You shut your mouth!' Armstrong shouted, 'or I'll shut it for you!'

Something happened at the back of the store and in a moment, a riot had broken out. Men were punching the troopers and then fighting each other. A brawl is always simmering just below the surface when diggers have a bit of rum in them and a fight starts. And when a fight starts, a riot often quickly follows, especially at night.

Armstrong went berserk. He had his whip back and was slashing around him. He was roaring, 'Order! Order! Get out, all of you! Get out or you'll all be under arrest!'

Martin was pushing men away from him and trying to keep out of the fighting when a trooper rushed over and grabbed his arm. Martin grabbed the man around the neck and threw him backwards, sending him crashing across the counter to land on his back amongst the goods that Armstrong had been searching. Martin was hit from behind by a trooper leaping onto his back. The next thing he knew he was under a heaving mass of troopers all trying to punch or kick him. Armstrong was snarling in his face: 'You're under arrest!' Another two troopers got his hands behind his back and snapped the handcuffs on.

Most of the diggers had melted away and the dozen or so who

remained in the wreck of the store were looking the worse for wear. Four others, including one of Sam's partners, Rex Dallen, were handcuffed and under arrest.

The police had evidently expected to make arrests because they had a spring cart parked outside. Armstrong ordered all five of the handcuffed men out to the cart and when they were huddled together on the floor with a trooper holding a pistol over them, he gave the order: 'Drive on.'

They drove past the police station at the edge of the field and continued down the road towards Ballarat. Once there, they were taken to a ramshackle, old wooden building that had been a barracks but which had been vandalised over the years by hundreds of wild inmates to the stage where it was hardly habitable.

They were locked into a long, bare ward with a parting message from the trooper in charge: 'Settle down for the night. It'll give you time to cool off. You'll be charged tomorrow.' There was nothing for it but to settle down on the few bare bunks lined up against the wall and wait for morning.

Martin spent a cold and sleepless night. He was thankful that he was wearing his heavy 'bluey' coat, the one he had picked up from the side of the road near Diggers Rest over a year ago. He was impatiently waiting for an officer of authority to come on the scene so that he could demand to be released to get back to his team and his work, but the morning dawned and there was no sign of movement. All the one trooper who was guarding them would say was: 'The Inspector will be here later. He'll deal with you when he comes.'

Martin started poking around the premises as best he could with a half-baked idea of escaping, but his comrades said, 'If you think you'll get away from these bastards, you're up the wrong street. For one thing, they'll be waiting for some excuse to shoot you. Many are the good men who've been shot escaping from this place.'

Martin sauntered the length and breadth of the large dormitory and found a door in the back wall that led to a latrine. He went through and used the facilities. There was another door that evidently led outside, but it was securely locked. A small window above a bench caught his eye. He climbed up and found that he could see down into a small exercise yard at the back of the barracks.

He was moving away from the window in preparation of going back inside to tell the others about the latrine when he saw a policeman come into the yard through a small door in the corner. There was just enough light to make out what he was doing. Martin watched with intense interest as the man went to the far corner and produced a bricklayer's trowel from under his coat which he used expertly to open up a hole in the ground. He fumbled with something as he cleaned out the last few handfuls of soil and then produced a small tin from his pocket which he deposited in the hole. Looking around furtively, he quickly filled the hole in and pressed the soil down with his booted foot.

Martin shrank back from the window and stepped down into the room, puzzled by what he had seen. The only conclusion possible was that whatever the trooper had hidden was illegal and valuable.

Martin told the others of the latrine and they soon all went to have a look for themselves. He decided against telling them about the trooper.

The middle of the day came and still no sign of any official move to deal with them. The other four men, all tough diggers, yelled for the trooper and demanded food and drink. All they got was the same response: 'The Inspector will deal with you when he comes.'

Inspector Armstrong finally arrived on the scene an hour later and they were taken to be interviewed by him one by one. He was sitting behind a desk with a notebook before him, freshly shaven and dressed immaculately in his uniform.

'Name?' he asked as Martin stood before him.

'Maynard, Martin Maynard.'

He then rattled out: Age? Address?

Martin told him who he was, that he was a carrier and had four horses to look after urgently.

'Oh, yes, I've heard of you. You're the Johnny who fought off the bushrangers and took their guns?'

'Yes, I did have a bit of trouble down at the Black Forest, but that was months ago now. I've had no trouble since,' Martin said.

'You think you're pretty smart, don't you. Why didn't you bring those outlaws back to me so they could be dealt with by the law? You know what you did was illegal, don't you?'

'No, I don't know that,' Martin replied. 'I thought a citizen had the right to protect himself and his property from theft or damage by villains.'

'I think you are too smart for your own good, and you're a dangerous man. That's what got you into trouble last night. You think you can come onto the goldfields and assault the police any time you feel like it, ' he sneered.

'Now give me a chance to explain my side, Inspector,' Martin said. 'I had nothing to do with what happened at Mellors's store last night. I went there as an innocent customer and got caught up in somebody else's brawl.'

'I don't think you're too bloody innocent, Mr bloody Maynard. You can explain everything to the magistrate; he'll be here in two days. Assaulting the police usually carries three months, at least.'

'But, Inspector, I've got four horses that just have to be looked after.

I can't leave them unattended for four days. If you're set on charging me, I'm entitled to bail.'

'You're only entitled to what I say you're entitled to, and I say you stay here until the magistrate decides what to do with you. Back to the dormitory, and stay there – and don't give us any trouble!'

When Sam and his mates got back to the tent late the night of the riot and told Nellie what had happened, she was frantic with worry. 'What will that mongrel Armstrong do to him while he's got him locked up and helpless?' she demanded.

Sam was worried, but he wasn't in the mood to let her rage too far.

'I'm worried too,' he said, 'but we're not going out to hang ourselves in desperation just yet. I'll go up and tell old Zac what's going on first thing in the morning and see if he needs a hand with the horses. As for Martin, he won't be happy, but he knows how to look after himself and I wouldn't be surprised to see him home before dinnertime.'

When Zac was roused out early the next morning and told what had happened, he exploded with anger. 'What?! How the hell did you blokes let that happen?' he demanded. 'Was Martin to blame? Tell me exactly what happened.'

As soon as Inspector Armstrong's name was mentioned, Zac said, 'Oh, he's involved, is he? That means trouble, big trouble. We'll have to work out what to do. In the meantime, I can look after the horses, that's as long as the feed hangs out.'

'But you'll have to find out whether he's been charged with anything and when he'll get out. You'll have to do that today, without fail,' said Sam.

As Sam turned to go back to his tent and his mates, Zac said, 'Another thing. As you go back, call in to Derek Miles's store and tell him what's going on. We might need him to help in some way. You never know what to do with that mongrel Armstrong in charge.'

Sam did as Zac had instructed him and got back to the tent as his partners were leaving for work. After talking it over, they decided that Sam should go to Ballarat and find out from the police what was happening to Martin and when he would be getting out.

Sam arrived back in the late afternoon and saw Zac and Derek before telling his mates what he had learnt.

'I can't understand why Armstrong is being so bloody minded about the deal. It's not as if it is a serious criminal offence or anything like that,' Jim said. 'I can't understand what he'd have against Martin.'

'I can,' Sam said. 'He's a nut case. He's so puffed up with arrogance because he's the big bloke around the diggings, he'd be jealous of Martin because of all the talk about him beating the bushrangers at their own game. It sounds a bit silly, but I'll bet that's what's in his mind.'

Much to Martin's surprise, the other four men who had been brought in with him were released late that afternoon after they had been interviewed by Armstrong. He was left in the dormitory on his own. After the others had been released, he was given bread and jam to eat and a canteen of water.

There was nothing to do in the dormitory and he filled in the time by trying to sleep between walking backwards and forwards from one end of the long room to the other for half hour periods.

He attracted the trooper's attention and asked him if he had a newspaper or something else to read. He wondered whether the man himself could read; he didn't seem very intelligent and he was inclined to be surly. He was a big, burly fellow in his early twenties.

Martin set himself to win over the trooper's goodwill, if not sympathy. He had a vivid mental picture of the first trooper hiding something under the ground in the corner of the yard and was convinced it was something of great value – maybe gold. He had decided to get into the yard during the night and dig up whatever was there.

It was hard going; the trooper was morose and short-tempered and Martin soon decided he had a chip on his shoulder about something, but he couldn't tell at first what it was; however, like most human beings, he was very interested in himself and his personal affairs. Once Martin got him talking about his home and his young days, he opened up and was soon talking about his job and the difficulties the police encountered on the diggings. He said his name was Pat Riley. He disliked being 'Joe'd' and couldn't understand why the diggers hated the police so strongly.

'Did you ever have a go at digging yourself, Pat?' Martin asked him.

'Yes, I did have a go for six months,' he replied, 'but the mob I was with didn't know anything about finding gold and we didn't make any money at all. When the chance came to get a good job with the police, I took it. At least we get paid regular and the work is not hard.'

'It was bad luck for you to fall in with a poor lot to start with,' Martin sympathised with him. 'A big, strong lad like you would be an asset to any gang. I'll bet you could shift some dirt in a day!'

He evidently liked being praised and admired and Martin sensed he was making progress. After a while, he asked him again for something to read and when he brought him a newspaper only a few days old, he thanked him profusely and made some nice remarks about being a civilised man and a gentleman.

Martin said, 'I'd like to pay you for the paper. It's good of you to get it for me. Here, take this ten bob for your trouble.'

The trooper's eyes popped open and he smiled in appreciation. 'Thanks, thanks a lot,' he said.

By this time, the sun was well down and it wouldn't be long before darkness set in. Martin was now convinced that if he was to get a look at what was hidden in the ground, he would have to act before morning. A premonition told him that it was now or never.

When the trooper brought him more bread and jam, Martin said to him, 'By hell; it's been a long, dull day shut up in this one room all the time. Could you see your way clear to give me an hour in the exercise yard out the back?'

'I wouldn't mind, but the Sergeant said you were to be kept in the dormitory.'

'He'd never know. Anyway, what harm could there be in it? I couldn't get out even if I wanted to, which I don't. I'll make a solemn promise that I won't try to escape or do anything to get you into trouble with your bosses,' Martin said.

'It will soon be dark, so there's no good in going out when you can't see anything,' Pat observed.

Martin chuckled as he said, 'I'm not going anywhere, so it won't matter whether it's dark or not. Tell you what, if you'll let me out the back door for half an hour and then lock me in again afterwards, there's a quid in it for you for your trouble.'

'All right, but don't you try any tricks. You can't get out, but if you try we'll shoot you,' Pat said as he opened the door and came into the dormitory. He walked through the long room and into the latrine where he produced a bunch of keys from his pocket and unlocked the back door.

'Thanks, thanks a lot,' Martin said as he gave him a friendly pat on the shoulder. 'I might get some sleep after a few turns around the yard. I'll just get my coat, it's cold out there. He was playing for time to pass so that Pat would get sick of watching him walking around the yard and go back inside. That would be his chance to dig up whatever was in the ground while he wasn't under the eye of the trooper.

Martin walked around the perimeter wall to act out the part of taking exercise and to have a quick look at the spot in the far corner where he had seen the trooper bury something.

Darkness was coming on rapidly and by the time he had walked around the yard five times, he knew that it would soon be pitch-black. His heart raced as he saw Pat turn back from the steps and go inside. He kept walking until he reached the corner. He glanced around as he reached into his trouser pocket and brought out his pocketknife. He thanked his lucky star that the police here in Ballarat were not as efficient as the warders in the convict gaols where no prisoner was allowed to keep a knife, or anything else, once they were locked up.

He could barely see the back door and hoped that Pat couldn't see him well enough to see what he was doing, if he was watching. Chances were, he thought, that he'll be huddled up in a corner waiting for me to come back inside.

He dropped to his knees and in the deep gloom rapidly dug down into the soil using his knife and his hands. A foot down, he struck a canvas bag which he got out without any trouble. It was a small bag but surprisingly heavy, and the top was folded over to keep the soil out. He got his hand inside and felt a small, flat tin which he pulled out. Judging by the weight, it contained gold. He slipped it into the deep side pocket of his 'bluey' coat.

There were three more tins, all of which he pocketed. He stuffed the bag back in the hole and dragged the dirt in with his hands. A quick press down with his foot and the job was done.

He did another lap around the yard, the weight of the tins heavy in his pockets. He sprinted up the steps into the latrine – Pat wasn't in sight. He closed the door and went through into the dormitory where he found Pat sitting on a bunk.

'Thanks, mate,' Martin said jovially. 'That has made me feel a lot better. I might get a bit of sleep tonight now.'

He had the pound note ready in his hand. As he handed it to Pat, he said, 'Don't forget to lock the back door. If the Sergeant finds it unlocked, he'll go off his head. Any chance of a loan of a light, mate?' he asked Pat. 'I'd like to read that paper for a bit before I settle down.'

Pat said, 'I'll see what's out here,' and returned a few minutes later with a storm lantern. Martin set it on an upturned box that was lying near the row of bunks and opened out the paper. Pat turned and left the room, saying, 'I'll be back for the lantern in a while.'

As soon as Martin felt it was safe, he crouched down behind the bunk to take a look at his booty. The tins were the same as the ones Zac used to send the gold to Melbourne. He didn't spend too much time examining them in case Pat came back unexpectedly, but he knew he had made a great find if he could get them out of the gaol without discovery when the time came.

⌦ — — ⌫

When Sam Jessup and Rex Dallen reported again to Zac Bellchambers that night, it was decided that something had to be done to get Martin out of gaol as a matter of urgency.

The next morning, Zac and Derek were waiting at the police station for Inspector Armstrong to come to work. He turned up midmorning and the Sergeant on duty told him that the two storekeepers were waiting to see him about Martin Maynard.

'What's that got to do with them?' he snarled. 'If they think they can tell me how to do my job, they're wasting their time.'

When the two were shown into his office, he met them with an offhand: 'Good day. What do you fellows want with me?'

Zac said, 'We want to discuss the Maynard case with you.'

'There's nothing to discuss,' he replied. 'He was arrested the night before last for assaulting police and dealing in sly grog, and now he's in the lockup waiting for the magistrate to come in a few days to hear charges against him. I expect him to get at least three months inside.'

'We are concerned that you may not know the full background to his case,' Zac said, 'and we're appealing to you to let him out on bail so that he can attend to his business, including the care of his four horses and, if necessary, to get legal advice.'

'Why should he be treated any different to other scum who go around assaulting the police? He's a well-known brawler and strong-arm man who is a danger to the community.'

'That's just the point, Inspector,' Derek said. 'All we're asking is that he be treated the same as any citizen is entitled to be treated. These charges you propose to lay against him are not criminal offences and normally he would be on bail within a few hours of being charged. Have you actually charged him yet?'

'No, he hasn't been formally charged,' the Inspector reluctantly answered. 'We're just waiting for the magistrate to come and then his staff will prepare the charges.'

'That's the whole point that we're concerned about,' Derek said. 'It could be a sticky legal mess if you hold him too long without charging him. As responsible businessmen and citizens of Ballarat, we feel you should know that Maynard is a wealthy man in his own right and is easily able to get the best lawyers in Melbourne. He's also got a few friends who are close to government circles who could be brought into play. What about reconsidering the issue of bail? Maybe you could let him out on our surety to guarantee that he will appear in court when the charges are formally laid.'

'Yes,' Zac said, 'that way he can look after his own horses before the feed runs out. There's only enough for another feed and then I don't know what we'll do. That's a matter that could affect you too, Inspector.

If it comes to a legal wrangle, the court might take a dim view of the police denying a businessman the right to care for his business, especially where animals are involved.'

David Armstrong was slowly realising the full implications of holding Martin Maynard under arrest for a long period without charges being laid, especially without legal advice. Suddenly he could see the possible implications: the Commissioner of Police, the Attorney-General, even the Governor might become involved. He gave in without further argument.

'Yes,' he said, 'I have reconsidered the case in view of what you have told me. There are good reasons why he should be released on bail. We can fix it up this morning, now if you like. You did say that you two would go surety, didn't you?'

The upshot was that the Sergeant went to the dormitory and said to Martin, 'You've been bailed, you can go now. Come on.'

Martin still had his bluey coat on so the tins of gold were distributed between the side pockets and his trouser pockets. He walked out with not the slightest hint of being searched or questioned.

He was met in the office by Zac. 'I've got a pony and sulky outside,' he said. 'Let's go.'

As they drove out onto the road towards the goldfield, Martin looked at Zac and said with a wide grin on his face: 'What's been happening? How the hell did you pull this off?'

Zac laughed heartily. 'We've had a very interesting morning. It's been one of those days that we'll laugh about until we finally cash our chips in.' He then gave Martin a detailed account of all that had happened.

'Well, all I can say is, thanks a lot. It's good to have mates. You've done well, extremely well!' and he burst out laughing again. 'But,' he continued, 'there's another chapter to the story. Just wait until you hear that and then you'll have something to laugh about!'

He pulled a tin out of his pocket and handed it to Zac. 'Feel that. What do you think it is?'

'By the look of it, and the weight, I'd say it's gold. Where did you get it?' Zac asked.

Martin then gave him an account of his experience in the gaol. They continued to discuss the episode and enjoyed the irony of it all as they drove the mile or two to Zac's store.

Martin immediately saw to his horses, giving them water and feed, and then joined Zac in his kitchen for a feed himself. He asked Zac to look at the gold and offered to share it with him, but he wouldn't hear of it.

'No, it's all yours,' he said. 'You were the one with the gumption to get it, and take the risk. You keep it all. There's one thing though that I will say seriously: keep all this gold for yourself. I think there's about eighty ounces of it, but don't ever tell anybody else about it. This is one of those things you never tell anybody.'

Neither Martin nor any of his friends ever found out what went on within the police, but Martin was never charged or summoned to court. The whole episode went dead and was never raised again.

Chapter 14

*I*t was with a great sense of relief that Martin left Ballarat that afternoon. He had a full load on board; empty barrels and kegs for
Moles & Keane and, secretly, gold to be deposited at the Bank
of New South Wales in Melbourne.

As usual, he had his rifle and pistols placed where he could quickly
put his hands on them if necessary. The horses were fresh and frisky
from their longer than usual stay at the goldfield and were striding out
enthusiastically. He was looking forward to reaching the first camp to
get some relaxation and a good night's sleep.

The year 1854 was drawing to a close and the gold rushes had
cooled to the stage where the traffic on the road had decreased markedly. It was still a busy road, but the days of a continuous line of traffic
from Ballarat to Melbourne were gone.

There were always a few dozen people camping overnight at the various staging camps, but not the throngs that Martin saw for the first few years of his business. He smiled as he remembered the characters he struck in those days and the amount of surplus luggage and goods of all types that the weary travellers threw away as it got too heavy for them to lug any further. He was still wearing the old bluey coat he picked up one morning near Diggers Rest, and he smiled again at the thought of how handy the deep pockets had been when he stole the buried gold from the gaol at Ballarat.

He reached his lodgings three days later early in the afternoon and parked the wagon behind the stables, unhitched the horses and went into the house. He knew immediately from the stricken look on Alice's face that something was wrong.

'Hello,' he said as he kissed her. 'What's the news?'

'It's bad,' she said, 'really bad as far as I'm concerned. My husband is coming back.'

He felt a stab of surprise and anger go through him as he took her in his arms and held her. She had tears streaming down her face and he could feel her sobbing.

'When is he coming?' he asked her.

'In three or four weeks,' she said. 'I've got a letter from him.'

'Let's sit down and talk about it before Gwen comes home from school,' he said. 'Does she know about it?'

'No, I haven't told her yet.'

She swung the kettle over the fire and threw some kindling on to get a quick boil. 'I'll get you something to eat. You must be starved,' she said. 'I've got some cold meat.'

In a few minutes, he was sitting at the table eating cold meat and bread, with pickles. 'At least we've got a few weeks to get used to the idea. It would have been an awkward situation if I'd got back to find him here, maybe waiting to attack me.'

'No,' she said, 'I doubt that he would give you trouble like that. For all his faults, he's got a fairly reasonable approach to life and would realise that he gave up all his rights when he left us in the lurch like he did. This is the letter,' she said, handing him a single page. It was addressed:

Dear Alice,

I know you will be surprised to get this letter from me, but I hope you will receive it in the same spirit that I send it. I know I did the wrong thing when I went off to the gold rush and left you and Gwen. I think I was a bit mad at the time and couldn't see things clearly. I know it will sound silly to you, but I never stopped loving you and Gwenny all this time.

I know I did you wrong, but I hope you will accept me if I come home. I'm still at the Ovens goldfield, but I can see now that this life is finished. I've got 600 pounds for all my work. I would like to come in about a month.

Please write to me,

Your loving husband,

Eric Bunce

Martin read the letter with interest and a degree of relief. At least he wasn't stony broke like most failed diggers; that was something to be really pleased about. He knew he had to be extremely careful what he said to Alice, and how he said it.

'When will Gwen be home?' he asked her. 'I don't suppose you want to talk about this in front of her.'

'She won't be long. I reckon she's gone to her friend's place to play on the way home.'

'We can talk some more tonight,' he said.

She asked him about the trip and why he was two days late getting back.

'I got arrested in the sly grog shop and put in gaol,' he said with a grin.

He was amused at the expression of utter amazement that came over her face.

'What!' she exclaimed. 'You in a grog shop, and getting arrested! I can't believe it. Tell me all about it.'

He gave her a carefully edited version of what had happened and how it had held him up. They chatted about the episode until Gwen came home from school when she too had to be told about the trip.

Martin knew instinctively that the news Alice had given him would trigger a defining period in his life. His mind was already working on the possibilities that would be open to him. The first one was whether to quit the carrying business and look for other openings on the gold-fields, or whether to look at opportunities in Melbourne. He knew that Victoria was entering a period of great growth. Zac had spoken of this several times, making the point that Melbourne, as the capital, would be a major growth area. Martin already understood this because of his experience in the split timber trade of Van Diemen's Land.

In spite of all the questions in his mind, he knew he had an obliga-tion to his two main customers, Zac Bellchambers and Derek Miles, to get the next load up to them as soon as possible. Whatever he decided to do, he would have to do the right thing by them.

The thought struck him that he would like to discuss his situation with his best mate Zac and he resolved to get back to Ballarat as soon as possible.

When Alice came to his bed late that night, she was very upset and wanted to talk of nothing else than what the return of her husband would mean to her and her daughter. He comforted her as best he could, but he was careful not to give her any ideas that he would consider taking her away from her husband.

'We've got to keep our heads and handle this as sensibly as we can,' he said to her. 'At least there are a couple of things that you can be very thankful for. Firstly, that he has given you time to work things out and secondly, that he is not broke – he has six hundred pounds. Used sensibly, that will be a buffer against any other problems that come up.'

Before she could answer this, he held her close and kissed her as he spoke again.

'I just want to say this. I am very fond of you and I admire you tremendously. I think you've done a wonderful job to manage as well as you have since Eric went off and left you and Gwen. I want to thank you as sincerely as I can for what you've done for me. You've been the perfect helper and I will never forget it – or you. You'll have a special place in my heart forever.

'That's all right for you,' she said with a sob. 'I don't feel just fondness for you; my problem is that I'm in love with you, deeply, and with my whole heart. How can I go with another man whom I will never love while you're in my heart?'

'Alice, Alice,' he said, 'don't make it too hard for yourself, or for both of us. Don't forget, I've had guilt feelings for a long time too; the way I came in here and took you over as if you were my wife and not another man's. You could have tried harder to find Eric. If we had put our minds to it, we could have found him, but I'm ashamed to say that I didn't want to.

'You'll have to decide how to handle Gwen as soon as you can. She is just as important in this situation as we are. After all, it is her father who's coming home. Does she know what the relationship between us has been for the past three years? She is fifteen now, so she probably knows a lot more than we think she does. That just makes it harder for you to handle. You might have to take her into your confidence and tell her more than you really want to. I hope you don't mind me talking like this, but I know how important it is. You have to think ten or twenty years ahead. I don't want to see you make a problem between you and your daughter that will haunt you for the rest of your life.'

'I'll try to think about it more while you're away next week,' she said. 'I know I'm not thinking straight now. All I can think about is parting from you. I don't know how I could handle it.'

'Yes, that's the way,' he said, 'give it more thought over several days. And I think you should consider taking Gwen into your confidence; your relationship with her is more important than your relationship with Eric, or for that matter, with me. One of these days, she will be giving you grandchildren, and you'll want things right between you then.'

At last she went back to her own bed. For the whole of the three years, she had never taken him into her bed because of the risk that Gwen might inadvertently discover that her mother was having an affair with the lodger. Martin smiled to himself as he thought about it. He always approved of the way Alice handled the situation and he supported her, and thought more of her because of it. After three years of such a situation, he knew that not more than one woman in a hundred would be able to continue with the subterfuge. It showed a remarkable strength of character. It occurred to him that Alice would eventually come to terms with the new situation she found herself in and would handle it with commonsense and strength.

The next morning, he was on the road early so as to be first in line at Moles & Keane. He told Cam Ralph that he was considering selling his rig and asked him to keep his eye out for a buyer and also to investigate the market to find out what the wagon and four horses would be worth.

Arthur Lees, the bank manager and by now an old friend, was surprised at the amount of gold Martin had to deposit. He was clearly intrigued by the eighty ounces and asked about it. Martin felt that he was being pumped and in his typical reserved way, he clammed up.

'It's just a deal between me and Zac Bellchambers,' he said. 'He knows all the details and I'm sure he can answer anything you want to know if you drop him a line.'

'The price of gold has risen again lately,' Mr Lees said. 'The price this week is three pounds seven shillings an ounce. That means your account will be over three thousand pounds in credit again. That is in addition to the money you've had on deposit with us, of course. Maybe it's time for you to think about putting a bit more on deposit to earn interest for you.'

Martin told him that he was considering selling his carrying business and quitting the goldfields. 'I've got a feeling that we've had the best of it, and now could be a good time to look for a change. I'll also be looking for somewhere else to live. My lodgings where I am now won't be available after a few more weeks. I don't know what I'll do yet, but maybe we could talk about it when I come back in about ten days,' Martin said.

'Yes, I'd be only too happy to talk with you. Please feel free to pick my brains any time you want to. I do know my way around business circles in Melbourne, if that's any use to you.'

As usual, Martin was back at his lodgings with Alice soon after midday and they had the afternoon together while Gwen was away at school. Martin sensed that she was starting to accept the inevitability of the return of her husband although she wouldn't admit as much in words. He had more sense than to press her too much on any aspect of the situation. He understood her anxiety and felt sorry for her. He would have done anything in his power to help her, but at this stage there was nothing he could see that would be the slightest help. He was convinced in his own mind that the best way he could help her would be to gradually get her to accept the situation and adjust herself to accept it with the best grace she could muster.

The afternoon and evening passed slowly and sadly for them both although they put on the best face they could for Gwen's sake.

As always on his trips to Ballarat, he was on the road early the first morning and spent the first night at Diggers Rest, by now a place of a hundred memories for him. There were twenty or thirty people in the camp that night, a far less number than the old days. As he crawled into his bed, he fancied he could hear the shouting and singing, the oaths and the firing of the wild nights of the old rushes.

He followed his old, well-established practice of resting the horses on good grass at his old camp south of the Black Forest. The last signs of the drought were gone and the country was lush with feed and water. The gum trees had recovered from the severe effects of the bushfire and were again a dense forest of cool greenery.

The creek at Gisborne was running strongly and the farms were lush with grass and crops. The Bush Inn was trading strongly although not as frantically as when Sam Jessup paid thirty shillings each for dinner for himself and Martin and Nellie Houseman on Martin's first trip to the goldfields in 1851.

He reached Zac's store at dinnertime two days later in time to join him for dinner. The two friends had a lot to talk about. Martin told him about losing his lodgings and how that had made him decide to sell his wagon and rig and retire from the carrying business.

Zac said, 'That doesn't surprise me. You've stuck at it day and night for the three years and you've done well. You've made as much, or more money than you could have made at gold mining, unless you'd been exceptionally lucky and struck a real shiner. The thing you have to think about now is hanging on to your money and not losing it.'

They talked for an hour, Zac saying that he too was thinking about quitting the goldfields to try something else. 'Like you,' he said, 'I've had a hard and busy life for the past years, but now I'm set for life if I manage my money properly. I'm not going to rush into anything in a hurry; the advantage we've both got now is that we can afford to sit on our money and live off the interest while we look for new opportunities.'

Martin told him about Arthur Lees's interest in the eighty ounces of gold he had to deposit to his own account in addition to the usual deposits for their partnership. 'I doubt that he will write to you, but if he does, you will know what it's all about.'

'I'll be surprised if he does,' Zac said, 'but it does raise an interesting question of what we should say if we are ever confronted by the police or some other authority. The legal position would be that it is stolen property and we'd have to prove otherwise.'

Martin chuckled as he said, 'It would be an interesting point. We'd be talking about gold stolen from diggers unknown, by the police as bribes and then stolen from the unknown police by another unknown person. It gets very involved and tangled, so I don't think we will ever have to make any explanations to the police.'

In due course, Martin took Derek Miles's freight down to him and, as usual, loaded up with empties. Derek was anxious to talk and Martin thanked him again for his help in getting him out of gaol. He told him he was thinking of quitting the carrying business and the goldfield.

'I think you would be wise to get out now if you can,' Derek replied. 'It's not your fault, but you have made an enemy of Armstrong, "The Monster" as he is known on the diggings, and he is well named. Knowing him as I do, I'd say he will wait his chance and try to get you in retaliation. He has shown in the past that he's got a long memory – like a bloody elephant.'

Martin returned to Zac's place and completed the load of empties. After another cup of tea and a further talk about their plans, he started for home where he found Alice still in a quandary and very unsettled. The only good news that Martin could see was that she had told Gwen about her father wanting to come home and had shown her his letter. Martin could only hope that it would be the start of a resolution of Alice's quandary and an even closer relationship with her daughter.

Late that night when she came to his bed, he told her how pleased he was that she had started to take Gwen into her confidence.

'She's a wonderful girl and you're lucky to have a daughter like her,' he said,' and I wouldn't be surprised if she finishes up being your best friend as well.'

'You could be right about that. Only time will tell,' she said. 'Once you're gone, she'll be my only friend.'

'I don't know how much you've told her about us, if anything, but do you think we ought to end this affair before too long in case she does wake up to what's going on between us?'

'No, I do not,' she said quickly. 'Rightly or wrongly, I'm going to have you as close to me as I can while you're here. Once you're gone, I'll never have the same kind of love in my life again, so don't ask me to give it up before I have to.'

He comforted her and assured her again of his abiding friendship and support.

The next day, Cam Ralph told him that he thought his rig would be worth five hundred pounds all up; that is a hundred pounds each for the horses and the same for the wagon. 'I don't know of anybody who might be interested right now,' he said, 'but it will remain a good business into the future, so it won't be long before you find a buyer.'

Arthur Lees said the same thing and advised Martin not to rush into any deal too quickly. 'Give yourself a few weeks,' he said. 'The first rule in business is to give events time to mature rather than doing everything in a rush.

'But I've had an idea about your need for accommodation. I've got an old client who has a hotel down at Port Melbourne that has a stables. That might suit you for a few weeks or months while you're getting your affairs resettled. Would you like to talk to him? I wouldn't mind taking you down today if that suits you.'

Martin was taken aback at the sudden proposal. He laughed as he said, 'First you're advising me to take things quietly and now you're pushing me along a bit, but thanks for the offer. Yes, I think I would like to have a look at the possibility.'

The upshot was that Arthur called for a cab and within the hour, they were on the premises of the Golden Swan Hotel at Port Melbourne, asking to see the proprietor, Mr Campbell Gunter.

They were shown to a private sitting room upstairs where Campbell Gunter was sitting in an armchair close to a fire burning in an open fireplace. As he stood up to greet Arthur, who was evidently a friend, Martin could see that he was an invalid. He was a slight man about fifty years of age and he stood with a stoop that made him look older. Although he was obviously in poor health, his face reflected a strong character. His features, including his finely formed Roman nose, were even and handsome. He greeted Martin with a smile, but his handshake was limp and brief.

Arthur Lees explained Martin's situation and his need for stables accommodation for four horses for a few weeks. A discussion about the details of Martin's operations ensued and Mr Gunter finished up suggesting that they go down to inspect the stables before talking about rental.

The stables were on the back of the property about a hundred yards behind the hotel which was a large, double storey, brick building that occupied almost the entire street frontage. Martin could see at once that there were stalls for eight horses and a chaff house as well as two large storage rooms, more space than he would want.

He said to Arthur Lees, 'This would suit me very well in the circumstances. I'd prefer something with a paddock, but this will only be a temporary arrangement for a few weeks.'

They went back upstairs to find that Mrs Gunter had joined her husband in the sitting room. She too greeted Arthur Lees as an old friend and he introduced Martin to her with a few brief words of explanation as to who he was. She was much younger than her husband and, unlike him, she looked to be in robust health. She was a beautiful woman whom Martin thought would be in her early thirties.

Within a few minutes, they had agreed on a weekly rental for the four horses, and Martin told them that he would let them know within a fortnight when he would be moving in.

Arthur Lees and Martin returned to the bank and Martin then walked on to where his team was parked at Moles & Keane's.

He arrived at Alice's place, fully loaded for another trip to Ballarat, about the middle of the afternoon to find her worried because he was later than usual in returning from his Melbourne day.

'It just goes to show how a reputation for strict routine and reliability can cause problems at times,' he said with a grin. 'The fact is that I've been held up by business.'

He told her about finding alternative accommodation at the Golden Swan, a piece of news that brought on another bout of weeping.

They had lunch and spent the afternoon together, mainly talking about their plans. He told her what Cam Ralph had said about the value of the rig. On a sudden impulse, he said to her, 'You and Eric should be buying it. It would be a good business for you.'

She was silent for a few minutes and Martin was wondering whether he had said something to upset her.

'I suppose Eric could handle it. He used to be a carrier around here in the old days; he's good with horses,' she said. 'But will he have enough money to buy it by the time he gets home?'

Martin reminded her that he claimed to have six hundred pounds from his gold digging and that it was unlikely he'd lose it all before he got home.

'If you're interested, I'll drop the price by a hundred pounds as a friendly gesture between me and you. I'd like to do something to help you. I've really valued your friendship over the years.'

Martin could see that she was interested and was mulling it over in her mind.

'The problem is that I can't do anything until he gets home and I find out whether he wants it,' she said.

'I can wait for a week or two,' he said. 'I've told the Golden Swan that I'll let them know in a fortnight when they can expect me to move in. In the meantime, I'm obliged to keep Zac and Derek supplied with flour so I'll be doing my trips as usual.'

They left the discussion at that point with Martin hoping to hear more of Eric when he returned from Ballarat in a week's time.

He had a good trip and was back home seven days after leaving. She still had no further word from her husband as to the timing of his return, but she told Martin she had written to him telling him about Martin's rig being for sale and suggesting that he buy it. Martin felt satisfied on two counts. Firstly, it was another sign that she was accepting her husband's return and secondly, that she was seriously interested in buying the rig, something that would give him a sense of satisfaction.

Now that the idea had occurred to him, he felt good about offering to reduce the price by a hundred pounds. He was genuinely fond of her and this would be a lasting expression of his feelings towards her.

Ten days later, he had completed another round trip and arrived home wondering what news would greet him.

She had received another letter from Eric. It was very short but the general tone was friendly:

> *Dear Alice,*
> *Thanks for writing to me. I know it took a lot of patience on your part. I would be interested in the carrying business if that is what you want. We can decide when I get home, in about a fortnight.*
> *Best regards to you and Gwen,*
> *Eric Bunce*

Martin again told her that it was important for him to continue servicing Zac and Derek and that he would be leaving in two days time to do what he hoped would be his last trip to Ballarat.

'If you and Eric buy the business, it will be important that you have my old connections to start with,' he told her. 'There is still plenty of work to be had, but not as much as in the old days.'

When Martin reached the goldfields, Zac had some ominous news for him: 'Inspector bloody Armstrong paid me a social call, asking about you. Where you were, how often you came to the field and when you were expected again.'

'What did you tell him?' Martin asked.

'Not the truth, that's for sure!' Zac said. 'I told him I didn't expect to see you for another week. I don't know what he's got in mind for you, but we can be sure that it won't be anything good. I'm not telling you to run away, but I do think this is a case where it would be sensible to make yourself scarce for a while. I don't think he can do anything official, but we know that bastard doesn't worry too much about mixing up official business with his own thuggery. My advice is: get unloaded as quickly as you can and get back on the road this afternoon.'

That is exactly what Martin did. Two hours later, he was trundling down the road to Melbourne, reaching the first camp well before the sun went down.

He was pleased to see about a dozen travellers in the camp already and he knew that more would arrive before sundown. He knew that if Armstrong was determined to interview him, for whatever reason, and he found out that he was in the camp, it was odds on that he would come looking for him in the night. There was safety in numbers; not even Armstrong would be silly enough to harm him in front of witnesses, but he decided to made provision to avoid being ambushed.

He parked the wagon where it would be surrounded by other campers and he arranged his bed so that he could have two pistols close to hand while he slept. He tethered the horses to trees with heavy halters so they couldn't break away if they were spooked by gunfire in the night, and he arranged some twiggy branches so that he would be warned if somebody tried to sneak up on him while he slept.

The camp settled down to sleep well before midnight and all stayed quiet for several hours. He drifted off into a light sleep but woke a couple of hours later when he fancied he heard horses on the road. He lay quietly, listening. He heard a twig rustle and snap. He peered through the flap and could make out the figure of a man approaching the wagon one step at a time.

He rolled off the bunk, leaving his blankets ruffled as if he was lying under them, and wriggled to the centre of the wagon. The man took ten minutes to finally reach the wagon and stood peering at it in the darkness. He then made the fatal mistake of feeling the blankets to assure himself that Martin was indeed under them. He put his hand over the blankets where it was seized in an iron grip by Martin who jerked with tremendous force, causing the assailant to fall forward and bash his head against the side of the wagon. He let out a cry of pain and collapsed onto the ground. Martin was over him in a second with a choke hold around his neck. As he pulled him over, a pistol fell out of his coat. Martin dealt him two heavy, open-handed blows to the face, one each side.

'Who are you and who sent you? Tell me or I'll kill you!' The man groaned as Martin got his hands around his scrawny neck and tightened his grip. 'Talk or you're done for,' he said in the man's ear.

'I didn't want to hurt you, but he made me,' he gasped as Martin let a little breath into his mouth.

Martin gripped tighter again. 'Tell me the name! Tell me or I'll strangle you this time!' He relaxed the grip enough to save the man from suffocating.

In a weak and tired voice, the man said, 'Armstrong.'

'What's your name?'

'Albert Sims.'

'How much did he pay you?' He tightened his grip again as the man was slow to answer. He again loosened his grip and shook him. 'Answer,' he said into the man's ear.

'He promised me fifty pounds' he panted.

Martin shook his head from side to side. 'Now hear this. Listen carefully because your life could depend on it.'

He screwed Sims's head around so that he could look directly into his face.

'Go back and tell Inspector Armstrong that Martin Maynard will be reporting this attempt to kill him to the Commissioner of Police in three days time. Now go!'

The man was barely able to get to his feet, but Martin slapped him again and made him stand up. He picked up the pistol and put it in his pocket.

'Get going,' Martin said again and gave him a push. He staggered off through the camp where several campers had heard enough to be wakened and were looking towards the wagon although they couldn't see much in the dark.

Two of them came over and asked, 'Having any trouble?'

'Just a bit. It's a thug trying to shoot me, but I was awake and caught him. He's on his way back to his boss at the Ballarat goldfields to report that he failed.'

After a while, the camp settled down and all was soon quiet.

At breakfast, the camp was agog with the news that an attempt had been made to shoot Martin, but he had saved himself, and probably others, by being alert and plucky. Martin repeated what he had told the two campers, taking care not to mention the police, but referring to the assassin's boss on the goldfields. He knew that it would get back to Armstrong within a few days of the travellers reaching Ballarat and he wanted Armstrong to know that he knew the full story.

He had a hearty breakfast with a group of the campers. They were a mixed bunch; a few were old diggers returning to the diggings after a trip to Melbourne and others were making their first trip to the goldfields to try the life of a gold miner as a change from the humdrum of their previous lives.

Martin bade them goodbye and resumed his homeward journey in a happy frame of mind. He felt that after the failed attack on him last night, he would have The Monster off his back forever.

He reached Flemington in the middle of the afternoon two days later where he had another shock awaiting him.

He had parked the wagon in the usual place behind the stables and was unhitching the horses when a man came around the corner of the building. Martin had a quick impression of a well set up man of average height with a brown beard who was walking towards him with his hand held out. 'Good day, I'm Eric Bunce.'

Martin felt a shock of apprehension sweep over him. He had often wondered what this meeting would be like; the return of the long lost husband to find another man ensconced in his home with an attractive wife who was convinced that she had been deserted for good was a recipe for trouble. He had more than half expected a fight. But this fellow seemed like a civilised individual who was acting agreeably. He returned the handshake and resumed his work with the horses.

'They look like a good team,' Eric said.

'Yes, they are good,' Martin replied. 'I brought two of them with me when I came over from Van Diemen's Land three years ago, and the other two I bought here almost two years ago. They've been on the road every week since then.'

Martin soon realised that Eric knew a bit about horses.

'Why do you use a team of four? I'd have thought that two would have been enough to handle that small wagon of yours.'

'I bought the extra two so that I could go on working when the road to Ballarat became almost impassable after the drought broke in '52. I have just gone on with the team of four ever since. I like to be on the road every week and by having four horses getting it easy as opposed to having two a bit overloaded, I can get away with it.'

By this time, he had the horses in their stalls and fed.

'Might be a good idea to go in and get something to eat,' he said. 'I'm as hungry as a horse myself.'

They walked across the yard and into the house together, Martin wondering how Alice would handle the situation.

She greeted him with a cheerful, 'Hello, you're back. I've got the kettle ready for a cup of tea. I suppose you're hungry.'

'Yes,' he replied, 'I am. I'll be pleased to have the rest of the afternoon off.'

They all sat around the table, sipping tea, with Martin tucking into a plate of cold meat and bread. The conversation stalled at that point and silence reigned for a few minutes. Martin, never good at small talk, was wondering what he could say to get it going again when Alice saved the day.

'Did you have a good trip?' she asked him.

He made a quick decision not to mention anything about the attack on him the first night out from the diggings.

'Yes,' he replied, 'everything went as normal. I got a full load home, so I'll gross a bit over a hundred pounds.'

'Eric and I have been talking about the business,' she said, 'and we are interested in buying it if you're still going to sell, and if we can agree on a price.'

'Good,' he said. 'Yes, I've made up my mind to have a change. It's a good business, but after three years, I want to try something else. Cam Ralph reckons it's worth five hundred pounds, but if you're interested, I'll take four hundred for a quick sale.'

'It looks as if we'll be able to make a deal then,' Eric said.

The talk continued for another hour while Eric asked Martin about the best way to manage the business, his contacts on the goldfields and other details that would help him get started. On Martin's suggestion, Eric agreed to travel into Melbourne the next morning to deal with Cam Ralph to learn that end of the business.

Eric produced four hundred pounds in banknotes and paid Martin out.

'We ought to have a drink to celebrate the deal,' Eric said. 'Can we have a beer?'

Martin could tell that Alice was subdued and not very enthusiastic, but she produced two bottles of beer and some glasses. Eric poured out and they were drinking and chatting when Gwen arrived home from school. Martin could tell that she too was feeling somewhat embarrassed and ill at ease about the changed circumstances in the house. She greeted him with a subdued, 'Hello, Mr Maynard, you're back,' and shortly afterwards disappeared into the front of the house.

There was an undercurrent of reserve during tea and as soon as he could, Martin said he was very tired and would go to his room. He was reading the newspaper when a faint tap came on the door and Gwen came into the hut.

'I feel that I want to say something to you. When will you be leaving?' she asked.

'The way things have turned out now, I'll be leaving in the morning,' he said. 'Your father is coming to Melbourne with me and he will take over the wagon as soon as we finish at the warehouse. I won't be coming back here.'

There were tears in her eyes as she said, 'Why did this have to happen? We were so happy until Father said he was coming home.' She stepped close and clung to him.

'Sit down for a minute. There's something I want to say to you,' he said. 'This has been a shock to us all. I suppose it was inevitable; it had to happen some time, but this has been a bit sudden.'

'Poor Mother,' she said. 'She's heartbroken.'

'That's what I wanted to talk to you about. I know you will, but I want you to help your mother as much as you can. She is going to need you as her best friend for a long time to come.

'The other thing is not so easy. That is, I strongly advise you as a friend …' and he paused at that point to interject on his train of thought, '… and I hope you'll always regard me as a good friend to both you and your mother. Give your father a chance to prove that he can do the right thing by you both. Just remember; if you're patient, one of these days he'll tell you why he went off like he did and never contacted you afterwards.'

'I'll try as best I can,' she said, 'but it's not going to be easy. Mother has talked to me and told me a lot. I have known for a long time that she's very fond of you, but now I know the full story. She's put Father into my room to sleep and I'm to sleep with her. I don't know how long that will last, but I guess she'll sort all that out later. But I know she wants to visit you tonight to say goodbye because it could be a bit awkward in the morning.'

He put his arm around her shoulders and said, 'Thanks for explaining that. I think you are handling this well. It's been a real test for both you and your mother, and you are coming through like a woman years older than your age. Good luck, dear girl. You'd better go now. I know you'll be all right.'

She kissed him and left the room.

Later that night, well after midnight, he became aware of Alice in his bed.

'What are you doing here?' he asked her in a low voice.

'I'm determined to be able to say goodbye properly and this is the only way I can do it. Now that Eric has turned up earlier than expected, I don't expect to have any private time with you – ever again.'

'Gwen has told me that you've spoken to her woman to woman, so I think I understand what you're doing.'

'Yes,' she said, 'I took your advice and talked to her about you, and her father, and me, and you were right; she does understand a lot more than I thought. You're a wise sort of a bird, aren't you?'

'Well, I've had a fair bit of experience, one way and another,' he said, 'and I'm very fond of both you and Gwen, and I'm very pleased and relieved that you are so close as a result of what has happened.'

They spent the next two hours whispering about the situation and the way it was working out as well as reminiscing about the last three years. It was a fond and sad farewell for them both, and she was quietly weeping when she left him to go and join Gwen in her own bed.

CHAPTER 15

*M*artin went to the stables early to feed the horses as he usually did before taking them out for an early start. Eric Bunce joined him a few minutes later.

'I thought you might be doing this,' he said. 'I may as well start as I intend to carry on.'

'Good idea,' Martin said. 'Get the horses used to you as soon as you can. As an old horse man yourself, you'll know about that.'

They had breakfast and Martin loaded his swag and his two big portmanteaux onto the wagon. He said goodbye to Alice and Gwen as Eric looked on. It was a restrained farewell with formal handshakes and good wishes expressed to each other, not like Alice's goodbye to him in his hut last night when she had clung to him, weeping bitterly until he had urged her to go back to her own bed.

The two men were riding on the driver's bench at the front of the wagon with Martin handling the reins. About a mile along the road, he stopped the team and handed the reins to Eric.

'I think it would be best if you took over the driving now. It will give the horses a chance to get used to your hands on the reins.'

They drove on in silence for a time.

'I suppose you wondered why I never came home sooner,' Eric said. 'It's none of your business, but I will say something. I got carried away completely by the gold fever and I guess I went a bit mad. I did well at first, but like a lot of others I got hooked on the grog. I lost all I'd made and I thought the best thing I could do was to stay away. I felt it was no good thinking about coming home broke with no chance of getting a start again. I got down pretty low, but about two years ago I got off the grog for good and gradually came good. I got in with some fine mates and we struck a couple of rich claims and I got ahead again. That was when I finally came to my senses and wrote to Alice.

'I'm not holding anything against you or her, but I didn't come down in the last shower so I've got a good idea what went on. In fact, it might surprise you to know that I think she was lucky you came on the scene. At least she had money and could live all right. Now that it's all worked out like this, I'll do the right thing by both of them, Alice and Gwen. It'd be silly to thank you, but I do wish you luck.'

Martin was flabbergasted by this speech and was silent for a minute. Then he said, 'I'm glad to hear you say that. I saw a lot of men on the goldfields like you and I understand what you've achieved and I admire you for it. But I can't help saying, even at the risk of upsetting you, that I couldn't understand how you could go off and leave a good woman like her, and a kid like Gwen, and not keep in touch somehow.'

'Well, like I said,' Eric replied, 'I went a bit mad, and got into a hell of a mess. But it's all over now and I'll try and rebuild my life. I'm determined to win Alice back and I want Gwen to be proud of me again.

That's why I want you to stay away from them both. What's happened has happened, and although I don't like it, I'm not holding a grudge against you, but I don't want to see you about our home ever again.'

'That's a good, straight message you're giving me,' Martin said with a grin. 'I've heard what you said and you can rest easy. I won't be giving you any cause for concern. I hope you do succeed in rebuilding your marriage, but in view of your tone to me, I'm bound to say that you've got to remember that it's all your own fault. Alice is a mighty fine woman and you didn't treat her right. If you can win her back, I say good luck to you.'

'Right,' Eric said. 'We've both had our say now, let that be the end of it.'

They met Cam Ralph and explained the deal they had made for Eric to take over the wagon and the business as a going concern. Cam agreed to continue with Eric where he was leaving off with Martin.

Martin then led the way to the loading bay where they unloaded the empty barrels and kegs, at the conclusion of which he took the reins and drove the rig around to the back of the warehouse where he usually tethered the horses while he did his banking. He was aware that Eric was nonplussed about why he didn't reload immediately while still at the platform. He said to him in a low voice, 'I've got something else to show you.'

When the team was tethered, Martin made sure nobody was watching them and then removed the floorboards from the false bottom on the wagon.

'You can see what this is,' he said as he transferred the containers into a small hand bag. 'There are only two people who know about this secret compartment on this wagon: me and Zac Bellchambers, my storekeeper mate at the diggings. I don't know what he'll want you to do, but I used to bring valuable stuff down to the bank for him and I kept it secret because of the bushrangers. If they ever found out about it, you could bet your last quid that they'd be out to rob you. That's all I can say about it. Zac might talk to you after he gets to know you, but there you are, I've shown you everything. I'll go down to the bank now and pick my swag up from the warehouse later. Goodbye and good luck!'

Eric had a slightly confused look on his face as he said goodbye and shook hands.

Martin met his friend Arthur Lees at the bank and delivered his last consignment of gold for deposit to his and Zac's joint account, and also to deposit the money from the sale of his rig to Eric Bunce. He told Arthur Lees about selling his business and the arrangements for Eric Bunce to carry on.

'At that rate then, you won't need the stabling for your horses at the Royal Swan after all?'

'No, but I'm planning on living there for a few weeks until I work out what to do next,' Martin said. 'I hope Mr Gunter won't be put out by the sudden change in our arrangements.'

'I doubt he'll be worried about it. He did understand that your arrangement with him wasn't final,' Arthur said, 'and the poor man has other worries; he is not well and doesn't seem to be getting any better. What are your immediate plans?' he asked Martin.

'I'll book into the Golden Swan today and settle down for a couple of weeks to find my feet after three hectic years as a carrier,' he replied. 'I'll live off that interest you'll be paying me,' he said with a grin.

'You'd better come in and have a yarn with me in a couple of days. I might be able to help you,' Arthur said.

With that Martin departed and walked up the street towards the warehouse. On the way, he hired a cab which took him there where he loaded his swag and luggage and gave the destination as the Golden Swan at Port Melbourne. Twenty minutes later, he was standing in the foyer of the hotel telling the porter who he was and that he wanted to book in.

'Mrs Gunter knew I'd be turning up one day about now,' he said whereupon the man went into an office that opened off the foyer and brought her out. She greeted Martin by name with a warm smile on her face.

'I wondered when we would see you again,' she said. 'Have you come to move in?'

'Yes,' he said, 'but I won't need the stabling for my horses now because I sold them yesterday.'

'Oh, right. How long are you planning to stay?' she asked him.

'A few weeks. I want to have a spell and look around Melbourne.'

'I think you'd be happy in a room with a view. It's nothing grand, but it's in a quiet part of the hotel and you'll have a view over the stables. As a horseman,' she continued with a smile, 'you'll be interested to see the traffic coming and going from the hotel. Come on up,' she said as she turned away, 'and I'll show you.'

She called the porter over to help with the swag and the cases and walked up the stairway that branched out at the top of the first landing to lead to the two separate wings of the building. She turned left to lead to the east wing and then down a corridor to a room in the north-eastern corner that had a view of the backyard and stables as well as a view of a large section of the town. It was a good sized room with a double bed and a washstand. There was a wardrobe in the corner and two comfortable chairs.

Martin glanced around the room. 'I'll be here on my own, I won't need a double bed.'

She smiled. 'If you're here for a rest, you may as well be comfortable. I won't charge you any more.'

She showed him where the bathroom was, halfway along the

corridor, and the sitting room not far from the top of the stairs. 'Dinner starts at six o'clock,' she said. 'The dining room is downstairs.'

She left, and the porter went with her. Martin was suddenly on his own with nothing to do.

Her mention of the time for dinner made him think of the time, and he realised he didn't own a timepiece of any sort. He had a sudden impulse to have a watch and that started him thinking of other personal desires, such as some smart city clothes and footwear.

He sorted out his clothes, putting on his best trousers and shirt, and packed the rest away in the wardrobe. He sat down on one of the chairs and took a good look out the window and across the view of the town. It was a sunny day and the impression the view gave him was of peace and quietness with hardly a sound to be heard. He idly speculated what the people in the houses were doing.

His mind turned to thinking about the situation he was now in. After the constant work and excitement of the past month, he felt disorientated by the lack of anything to do; he had only finished work an hour or two ago and already he was feeling slightly lost and nervous.

He thought the first thing would be to get himself organised into life in the city for a time. He would certainly be able to afford anything he wanted. He had made a good start, moving into a good hotel, and he would go out this afternoon and buy a few things, including a watch. Yes, that was it, a watch would be very necessary for a city man.

He suddenly thought about food. He knew it was a little after midday, the time he normally had something to eat, usually only a snack while he was on the road, but when at home Alice always served up a dinner of meat and vegetables at this time. He decided to go downstairs and look for the dining room.

He sauntered along the corridor, exploring as he went. He found the bathroom with its big bath on legs about a foot high and a long bench along one wall with four mirrors fixed to the wall.

He found the sitting room; a long, rectangular room with a big table in the middle and sofas and stuffed chairs around the walls. A big window looked out onto the street at the front of the hotel. He noted that there were several newspapers lying on the table.

He proceeded downstairs and asked the porter where to find the dining room.

'Along the hall that way, sir,' he said, pointing to the southern side of the building.

There were people scattered around the large dining room. Lunch wasn't as popular a meal as dinner was at that time in Melbourne; nevertheless, a middle-class hotel like the Golden Swan always had a decent number of diners for lunch most days.

As he sat down at the table and saw the snowy white tablecloth and table napkins with the cutlery service carefully set on each side of the place, he remembered the occasions at Ashburton when he and the Smith boys would be called up to the manor house to act as waiters when Sir Reginald and Lady Palliser were entertaining. It was all a long time ago, but the memory was fresh in his mind. He could still see a picture of the great dining room, all the boys and girls from the estate who had been pressed into service standing around the walls dressed in house uniform, waiting to serve each course as the dinner slowly worked its way through the seven courses that were the standard procedure for important occasions. Equally remembered was the skylarking that went on out in the kitchen with the boys sneaking drinks off the trays as they were carried out, and the girls allowing themselves to be caught in the butler's pantry for the kissing and cuddling before the fearsome butler came rushing in to catch them.

The memories caused him to smile as the waitress handed him a menu to choose the dish he fancied for his midday meal. He chose the roast lamb with mint sauce and vegetables. A feeling of comfortable wellbeing came over him as he unhurriedly ate the meal, and at the end he felt as if he were truly on holiday. He returned to his room to freshen up before going uptown to start his shopping.

He asked the porter how to get a cab to take him into the town and was asked to wait while that worthy character went out into the street and, putting his fingers to his mouth, let out a sharp whistle which was quickly answered by a hansom cab appearing at the kerb.

He was soon walking along Swanston Street, wondering where to start. He could see many upmarket shops with windows crammed full of fashionable clothes for both men and women. He kept his eyes open for a shop that sold watches. He soon found one and then went looking for shops that sold suits of men's clothes.

By the time he returned to his room at five o'clock, he had a veritable swag of booty from his first shopping expedition. He knew it was five o'clock because he pulled the handsome watch from his pocket to check the time.

With some trepidation, he took a bath. The bathroom was a formidable place and needed strong nerves to tackle, but by using his imagination and undoubted courage, he worked out how to put some kindling in the bath heater and run the water into the bath. He emerged after fifteen minutes cleaner and fresher than he had been since leaving Norwood over three years ago.

He dressed in his new suit and boots and after killing more time in the sitting room, he went back to the dining room. He was surprised to find Mrs Gunter hovering around the waitress who was again on duty at the door.

'Good evening, Mr Maynard,' she greeted him, her eyes sweeping over him from top to bottom. 'Have you had a good afternoon?'

'Yes, thank you, very pleasant,' he replied.

'Would you like to join me at my table?' she asked with a smile.

'Why, yes, I would,' he replied, returning the smile.

The smile was genuine because as he dressed in his room and came downstairs, he had felt the first tinges of loneliness, and the prospect of having company at dinner, especially with a beautiful and interesting woman like Mrs Gunter, was pleasing.

She led the way over to her usual table. It was in the middle of the room and allowed her to keep an eye on what was happening.

'I can see that you have been shopping,' she said, smiling again. 'Your suit looks very handsome and a great fit.'

'Thank you,' he said. 'It's a bit daunting, venturing into those upmarket shops in Swanston Street, but I managed it somehow.'

'That's when you should have your wife with you. Wives are great at helping their husbands buy clothes.'

He laughed as he said, 'I haven't got a wife. I'm just a poor man still on his own.'

'That's too bad,' she said. 'Either you're too timid or the girls where you live are too shy.'

'No,' he chuckled, 'I can't blame the girls. I've been too busy working all these years. It's all my own fault.'

'Would you like a glass of wine with your meal? I like to have one at dinner.'

'Yes, I would,' he said. 'Allow me to order a bottle from the waiter.'

'Oh, thank you.'

That was the start of a very pleasant evening for Martin. It was not that he was used to dining formally in hotels, but he was blessed by nature with a practical approach to every aspect of life, and he had the gift of being a relaxed person in whatever company he found himself in.

She was taken by him and interested in his background. She gradually drew him out to talk about his young days of schooling and growing up. Martin was not a loquacious man, indeed most people thought he was a quiet man, but like a lot of quiet people he was eloquent. He was intelligent and well-informed on a variety of subjects. He told her about Ashburton and the life there. He told her enough for her to believe that he came from a good yeoman class family and that he was a man of substance. He didn't mention anything about how he came to be in Van Diemen's Land.

After about an hour, she said, 'Thank you for your company, and the wine. I must go to attend to my husband now. He is not well and he needs me.'

'Thank you,' he replied, 'I've enjoyed talking to you.'

After breakfast the next morning, Martin walked the mile or so into town to get a look at the rapidly growing city and to stretch his legs for exercise. Once in Flinders Street, he found a barber and had his beard shaved off. It was the first time he had been beardless since being arrested in England prior to his trial. He hardly recognised the fresh and clean face that looked back at him from the mirror after the barber had finished. He then had to purchase a razor and shaving equipment so that he could keep his new look by shaving at least once a week.

He filled in the morning by sauntering around the city streets before walking back to the hotel in time for lunch in the dining room, after which he settled down in his room to write letters to his mother in England and to the Drewitts in Van Diemen's Land. He had a lot to tell them about his change of life from the goldfields to the city, for a time at least.

In his letter to his mother and sisters, he told them about the booming economy in Victoria as a result of the gold rushes and the huge amount of money being invested in the new colony that was creating work for thousands of tradesmen, including blacksmiths. He suggested that his brother-in-law George Latimer and his sister Anne should think about emigrating and offered to help them if they decided to make the break from their old home.

He had sent several amounts of money to his mother over the past three years and would send her more in a few days. He told them to address letters to him as 'Care of the Melbourne Post Office'.

As with his previous letters to the Drewitts, he addressed it to 'Mr and Mrs Drewitt and all at Norwood'. He couldn't tell them much more than what he had already written to his family in England. He told them where he was living and a little about Melbourne, how it was growing rapidly and that he had been told that the demand for timber was very strong and likely to increase. He knew that would interest Charles Drewitt, and he had a shrewd expectation that he might hear something from him in respect to timber.

Martin didn't get an opportunity to speak to Mrs Gunter again for the next few days, but he caught sight of her several times in the dining room.

He knew that the big public bar that occupied a large part of the northern side of the ground floor did a roaring trade, especially after five o'clock in the evenings, but he had ventured in there only a couple of times. He was not one to drink in a bar unless with friends and so far he hadn't made any drinking friends in Melbourne.

One evening, he returned to the hotel as the evening trade was going full blast and met Mrs Gunter in the foyer. She was intrigued to see him clean-shaven and couldn't take her eyes off his handsome and fresh complexioned face. He was chatting to her when a ruckus broke out in the bar that could easily be heard from where they were standing. Suddenly a group of men burst out from the bar through the door that gave access off the internal hallway, swearing and yelling; a running fight was in progress between two or three of them and the others were urging them on.

The porter suddenly appeared and tried to get them to return to the bar, but without success. One of the assailants turned around and felled him with a punch to the head. Mrs Gunter was frightened and very agitated, calling out for help from the other staff.

Martin ran over to the milling group of men, calling on them to quieten down and return to the bar. One of them turned on him, throwing a punch at his head as he did so. This was the kind of combat that Martin had learned as a boy from Petala Smith, the gypsy horse steward.

He calmly caught the puncher by the wrist and jerked him forward, stepping to one side as he did so. The surprised man flew past Martin and crashed into the wall. One of his mates saw Martin handling him and he too rushed in to attack him. He got the same treatment and crashed headlong into the first assailant as he struggled to regain his feet.

Martin look around in time to see another hooligan coming at him, so he grabbed him by the arm and gave him the big jerk forward, turning his shoulder and dropping to one knee as he did so. He tumbled over Martin's back and crashed to the floor. Martin caught sight of the other two turning to scramble back through the door into the bar and ran at them full pelt, getting his arms into position for the battering ram contact. The closest man caught the full force across his shoulders and crashed into his mate, bringing them both down as they crashed through the door into the bar.

Apart from looking a bit dishevelled and puffing for breath, Martin was quite composed and was feeling exhilarated; he enjoyed a bit of genuine brawling and knew that he was good at it.

The porter and two other hotel employees had arrived on the scene to join Mrs Gunter. They were all looking at Martin in disbelief at what they had just seen. When she could speak, Mrs Gunter said, 'Thank you for your help. You happened to be here at the right time. Get those animals out of here!' she ordered the hotel men.

One man had to be dragged back to the bar. The other two meekly submitted to being escorted after him.

She turned to Martin, still upset and near tears. 'Thank you again,' she said. 'I don't know how you did it, but it's the best thing that's happened to those roughnecks for a long time. Will you come down to the office for a minute?' and she led the way along the hallway towards the dining room end of the hotel.

'I think we both need a drink after that. You'll join me, won't you?'

He laughed. 'How could I refuse? A pretty maiden in distress can't be refused.'

'What would you like?'

'A sip of the miners medicine would be nice,' he said. 'I'll have a rum, please.'

A waitress appeared as if by magic and Mrs Gunter sent her for a bottle of rum and glasses and a pitcher of water.

'Sit down,' she said, indicating a sofa.

The drinks arrived quickly and she poured a good stiff one for him and a small one for herself which she watered heavily. Martin took a little water in his and held the glass up in a toast. 'Happy days,' he said, and took a sip.

'Well,' she said with a smile, 'I've seen another side of you. Wherever did you learn to fight like that? You'll have to tell me about it.'

He chuckled as he told her about Petala Smith and the way he had taught Martin and his own boys to wrestle and how that led to the advanced unarmed combat.

'It's not something you use in contest wrestling or boxing,' he said.

'In fact, you have to be careful how you use it because you can easily injure people. It's not hard to break an arm or even a leg, so you have to be careful.'

'I wouldn't care if a few arms and legs were broken around here. A lot of the men who drink here are wharf labourers and tradesmen and that sort. Many of them are hooligan types and they like fighting. Since my husband has been ill, things in that side of the hotel have got out of control and it's the worry of my life. I wish I had somebody like you to help me.'

He grinned as he said, 'I don't think I want a job as a pub chucker-outer, but I don't mind giving you a hand while I'm here.'

'I hope I don't have to call on you, but if I do, I will. I think that episode tonight will go the rounds of the bar and have a good effect on them. Most of them are cowards and won't come up against anybody they think can best them,' she said.

'Anyway, have another drink, and you'll have to join me for dinner again tonight. I'd like to hear more about your Petala Smith and his boys.'

'He's got a couple of very pretty girls too,' Martin said with another wide grin.

'All right,' she said with a smile, 'I'll hear about them too if that's where your interest lies. I'm going up to visit my husband for a while. We usually have a quiet drink about now. I'll see you in the dining room in an hour.'

Martin went to his room to fill in the time and then joined her again an hour later. She was genuinely interested in the life at Ashburton and asked him many questions.

'Of course, the lives of the family who owned the estate were separate and different to ours,' he told her, 'but they intertwined to a remarkable extent. The Squire is like the head of the family and everybody on the estate is part of that. I had a good life as a boy and a lad, and I got the benefit of a good education which not many did in England. Even so, I wasn't impressed by the way I was tipped out at a young age when my father died.'

'Are you a natural born Australian, or are you like me, a jimmy-grant?' he asked her.

'Yes, I'm a pure Merino,' she said. 'My father was an Englishman, I was reared on a farm not far from Bendigo and grew up in that district.'

Martin had another enjoyable evening in her company and was disappointed when she had to retire to go to her husband again. As she got up to go, she said, 'I'd like you to come upstairs to see Campbell in the morning. We usually have coffee at half past ten. Would you come?'

'Yes, I'd be pleased to,' he said.

When he entered the Gunters' private sitting room the next morning, he was surprised to see how much worse he was than on his first visit a month ago. They shook hands and he said in a muted voice, 'My wife has told me how helpful you were in handling those ruffians last night. I want to thank you. The way things are going with me, I'd like to have a man like you about all the time to help her. How long are you planning on staying here?'

Martin told him how he was situated and that he wanted time to look around to find a business he could get into. 'But I'm not planning to rush into anything,' he said. 'If it takes six months, I won't care. I'm securely placed and will have an income to keep me going.'

'Maybe we could work something out between us,' Mr Gunter said. 'Would you be interested?'

Martin thought quickly and said, 'Yes, I would be. I've got the time to fill in and I don't like being idle, but whether I'd be any good at hotel work, I don't know.'

Campbell turned to his wife and said, 'What do you think, Joan?'

'I'd like to have the help,' she said quickly. 'Apart from handling the staff, the office and the banking are the biggest worry for me. Since you haven't been well enough to do it, I'm afraid things have gone back a bit. Could we give it a trial for a week or two?'

'If Mr Maynard is willing, I would be too,' he said. 'I think it might work. Arthur Lees gave you a good reference and I've got faith in his judgement. What say you give it a two week trial in return for your board and lodgings, and we'll see how it pans out.'

Martin smiled broadly as he agreed. 'I didn't expect to get a job when I came up for coffee,' he said, 'but I'll do it. The first thing is, can we get onto a first name basis? I'm not used to being called Mr Maynard in my previous business.'

They all laughed as she said, 'Yes, I think that is sensible. I'm Joan and he is Campbell, often called Cam.'

'Now,' she said, 'it's time for our coffee. I'll just run down and get the girl to bring it up.'

They spent another half hour together before Martin could see that the older man was tiring noticeably, so Martin made a diplomatic departure.

He found Joan in the office later in the morning and asked her, 'When would you like to start showing me the job?'

'Now,' she said with a smile. 'What do you want to start with?'

'It's occurred to me that the staff will have to be told something. If you want me to deal with them, I'll have to have some standing and authority. What have you got in mind?'

'Let's talk about it,' she said. 'It's the bar staff and the men I want you to deal with mainly. We used to have a good head barman who could keep control in that department, but he's left to go to the goldfields and the man I've got now is a shifty character – not up to the job.'

'Why not say that I'm acting manager while Campbell is ill?' he asked. 'That would be plausible and would give me all the authority I need. Naturally, I won't do anything without consulting you.'

'Yes, that will do. I'll take you around now and introduce you to them. We'll have time to do it before lunch.'

'We'll start in the kitchen,' she said. 'The head cook is Mrs Mary McGinty.'

Mary McGinty would have passed as an elder sister for Henrietta Smith, Martin thought. She had the same purposeful and no nonsense manner and the same square cut figure.

The head waitress was Eleanor Whitehouse; a pretty, brown-haired woman in her late thirties with a ready smile and a quiet voice.

The porter's name was Logie Jenson. He was an agreeable fellow about fifty-five, and Martin knew from his encounter with the hooligans that he was not very good at fighting.

There was another man out in the stables who shared all the stable-man's and handyman's duties with Logie. His name was Ken Lowrie and he was a fifty year old ex-boundary rider.

The head barman was Steve Carmichael, a squinty-eyed man of forty who looked strong and tough, but whom Martin picked as a faint-hearted coward. He greeted Martin with a subdued voice and a close look. He had evidently heard all about the fight in the hallway and was apprehensive about what to expect from Martin.

Martin asked him how many barmen he had on staff and he replied that he had six. 'It gets pretty hectic here at times,' he said. 'We need them all when it gets like that.'

'Yes,' Martin said, 'I can understand that, and I'll be interested to see how it goes. I'll come back tomorrow morning and you can show me the bar set-up and how you manage things. I'll see you then if not before.'

Martin and Joan returned to the office where she said, 'You've met most of them. There are three more housemaids; they spend most of their time upstairs, making beds, cleaning and the like. We usually have ten or more guests staying at any time, often more. There is a lot of work to do. We'll go in and get our lunch soon,' she said.

'I suppose that's another thing we should think about too,' said Martin. 'If I'm to be on the staff here, it may not be wise for us to be seen dining together at every meal. Don't get me wrong,' he chuckled, 'I enjoy eating with you, but for the sake of propriety, it might be better if I have my own place in the dining room. But you will invite me occasionally, won't you?'

Her cheeks flushed. 'Yes, I suppose you're right. I'll tell Eleanor to put you at the side table.' She looked up at him and said, more seriously than she meant to be, 'Where did you learn all that?'

He smiled again as he said, 'Don't forget, I've lived close to quality and I know a fair bit about how they do things.'

When they went into the dining room, Joan said to Eleanor, 'Mr Maynard will be having lunch with me today, but I want you to set a place for him at number seven, over there near the wall, for his own place for his meals.'

During the afternoon, Joan showed him how she managed the cash and did the banking. Steve Carmichael brought her the cash takings from the bar every morning, already counted, and to this she added the takings from the house and dining room. It was all checked and then taken to the bank. The Gunters had banked with the Bank of New South Wales for many years and as Martin knew, Arthur Lees was a personal friend.

About three o'clock, Joan said, 'I think we should leave the rest for today. You'll see it all tomorrow morning and I've got the doctor coming to see Campbell at four o'clock.'

'Oh, that's a worry for you,' Martin said. 'How is he? Is he making a recovery?'

She frowned as she said, 'No, I'm afraid he is not. As a matter of fact, I'm very worried about him. He seems to be getting worse.'

They parted and Martin went to his room where he made himself comfortable with an *Age* he borrowed from the upstairs sitting room. He read until a little after five o'clock when he went downstairs and along the hallway to the bar. It was already well filled and the barmen were busy. Martin struck up a conversation with a man he judged to be a tradesman of some sort, and when he told him he was just back from the goldfields, the talk flowed easily. He wanted to know how it was on the fields at present and he had lots of questions. Martin had noticed that everybody in Melbourne loved to talk about gold and where it came from and, increasingly, where it was being spent.

While he talked to his new friend, he kept an eye on the barmen. They seemed to be efficient enough, but he noticed they all looked surly and resentful about the work they were doing. He drank four glasses of beer and then it was time to go for dinner.

When he went to the dining room, he found that Eleanor had him sitting at the head of table seven from where he had a good view of the whole room. He thanked her and told her he liked the arrangement.

He thought Joan looked worried when he saw her in the office the next morning. He asked her how Campbell was after seeing the doctor.

'No good,' she said. 'I'm getting a nurse in today to see if that will make a difference. I would like you to come up for coffee this morning, that will be good for him. He likes to feel that he is involved in whatever is going on around the hotel.'

When he went up for coffee, he could see that Campbell was no better. He tried to be as cheerful as possible and made a point of telling him about meeting all the staff yesterday afternoon and that he was quickly getting a feel for the place.

'That's good,' Campbell said in a quiet voice. 'It's like any other business; the main thing is to keep an eye on the staff to see that they're not robbing you. It's not always easy to keep a check on the grog, and the food in the kitchen. They're the two places where they can get at you.'

Martin stayed around for twenty minutes and then found a reason to go back to the office.

He had a session with Steve Carmichael during the morning and had a good look at the system of stock control he was using. The kegs of beer were delivered by the brewery and put down into a cellar under the bar. When a new keg was needed, it was rolled up a ramp and placed at one of the beer stations from where it was tapped in preparation for being sold over the bar. The cases of wines and spirits were delivered by the merchants and also stored in a lock up room in the cellar.

The next morning, after he had checked and organised the cash under Joan's supervision, he suggested to her that he should take the money to the bank himself. She readily agreed and told him to ask Logie Jenson to have the pony trap they kept on the premises brought around to the front of the hotel.

He drove the little vehicle to the bank, found a hitching rail nearby where he could leave the pony and entered the bank. The head teller, who had welcomed him many times over the last three years, didn't know him with a shaved face and new clothes. After a minute, he quickly ducked back into Arthur Lees's office and the two of them reappeared very quickly with broad smiles on their faces.

Martin told Arthur that he had been persuaded to take a job with the hotel on a trial basis and quickly filled him in on the main details.

'I'm delighted to hear you tell me that,' he said. 'I am very worried about Campbell and Joan. I'm afraid he won't be around for too much longer and Joan certainly needs somebody like you around to help her.'

They discussed the job for a while. 'Do you mind if I make a suggestion that could help you keep some sort of check on the stock and the cash flow averages?' asked Arthur.

'No, I don't mind,' Martin said quickly. 'I'd be pleased for any help you can give me.'

Arthur reached into a desk drawer and pulled out some sheets of paper.

'If you make up sheets like these and record the cash takings every day from the different sections of the business, you can quickly see if they are declining. You'll be a jump ahead of any of your staff who might be trying to rob you. Another one is for carefully recording all the kegs of beer that are bought against the number that are tapped in the bar. To do that, you'll need to make the bar staff record every barrel they tap, the date and time and somebody's signature or initials. The same applies to bottles of wine and spirits that are taken from the cellar to stock the bar. It can be done in an ordinary exercise book in a few minutes, and you will soon be able to work out roughly how much cash should be coming in across the bar. Once you get the hang of it, you'll be surprised what control it gives you. It's what they call "constant auditing". We do it all the time in the bank.'

They completed their business and Martin departed with Arthur's words in his ears. 'Come and see me any time. I'm only too willing to help you in any way I can,' Arthur said.

When Martin got back to the hotel, he showed Joan what Arthur Lees had suggested and asked her approval to instigate the system throughout the hotel, starting at the bar.

'Yes,' she said. 'If you think it's a good idea, try it. If we don't like it after a few weeks or months, we can drop it.'

The next two weeks passed very quickly and Martin asked Joan what she wanted him to do – if anything – in connection with the job. He knew Campbell was growing weaker every day and he didn't like the idea of troubling him. He told her he was willing to go along on the same arrangement for a few more weeks if that was what she wanted.

'No, it isn't what I want,' she said firmly. 'I want you to be appointed manager permanently for a one year contract. If you want to leave after a year, then that will be your privilege. I'll talk to Campbell about it; I can do it without stressing him too much. Would six hundred pounds plus board and lodgings be a fair offer? What do you think?'

'I think I'd be happy for a year on that arrangement,' he said with a grin.

CHAPTER 16

*E*arly one morning, Martin was awakened by a knocking on his
bedroom door. It was one of the nurses who had been on duty
with Campbell for the past month. She told him that Mr Gunter
had passed away and that Mrs Gunter would like him to come
to her sitting room. He pulled on some clothes as quickly as he
could and went to her. When he walked into the room, he took
her hand and she clung to him.

Joan was obviously deeply grieved by Campbell's death, and Martin
saw that she truly loved him. There was no doubting the genuineness
of her grief.

'Oh, Joan, I'm so sorry,' he said. 'If there's anything I can do, you
know that you only have to ask me.'

'I hope I am not too much of a burden to you,' she said, 'but I will
need you to help me. I haven't got anybody else who's close to me.

'Don't talk about burdens, dear friend. You'll never be a burden to me. I'll help you to get through this as best I can. Have you any family, or any relatives here in Melbourne we should let know? Maybe there's somebody who could come to be with you?' he asked her.

'No,' she said, 'I was an only child and neither Father nor Mother had any relatives in Australia. It was the same with Campbell. He came out to Australia in 1824 as a lieutenant with the British Army and has no relatives here. He did have a sister who was much younger than him, but she disappeared from the family circle when she was a young woman. She hasn't been heard of since.'

'In that case then, all we need do is let your lawyers, and Arthur Lees, know. There'll be legal things that will have to be done. We'll have to think about a funeral too, but I can go to see the undertakers first thing in the morning.'

The nurse came into the room. 'There's nothing more I can do now, Mrs Gunter,' she said. 'Is there anything I can do for you before I go?'

'No, not really. Mr Maynard will be here to help me,' she said, and then as the thought struck her, she added, 'Yes, there is something. Mr Maynard will have to see the undertakers. Can you recommend somebody?'

The nurse gave them a name and address which Martin scribbled down in a notebook he had with him.

⚓ — — ⚓

It was a small funeral, only about twenty business friends and acquaintances, like Arthur Lees and Mr Waterhouse – the lawyer – and a few other merchants Campbell had done business with over the years. The funeral was held at ten o'clock; Martin kept the hotel closed until midday as a mark of respect.

The lawyer and four of Campbell's closest friends came back to the hotel after the funeral and gathered in the sitting room for the reading of the will. It was a very simple document that left all his worldly possessions, including the Golden Swan, to Joan. Arthur Lees was named as the sole executor.

After the shock of Campbell's death and the sadness of the funeral, it took Joan a long time to get some semblance of balance back into her life. She told Martin one day that the only lifesaver that got her through that dreadful time was his presence on the scene to take the responsibility for the hotel from her shoulders.

'I do know how lucky I was the day you came into our lives, and I appreciate all you've done for me,' she said with a catch in her voice.

A sense of sadness clung to Joan and Martin for several weeks after the funeral. Martin tried to make life as pleasant and easy as possible for her, but as always at a time of mourning, only time itself can heal the pain of readjustment. Life must go on.

Martin had put the continuous audit in place throughout the business and he carefully recorded the figures every day. He had no way of knowing what the cash flows were over the past year, but his record sheets already showed clearly that they were rising under his management.

Steve Carmichael couldn't hide his resentment at Martin's presence and his authoritarian style of management. Martin always kept a civilised and pleasant tone in his voice, but he made all the staff understand that they were to do things his way. When Steve showed signs of rebellion, Martin considered sacking him straight away, but on reflection he decided to try the psychological approach. After all, he was the most experienced barman in the hotel and it would be difficult to find anybody better.

Martin raised Steve's wages by two pounds a week and told him that the strict recording systems were here to stay and if he couldn't handle it, he was free to leave at any time. Steve quickly thought he could handle the paperwork, and in a short time he had a smile on his face and an agreeable tone in his voice. While he was on that path, Martin informed him that the bar staff were surly and rude to customers and that he would have to find a way to make them change their style.

Martin was also unhappy at the number of fights in the bar. 'That sort of thing drives customers away fast,' he told Steve and the other barmen when he had them assembled one morning before opening time. 'At the first sign of a fight breaking out, the offenders have to be thrown out onto the street. Our aim must be to have this bar become known as a safe and civilised place to come for a drink, not as a blood house as it is known now.' He offered to teach them how to handle half drunk and cantankerous customers.

'I can soon show you a few holds that will give you mastery over them,' he said.

One of the barmen immediately spoke up. 'Yes, boss, you could show us a few tricks. It's not easy handling those fellows. They are tough and wild and the trouble is, they like fighting.'

'Right, we'll start now if you like, and we'll take half an hour every morning for the rest of the week. If you get sick of it, tell me and we'll talk about it again.

'There are two simple principles you've got to learn and remember. The first is to distract their attention somehow. In other words, con them. I often use yelling at them, or getting them to look somewhere else so that I can get a quick one in while they're distracted. The other one is to use their strength against them in a way that again takes them by surprise. If a man is swinging a punch at you, grab his hand and pull him towards you. He will be taken by surprise and lose all control. Nine times out of ten, he will fall over and then you've got a huge advantage over him, both physically and psychologically.

'The oldest trick in the book is to con a man to shake hands, then grab his hand and pull it towards you hard. By the time he recovers from his surprise, you'll have his arm up behind his back and he's heading for the door. The main things are to keep your nerve and practise, practise, practise.

'One last thing. You might be tempted to get big ideas about yourself, how good you are and that kind of foolishness, and deliberately hurt people. That is assault and it can get you into prison fast, so be careful what you do. Only ever use enough force to get control. I won't have thuggery of any kind. I want this hotel to be a friendly, safe and civilised place where people can come for a quiet drink and a good time.'

As it turned out, the men enjoyed the training they did and took immense pride in the skills they learnt. Even after the first two weeks when Martin was satisfied that they had learnt enough to handle themselves creditably, they asked him to continue the training for a couple of mornings a week.

Martin had the satisfaction of seeing the behaviour of the patrons in the bar improve markedly. Once the word had gone around that the barmen would not tolerate brawling, and that they could throw even the toughest men out, the new order was accepted. Better still from Martin's point of view, the record sheets showed that cash takings were increasing every week.

Martin took Arthur Lees up on his offer of advice and help and spent an hour every month discussing his own and the hotel's affairs with him. The two had been friends for a long time and grew even closer as the months went by.

Martin was worried that Joan was taking a long time to recover her balance after Campbell's death and that she needed some interests outside the hotel business. He mentioned this to Arthur one day and asked if there was somewhere he could take her where she would meet a completely different set of people.

'Yes,' Arthur said immediately, 'you can take her to the races. My wife and I often go and we would be delighted to have you both with us. Let's start now,' he said with a grin. 'Will you bring Mrs Gunter to the races on Saturday? We'll pick you up at the Golden Swan at midday and return you in the evening.'

Martin laughed and said, 'Thanks, we'll be glad to accept. You're a man of action when the occasion demands it, aren't you?'

Joan was surprised when Martin told her that he had accepted an invitation for the two of them, but she raised no objection.

'I'll have to see what I've got to wear,' she said. 'It's a long time since I went anywhere like that and my old dresses are out of fashion now.'

The next morning she had Logie drive her into the city in the pony trap and came home at lunchtime laden with parcels.

Martin had his good suit brushed and pressed so that he would look the part as well. He had a good smile to himself at the thought of how much his life had changed since the day he stepped ashore at Hobart as a convict not much more than ten years ago.

Both Joan and Martin enjoyed their day at the races immensely. Arthur and Barbara Lees were great hosts and good company. Joan had enjoyed the outing so much that she didn't want them to go. 'Why don't you stay and have dinner as our guests?' she asked. 'You can ask the cab to come for you at, say, ten o'clock.'

They agreed, so the party went on all through dinner and afterwards upstairs in the sitting room. When the Lees had finally departed, Joan turned to Martin and said, 'What a lovely day it's been. Thank you so much for thinking of it. I know it's well and truly time I started to snap out of this black hole I've been in, and once again it has been you who's got things rolling.'

Martin knew that she had a very good opinion of him as he did of her; he found her very attractive physically and he revelled in her company. She was a lively and vivacious woman who liked a joke and a good laugh. In addition to that aspect of their relationship, he had developed a great respect for her business abilities. She handled the staff with competence and dignity and they, in return, liked and respected her. He was tempted to build a closer relationship with her, but thought that not enough time had passed since the death of her husband and that he should wait for a more appropriate time.

They worked closely every day and got on well together. From their first meeting, she had found his slight reserve in manner coupled with a strong sense of humour very attractive and the truth was that she was already well on the way to being in love with him. She knew she was nine years older than him and that in ordinary circumstances, this would preclude any thought of marriage between them, but like all women in love – or falling in love – that little problem became less important as the weeks passed.

They were now quite relaxed in each other's company and as the weeks passed, she wondered why he had never made any further advances to her; she felt sure that he found her attractive. The idea gradually developed in her mind that he was being put off by the proprieties of their situation, or that he was too shy to press his attentions on her. She had the benefit of a life experience that included being brought up in a relatively well-off family and mixing with people of a similar background, of spending three years at an exclusive girls school and then of twenty years of marriage. Her parents had urged her to marry Campbell Gunter even though he was fifteen years older than her; he had the right social background and was well-off as a result of being given a land grant that joined her parents' property because of his army service. She thought about her present situation a lot, and Martin Maynard seemed to fit into her future naturally.

The outing to the races had sparked off more interest by them both in going out. They had more days at the races together and took the opportunity to attend shows at the several theatres in the city as they came on.

A couple of months had passed since their first day at the races when one night they returned home together from a late show. She asked him to go up to her sitting room where she had a light supper waiting for them. She asked him to open a bottle of wine and poured drinks for them both. Martin was intrigued by this display of intimacy and wondered where it was leading. She chatted on about the show and other functions they had attended together and poured more drinks, encouraging him to partake.

She moved over to sit beside him on the sofa and said, 'I just want to thank you again for helping me over the past few months. You are a wonderful man and I have grown very fond of you.'

Martin coloured up at this and mumbled, 'I'm very fond of you, too,' and put his arms around her. He kissed her and she responded without reserve. He felt himself stirring with desire and crushed her to himself. After a minute, he disentangled himself and held her so that he was looking into her face.

'If you get me stirred up like that, I doubt I can restrain myself like a gentleman should.'

'I don't know that I want you to restrain yourself,' she said with a mischievous smile on her face.

'Is this an invitation?' he asked. He gave a muffled chuckle while his heart was beating like a plover's wings.

'Yes, I suppose you could call it that,' she said. She stood up. 'You'll come to my room, won't you? We'll be secure and private there. Come on.'

A lamp was burning in her bedroom, turned down low. Martin helped her out of her dress and then left her to take the rest off herself. He threw his clothes off frantically and turned to see her standing near the bed. He took her in his arms and kissed her before they fell into the bed in each other's arms.

After the first gust of passion had been satisfied, they lay close together with her arms around his neck.

'I know now that I do love you,' she said in a low voice. 'I've felt it coming on for quite a while and now I am certain that I love you.'

'I've had strong symptoms of love for you for a long time too,' he said, 'but under the circumstances, I had to wait for the appropriate time. Thank goodness you had enough sense to lead the way.'

'My darling man, you needn't have waited so long,' she said.

'While we're talking about us, and things like that,' he said with a smile, 'I don't want to wait too long for the next big thing. Will you marry me?'

'Of course I will,' she said with a little laugh. 'Just you try to get away!'

'That's the cue for a gentleman to kiss his lady,' he said as he pulled her to him again.

Later, after they had both dozed for a while, he asked her how soon they could marry.

'Soon,' she said. 'As soon as possible as far as I'm concerned. Have you any relatives or close friends you would want at our wedding?' she asked.

'No, not really,' he replied. 'The only one I can think of in Melbourne is Arthur Lees. I've got a few friends in Van Diemen's Land, but it's not practicable for them to come to Melbourne, and I don't suppose you want to go over there to get married,' he said with a laugh.

'Well, no, I don't, but I wouldn't mind going there for a trip some day. I've heard it's beautiful.'

They married in a church only two blocks away from the hotel on Saturday the first of November 1855 and had a dozen friends in to a small luncheon afterwards. Arthur Lees proposed the toast to the bride and groom and a happy time was had by all. There was no thought of going away for a wedding trip because of the responsibility of keeping the hotel running. There had to be at least one of them on the job at all times.

Joan had her private suite, including her bedroom, redecorated and refurnished, so she felt that as if it was a completely new start. It was the happiest period in her life. After a few weeks of Martin's vigorous lovemaking, she knew she was the luckiest woman in the world. She bloomed and became more beautiful than ever and her happiness showed in her face and her vitality.

After the first year, they still delighted in each other's company even though they worked closely every day. The excitement was ever present for them.

Martin had several letters from his family in England. Life was going on in much the same way for them, with his mother now approaching old age in her sixties. She was very appreciative of the money he had been sending her and assured him it had made her life a great deal more comfortable.

His sister and brother-in-law were seriously considering emigrating, but they couldn't make up their minds at present. Martin strongly believed that it was on account of their mother; they didn't want to leave her with only his youngest sister living nearby, even though she too had a family of three children. Martin felt impatient at their conservative attitude to the idea of emigration. If they had any brains at all, they'd all up stakes and come to Australia, he thought.

The biggest shock he had felt since his marriage was when he had a letter from Charles Drewitt telling him that Mrs Drewitt had taken ill early last year and had died in the spring. He felt genuine sympathy for his friend, the 'Squire', and wrote to him trying to express his shock and dismay.

That news was lightened somewhat by another letter six months later telling him that Rebecca had married a young mining engineer and was living in Launceston. Martin had always had a special feeling for Rebecca, and deep in his heart he had harboured secret thoughts about her and her future.

The hotel continued to prosper and was making more money than it ever did, even at the height of the gold rushes. Gold still brought great wealth to Melbourne and was making the colony surge ahead in many ways, not the least being at Port Melbourne. There was now a railway running from the city a couple of miles down the river to the port. It was nothing unusual to have fifty or more ships berthed in Hobsons Bay, waiting a turn at the wharves for unloading and loading. Hundreds of men were employed as wharfies, labourers and tradesmen of all descriptions. One or two hundred of them patronised the Golden Swan on a daily basis and, under Martin's management, it had made a name as a congenial watering hole where good drink was served in civilised surroundings and safety. It was widely known that brawling and riotous behaviour were not tolerated on the premises and this was a good drawcard for many.

Joan kept up the standard of the dining room and the accommodation side of the Golden Swan, and it had built up a loyal following of country people who periodically came to Melbourne for business and recreation. The place was always full for the big Melbourne races and other big events of special interest to the squatters.

During the first few months of her marriage to Martin, Joan wondered if she would become pregnant to him. She had never had a baby and now that her child-bearing days were drawing to a close, she daydreamed again about becoming a mother. She didn't know why she and Campbell had never had children and supposed that it was because one of them, or maybe both, lacked the natural ability to conceive.

Martin's attitude to parenthood was: 'If it happens, wonderful, but if it doesn't, you're still my beautiful wife.' He sympathised with her longing, but never encouraged her to dwell on it.

Another letter arrived from Norwood. This time it was from Charles Drewitt asking Martin to make certain inquiries in the timber trading circles in Melbourne with regard to the future prospects for timber sales. Martin raised the matter with Arthur Lees at their next meeting, asking him for introductions to people in the trade who could be relied upon for sound information.

Martin travelled all over Melbourne seeing the people Arthur had recommended and listening to their forecasts for the future of building activity in Melbourne and the regions of the State of Victoria. Almost without exception, they were full of confidence in the future of the state and the prospects for building for many years to come.

'Everything that has happened during the gold rushes, and now the deep mining of gold, points to a continuation of these good times,' one of them said, 'and the way Melbourne is growing, it will take years, probably decades, before the demand for houses and other buildings is met. If you've got good quality timber at competitive prices, you can't go wrong. I know that you've got good timber in Van Diemen's Land, but you'll have to supply it as sawn timber cut to the required sizes; the days of split palings and stuff like that will soon be gone, never to return.'

This opinion was supported wherever Martin went and he reported as much to Charles Drewitt by letter within a couple of weeks. He finished his letter by saying that if Charles was looking for a business partner to be located in Melbourne, he would be interested in any proposition he might be thinking about.

A further letter came a couple of weeks later. Charles was well aware that the market for split timber was drying up and he was seriously looking at starting a large sawmill to provide the kind of timber that would be required. It would be too big an investment for any one person and if his investigations were favourable, he would be looking for partners, or maybe floating a company by issuing shares. He expressed a willingness to be associated with Martin and asked him to look around sawmills in Victoria to see what they had in the way of modern machinery.

'If we were to undertake a project like this, we would have to get the best machinery that is available, so anything you can find out would be very valuable information,' he wrote.

Once again Martin turned to Arthur Lees for suggestions.

'I wouldn't recommend that you go off to travel around the state,' Arthur said. 'There are engineers here in Melbourne who are experts on all kinds of machinery, including sawmilling machines. I can give you introductions to three good men I know who would be able to help you. One fellow especially I think would be your best bet. He's a Canadian, and I know he's had a lot of experience in his own country. His name is Alexander Wright. I'll arrange for you to meet him within the next few days.'

Alexander Wright and Martin got on well right from their first meeting. They were about the same age and in many respects were similar in personality. As usual with Martin, he told Alexander in uncomplicated terms what his interest in timber was and that he wanted information and advice regarding modern sawmilling machinery suitable for installation in a new mill in Van Diemen's Land.

'I think I can help you with that,' Alexander said in his Canadian accent, 'but first, you had better start calling me Lex. I'm not a man very strong on formality.'

Martin laughed and said, 'Yes, that is what I am used to myself. I've spent a lot of time on the goldfields and there's not much formality up there, I can assure you.'

'There's something I can show you,' Lex said. 'Not too far from where we are today, I've supplied machinery for a small sawmill here in Melbourne that you should have a look at to give you some idea of what I can do. It's down at Port Melbourne and they bring their logs up from Gippsland by ship. I can take you there any day that suits you.'

Martin laughed heartily. 'Port Melbourne! That's my home address. Yes, I do want to see it. I can go tomorrow if that suits you.'

The next day, Lex picked Martin up from the hotel in a fancy trap drawn by a high stepping horse and drove him two miles down the road to the mill. It was situated on a wharf on the side of the river and a small steamship was berthed at the wharf only thirty yards from the mill. They arrived in time to see a small log being winched out of the ship and up to the mill by means of a long puller chain powered by the same steam engine that powered the mill.

They stayed at the mill for a couple of hours, watching the logs being pulled up from the wharf and manoeuvred onto the breaking down bench where they were reduced to large billets before being put through the reduction benches. The various sized pieces of timber, all of a remarkably uniform size, were then transferred out to the yard where they were carefully stacked.

'This is a small operation,' Lex said. 'It's really a trial run. The men who set this up were worried about how they would manage the shipping of the logs. As you can see, the logs are rather small; they've got to be because of the shipping.'

'Yes, I had noticed that. The logs in our forests are giants by comparison,' said Martin. 'If we reach the stage of getting really serious about this venture, I think you would need to go to Van Diemen's Land and see the trees we would be handling before making any decisions about machinery.'

'I wouldn't mind doing that,' Lex said enthusiastically. 'I've heard it is a beautiful place, and full of wonderful forests.'

Martin reported all this to Charles Drewitt in a long letter. He reported the advice that Arthur Lees had given him, the outcome of his talks with the timber merchants and how impressed he was with Alexander Wright. He told him he had suggested to Alexander that he travel to Van Diemen's Land to look at the forests. The tone of his letter was optimistic, and supportive of the idea of getting into the timber trade.

The name of Van Diemen's Land was changed when it became Tasmania in 1856 after achieving full self-government under a bicameral parliament. This important change was achieved not without some heart burning on the part of the older and more conservative residents of the island, but with joy for all those who wanted to remove any vestige of the old convict system that was the foundation of the colony. Charles Drewitt and Martin Maynard had their own private thoughts on the issue that would not concur with those of many of the people who had campaigned so strenuously to put a stop to convict transportation, a system that had made it possible for them both to escape a life of deprivation in England to get a new start – and eventual success and wealth – in Van Diemen's Land. But both of them were realists who understood that the new world was a constantly changing place and would continue to change for as far ahead as anybody could see. They both adopted the new name and started to use it immediately.

In spite of the fact that Martin was now spending a lot of time thinking about going into business as a timber merchant, he never let his attention to the hotel stray too far. He and Joan continued to work as a well-matched team and all the sections of the business were doing well. Between them, they had become very well-off and enjoyed living well. They continued to enjoy a full social life with days at the races and evenings dining out at fashionable restaurants in the city with friends. Melbourne had a number of theatres and there was always a selection of shows to be seen.

Martin and Joan had now been married for two years as they prepared for Christmas 1857. Melbourne was booming and Port Melbourne was getting its full share of the business.

The huge wealth generated from the goldfields had given the colony's economy a boost that resulted in more taxes flowing into the treasury coffers, and this in turn had made money available to upgrade all the roads around Melbourne and out into the regional districts. The main streets were being macadamised and communications were being upgraded by the arrival of the electric telegraph. The Port Phillip Heads were already connected to the city, so the merchants were able to be prepared to handle the arrival at Hobsons Bay of the ships that were bringing an ever increasing stream of imports.

Wages were high and customers at the Golden Swan liked to spend a fair share of their money on beer. The streets were full of imported New York buggies, and ice imported from Boston was on sale at five shillings a pound. Gas was being generated in Melbourne and rapidly connected to the suburbs. The city streets were lit by gas, a wonderfully modern innovation that was a source of pride for all Melburnians.

Since the famous clipper ship, the *James Baines*, had startled the world by sailing from Liverpool to Melbourne in sixty-five days with the 1854 Christmas mails aboard, the postal services between Australia and England had continued to improve. Martin was now able to receive letters from his family at Strathfield three times a year.

He received another letter from Charles Drewitt in connection with the sawmilling proposal. He had decided to travel to Melbourne himself to see the people Martin had been dealing with and said that he would travel across the Strait by the new steamer now running a regular service from Launceston every week.

Joan was excited at the prospect of meeting Martin's old employer. Martin had long ago told her the true account of his conviction and transportation in order to get to Van Diemen's Land, and of his experiences as a convict. She was intrigued by the story and never doubted his account. In fact, her admiration for him as a person went even higher.

'I'm telling you now,' he said, 'because you can be sure that some time in the future you will hear that I was a convict, and I don't want you hurt by the thought that I wasn't open and honest with you from our earliest meeting. I'm not the least bit ashamed by what I did. In fact, it's just the opposite. I don't want you to think I'm a boaster, and I might hasten to say that I would never talk like this to anybody else, but privately I'm proud of what I've achieved.'

'Don't think that I might doubt you,' she said. 'I picked you from the start as a special man, and nothing that you've told me alters that first impression. All it's done is confirm what I thought of you in the first place.'

'I'll be interested to hear what you think of Charles Drewitt,' he said. 'He's one of the best men I've ever known, but not everybody takes to him at first. He can be very offhand and even a bit arrogant, but he's solid gold, I can assure you of that.'

'If that's what you think of him, my darling husband, I'll give him a fair hearing and the benefit of the doubt,' she laughed.

When he arrived and met Joan, they took to each other like father and daughter. She made a fuss of him and made sure the staff waited on him hand and foot, giving him all the respect and honour of a visiting person of great importance.

Thanks to all his years of hardship and struggle, and eventual success and wealth, Charles had a strong understanding of the vicissitudes of life and was able to judge a person as to their value as a human being. He quickly judged Joan to be a person of innate quality. He also felt a sense of thankfulness and happiness that Martin had arrived at a great success early in life.

Martin lost no time in taking Charles to renew his acquaintance with Arthur Lees. Arthur, as usual, met them in his office. To mark the occasion, he had his staff arrange a special morning coffee function to which he invited several of the leading timber merchants.

The two old friends talked at first of old times and business that had been transacted between them, and then the talk turned to the proposed sawmilling project.

'I'm surprised, although I shouldn't be, that you are still looking for new business opportunities after all these years, but then you always were a goer, weren't you?' Arthur said.

Charles laughed in a relaxed gesture of goodwill. 'Yes, I've not changed. I plead guilty. I'm still looking for the excitement of doing things and having a go. One of these days, I'll be called to account, I know that, but in the meantime I'll enjoy it while I can.'

Martin was struck by this statement; he had never heard Charles

Drewitt speak in that philosophical way before. A sudden feeling of predestined fate swept into his mind but was as quickly swept aside.

After meeting Arthur, Martin took Charles to meet Alexander Wright. Charles again demonstrated that he had a full grasp of the details of the proposal, particularly in relation to the importance of having markets secured before production started. This meeting finished with an invitation from Charles for Lex to stay at Norwood for however long it took for him to get a good look at the forests in the Don district.

The three of them – Martin, Joan and Charles – had a celebratory dinner at the Golden Swan that night. It was a good night for them all. Joan felt that she was getting to know Martin's family and instinctively saw Charles as a father, Martin felt relieved that Joan and Charles had hit it off so successfully and Charles felt a glow of satisfaction that Martin, a man whom he had come to regard as a son, was doing so well.

A week after Charles had departed to return home, Joan complained of a headache and nausea. They put it down to the infectious colds that were sweeping Melbourne at the time and she went to bed for a couple of days with lemon drinks and an extra blanket on the bed.

She recovered quickly, but three weeks later she had the same symptoms. Again she took to her bed for a couple of days to rest and again threw off whatever it was.

When it happened again a few weeks later, Martin insisted she have the doctor. After the doctor had completed his consultation with her, Martin hurried up to her room to hear what his prognosis was.

'He said it was just a little infection that is going around Melbourne at present. He told me to rest and to drink lemon to ease the congestion,' she said.

A week later, she told Martin that while she was bathing she had felt a small lump in her left breast and was apprehensive about what it was. He felt her breast and agreed that there was something like a lump. Neither of them had ever heard of anything like that being a problem.

Martin stewed over the news for three days before saying to Joan, 'I want you to ask the doctor about the lump. Let's see what he thinks of it.'

'I don't like asking him. What will he think?'

'I don't know, but the important thing is we want to know whether it's important. If you feel too embarrassed to ask him, then let me ask him.'

'No, I'll talk to him myself,' she insisted. 'It's not my embarrassment I'm thinking about, but his. Some doctors are funny about womens' problems.'

The doctor examined her breast but was unable to say what the lump was and whether it had any significance.

'These lumps come and go on various parts from time to time,' he said. 'I doubt that it's important. It's not very big and my expectation is that it will disappear after a time.'

'That's good news,' Martin said when he was told. 'I thought that could be the case.'

'You're as sound as a bell,' he chuckled as he took her in his arms, 'and good-looking too, my lovely wife.'

Martin had increased his understanding of the timber trade and the prospects for the long-term future of the construction industry in Melbourne. He had been thinking continuously about Charles Drewitt's proposal for a mill to supply Melbourne with timber and had become more convinced than ever of its soundness.

He wrote again to Charles, telling him of his increased belief in the proposal and suggesting that they should establish a large warehousing operation in Melbourne themselves in addition to supplying the builders who had signed up for contracts. He believed they could build a big trade on the basis of providing a continuous and ready supply on demand at competitive prices.

Charles replied a fortnight later, agreeing with Martin's assessment of the situation, saying that his main backers were in agreement and that Martin should now assume that the proposal would go ahead. The syndicate, as Charles referred to them, believed the best approach would be to set up a company and issue shares that could be traded in the future. Charles would be acting as chairman of the interim board of which Martin would be a member with special responsibility as the Melbourne representative. The legal work of setting up the company would be done by Mr Algernon Stackhouse of Launceston, and it was planned to have a prospectus out for investors within a month.

Charles urged Martin to arrange for Alexander Wright to make his visit to Van Diemen's Land as soon as possible so that work on planning the mill could be started. Lex made the voyage to Launceston a week later where he was met by Charles and taken to Norwood by a new light coach Charles had recently had made by Thomas Carter. It was drawn by two well-bred, grey horses and because of the recent upgrading of the road from Launceston to the Mersey, it was possible to drive to the Don in one day. Lex returned at the end of two weeks full of enthusiasm for the sawmill proposal.

'You were right about the forests,' he said. 'There are enough trees on the north coast to keep a large mill cutting forever. I'll have my recommendations and estimates ready for you in a week from now.'

He was as good as his word and that made it possible to have the prospectus out a month later. Martin took it to Arthur Lees to get his advice and comments. A day or two later, Martin was in his office on business for the Golden Swan when he said that he'd read the proposal and liked the idea, albeit with some reservations.

'The key to success will be the quality of the management that takes control. If they are competent, it will be a money spinner, but if you get the wrong man in charge it might be a different story,' he said. 'How much are you thinking about putting into it?' he asked Martin.

'I think I'll buy two thousand pounds worth of shares,' he replied.

'That's a big investment. Do you really think that's wise at this stage of the company's development?'

'Under the circumstances, with me being a director, I feel I should make a decent investment,' Martin replied.

'That's where I'd like to talk to you as an old friend, and as your financial adviser, if you don't mind,' Arthur said.

'No, of course I don't mind. You should know me well enough to know that I want your straight talking advice, not some soft soap words to make me feel good.'

'Right, I do know you pretty well and I'm not surprised to hear you say that. It's just that you may be thinking you want to keep up with Charles Drewitt and some of his wealthy friends. There's no need for you to do that; if you want more shares later, I don't think you'll have any problem getting them.

'Your best course is to take what is a reasonable and appropriate level of risk in the new company and wait to see how it pans out. As I said, it's going to depend on the management. Too often a new company like this gets into trouble in the first two or three years and a lot of money is lost; but more importantly, if that happens, a shareholder with a smaller stake – like you – is then in a position to buy a much bigger stake, and maybe control of the company, at a low price.'

'I must say, I haven't thought like that, and not that far ahead. But I can understand what you're saying. On reflection, I think I'll cut back to one thousand pounds worth of shares.'

CHAPTER 17

A month after consulting the doctor about the lump in her breast, Joan suffered another attack of a heavy cold and headaches and had to take to her bed. Martin sent for Doctor Trebilco immediately and waited outside the bedroom while he examined Joan.

'What do you think the trouble is, Doctor Trebilco?' he asked. 'For her to be going down like this every few weeks must indicate that something is not right.'

'Yes, it is a worry,' the doctor said, 'but I can see nothing wrong that would be causing this trouble. These things come and go at times without any apparent reason.'

'Would you recommend we seek a second opinion?'

'Yes, I can recommend a senior doctor whom I know well. He's a good man, but whether he can help remains to be seen. You would have to take your wife to him; he wouldn't do house calls out here at Port Melbourne.'

The arrangements were made for Joan to see Doctor Bellinger in his Collins Street rooms in three days time, an arrangement that indicated the urgency of the case, but he wasn't able to give them any more help than Doctor Trebilco had offered. He prescribed bed for a week and a special tonic he prescribed and had made up in his dispensary.

Martin had a feeling of hopelessness come over him. His instinct told him that Joan had a serious problem, but he had no idea what it could be and he didn't know where to turn to next for advice that he could rely on.

By the end of the week, Joan had recovered enough to get up and come downstairs for an hour at a time. They had four happy weeks while she seemed to make a full recovery, but one morning she woke up with the same old fever and listlessness. Martin immediately went round to Doctor Trebilco's rooms and demanded he arrange another consultation with Doctor Bellinger for as soon as possible.

Martin insisted on speaking to the doctor after the consultation, but he got no satisfaction from the conversation.

'The position is that we can't determine what is causing these symptoms in your wife, Mr Maynard. The lump in her breast is still there, but it hasn't grown any bigger. If she is developing what we call a growth then we can't be sure until it grows bigger, and even then, I am sorry to say, there is not a lot we can do. If it comes to a matter of controlling pain, we can give her a measure of relief by giving her laudanum, but she is a long way from that condition.'

Martin was alarmed. 'Good God, man! Are you telling me that my wife has a terminal illness?' he asked.

'No, I'm not! Doctor Bellinger snapped. 'I'm telling you that we can't diagnose her case. All we can advise is that you make life as easy and pleasant as you can for your wife for the next few months and see what happens.'

'Isn't there anything we can do? What about seeing other doctors in Melbourne? I don't want to be rude or hurt your feelings, but you can see the quandary I'm in. If there's any chance of getting help for her, I will do anything. I don't care what it costs.

'I understand how you feel, Mr Maynard. We doctors are not without sympathy for the people we don't know how to help. I am very sorry for your wife, and for you, but I'd be derelict in my duty to be less than honest with you. Yes, I can arrange for another doctor to see her, or even two doctors together, but it will cost a great deal of money and I have to tell you that there is little chance they can do anything more than Doctor Trebilco and I have done.'

'Thanks for being honest with me,' Martin said. 'I appreciate that, and even if it is an apparent waste of money I want you to organise a consultation with your two colleagues.'

Martin was determined not to let Joan see how worried he was. He was very careful how he worded the information that she was to have a consultation with two more doctors. If she had any suspicions that things were not going as well as they had hoped for, she gave no sign of it.

The consultation took place a fortnight later. It was another two days before the two doctors would give their considered opinions which were dressed up in a deal of medical phraseology that sounded impressive, but at the end it was nothing more than what the others had said. Martin had to accept the fact that medical science could not tell him what was wrong with his wife. They supported Doctor Bellinger's advice that Joan should not work too hard and that she should avoid all stress and worry. This made Martin all the more careful of what he said to Joan.

He took the line that whatever it was that was troubling her, it was bound to pass in a few months and she would be well again.

'Nature has a great ability to heal our bodies,' he said to her. 'I've seen men badly hurt in accidents and look like hopeless cases, yet in a few months they had healed and were strong and fit again. My youngest sister had terrible stomach cramps for months when she was eighteen and my mother was frantic with worry, but she came right in the end and has been well ever since.'

Whatever Joan thought privately, she didn't say anything to Martin that would worry him; but, unknown to him, she did send for her lawyer to make sure her affairs were in order.

Martin apologised to Joan for the fact that he had become obligated to spend a certain amount of time away from the hotel on company business. He felt he shouldn't be leaving her to cope alone, even for the odd day now and then, but she disagreed with him on this issue. She told him in no uncertain terms that he was to attend to his company responsibilities without regard to her.

'I want you to do your job as a director of the company properly,' she said. 'That is your long-term goal in life; to make your company as successful as possible. I'm proud that other men, like Charles and Arthur, have the faith in you to give you a leading role, and I want you to measure up to their expectations. If I can't cope on my own, we may have to find a capable woman to help me, but we can look at that later if it becomes necessary.'

Martin had to put his submissions to the interim board by way of letters through Charles Drewitt because it was not practical for him to travel to attend the board meetings in Launceston. Concern for Joan being uppermost in his mind, he wouldn't consider spending a whole week away from her even if he never got to a board meeting.

Martin's main consideration at this time was to identify and secure a site in Melbourne for a timber warehousing business. He eventually decided that Williamstown would be a better site for a depot than trying to get closer to the city because land was much cheaper there than on the banks of the Yarra. He bought two acres close to the new wharf at Williamstown that would be easily accessible by wagon from an already built road.

In his letter to Charles, telling him what he had done, he said: 'Two acres may appear to be slightly more than we need, but in view of our long-term aims, I regard it as a good investment. Apart from the fact that land everywhere in and around Melbourne is rapidly increasing in value every year, there are other considerations. If, at some time in the future, it suits us to sell part of it to another investor, we could do so while showing a profit. Williamstown is bound to become an important industrial centre and is central enough to be reasonably convenient for our customers.'

Alexander Wright had produced a comprehensive plan to build a sawmill at the Don that would be capable of milling three hundred thousand super feet of logs a year, producing scantling timbers for use as framing as well as boards. It would be fitted out with the latest American equipment and would be powered by a powerful Marshall steam engine from England. He went to Launceston to discuss the plan with the board and returned to tell Martin that it had been accepted and that the machinery would arrive in Melbourne within six months.

'Things are starting to move now, Martin,' Lex told him. 'With a bit of luck, we'll have your sawmill built and in operation before the end of 1858.'

As soon as this decision had been taken, the new company issued shares to the public. Martin paid his one thousand pounds and received a certificate for one thousand shares. He soon after learnt that he was amongst the top five investors in the company and that his position as a director had been confirmed by the board.

The board appointed Charles Drewitt as chairman and George Perkins, another large shareholder, as managing director, a decision that Martin had no hand in because he was not prepared to leave Joan for the time it would take to travel to Launceston and back. He would have liked to make the trip to his old home at Norwood and take a look at the proposed site for the mill, but he felt the time was not opportune.

Joan's health continued to be uncertain. Sometimes she would be well and like her old self for weeks at a time and then she would suffer more weeks of dreadful fatigue and despondency. All the doctors could do was to prescribe tonics of various kinds that were meant to stimulate her system so that she could throw off the affliction that was troubling her.

She agreed to engage a personal assistant to help her with the routine running of the hotel. Martin was still spending a lot of time in managing the hotel, but there were many days when he was obliged to be away.

They engaged a forty year old woman who had been a nurse since the age of fifteen but now wanted a change of lifestyle. Her name was Gladys Weatherall and she was a widow, her husband having been killed in a goldmine at Bendigo two years previously. She was not engaged as a nurse, but Martin thought her nursing background would be an added bonus. She proved to be the ideal person for the job and soon became a good friend to Joan. With her nursing training to help her, she soon grasped the routine of running a busy, middle-class hotel.

Alexander Wright fulfilled his promise to have the machinery in Melbourne within six months of lodging the order with him, and from there it was sent by the *Water Witch* – still sailing Bass Strait after all those early years – directly to the Don River.

The managing director, George Perkins, had engaged a contractor to build the mill and Alex Wright sent a small team of mechanics, working under the direction of an engineer, to install the machinery. It was a big project and tested the contractors to the limit of their skills.

Substantial excavations were needed to level a large terrace on the banks of the river where the mill would be built. Big trees had to be laboriously winched from the river up the bank to be placed in the ground as platforms to which the big saws would be anchored. Similar heavy platforms were required to accommodate the steam engine, easily the biggest in Tasmania at that time. Finally, a substantial wooden building with a paling roof was built over the assembled machinery.

The day the first head of steam was raised to drive the steam engine was an event of great importance to the company and the district of Devon. A large crowd of people from far and wide came to see the engine start up, at first idling over at a restrained pace, but soon showing the power it could put out when the throttle was opened up. The heavy driving belt was fitted from the steam engine's flywheel to the main breaking down saws and started up. The saws started with a whine that quickly became a constant snarl, and when the first log was run through them the locals heard a noise they would come to know well over the years; a series of piercing, intermittent screams as the saws ripped through the tough, Tasmanian eucalypt logs.

The first week was spent in testing the machinery and making final adjustments. The sawmill hands had to be trained to do their various jobs.

The new mill shipped the first load of sawn timber to Melbourne in the spring of 1858. Martin was on the wharf to see the first large bundles of timber swung out of the hold of the *Water Witch* and lowered onto a wagon. As the first wagon pulled away from the wharf, a second one moved into position to receive a further load. It was taken to the company depot only a mile away from the wharf where it was sorted into heaps according to size inside a large warehouse.

The whole system, from the milling of the timber at the Don, the shipping across Bass Strait and the warehousing at Williamstown, was soon running smoothly enough, albeit in a modest way. It would take time to build up to large volumes. Martin was rapidly increasing sales and he wanted more stocks of timber.

Christmas was a quiet affair for Martin and Joan that year. Joan's health continued to be a great worry for them both and it was not a time for celebration.

'I am so disappointed that things have turned out like this,' Joan said. 'Somehow I feel guilty that I have become a burden to you and that I shouldn't have married you.'

'Don't say that!' Martin exclaimed. 'It's not your fault you've been stricken with a health problem. Please don't ever think that I find you a burden, I don't. I love you, and I want to be with you always.'

'You're too good for me, that's something else. You should have had a younger wife who could give you children and be around forever to share your life.'

Martin was shocked. 'Don't talk like that,' he said sternly to her. 'You'll hurt my feelings terribly if you do. I don't want to hear that kind of talk because it's not true.'

Joan looked up at him and saw the tears in his eyes. Guilt and remorse struck her. She broke down and wept bitterly. 'Please forgive me, darling,' she wailed. 'I shouldn't have said that. In my heart, I know you love me deeply, as I do you. It's just that I'm so down, and it seems so unfair, but I'll be all right soon. If we are to be parted, I want every day we've got together to be good.'

'Yes, that's the way,' he replied. 'I'm not accepting that we will be parted, but you're right when you say that we've got to enjoy every day. That's the way God meant us to live, and that's the way I want it.'

That was the first time they had actually referred to the possibility that she might die, and it was a traumatic experience for them both. They both had tears on their cheeks and were clinging to each other.

'We've got to help each other,' he said softly. 'I'll give you as much strength as I can and I want you to give me what you can spare. I'm bewildered and frightened too. I can't imagine living without you. You were the best thing that ever happened to me in my life, and you must believe me when I say that.'

'I know you love me, I really know that. We'll go on helping each other,' she said.

Somehow, that opening up of their souls to each other did help them to maintain a brave front to the world. Gladys Weatherall and all their friends knew that something was dreadfully wrong with Joan, but she bravely kept a smile on her face and hid her troubles from them all. It was only at night, lying in Martins arms, that sometimes a tear would escape her.

She was stricken down again in March and the same old round of doctors looked at her and shook their heads, muttering silly things that Martin had long ago given up trying to understand.

She lost weight at a faster rate, and after a month she was little more than skin and bone. About the middle of April, Gladys spoke to Martin to warn him that the end was near.

'I know it's not my place,' she said, 'but I've had a lot of experience and I just feel that I've got to say something to you about Joan.'

'I think I know what you're going to say. I know she won't be with us for much longer. I'll appreciate anything you can do to make to make her time as comfortable as possible. It's going to be hard on us all, but we'll manage somehow.'

The end came in the last week of April. She slipped away quietly one evening while Martin was sitting beside her bed with Gladys waiting out in the sitting room. He went out to tell her that Joan was gone, and to his own distress burst out in a cry like a wounded animal. Gladys did all she could to help him regain control and tried to comfort him.

'You did everything that was humanly possible,' she said. 'I've never seen another man support a wife so well and so bravely. Please accept my sincere and heartfelt sympathy.'

The funeral was held at the same small church where they were married. With their few close friends and the hotel staff, the church was filled. Then she was laid alongside her first husband, Campbell Gunter. It was a sad day for them all.

The same small group that had come back to the hotel after Campbell's funeral came again. The lawyer produced a will that, unbeknownst to Martin, Joan had made only a few months ago. It was very short and simple; she left all her worldly possessions to Martin.

Arthur Lees and his other friends were very supportive and urged Martin to take things quietly for a while to give himself a chance to get back onto an even keel. 'I know there's no need to tell you, but I will,' Arthur said. 'If there's anything that Barbara or I can do, we hope you'll ask us.'

'Thanks,' Martin replied. 'I value your friendship above all others, and I thank you both for your friendship towards Joan. She was very fond of you both and we had some good times together.'

For the first month after Joan's death, Martin was in a state of numbed shock. He had been expecting to lose her for months, but when the final curtain fell, he found it very hard to accept the reality that he would never see her again and that he was once again facing life on his own.

Gladys Weatherall had become very proficient in her job as personal assistant to Joan. She provided great support for Martin too and he felt confident in leaving her in charge while he was away attending to his responsibilities as the Resident Director of the Don Timber Company.

The year 1859 continued to bring bad news. Martin had a letter from Charles Drewitt telling him that Rebecca's husband, Richard Stamford, had been drowned in the South Esk River while engaged in a mineral exploration project in the Fingal Valley. She had moved back to Norwood with her small daughter to live with Charles and her younger sister, Sarah. Martin struggled with his best attempt to write short letters of condolence to them both.

Martin continued to be disappointed by the small amount of timber he was receiving from the mill at the Don and raised this in his letters to Charles.

'I am selling all that comes over with no trouble and I am sure that I could sell a lot more, but the small amounts we are landing are very disappointing and well below the capacity of the mill to produce. I hesitate to accept new orders in case I'm unable to deliver.'

He discussed these worries with Alexander Wright, asking him how long it would take for the new mill to get up to full production.

'That depends on how quickly the mill workers learn to use the plant. And also how good your manager is at getting things organised to best advantage,' said Lex. 'Why don't you go over and have a look at it yourself? You've worked in the same forests they're cutting and you've been involved in exporting to both Melbourne and Adelaide. You would have a good idea whether it's being well-managed.'

'Yes,' Martin said, 'I'm very tempted to do that. Apart from anything else, a trip over there would do me good. I must admit I'm not feeling terribly enthusiastic about anything at the moment.'

Martin had a few loose ends to tidy up before he could think about taking the trip to Tasmania. He had a comprehensive review of the hotel account with Arthur Lees during which he became aware of how rich he was as a result of his inheritance from Joan.

'The hotel property is debt free,' Arthur told him, 'and in addition to that, there are over eight thousand pounds credit in the trading account. Campbell and Joan did well with the hotel from when they bought it in 1845, but the big boost came after the gold rushes began. They were making big profits every year right through and then when you came on the scene, the profits went up again. I think the hotel is worth about sixty thousand pounds, so all up, including what you were worth when you sold your carrying business, you would have a gross worth of about eighty thousand pounds.'

'I can hardly believe it,' Martin said. 'The great tragedy is that poor Joan died before she could enjoy it to the full. There are so many things we could have done together, like a nice trip to England. I would have liked her to see the old country where we all came from, and other parts of the world too. It's going to be so much easier to travel around the world now that steamships are coming on the scene.'

'You will probably do those things yourself in time. You're still under forty, so you've got a long way to go before you grow old,' said Arthur.

'Yes, I might, but my biggest worry at present is the timber company. Things are not going as well as they should. I'm going over to Tasmania in a week or two to see for myself what is happening.'

'I think that's a good idea,' Arthur agreed, 'but just one word of caution: Don't be persuaded into putting more money into the business just yet. If the original estimates are not working then there's something wrong, and that could be an expensive thing to fix. Get that all fixed before you are persuaded to undertake any rescue mission.'

'Yes, I understand. I'll be interested to see Charles Drewitt and hear what he thinks. He's got more money invested in it than anybody else and he's a very good money manager, so I hope he can see what needs to be done.'

A fortnight later, Martin travelled to Launceston on the SS *Troalla*, a fine ship of five hundred tons which provided cabin accommodation and a dining saloon.

Martin reflected on his last crossing of Bass Strait on the *Water Witch* in 1851 and smiled at the memory of Nellie Houseman in the packing case and how he had rescued her. I wonder what they are all doing now, he thought as he lay in his bunk listening to the rhythmic thump of the steam engine.

He had written to Charles telling him when he would be arriving and that he would travel to Norwood by coach from Launceston. His arrival was a great event for all the old hands of Norwood, most of whom were still on the scene. Charles was a lonely figure without his wife Leah, Rebecca was a quiet and somewhat reserved widow with a little daughter, Sarah was a fine looking young woman of marriageable age and Henrietta Smith was a well-preserved matron of forty-six, still in charge of the kitchen and a force to be reckoned with in the Norwood establishment.

Martin got an opportunity to speak privately with Rebecca for a minute as they moved along the hallway to the dining room.

'I was very sorry to hear of your bad luck in losing your husband. Please accept my sincere sympathy,' he said in a quiet voice.

'Thank you,' she said. 'I was sad to hear you had lost your wife. It must have been terrible for you. It makes you wonder why these things have to happen.'

Any awkwardness at the changed social status of Martin from his previous life at Norwood was brushed aside by Charles's warm welcome into the family circle. He was shown to a spare bedroom and was placed at Charles's right at the dining table. After the first few minutes, the talk flowed. The family wanted Martin to talk about his days on the goldfields and on the roads with his wagon.

When the meal was finished and the family were settling themselves in the sitting room to continue talking, Martin said, 'Would you mind if I just slip out to the kitchen to say hello to Mrs Smith and the others?'

'No, of course not,' they all said together. 'Go and see them.'

Henrietta greeted him with a massive hug and an enthusiastic kiss on both cheeks. 'It's good to see you, Martin,' she said. 'It's very good to see you. Welcome home.'

'Thanks,' he said with a happy smile, 'it feels like a homecoming. I did miss you all and thought a lot about you and the old place.'

'How are you, really?' she asked. 'I was sad to hear about your bad luck, your wife dying after only three years.'

'It's been hard. The worst thing that's ever happened to me, but I suppose I'll survive, somehow.'

'Life can be hard at times. You never know what's going to happen next. Look at Rebecca; her husband swept away in a flood and gone in a minute.'

'How are things with you? I see you're still here.'

She laughed as she said, 'Yes, still here. I reckon I'll live my life here and die on the job. I'm on the lookout for a proposal from a rich gent, so watch out!'

They chatted about old times and old friends. Joyce was happily married to her boatbuilder husband at Port Sorell and had three children. Ellen had married a nice boy from the village and had two children. Allan Freeman still worked on Norwood as the farm overseer, but Jock Masters had left to take a job in the new sawmill.

'How long are you staying?' she asked.

'Only a few days, a week at most. I want to have a look at the new mill and a few other things, but I've got to get back to look after my business.'

'We'll get a chance to talk again before you go, I hope,' she said.

He returned to the sitting room to find the family reading and Charles dozing in his big armchair. He had noticed that Charles was lacking a bit of his old spark and vigour and said to him, 'How are you keeping these days?'

'Oh, not too bad, I suppose,' he replied. 'I turned sixty a few weeks ago, and I have to admit I'm not as frisky as I used to be.'

Another hour passed in talk. Martin didn't get a chance to speak to Charles about business in a serious way. The girls spoke about the big day when the new mill was started up for the first time and about the crowd of spectators that turned up to see the biggest steam engine in Tasmania.

'I think I'll get a cup of tea for us before we go to bed,' Rebecca said. 'I'll go out and swing the kettle.'

'I'll give you a hand,' Sarah said as she followed her sister out to the kitchen.

'How's the mill going?' Martin asked Charles. 'Have the start up problems been ironed out yet?'

'No, not completely. I'm worried about a few things, as I know you are, but we can talk about that while you're here. I'm not sure we've got the right people running things,' he went on, 'but it won't be easy to make changes at this stage.'

The girls came back into the room with tea and cake and no more was said between the two men about business.

Charles was the first to retire. Getting to his feet, he said, 'I'll think I'll go and fall into bed. I'm bushed again tonight, must be cracking up!'

Martin sat with Rebecca and Sarah for a few minutes, sipping the last of the tea. Suddenly, Charles called out from his bedroom in a strangled voice: 'Sarah! Sarah!'

She jumped up and ran to him. A minute later, she screamed for Rebecca.

Martin jumped up, suddenly full of foreboding, and he was in the hall by the time Rebecca called for him. He hurried along the hall towards the front of the house where he could see light streaming from a bedroom door.

He entered the room to see Charles undressed except for a shirt, sprawled across the bed, his huge bulk making the bed look small. Sarah had a pillow under his head and was trying to hold him. Rebecca was on his other side and the two of them were trying to lift him up into a sitting position. He was clutching at his chest, and as Martin bent over him to assist the girls, he heard the last breath leave his body. Charles collapsed into a heap on the bed. His head fell back and his mouth fell open in a grotesque yawn.

'I think he's gone,' Martin said in a quiet voice. 'There's nothing we can do.'

The two women broke down into uncontrolled weeping, overcome by shock. Martin tried to get him fully laid back on the bed, and put his hand under his chin to shut his mouth.

'We'll have to put something around his head,' he said. 'Perhaps we ought to get Mrs Smith; she'll know what to do.'

'I'll go,' Sarah said, and left the room.

'Oh dear, what a terrible thing to happen,' Rebecca said. 'I can't believe it, to happen so suddenly like this.'

'Yes, it's a shock all right. None of us would have dreamt of anything like this happening when we were all so happy tonight,' Martin said.

Mrs Smith came bustling into the room. She glanced at Charles and put her hand on the side of his throat. 'He's gone. Poor man … and so sudden.' They stood silently for a minute or two and then she said, 'I'll get something to put around his head,' and left the room to return within a minute with a wide bandage which she deftly tied around his head to keep his mouth closed.

'What do we do now?' Rebecca asked in a tremulous voice while looking at Martin.

'There are things we'll have to attend to tonight; some others can wait until morning. First, we'll have to let the doctor know what has happened, and then somebody will lay him out properly,' he said, looking at Henrietta Smith.

'Mrs Little up at the village usually does that,' she said. 'We'll have to get her tonight. It needs to be done fairly quickly.'

'I think we'd better get Allan Freeman out to go to the doctor's and Mrs Little's,' Martin said. 'I'll go and get him now.'

Martin went out through the house, past the kitchen and up the garden path that led to the gate opening out onto the spacious farmyard. Allan was still living in the same old hut. Within five minutes, Martin had him awake and they were shaking hands in the light of a lantern Allan had hurriedly lit.'

'It's good to see you back on the old place again, Martin,' he said.

'Yes, it is good to be back, but a dreadful shock for us all. Mr Drewitt has had a heart attack and died.'

'What?!' Allan gasped. 'You mean now, tonight?'

'Yes, just a few minutes ago. That's why I've come to wake you up.'

He quickly told him what to do and then returned to the sitting room where Henrietta and the two girls were waiting. He told them that Allan was on his way to the village to wake the doctor and Mrs Little.

'I expect they'll both be here in a short time,' he said. 'I suppose we can only wait. There's nothing else we can do in the meantime.'

'I'll go and swing the kettle,' Henrietta said. 'They might like a cup of tea when they come.'

When she left the room, Martin said, 'This must be a terrible shock for both of you. Please accept my heartfelt sympathy. I am shocked and terribly sad to see him gone. He was a great man, and he did a lot for me.' His voice choked up as he continued: 'I became very fond of him over the years. He was like a father to me.'

Rebecca had a sob in her voice as she said, 'He thought a lot of you too. I think he saw you as a son.'

'It makes that terrible time when Mother died come back again, all too soon,' said Sarah, tears streaming down her face.

Presently the doctor came and offered his sympathy to the girls. 'I had been seeing him often and knew he was in danger of having a heart attack, so there is no question about what I'll put on the death certificate. I'm just sad to see him taken. He was a good man.'

They sat in the sitting room for another couple of hours while the girls talked about their parents and their happy lives at Norwood until later, when Mrs Little arrived on the scene, Martin persuaded them to go to bed.

CHAPTER 18

*M*artin spent a sad and restless night after finally getting to bed about 2 am. His mind was full of memories of that first day many years ago when he was picked up by Charles Drewitt from Mr Fenton's farm and brought to Norwood. He had a compelling mental picture of a large, judgelike figure of a man, sitting beside him in the chaise cart climbing the hill from Forth. He remembered exactly what he had said: 'If you do the right thing by me, I'll do the right thing by you'.

The doctor had left after writing out a death certificate and giving it to Martin. 'I'm not surprised he finished up like this,' he said. 'He was always too heavy, and these last few years he stopped all physical work that used to keep him reasonably fit and then got too soft. He did well to reach sixty, I'd say.'

And then he had said something that Martin was to hear many times during the next few days: 'But he was a great man, a greater man than most people knew about. He had a mixed reputation, but he did a lot for the colony and especially for this district'.

Mrs Little had been the last to leave. 'Poor man,' she had said. 'He was taken very suddenly, but if your time is up, it is the best way to go. Quick, not like his poor wife; she took months to go.'

At daybreak, Martin was up and asking Allan Freeman to harness up the pony and trap for him to go to the village. He roused Earnest Valentine up out of bed an hour before his usual time. As soon as he saw Martin, he said, 'Is there something wrong?'

Martin gave him the sad news and a few details about Charles's passing.

'If you're looking for a will, I reckon I know where it will be,' Earnest said. 'It'll be in that big desk of his in the front room where he spent a lot of time working on his business affairs. Yes, I'd have a look for it when you go back to the house if I were you. The girls might know something.'

'I'm just assuming that Mr Stackhouse in Launceston is still his solicitor,' Martin said.

'Yes,' Earnest said, 'he's had him for a long time.'

Martin saw the minister of the little church that Charles Drewitt had financed all those years ago. The minister responded immediately. 'I'll be out to visit the family first thing this morning.'

Martin saw the mill manager and then a few other people about the village and told them the sad news. He knew that the countryside for miles around would know by dinnertime that day.

When he returned to Norwood, he told the two sisters what Earnest Valentine had said. 'I think we should find the will if it is there in case your father left any last instructions about his funeral, or anything else that we should do,' said Martin.

They all went up to the front room and Sarah opened the big desk. 'He had this desk made especially for him in Launceston by Thomas Carter,' she said. 'It's a beautiful piece.'

It didn't take long for them to locate the will. It was in a small drawer with the title deeds to Norwood and a few other valuable papers. Sarah opened the single sheet document and glanced through it. 'You're named as the first executor,' she said to Martin.

He was flabbergasted. He turned red in the face and said, 'What?! Me? I can't believe it. Why would he do that?'

'I told you he thought a lot of you,' Rebecca said. 'We all do. Sarah and I will be delighted that you're looking after Father's affairs.'

'Who else is named?' she asked Sarah. 'There's usually more than one.'

After a moment's study, Sarah said, 'James Fenton of Forth.'

'Oh yes, I'm not surprised. They were good friends and Father had a high opinion of him as a man as well as of his business ability,' said Rebecca.

Martin quickly gathered his wits after the surprise of being named as executor of his old friend's will. 'I suppose we should read it properly now,' he said. 'There might be some instructions from your father about things he wants done quickly.'

Sarah handed the document to him. 'You read it.'

For a wealthy man, it was a short will. Apart from a small bequest to the local church and to the library – a special interest of Mrs Drewitt's – several Devon district sporting clubs were given fifty pounds each. The residual of his estate was to be shared equally by his two daughters.

'That's simple and straightforward. It shouldn't give you any trouble,' she said to Martin.

'That's right, except for the timber company,' he said. 'I believe things aren't going too well there and it's losing money, but I won't know the full story for a few days. As a matter of fact, that's why I'm here now. I've come over to check things out.'

The sisters expressed surprise at that. 'Father never mentioned it,' Sarah said. 'It can't be too serious.'

'I don't know yet. I'll know more in a few days,' he said.

Charles Drewitt was buried in the local churchyard two days later with the biggest crowd of mourners the Devon district had ever seen. He was lauded by the minister during the service and by the editorials in all the newspapers in Tasmania. Reference was made to his humble beginnings in the colony, but no direct reference was made to him being a convict. He was laid to rest with praise heaped on him for his success in business which had brought about many jobs and the economic development of the colony to the benefit of Tasmania but especially for the Devon district.

Martin explained to the girls the importance of him getting to see his fellow executor James Fenton, now living in Launceston, and the family solicitor Mr Algernon Stackhouse as soon as he could. He left Norwood in the light carriage drawn by two horses early on the day after the funeral and reached the town in the late afternoon.

He arrived at Mr Stackhouse's office only minutes before he was to leave for home, and after a short discussion they arranged to meet the next morning .

Martin called on James Fenton that evening. He told him he had been named in the will as an executor and showed him the document. James too expressed surprise that he had been chosen by his old friend, but indicated that he would willingly serve to the best of his abilities.

Martin told him that the only problem they might have was in sorting out the problems at the new sawmill. Charles was far and away the biggest investor in the company and if the business was losing money, which Martin feared was the case, then the executors would have a special obligation to sort out the mess as quickly as possible.

James Fenton was pleased to meet Martin again and was soon reminding him of his early visits to the farm at Forth in the company of Nathanial Kentish and of Martin's service on the survey gang in the depths of the forests at Kentish Plains.

'I'm glad you remember that,' Martin said to him. 'I have thought a lot over the years about what happened to me at that time, and it took me quite a while to work out just how much you and Mr Kentish, with Charles Drewitt, did to help me. I understand it all now, and I thank you sincerely.'

James Fenton laughed. 'We picked you for a good one and as things have turned out, we were right.'

They arranged to meet at the solicitor's office the next morning.

☙ — — ❧

Martin handed the will to Mr Stackhouse. 'We found this in his desk the morning after he died. He evidently chose to keep it in his own office rather than with you, or as some do, at their bank.'

Mr Stackhouse smiled as he said, 'Charles always had his own way of doing things. I knew where it was.'

He agreed to get his office to make two copies so that both Martin and Mr Fenton would have a copy when they left. He went through the clauses of the will and explained how Charles's wishes would be carried out.

'It is all straightforward,' he said. 'All we will need to do is have the names on the title deeds to the various properties altered and the shares he owned transferred to the two daughters.'

'That's the part that we'll need to take care to deal with quickly,'

Martin said. 'As a matter of fact, that is how I happened to be in the house when he died. I've come over from Melbourne to have a look at the company sawmill operation. It is not going according to the plan and budget we started with. Charles said as much himself during the few minutes discussion we had that evening. He said we had a problem, but it may not be easy to fix. I don't know what he meant by that.'

'I've got a shrewd idea of what he meant. The manager is closely related to one of the directors; a son-in-law, I believe,' Mr Stackhouse said.

'Could you take us through the share registry?' Martin asked. 'We're representing the biggest shareholder, plus there's my own standing as a director and a shareholder. It's important for us to have an accurate overview of the company.'

'Of course,' Mr Stackhouse said as he produced the big, leather bound book that was the official share register of the Don Timber Company.

Charles Drewitt was easily the biggest shareholder with ten thousand shares with the next biggest being a Launceston timber merchant, George Perkins, with five thousand shares. After that the holdings tailed off to many with only a few hundred and some, like Martin, with one or two thousand.

'I'm not a shareholder,' James Fenton said. 'It wasn't convenient for me when the company was floated, but I wouldn't mind buying a parcel if the opportunity came up at the right price.'

'Your opportunity might come along quicker than you expect,' Mr Stackhouse said with a smile.

'As company secretary, could you brief us on the financial position of the company now?' Martin asked him.

'Yes, you're entitled to that, both as Charles Drewitt's executors, and in your case as a shareholder and director.'

He produced a financial statement that had been submitted to the last board meeting only three weeks ago. It showed that the business was not running anything like the plan that was in place when operations began almost a year ago.

'In view of what you've shown us this morning, and if Mr Fenton agrees, I suggest that you don't proceed to transfer the shares into the daughters' names for a few months until the company is on a sound footing,' said Martin.

'I certainly agree with that,' Mr Fenton said. 'We'll have to be very careful how we handle this. We may have to consider liquidating the share holding rather than saddle the daughters with a loss making investment that might go on for years.'

They discussed all aspects of the situation and agreed that Martin and Mr Fenton would take a close look at the operation of the mill as soon as possible. They also recommended that Martin make every endeavour to attend the next Board meeting in Launceston in a month's time.

When the two men got away from the solicitor's office, Martin asked Mr Fenton whether he would be available to travel to the Don in the near future. He explained his own responsibilities to the hotel and to the company timber business in Melbourne and said he wanted to get home as soon as possible.

Mr Fenton was agreeable to drop his own affairs for a couple of days to devote himself to his old friend's business and offered to go back to Norwood with Martin that same day, returning to Launceston a couple of days later so that Martin could catch the next steamer to Melbourne. The upshot was that two hours later they were bowling along the Westbury Road in the direction of the Don and Norwood.

By travelling all day, only stopping to rest the horses; and by taking advantage of the long, early summer evening, they reached Norwood at nine o'clock that night. Rebecca and Sarah were surprised to see Mr Fenton, but with the capable help of Henrietta Smith in the kitchen and their own capacity as country hostesses, they coped with ease and grace.

Martin and James were in the sawmill yard at half past eight the next morning.

'I want to get a good feel of how this business is being run,' Martin had said as they travelled the mile or so from Norwood to the mill in the chaise cart, 'and to see how well-organised they are to start the day will be an important pointer to the rest.'

As Martin had expected, the mill was not a hive of activity at that hour of the morning. When he asked the foreman who met them in the yard why the saws were not going, he replied, 'We do other work first thing of a morning. It takes an hour or two to get steam up for the engine.'

The manager arrived at nine o'clock. His name was Greg Samson and he was a tall, gaunt looking man in his forties with a slight stoop and a bristly personality that he didn't bother to hide.

'I didn't know you were coming,' he said brusquely. 'It would have been good if I'd known you were coming so early this morning.'

'Sorry about that,' Martin said with a smile. 'Fact was, we didn't get back from Launceston until late last night and we're anxious to see all we can today so we can get back on the road tomorrow.'

'What do you want to see?' he asked, somewhat ungraciously.

'We want to see all we can about your operation here,' James Fenton said. 'We're here as executors of Mr Drewitt's estate. Mr Maynard is a large shareholder and a director of the company as well as being the Melbourne manager.'

At this, Greg Samson took a breath and some of the tension eased. 'Have you got any concerns?' he asked, looking at Martin.

'To be frank, yes, we have,' Martin said. 'I've been very disappointed at the small amount of timber you've been sending me. I could have sold twice or three times as much if I'd had it.'

'Well, you've got to remember we are only just starting and it is taking a while to get things running properly,' Samson explained.

'When my friend Alexander Wright inspected our forests, and this site, he recommended certain machinery that would have the capacity to mill three hundred thousand super feet of timber a year, and allowance was made in the plan for a training and running-in period, but so far you haven't looked like reaching that target,' Martin said.

'Oh, these bloody experts!' Samson burst out. 'They all think they know everything, but put them on the job here and see how they go.'

By this time, the mill had started sawing and the saws were screaming through the first of the logs for the day. Martin and James turned and strolled into the mill with Samson trailing along. The men seemed to be cheerful enough and gave Martin a cheery wave and a shouted 'Good day'. After a few minutes, they moved outside where it was easier to talk.

'I'd like to start at the bank of the river and follow your production system right through to the marshalling yard,' Martin said.

They moved down to the river bank where several logs were tied up to a mooring post at the edge of the water.

'Have you got a catch-all net or something to stop any stray logs being carried downstream past the mill?' Martin asked Samson.

'No, but we don't lose many,' he replied. 'We know when to expect them.'

Martin noticed that there were only a couple of logs waiting outside the mill to be moved on to the breaking down platform, so he questioned Samson about it. His answer was that it was mostly just as quick to pull them straight from the river as they were needed. So it was, all through the mill. At every stage, it was obvious that the system could be speeded up by better management .

Before they left that afternoon, Martin said to Samson, 'We will be making a report to the board with suggestions for streamlining the system you're using. We've got to get a lot more logs into the mill and sawn timber out. At the rate of production you've got now, the mill will be broke and out of business inside twelve months. Just as a suggestion for you to start with, we would like you to bring a man on duty at five o'clock in the morning to get steam up on the boiler so that the saws can start at half past seven sharp every morning. Another suggestion for you is to get the men themselves to make suggestions on how to speed things up. You might be surprised at what they'll come up with if you give them a chance.'

Greg Samson was barely able to conceal his pleasure at their departure when they left several hours later to return to Norwood.

⚐ — — ⚑

Afternoon tea was served in the dining room where James Fenton reminisced with Rebecca and Sarah about the old days at the Don and Forth. A happy couple of hours were spent between them all and many fond memories were recalled.

Rebecca had her little girl Enid with her. She was only one year old, yet Martin was intrigued by her likeness to her mother. Some of the Drewitt features already showed in the way she moved around, even though she was only crawling.

Martin was anxious to get a few minutes alone with Rebecca, and late in the afternoon he got lucky. James went outside with Sarah to see something in the garden and the two were gone for a quarter of an hour, leaving Martin and Rebecca alone in the sitting room.

'I've been hoping to get a few minutes with you,' Martin said.

She looked at him inquiringly with a quick glance.

'The trouble is, the way we are situated at present, I seldom ever get a chance to see you, let alone talk to you, so I've got to grab the opportunity when it comes along.'

'Is there something wrong?' she asked.

'No, there's nothing,' he said. 'It's just about us – you and me. The first thing I want to say is that I hope nothing I say to you now will upset you, or hurt your feelings, or seem to be in bad taste.'

She was silent for a minute, then said, 'You had better say what it is before the others come back; you may not have more than a minute.'

'It's just that you and I have finished up in the same situation – something disastrous for young people like us. That's what has made me speak now. But there's something else. I doubt you ever had any idea, but in the old days before I left here to go seek my fortune, I was very fond of you.'

He gave an awkward chuckle and said, 'I'm sorry I'm sounding like a jumbled up fool, but I want to know if you would be upset if I were to speak to you about marriage. Not now; it's too soon for both of us, but in a few months when our lives have settled down to a balanced pattern again.'

To his immense relief and joy, she smiled.

'You haven't hurt my feelings,' she said. 'I think you are paying me a compliment. No, you won't hurt my feelings if you speak to me again at the appropriate time. Now would be too soon to talk of such things, but later, yes. In the meantime, you may write to me.'

'Thanks,' he said as he held out his hand. She took it and shook it warmly, the first intimate contact between them. He saw a trace of a tear in her eye and he felt one dangerously close to his own.

Martin and James left in the carriage the next morning to return to Launceston, taking Allan Freeman with them to bring the carriage home. That evening, Martin and James worked together in the Fenton residence on the draft of a report that would be presented to the next board meeting.

He arrived back at the Golden Swan two days later and, to his great satisfaction, found that everything had gone well while he was away. He could see that Gladys Weatherall was pleased and proud of the fact that she could report that everything about the hotel had run with the usual efficiency and success, even though they had been surprised by Martin's extended absence. She laid the daily trading figures and stock reports before him which supported her good report.

'Well done,' Martin said, 'you've done well, as I knew you would. I'm sorry I had no way of letting you know how long I would be getting back; it was a completely unexpected circumstance . It's not often in life that you go to visit an old friend and he dies that same night!'

She was shocked. 'You poor man,' she said. 'What an experience, especially after what you've been through these last few months. You'll be pleased to be home. There's a letter here for you. I think it's from the lawyer. It might be important.'

He took the letter to his room and sat down to open it with a strong sense of foreboding. He saw at once that it was from Mr Nigel Waterhouse, his solicitor. He was asking Martin to call on him as soon as possible to discuss an important family matter.

Martin went to the lawyer's office in Collins Street the next morning and was immediately shown in to see him.

'I don't quite know what to make of this,' Nigel said, 'but I am apprehensive enough to bring it to your notice as a matter of importance. A few days ago, I had a young Scotsman call on me. He claims to be Campbell Gunter's nephew and he has come out from Scotland to find his uncle, looking for assistance to get a start in life. He didn't know his uncle had died or that his widow had remarried and subsequently died. As I say, I don't quite know what to make of it all, but I am apprehensive. There are plenty of shysters about this town who would lead him into making claims against you if they got the sniff of money, especially a large fortune like you now control.'

'Of course I'm surprised, 'Martin said. 'And like you, I don't know what to think. I never knew this person existed. I'm certain my late wife didn't know about him either. She told me that Campbell did have a sister who was years younger than him, but she disappeared from the family scene after he came out to Australia as a soldier, and she has never been heard of since. What sort of a bloke is he? Would he have any claim on me after all that has happened?'

The lawyer looked thoughtful and paused before answering. 'To answer your second question first: no, I think not, decidedly. But knowing how the law can be wrangled around and manipulated by unscrupulous shysters, I am apprehensive about the inconvenience and expense you could be put to.

'As for the first question: he says his name is Garth Gunter and he is thirty years old. I didn't know what to make of him when he came in here; he was hard to sum up. I think my advice would be to do nothing for a while and see what happens.'

'I'll take your advice for the time being, but I don't like having loose ends hanging around me. If there is a danger he could spring a sudden claim on me sometime in the future, I'd rather get everything sorted out quickly and have done with it. Can you find out any more about him?'

'Not quickly; communicating with Scotland is a very slow and tedious business,' he said. 'Let's wait for a couple of weeks at least and see what happens.'

With that, Martin went about his business, albeit with forebodings of problems to come.

He continued on that morning to the company depot at Williamstown with some trepidation that he may not find a good report there; but again, the business had run along without him quite well. He was particularly pleased because he had left a new man in charge who had only been on the job for two months and this experience had been good for him as well as giving Martin confidence in him.

His name was Reuben Ralston; a thickset, strongly built man who had served an apprenticeship with a Melbourne builder as a boy and had stayed in the industry for another ten years. Martin first met him when he was buying timber for his boss and had got to know him over a period of months. When he was looking for a man he could train to take a senior position in the business, he offered Reuben the job. By that time, Reuben had been looking for a change and was glad to take the opportunity, partly because of the increased pay that Martin offered him. Martin believed in paying his key people well, and his experience in his days on the goldfields, and then in the hotel, had proved that it was a good policy. Reuben's only complaint was that he had been unable to supply his customers with all the timber they wanted.

'I hope that situation will improve over the coming months,' Martin told him. 'We're looking at improving the performance of the sawmill, but it will take a while to get going.'

Martin called on his old friend Arthur Lees within the first few days of his return and gave him a full account of his trip to Tasmania. He was shocked to hear of Charles Drewitt's sudden death and immediately asked Martin how that would affect the Don Timber Company. Martin told him of his worries on that account and what he was doing to resolve the problems. His other friend, Alexander Wright, was equally interested in how the mill was performing.

'The mill machinery is running well and is doing what you said it would, but the production is disappointing,' Martin told him, then explained what he was doing about it. Once again, Martin was pleased to have the advice of his friends, both of whom he knew he could rely on.

'I'll see what comes out of my first board meeting,' Martin told Lex. 'I might ask you to make another trip to Tasmania to give them the benefit of your experience.'

'You know I'll do anything I can to help,' Lex replied. 'Sometimes an outsider's eyes can see things that people who are too close to the situation can't see.'

A week after returning home, Martin wrote to Rebecca for the first time. He tried to strike a balance between a private and confidential tone and a newsy account of his daily life. He told her he would be in Launceston for the board meeting in about two weeks time but that he didn't expect to see her because of the need to return to Melbourne.

Another letter from Mr Waterhouse arrived, telling Martin that he had received a communication from a lawyer representing Garth Gunter demanding a share of the Gunter fortune. Once again, Mr Waterhouse asked Martin to call on him at his earliest convenience. Martin was in his office early the next day where he found an angry and frustrated lawyer.

'As I told you when this first blew up, I don't believe the fellow can succeed with a claim against you, but if they persist by threatening to take you to the courts, then I don't doubt they could cause you a lot of trouble – and expense,' said Mr Waterhouse.

'What is our next move to be?' Martin asked.

'Firstly, we've got to reject their claim out of hand. It has no basis in law and you have no legal responsibility for your late wife's nephew, even if he can prove to be who he claims to be. I think we've got to meet this claim with an uncompromising refusal to give it any legal standing whatsoever. Whether you would want to meet the fellow face to face and consider giving him any other help is another matter entirely, one for you alone to consider. Maybe you could help him get a good job; that may be enough to get him off your back.'

'Before I do anything, I must be sure he is the genuine article,' Martin said. 'I wouldn't mind meeting him if he can convince you that he is who he claims to be. What is your advice on that approach?'

'I don't like the way he has run to another lawyer, especially the one he has chosen, and I am concerned at what has happened so quickly. If he wanted to meet you as a family connection, why didn't he ask me to arrange a meeting for him? But I suppose we can't get into trouble by agreeing to talk to him on the condition that he can prove his identity,' Mr Waterhouse said. 'If you want me to, I'll arrange it.'

'Thanks,' Martin said. 'I'll wait to hear from you.'

Martin made the trip to Tasmania a few days later. As things turned out, the steamer got him to Launceston the day before the meeting. He booked into the Brisbane Hotel, the leading hotel in the town. He felt now that he could afford the luxuries of life and, in addition, he was well aware of the importance of a good address in business and social life. His fellow directors would be much more impressed by him staying at the top hotel in town rather than bunking down at his old mate's house. Thanks to his parents' influence, and his young days on Ashburton, he had never been overawed by social standing and he had learned during his crowded life that wealth alone was seldom a true indicator of a person's inner quality.

The board meeting was held at Mr Stackhouse's offices in St John Street. The boardroom was at the rear of the offices and the dominating piece of furniture was the long deal table and chairs that took up all the middle space in the room.

Martin was greeted warmly by Mr Stackhouse and introduced to the other directors. Mr George Perkins, the senior partner in a Launceston firm of sawmillers and the Vice Chairman of the Don Timber Company, was at the head of the table. Another Launceston merchant, Mr Lindsay Thomas, together with Mr Gerald Robertson, a Longford property owner, made up the rest of the board.

The meeting opened with appropriate references to the passing of the Company Chairman, Mr Charles Drewitt, and the directors stood for a minute's silence as a mark of respect. The chairman then referred to the need to appoint a new chairman and within a minute, Mr Perkins had been appointed. Martin assumed that the other directors had decided amongst themselves what they wanted because Mr Robertson was immediately nominated and appointed Vice Chairman.

The company secretary then gave a report on the state of affairs and the financial position of the company and concluded his report by laying on the table a report by Mr Martin Maynard and Mr James Fenton, executors of the estate of the late Charles Drewitt on a visit they had made to the mill.

Martin had discussed the most appropriate tactics for him to adopt at the meeting with Arthur Lees, and he knew that this was the moment for him to make his presence felt.

'Mr Chairman,' he said, 'could I be given an opportunity at this stage to say a few words in relation to my visit to the mill and also in relation to my role as a director of the company?'

'Yes, Mr Maynard, we will be interested to hear what you have to say. We've been disappointed that we haven't had the benefit of your direct input into our deliberations up to this point.'

Martin was determined to keep cool and not get embroiled in useless backbiting before the important business discussions had to be addressed.

'Thank you, Mr Chairman. I apologise for not attending a board meeting earlier. I know that Mr Drewitt has explained my position to you . The fact that crossing Bass Strait is a voyage that can take anything from a day and a half to a fortnight, plus that I had a very ill wife who I was loath to leave even for a day, explains why you haven't seen me at the earlier meetings. Sadly, my wife has now died; however, attending future meetings will be a different matter. Now that the new steamer service has been established, I will be able to come to Tasmania and return within four or five days with certainty.

'As for the visit to the mill, when Mr Fenton and I discovered that we had been appointed as Mr Drewitt's executors, along with the knowledge I had that he was by far the biggest shareholder in the company and by the further knowledge I had by virtue of my position as the Melbourne director that the mill is not performing anywhere near its planned budget, we felt that before we could decide whether to liquidate the Drewitt estate shareholding or continue with it, we needed to see for ourselves how things were going at the mill. We discussed this with Mr Stackhouse and he, very kindly, indicated his approval.

'This report tabled today has been written by Mr Fenton and myself. The main thrust of it is that, in our opinion, the mill is not being managed in a way that can achieve the production essential to making a profit. If you are agreeable, I can go through the detailed report with you.'

A deep silence prevailed for a minute.

Martin had worked out for himself that the other directors wouldn't want to see the Drewitt shareholding liquidated because that would immediately devalue their own shares, and possibly be the end of the company.

'Ahem,' the chairman finally said. 'Well, yes, we'll need to discuss the report.' Turning to Mr Stackhouse, he said, 'Do you have anything from a professional point of view that you'd like to say at this stage?'

Mr Stackhouse was in no hurry to start talking. He looked around the table at each director and then said, 'You'll recall that we discussed the importance of getting the mill up to full production as soon as possible and that a really capable and experienced sawmiller would be essential to train the workers and get the necessary systems established. My only comment at this stage is to suggest that you keep that in mind while we discuss the report.'

The discussions went on until a halt was called for lunch. They all went together to a nearby hotel and had a meal. That at least was good, Martin thought, because it gave them a chance to get to know him.

After lunch, the new vice chairman, Gerald Robertson, said that he felt he had a clash of interests in the discussion because his son-in-law was the manager of the mill. He then offered to withdraw from the meeting. Martin could see that this could cause a dangerous rift in the board and suggested he stay. 'Certainly our report is critical of the management; I'd be a hypocrite to suggest anything else,' he said, 'but we are not looking to have Greg Samson sacked at this stage. What can we do to get better systems in place?'

Mr Lindsay Thomas, who had been relatively quiet during the morning's discussions, then spoke up.

'It seems to me that Mr Maynard has a good grip on things and he obviously has access to good professional advice. I suggest we appoint him managing director and review the position in six months time. I know this is tantamount to asking Mr Perkins to give up his formal position as managing director, but I know him well enough to believe that he will agree with what I am suggesting. In the meantime, Mr Samson is to be clearly instructed by the chairman and secretary that Mr Maynard will be laying down the overall management of the mill.'

George Perkins made some noises in his throat that indicated he was going to speak, but he hesitated for a few seconds before saying anything.

'I am not the least bit concerned about relinquishing the position of managing director,' he said. 'However, there are one or two aspects that I feel bound to mention. From the first day of our association and the development of the company, everything has been dominated by Charles Drewitt. I know he was a brilliant businessman and that he had the power through his great wealth, but he was also very domineering and we have been left with one or two fundamental mistakes that will haunt us for the next few years until we can build strength enough to rectify them. The worst was his insistence on building the mill on the Don River and not on one of the bigger rivers on the north-west coast. The way things are turning out now is a continuation of the dominance of the Drewitt family. I can only hope that Mr Maynard, through his position as managing director and his connection with the family, will be able to bring a bit more balance to the scene.'

This outburst was followed by a silence at the table. After a few seconds, the chairman said, 'All those who agree to the motion to appoint Mr Maynard managing director indicate accordingly.'

In a short space of time this was agreed to and suddenly Martin found himself in a position of great power in the Don Timber Company. The meeting closed soon after.

As the directors stood around chatting and enjoying a cup of tea after the meeting, a clerk came up to Martin and handed him a note. As soon as he could look at it privately, he saw that it was from James Fenton, asking him to call at his home as soon as it was convenient. Martin hired a cab and was driven to James Fenton's home on High Street.

'Come into the sitting room,' James said. 'We've had a special friend call on us.'

Martin walked into the sitting room and was surprised to see Rebecca sitting on the sofa.

'What a surprise!' he said as he held out his hand. 'This is an unexpected pleasure to see you again so soon.'

She laughed and said, 'You never know who you'll run into when you venture away from home.'

Mr Fenton's daughter Elise was serving afternoon tea, so Martin had to accept a cup. The company chatted enthusiastically about the weather and other trivial matters and Martin was pressed to stay for dinner, an invitation he was pleased to accept.

'Are you staying in town?' Martin asked Rebecca.

'Yes,' she said with a smile, 'I'm staying here with the Fentons for a couple of days.'

That set Martin's mind to pondering the circumstances of this happy meeting. She would have known from his letter that he would be in Launceston this day. Could she, by some chance, have organised a visit to coincide with his? His heart leapt. It would be a wonderful stroke of good fortune if she thought enough of him to come all the way from Norwood to see him, just for a few hours.

Later in the afternoon when the tea cups had been cleared away, James suggested they have a drink before dinner. He poured sherry for the two ladies and whisky for Martin and himself.

'How did you enjoy your first board meeting?' he asked Martin as he handed him a glass.

Martin gave an ironic laugh and shook his head. 'By and large, I enjoyed it quite well,' he said, 'but I've got myself another job out of it.'

They looked at him expectantly.

He laughed again. 'You're looking at the new Managing Director of the Don Timber Company. I don't quite know how it happened, but it did. If the sawmill fails to get going properly, I'll get the blame.'

'Regardless of how it happened, I think it was a good decision by the board,' James said. 'Congratulations. I know you'll do well.'

The talk carried on at a fast rate with Martin giving them an account of the day's work and trying to answer their questions.

Elise left the room to attend to business in the kitchen and James followed her out a couple of minutes later, leaving Martin and Rebecca alone. Martin turned to her and said, 'What a lovely surprise. I never thought for a moment that I'd see you this trip.'

She chuckled and said, 'I just thought it might be a good idea to let you know that I heard what you said the other day.'

'Thank you. You've made me a very happy man. I will be waiting impatiently for the next six months to pass.'

'That's to be the time, is it?' she said with a whimsical laugh.

'That's too long for me,' he said, 'but we've got to think of the others and what they might think.'

'Now that you've taken this new position in the company, does that mean you'll be coming over more often?' she asked.

'Yes, I'll have to come often, especially at first while I'm getting Greg Samson trained into being a competent manager.'

'You know, you'll always be welcome at Norwood, don't you? You'll always come and stay with us?'

'You'd find it hard to keep me away.'

'If I can help in any way, I hope you ask me,' she said.

Dinner was a happy time together for them all. When the meal was over, James invited Martin to go out to his office for a few minutes. 'I've got something you'll be interested in,' he said. 'You got a bit of a surprise when you came here this afternoon, didn't you?'

'Yes, I did. A very pleasant surprise,' Martin replied. 'I sensed you were in a conspiratorial mood from the look on your face. You must have been in on the surprise from the start?'

James had a wide smile as he replied, 'No, we didn't know anything until she knocked on the door and asked if she could stay for a couple of days. It wasn't until she suggested to us that it would be a good idea to ask you to come for afternoon tea that I dropped to what was in her mind. I might say I'll be delighted if it turns out the way I think it will.'

'There is something between us, but we can't say anything for a few months for obvious reasons, not the least being that it's only four months since my wife died. But that aside, thanks again for being helpful to me, and Rebecca too.'

James's smile revealed that he was enjoying the situation. 'That's what friends are for,' he said. 'One thing I do know; Charles would be pleased. He looked upon you as a son for years, and if you and Rebecca team up, you will be his son.'

'We want to keep it secret for a few months and I know that you and Elise will help us do that,' Martin said.

'Of course. Your secret will be safe with us.'

CHAPTER 19

*M*artin boarded the steamer the next morning to return to Melbourne. On board the ship, he met several businessmen from different parts of the state who were travelling to the mainland on business. They were all rejoicing at the latest improvement in communication between their new state of Tasmania and the rest of the country.

Martin arrived back at the Golden Swan in time for lunch the next day and was immediately back into his own business affairs. Another letter from Mr Waterhouse confirmed Martin's worst forebodings that Garth Gunter had fallen into the clutches of a shabby shyster who was on the hunt for gold. He again asked Martin to call as soon as possible.

Martin went to his office within a few hours and was given the ominous news that the lawyer, a well-known shyster by the name of Solman

Lewes, was preparing to apply to the court to have the entire Gunter fortune sequestered pending the settlement of a claim by Garth Gunter for a share of the estate.

'What does it mean?' Martin asked. 'Can they succeed with a blatant gold-digging move like this?'

'Unhappily, they might. It depends on whether they can convince the court that the young man has a genuine claim to a share of his uncle's estate.'

'Have you made any progress towards arranging a meeting with him?' Martin asked.

'Yes, Solman Lewes says he has proof of identity with him and he is quite agreeable to producing it and talking to us. We can meet later this week if that suits you.'

Martin agreed to attend Mr Waterhouse's office on Thursday morning to meet Garth Gunter. He prepared for the meeting with mixed feelings. On the one hand, he had feelings of sympathy towards a young man looking for a fresh start in Australia, but his common sense told him to be very wary of becoming entangled in anything like a family feud. He felt a strong sense of obligation to Joan – and even to Campbell Gunter himself – not to allow any part of their fortune that they had worked so hard to build to be frittered away on a worthless opportunist.

Martin's life had become full of anxieties and he felt the chill winds of foreboding that his good fortune of recent years was running out. Often he would lay in his bed of a night, reflecting on his life since he gave up his business on the goldfields. The tragedy of that period in his life was losing Joan, an event that still caused him great sadness. He felt a keen sense of resentment on her behalf that life had dealt with her unjustly; firstly the deprivation she must have felt at not having children and then when she found real happiness with him, she was taken at far too young an age.

He had rationalised his genuine feelings of love for Joan and his sadness at losing her with his new relationship with Rebecca. He felt no reservations about what he was doing; he was a man with a big heart and he knew that he had loved Joan unreservedly for the few short years they had together, but for many years Rebecca had occupied a special place in his heart, albeit secretly. He knew he would also love her unreservedly for the rest of his life, and his only worry was that his life was turning down a road to happiness that he may not deserve; he still harboured secret guilt feelings about Joyce Salmon and Sarah Bunce. Is all this too good to last? he wondered.

The first person to attract his attention as he entered Mr Waterhouse's conference room on Thursday morning was a heavily built, short, swarthy man with a brooding face dominated by a long nose. He immediately assumed, correctly, that this was Solman Lewes, the lawyer Nigel Waterhouse had described as a shyster.

Sitting next to him was a much younger man dressed in a suit that had seen better days, and boots that were showing signs of wear around the toes and heels. He had longish, red hair and an open face with a remarkable resemblance to the late Campbell Gunter. Martin realised he was looking at Garth Gunter.

Mr Waterhouse introduced them both to Martin and suggested they sit around a boardroom table at the other end of the room. He took the chair at the end of the table that would be occupied by the chairman.

Mr Waterhouse opened proceedings with a short summation of the circumstances and reasons for the meeting. 'In the circumstances of the demand made by Mr Gunter against Mr Maynard, the first fact to be established is that Mr Gunter is who he claims to be. I have seen his passport and other papers he has with him and I am prepared to say at this stage that I believe he is Garth Gunter, nephew of the late Campbell Gunter. Turning to Martin he asked, 'Mr Maynard, are you prepared to accept that as an established identification?'

Martin smiled. 'I can see a strong family resemblance to Campbell and that, in addition to what you have told me, makes me believe in him.'

'Well, that settles that,' Mr Waterhouse said. 'The next matter is Mr Gunter's claim for a share of the Gunter estate following the deaths of both Mr Campbell Gunter and his widow Joan who was married to Mr Maynard for three years before she died. Mr Maynard rejects that claim as having no basis in law, or in any other way.'

Mr Lewes then launched into a rambling submission in relation to the laws of inheritance and reasons why a properly constituted court would find that Garth did have an entitlement to part of the estate.

Martin said, 'If I may say a few words at this stage, Mr Waterhouse. Firstly, I am surprised that Garth has made no attempt to meet me to inquire after his uncle and aunt, people whom I am sure he never met while they were alive and of whom he knows nothing. I have no responsibility whatsoever for Garth, but in the ordinary course of decency towards any member of the Gunter family, I would have been pleased to meet him and, if possible, give him a hand to settle into a new life in Australia. I may have been able to help him get a job. I will still help him in that regard, but Mr Waterhouse has stated my position as regards the estate. It is because of these feelings that I can't understand why he has chosen to open our acquaintanceship with a threatened court action.'

'That seems to be as far as we can go,' Mr Waterhouse said. 'If there's nothing else, we can close this meeting.'

For the first time, Garth entered the conversation.

'I didn't know about you,' he stuttered in his broad Scotch accent.

'If I had, I would have tried to find you. I'll still talk to you if you want me to.'

'I'll talk to you, man-to-man, but not with your lawyer,' Martin said.

Mr Waterhouse entered the discussion again, to save the day for Garth. 'I suggest, Mr Lewes,' he said, 'that we leave these two young men together for an hour to get acquainted without our presence.'

Solman Lewes reluctantly agreed to this, and standing up said, 'I'll see you back in my office this afternoon, Garth.' He then left.

Martin stood up. 'Let's just sit here for a while and talk. What's your story, and why are you hell-bent on taking me to court to upset the last wishes of two relatives who were very good, decent and kind people.'

When Garth got started, he soon gave Martin an account of his life. His mother was only nineteen when he was born. She had been deceived and seduced by an older man who deserted her as soon as he discovered she was pregnant. Her parents kicked her out and for the next ten years, she eked out the most terrible existence. When Garth was ten, she married a widower who was ten years older than her. Life was a little better for the next twelve years, but after he died they were poor again. He had only a rudimentary education and found it impossible to get on in Scotland.

Towards the end of her life, his mother told him about his uncle in Australia. After she died, he was desperate to get a start at a long-term job. He somehow managed to get enough money to buy a steerage ticket to Melbourne and came out to Australia to find his uncle.

'How did you fall in with a poor type like Lewes?' Martin asked him.

'Accidentally,' he replied. 'The woman I was boarding with at Mentone sent me to him because she said he would know how to find my uncle. It took him about a month to track Uncle Campbell down only to find that he was dead.'

They chatted on for another half hour. Martin was reasonably well-impressed by him. He could see a great similarity between himself and Garth; they had both left their homelands because of hopeless opportunities for a decent life.

'I'm still prepared to help you get a job. If you're prepared to work, you'll get on here in Australia. This is the land of opportunity. But if you take my advice, you'll cut loose from that shyster of a lawyer and keep away from people like that.'

'That may not be so easy,' Garth replied. 'I'm sort of tied to him. He made me sign a paper to pay a percentage of anything he got for me from the estate.'

'Bloody oath!' Martin exploded. 'That was a mad-headed, stupid thing to do! God knows where that will lead; to big trouble, I'd say.'

At Martin's suggestion, they exchanged addresses and agreed to keep in touch.

Martin's worst fears came to haunt him. A fortnight after the meeting in Mr Waterhouse's office, official papers were served on him to defend an action in the Supreme Court to have the Gunter estate sequestered pending the resolution of claims by a previously unknown relative.

'What does it mean if they win and the estate is sequestered?' he asked Mr Waterhouse.

'It means that you cannot sell, or dispose of, any part of the estate without court approval. It is more involved than it sounds. I can assure you that you will find it very frustrating and a problem in business.'

'What can I do?' he asked in exasperation.

'Nothing,' Mr Waterhouse replied. 'Except get the best King's Counsel in Melbourne. The case will be fought out, no holds barred, when it comes on in several months time. It is going to cost you a great deal of money, but I don't think he can win. My guess is that Lewes is punting on you agreeing to settling out of court before the case comes on rather than you risking a big award against you. That way he will still make a nice fee whichever way it goes. That's the way shysters like him operate.'

In spite of his mounting worries, Martin had to carry on his increasing business interests as best he could. On his next visit to his bank, his old friend Arthur Lees told him that the bank had been officially notified that the Gunter estate was the subject of an application for sequestration and that they were obliged to report to the court any large transactions that Martin might make.

Martin visited Tasmania several times during the next few months and he and Rebecca announced their engagement in the spring. They were married on the first of November 1860. They both wanted to be married in the little church at the Don and the reception was held on the lawns at Norwood. Henrietta Smith was in her glory, supervising every detail of the magnificent repast she had planned with Rebecca and Sarah. Friends came from far and wide and every bed in the house and huts and in many of the homes in the village were filled by those who could not travel home in the one day.

The happy couple left Norwood the next morning to travel to Launceston in preparation to catch the steamer to Melbourne from where they travelled, in comfort and style, to the goldfields and then to Adelaide. They were away for a month.

By this time, the two sisters had talked through their plans for the future. Sarah was keen to travel and make her way to England in the new steamship, the *Great Britain* and was planning to stay there for at least a year.

Both Rebecca and Martin wanted to make Norwood their home and the sisters agreed to split the estate in a way that would give Rebecca sole ownership of the old place.

After Martin and Rebecca came home from their wedding trip, they settled into life at Norwood with the greatest of ease and enjoyment. Rebecca had achieved her longstanding wish to live at her old home and Martin was more than happy to take up the life of a farmer again, albeit with a lot of outside business interests to keep him occupied. The Don Timber Company affairs were still unsatisfactory and demanded a great deal of his attention.

A month after they returned home, Martin was advised by his Melbourne lawyer Mr Waterhouse that the application for sequestration of the Gunter estate was set down for hearing in the second week of January. Martin knew that the *Water Witch* was to sail with a load of timber for Melbourne the week before that and he decided to travel over with her. Rebecca insisted on going with him.

'It will be my last chance to take a trip on the old girl,' she said. 'For all the years Father had her, we only ever got a few trips. We can come home on the steamer.'

When the day for the trip came, Martin and Rebecca went aboard a half hour before the ship was to sail.

'The weather's a bit dicey,' Captain Peters said. 'It's been a light northerly all day, but there's a change not far off and I expect it to go around to the west.'

The afternoon was well-advanced by the time the *Water Witch* had sailed the few miles downriver from the mill to the heads. The little wind the sails picked up was a very weak westerly coming in short puffs that lasted only a few minutes.

'Once we're out in the Strait, away from the shore, the wind will pick up and I expect a fast crossing,' the captain said; however, as they got close to the heads and could get a good view of the open sea, Rebecca sensed that the captain and his mates were suddenly concerned about the weather. She and Martin were standing in a corner of the quarter-deck, not far from the wheel, when the captain cried out in alarm.

'Look at that!' he croaked, pointing to the north-west. 'Only about a mile out on their port quarter they could see an immense, black cloud hundreds of feet high, full of swirling vapours. Thunderclaps were rolling across the water and they could see lightning flashing inside it. The huge storm was bearing down on them and it was plain to see that they had no chance of escaping it.

'The only thing we can try in the few minutes we've got is to turn the ship around. We might be able to run back upriver ahead of it,' said the captain.

But there was not enough wind in the mouth of the river to push her around to point upstream. All he succeeded in doing was getting the ship beam onto the full force of the raging storm when it struck ten minutes later.

The five seamen and the mates tried desperately to lower the sails before the storm struck, but the job was only half done in time. The tornado winds pushed the ship over until the masts were only a few feet above the water. The sea in the mouth of the river had been suddenly whipped into a maelstrom. All those on the steeply sloping decks, including Martin and Rebecca, were frantically clinging to anything that would save them from falling into the water.

As well as the holds being packed full of timber, there were several smaller stacks on deck. These soon broke away from the securing ropes and slid down to hang over the side of the vessel, dragging her over still further.

The ship struck with a crash against the reef on the eastern side of the river mouth and huge waves swept across her, dragging away the broken packs of timber and anything else that was loose on deck.

With a wild scream, one of the seamen was washed overboard to be immediately sucked under the raging waves.

Martin and Rebecca clung to a grating at the foot of the mainmast. He put his mouth close to her ear and yelled: 'Just hang on! It might ease after a few minutes if we can hang on!'

He tried to put his arm around her shoulders, but she pushed it away and screamed at him, 'Just hang on! Hang on!'

The storm raged as if it would never stop. Martin could see the first mate clinging to a low railing near the wheel, but he couldn't see the captain. The minutes dragged by while the wind howled through what rigging was left.

At last the force of the tornado started to slacken off until, after an hour, it was back to gale force. The ship was lying up on the reef with the waves washing over the stern end which was in the deeper water.

As soon as the wind had abated a little, the mate struggled forward to loosen the ropes that secured a strong lifeboat slung in davits on the foredeck. He had secured himself to the deck with a life rope around his waist, but the ropes holding the boat were too securely knotted to be undone easily. Martin started to work his way around the deck to go to his assistance. As he got within a few feet of the lifeboat, he stood up to take the final few steps. Another gust of wind struck, blowing out the remnants of the mainsail, bringing it down to crash against him. He slipped down the steeply sloping deck and over the side, striking his head on the side of the ship as he fell.

Rebecca screamed and crawled to the side of the deck to look down into the water. The water on that lee side of the ship was somewhat quieter than on the weather side but was still very rough. Rebecca could see Martin feebly struggling with his head more often under water than above it. She was terrified and numb with panic, but quickly looked around for a rope or a lifebuoy to throw to him, but there was nothing of any use in sight.

Her distress drove her mind to find a way to help him. She was a good swimmer, but she knew she wouldn't last more than a few minutes in that water fully clothed. She kicked off her shoes and dragged off the jodhpurs she was wearing as quickly as she could; then, flinging her coat to one side, she jumped into the water to finish up close enough to grab Martin by wrapping an arm around his neck.

In the meantime, the mate had seen both Martin and Rebecca go into the water. By a superhuman effort, he managed to get the cover off the lifeboat and quickly retrieve a stout rope from inside. He crawled and slipped down the deck to the side and cast the rope across the two in the water, just a few feet below him. Rebecca caught the rope and hung onto it with all the strength in her free arm. The mate pulled them closer to the ship, but he knew that it was a desperate race against time to get them out of the water. Suddenly, another seaman appeared by his side.

'Where are the rest?' he yelled at the man.

'There are two up on the foredeck, the others are gone!' he yelled in reply.

'Help me get these two out! Get more rope from the lifeboat!'

Another seaman came on the scene and the mate quickly fixed a lifeline around his waist. 'Go over the side and help her,' he ordered him. 'You'll have to be quick, she's nearly done. We'll keep you safe.'

The seaman was a strong swimmer and succeeded in getting a rope around Martin's chest. The two men on the deck above them hauled him up and tied him to the railing before quickly pulling Rebecca up to join him. She was exhausted and unable to help herself, so the mate tied her securely alongside Martin while he and the seaman worked frantically to get the lifeboat into the water.

Ten minutes later, it crashed down into the water and miraculously stayed upright, surging against the side of the stricken ship. By this time, the summer daylight was fading fast and darkness was descending. The tornado had abated to a gale force wind, but they were still in perilous danger.

Martin was in deep shock, almost unconscious. His eyes were open, but he couldn't speak. He was staring into space and gave no response to Rebecca when she tried to talk to him. She herself shivered with cold and exhaustion. The wind was bitterly cold and she had no protection where she was lying, tied to the railing to prevent her being swept into the sea again.

The mate sent a man to find Rebecca's clothes, but he returned within a couple of minutes to say that all was gone. Everything on the decks had been blown or washed away.

The mate said, 'Look after these two while I try to get down to the skipper's cabin; there will be blankets and clothes there, but God knows what condition they'll be in.'

He came back a few minutes later with two blankets and some men's clothes, miraculously still dry. He helped Rebecca struggle into a pair of trousers and pulled a heavy, woollen jumper over her head and draped a blanket around her shoulders. He draped the other blanket around Martin and said, 'We'll try to get into the boat and get away, but I'll have to check the ship first to see if the Captain and the other seamen are still on board. If we can get back into the river, we might have a chance, but it's going to be a battle.'

Getting Martin into the boat and then being manhandled in herself was a nightmare experience that Rebecca remembered with dread for the rest of her long life. After the greatest difficulty, the mate and three seamen, together with Martin and Rebecca, were in the boat. The captain and two other men were gone. As soon as they pulled out from the leeside of the wreck, the gale struck them again. Fortunately, the wind was behind them and after the first ten minutes of frenzied rowing, it helped to propel the boat upstream.

With four men rowing and the wind behind them, they reached the Don jetty an hour later, all utterly exhausted and in varying degrees of shock. Martin was still comatose and incapable of standing up.

Help was quickly organised in the village and Martin and Rebecca were home at Norwood an hour later.

Henrietta Smith took charge and soon had warm beds organised for them. Doctor Greeves had accompanied them home and stayed for two hours to watch over Martin. 'Apart from the massive lump on the side of his head, I can't see anything wrong,' he said. 'He's obviously in a bad way, but I think it is just severe concussion. You never know how long it will take a person to come out of concussion; sometimes only a few hours, but sometimes it can take weeks.'

Rebecca had stood up to the experience remarkably well. Within a couple of hours of reaching home and regaining her normal body warmth, she felt in full control of herself physically and mentally. Her only worry was about Martin. The experience brought back the awful memories of a previous tragedy in her life when her first husband was drowned in the South Esk River. As she lay in the warm bed, she thanked God that she had insisted on going with Martin in the ship. She knew that if she hadn't been on hand to jump into the sea to rescue him, he would have drowned along with the other unfortunate men who had been lost.

Rebecca knew that it was important for Martin, or his representative, to appear in the court in Melbourne when Garth Gunter's application for sequestration of the Campbell Gunter estate came up. He certainly would be in no condition to travel to Melbourne in time for the hearing next week. She agonised over the problem facing her until she thought of Mr Algernon Stackhouse, their lawyer in Launceston. Maybe he could send somebody to Melbourne on the new steamer so as to be there in time?

Even though by this time it was midnight, something had to be arranged. It was imperative that somebody be on the road to Launceston at daybreak the next morning. She called out to Henrietta whom she knew was watching over Martin in the next room. Within half an hour, Allan Freeman had been roused out of bed and told to have the carriage and himself ready to leave at daybreak for Launceston with an important letter for Mr Stackhouse.

Henrietta was tut-tutting and mumbling while Rebecca went to the big desk in the front room to write to Algernon Stackhouse. She set out the circumstances in clear and concise language and stressed the importance of the case to her husband. She told him that a substantial fortune, in excess of fifty thousand pounds, was at stake and pressed him to take personal responsibility to contact Mr Waterhouse as a matter of urgency. She told him about the shipwreck and the present state of Martin's health and asked him to let her know what action he proposed taking by a return message with Allan Freeman.

The doctor left at eleven o'clock and Martin seemed to be sleeping naturally. Rebecca went back to her bed at one o'clock in the morning. In spite of all the exhaustion and drama of the past eight hours, she was restless and spent a wakeful night. She heard the coach go down the drive at six o'clock and then drifted into a light sleep.

Doctor Greeves came again at nine o'clock, by which time Martin had his eyes open but was still deeply concussed and not in possession of his full faculties. The doctor carried out certain basic tests in relation to his eyesight and hearing as well as feeling in his limbs.

'I know you must be very worried about him, but I believe he will emerge from this concussion within a day or two at most. Whatever

happens, he will have to rest for a few weeks. In the meantime, I will
be in twice a day to keep an eye on him. If anything happens that you
want me, send word and I'll come as quickly as I can.'

As it turned out, it was another twenty-four hours before Martin
showed signs of recovery. Rebecca noticed a gradual lightening up of
his eyes and then she was convinced that he recognised her. He drifted
in and out of awareness for another half day and then started mumbling
questions to her. Another day after that and he was conscious and in
full possession of his memory.

As soon as he realised what was happening, he wanted to jump out
of bed and get back to business. Rebecca pushed him down into the
bed, saying, 'No, you're not going anywhere until the doctor says you
can. He'll be here again tomorrow morning and then we'll see.'

'But what about the trip to Melbourne?' he said. 'You know I've got
to be there, no matter what happens.'

'I've got all that fixed, for the time being at least,' she said.

She told him about sending the letter to Mr Stackhouse and about
his reply that he would be on the steamer to Melbourne the next day.
He would be contacting Mr Waterhouse on arrival and would stay as
long as necessary to assist with the case.

Martin had a look of incredulity on his face and gasped out, 'You're
wonderful. I love you,' and pulled her down into his arms.

The doctor spoke very sternly to Martin the next morning and
impressed on him the importance of taking a couple of weeks to rest
up before plunging back into work.

'The world won't stop while you act sensibly for a couple of weeks,
even if you think it might,' he said. 'In fact, you'll probably find that
your affairs will proceed better than you expect even though you're
not there.'

A letter arrived from Mr Stackhouse a few days later, telling them that in view of the circumstances, including the shipwreck and Martin's state of health, the court had agreed to postpone the application for three months. He pressed Martin to come to his office at the first opportunity to discuss the sequestration application and also the urgent matters in connection with the Don Timber Company.

News of the wreck of the *Water Witch* and Rebecca's heroism in saving her husband from drowning quickly spread around the surrounding districts, including Launceston. A reporter from *The Examiner* travelled all the way to Norwood to get a personal interview with her. Rebecca was a reluctant heroine and shrank from front page exposure, but out of common courtesy she had to meet the reporter when he came to Norwood. He also spoke to Martin while there. The result was a front page story the next week with a full account of the wreck, including the fact that three lives had been lost and that Rebecca's bravery had saved her husband from certain death. Martin also featured as the same man who almost single-handedly captured a gang of bushrangers ten years previously.

Martin impatiently rested at home for the next two weeks and then travelled to Launceston to see Mr Stackhouse.

'I'm pleased you're back on your feet again, and I'm pleased you've come to see me,' he said. 'I can report to you about the case in Melbourne. As it turned out, things went well for us. Losing the *Water Witch* was a terrible disaster for the company, but I think the delay in the case brought about indirectly by that event has given you time to extricate yourself from a very worrying situation. I don't think Garth Gunter and his Mr Lewes can succeed in winning a share of the estate, but they can certainly cause you a lot of trouble and expense while the case drags on, which might be for years. The worst aspect of it is that you will be denied access to your inheritance, a large amount of capital that you could well need to help you deal with other problems you may have to deal with soon.'

'What problems are you talking about?' Martin asked.

'Problems with the company. The *Water Witch* wasn't insured and her loss could well put the future of the company in serious doubt,' Mr Stackhouse said. 'But let's finish with the Melbourne case before we get on to that.

'As I said a moment ago, that case could drag on for a long time and will surely impinge on your ability to conduct your affairs as you want. To put it bluntly, I think you should get out as quickly as you can, even if it means buying your way out by giving Garth Gunter money. What was your assessment of him when you spoke to him in Melbourne?'

'I thought he was basically a decent young man, poorly educated, desperate to get away from Britain because of its poverty and hopelessness, who foolishly allowed himself to fall into the power of an unprincipled shyster. He is convinced that he is tied to Lewes because he signed a contract to pay him a percentage of anything he gets from the estate. He didn't even know his uncle was a rich man until Lewes found out and told him.'

'To my mind, what you've just said makes the situation worse. If he's a naïve simpleton, Lewes could manipulate him for years. Lewes thinks you will pay up big to get him off your back some time in the future. Better to pay a small amount now than a big amount later.'

'What do you suggest?' Martin asked.

'Offer to pay three thousand pounds on condition that Garth Gunter signs an irrevocable agreement to withdraw his application for sequestration and to drop all claims against his uncle's estate for all time, an agreement to be drawn up by us; that is, Mr Waterhouse and myself.'

'What are the advantages to me?' Martin asked.

'Firstly, you'll cut off the expensive legal costs. Just having a King's Counsel in court to fight the application will cost you thousands.'

'Do you think Mr Waterhouse is of the same mind?' Martin asked.

'Yes, I took the liberty of discussing it with him. We are agreed on that,' Mr Stackhouse said.

'Righto, I will take your advice. How soon can we get it done?'

'I'll get in touch with Mr Waterhouse this week. We've got three months to get it tidied up,' Mr Stackhouse said. 'Getting back to the company affairs,' he continued, 'I'm afraid we're running into troubles, and the loss of the *Water Witch* is going to compound them. The immediate problem is a sagging market for timber. It may only last for a few months, or it may be years before the economy picks up again.'

Martin thought of the endless discussions about economics that he and Zac Bellchambers used to have in the old store on the goldfields at Ballarat. His own faith in the timber industry was as strong as ever, indeed stronger because of what he had learned from Arthur Lees and Lex Wright, but he knew that many of their shareholders would panic at the first sign of a downturn, particularly if the dividends started falling.

'If the situation is as serious as you say,' Martin said, 'we should ask the chairman to call an urgent board meeting.'

Mr Stackhouse agreed to get to work immediately with the aim of organising a meeting for the next week.

The board was shocked to learn that the *Water Witch* was not properly insured and wasted half an hour on blaming each other before getting to grips with the biggest problem: how to help the company survive the next six months. Sales were bound to be down because of the difficulty of getting the timber to Melbourne without their own ship.

After an acrimonious discussion, it was agreed to take urgent steps to order a new steamship designed to work out of the River Don. There was some discussion of raising more capital to finance the purchase of the new ship, but no firm decisions were made. Martin, as managing director, was given authority to enter into contracts to charter other ships to carry on the trade pending the arrival of the new vessel.

Martin left the meeting with a nagging worry that events were conspiring against the company and that the immediate future did not look good.

It wasn't long before the news that the company was in financial trouble over the loss of the *Water Witch* went the rounds of the shareholders, and some looked to sell their shares while they were still worth something. Martin had a long-term interest in increasing his shareholding in the company but was not prepared to buy more shares at that time because of the uncertain future and his problems with his inheritance.

The next board meeting, called to discuss ways and means of financing the purchase of the new steamship, was an acrimonious affair and finished up with the question undecided.

A week later, Martin received a message from the chairman of the board, George Perkins, through Mr Stackhouse, that he wanted to quit the company and was offering to sell his shares at considerably less than face value.

Martin and Rebecca discussed the issue at great length. They both sensed that a decision to commit themselves further to the timber industry at that stage would be a commitment for life, one that would affect not only themselves but their children that they hoped to have in the years ahead.

'What do you really think of the future for timber?' she asked. 'And more importantly, what's in your heart? Do you really want to make a commitment like this?'

'Yes,' he replied, 'I believe I do. The way I see it, I can exchange the Royal Swan for a timber company, and I am ready to do that. We can plan to spend our lives here at Norwood and work for the future timber industry.'

Martin knew that the purchase of the shares would put a strain on his cash reserves, but he had the security of his inheritance from Joan. He sent word to Mr Stackhouse to close the deal.

A month later, he had a letter from Mr Waterhouse telling him that Garth Gunter, still under Mr Lewes's advice, had agreed to accept four thousand pounds in full and final settlement of his claim on the Gunter estate in return for which he would withdraw his application for a sequestration order and sign an appropriate, irrevocable settlement agreement. That news gave Martin and Rebecca renewed faith in the future. With the financial security they would gain from the sale of the Royal Swan, Martin would be able to rebuild the Don Timber Company.

The downturn in the markets affected the timber trade and prices fell dramatically. The company stopped paying dividends and the shareholders, spoilt by years of easy profits, soon started complaining. Some decided to sell their shares for a quick return. Martin had been gradually accumulating more shares as the years went on and was willing to buy more, but his business sense told him that this wasn't the time for buying.

The news from the markets continued to be bad and, as always in a recession, prices plunged lower and lower until finally the market started to recover. Martin then bought shares at bargain prices and finished up owning eighty per cent – and full control – of the company.

As the months and years rolled by, Martin and Rebecca fulfilled their ambitions to establish a family at Norwood. Rebecca's little daughter Enid had been calling Martin 'Father' from the day they married, and they were overjoyed when they knew that they were soon to be parents in their own right. Their first child, a son, was born at Norwood and was named Charles Martin Maynard. Henrietta once again took charge of catering for a big lunch at Norwood after the little boy was christened in the same church where his parents had been married.

Over the next twenty years, Martin built a huge timber business with mills right across the north coast and enough ships to carry the product around the country. While these things were happening, Martin and Rebecca's family grew with the arrival of another boy and two girls.

Rebecca was in her element as the mother of a large family on the magnificent Norwood Estate. The wealth that her father and her husband had accumulated made it possible to install all the modern facilities for gracious living at Norwood. Before Henrietta Smith finally retired to live in her own cottage at the Don, the big kitchen had been upgraded with a large, wood burning range that had a hot water system installed with it to serve not only the kitchen but also the two bathrooms that were installed in the house.

As the children grew up, they started their schooling at the new Don school that had been provided by a mixture of government money and a large amount of private donations by men like Martin Maynard and his friends.

As the girls reached twelve, Rebecca employed tutors to take them on to a higher standard than the local school could provide. She thought they were too young to be sent away to boarding school at that age. When the boys reached twelve, they were sent to the Wesleyan Horton College at Ross, as boarders. It was a big wrench for them to be sent so far away from home and, like many other boys and girls, they suffered the agonies of homesickness. While the boys were having their private weeps at school; their parents, especially Rebecca, were suffering similar agonies of separation at home. At the commencement and at the end of terms, the carriage would be dispatched to Ross to take the boys to school or bring them home. It was always a time of anticipation and excitement.

Being the eldest, Charles was the first to start, and he had to learn about school life amongst a large number of strangers – the hard way. His brothers, James Henry and Arthur Zacariah, found it much easier.

When Charles had been at the college for five years and was seventeen, he was ready to leave school. One of the greatest satisfactions in Martin's life was that he had been able to give his children a good education. He thought of it as another blessing bestowed on him and his family by Van Diemen's Land, now Tasmania. He had been lucky as a boy that his father was employed by an enlightened employer who educated his own children and included the children of his employees in the little school he established on the estate, an unusual thing for the times. Martin was doubly lucky that his parents were literate themselves and wanted their children to get as much education as possible.

Charles particularly wanted his parents to attend the end of year 'speech night' at the end of his final year. He had written to his father asking him to be there and to make sure that his mother was there as well. 'All the other parents will be there', he had written, 'and we would like you to be with us for the occasion'. Martin was touched by the letter and by his son's request. He was a man who had never put much importance on the class distinctions that were so pronounced in Britain and to a greater or lesser degree in Tasmania.

As his children reached the age of fourteen, he had told them the story of his life so that they would be saved embarrassment when, in time, they were inevitably made aware of the convict connection.

'Your grandfather, a great man who founded the fortune that our family is built upon, was a convict, and I was a convict. You must learn to understand that the quality of a man or of a family is not determined by an accident of birth – that is in the lap of the gods – but by his achievements. That is another matter entirely.'

Martin and Rebecca were part of the gathering of parents and relatives of the boys of Horton College on speech night 1877. As they sat in a seat reserved for parents, Martin reflected ironically that the gathering included the bluebloods of the Tasmanian landed gentry, most of whom were the descendants of army officers and other government men who had been given grants of land in the early days of the colony and now considered themselves to be the aristocracy of this new land. Sprinkled amongst them were people like himself and Rebecca, descended from convicts who had hauled themselves up from abject poverty to success and, in their case, great wealth.

As he found himself doing more often as he grew older, thoughts of his boyhood came into his mind; of his father and mother, of the days after he was cast out from Ashburton and his hopeless struggle to find employment, of his desperate decision – with the help of his brother-in-law – to get himself transported to Van Diemen's Land. These daydreams always ended in a stream of faces drifting past the mirror of his memories. Thomas Carter, his convict friend from the day they were both convicted at Lancaster in 1842. The harsh months in the hulk, the tedious voyage to Hobart, the long march to Deloraine. Then Nathaniel Kentish and the impenetrable forests out past Kimberley's Ford. The next stage of his life featured people like James Fenton, Charles Drewitt, Sam Jessup, Zac Bellchambers, Alice Bunce, Cam Ralph, Arthur Lees, Joan Gunter, Alex Wright and Rebecca, Rebecca again and again.

Dr Allwright, the headmaster, came onto the stage and the hall went quiet. He made the first speech, reviewing the past year and talking about the school and their plans for the future. Then it came time to award the prizes to the outstanding students, both in academic studies and sport.

'Our main award, the Horton Scholarship which goes to the best all-round student for the year, this year goes to another outstanding student who will join the ranks of the distinguished list of winners going back to the year this college was established in 1855. All I can say about this boy is that, like a lot of our best students, he didn't cover himself in glory the first couple of years he was here. In fact, there were one or two incidents that were best forgotten, but as he grew older he improved in every respect and for the past two years he has developed into an outstanding student and a fine young man. I am very proud of him. That young man is Charles Martin Maynard.'

Martin felt a surge of surprise and immense pleasure sweep through him. He glanced at Rebecca and saw that her eyes were moist and she had a look of joy and pride on her face. Reaching out, he took her hand and they squeezed hard.

Martin's mind wasn't concentrating all the time over the next hour of the prize giving ceremony except that he did hear James's name called to the stage to receive a prize for being the most successful bowler in the cricket team. He smiled to himself as he remembered the boys and girls at Ashburton playing in the long, summer evenings.

The night finished with a lavish supper and with the assembled parents and relatives talking and laughing together in pride and happiness for their sons.

Martin and Rebecca went back to the hotel where they were staying overnight, tired but happy. As they lay in each other's arms, she said, 'We've done well, haven't we? Father would be pleased.'

'My darling wife, we have done well and the gods have been kind to us. We've been richly blessed,' he said. Then, with one of his characteristic chuckles, he said, 'I always knew that Van Diemen's Land was the place for me.'

New Releases…Also from Sid Harta Publishers

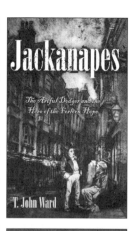

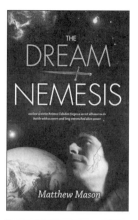

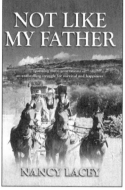

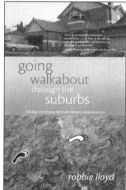

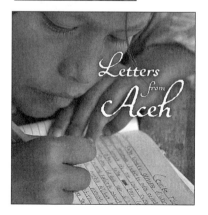

Best-selling titles by Kerry B. Collison

Readers are invited to visit our publishing websites at:
http://www.sidharta.com.au
http://www.publisher-guidelines.com/
http://temple-house.com/

Kerry B. Collison's home pages:
http://www.authorsden.com/visit/author.asp?AuthorID=2239
http://www.expat.or.id/sponsors/collison.html
http://clubs.yahoo.com/clubs/asianintelligencesresources
email: author@sidharta.com.au

Purchase Sid Harta titles online at
http://www.sidharta.com.au